Petals from the Sky

ALSO BY MINGMEI YIP

Peach Blossom Pavilion

Petals from the Sky

Mingmei Yip

KENSINGTON BOOKS
www.kensingtonbooks.com

To Geoffrey, loving husband and precious treasure

A thousand miles apart, yet the same moon shines over us all.
—Su Dongpo (1036–1101), Song dynasty poet

ACKNOWLEDGMENTS

In writing a novel, between the first word and the last one, there is a long, head-scratching, and pencil-biting process of filling in the hundreds of pages in between.

This daunting task, seemingly solitary, could not have been completed without the help and support of many others.

First and foremost, I owe each of these 338 pages of *Petals from the Sky* to my husband, Geoffrey Redmond, an endocrinologist specializing in women's hormones, himself an excellent writer with six books to his credit. Geoffrey is always my first reader, friendly critic, and trusted adviser, literary and otherwise.

I owe my ability to cheerfully complete my work to the great support and contagious enthusiasm of my agent, Susan Crawford, and my editor, Audrey LaFehr, whose appreciation and kindness would be any writer's elixir.

I also want to give special thanks to my other Kensington supporters: Karen Auerbach, Maureen Cuddy, and Martin Biro, whose hard work and generosity contributed to the success of my first novel, *Peach Blossom Pavilion.*

I must mention some of the many other writers and writing instructors who helped me along a writer's arduous, yet wonderful, path:

Neal Chandler, director of Cleveland State University's Imagination Workshop, and a writing teacher par excellence.

Lewis Frumkes, director of Marymount Manhattan College's Writing Center, who graciously invited me to many of Marymount's literary events, where I was privileged to meet some of the great authors of our time.

Max Byrd, author of historical novels and workshop director of the Squaw Valley Community of Writers.

Karen Joy Fowler, *New York Times* best-selling author of *The Jane Austin Book Club,* and instructor at the Imagination Workshop.

Andre Dubus III, author of *House of Sand and Fog,* an Oprah's Book Club selection, and instructor at the Imagination Workshop.

Ray Strait, instructor, Palm Springs Writers' Conference.

Kitty Griffin, my German "sister," fellow children's book writer, and coauthor of *The Foot-Stomping Adventures of Clementine Sweet,* whose generosity and kindness are rarely matched.

Lee Kochenderfer, author of young adult fiction—though our encounter was brief, her support for me has been more than generous.

Ellen Scordato, instructor and virtuoso grammarian, New School University, who patiently and generously answered my questions and solved my many puzzles of grammar that have no equivalent in my native Chinese.

Victor Turks, gracious host during my event at the City College of San Francisco.

My writer friends Sheila Weinstein, Esta Fischer, Chun Yu, Kathleen Spiveck, Baixi Su, and Shobhan Bantwal, for their generous help and delightful friendship.

Hannelore Hahn, founder and executive director—and her daughter Elizabeth Julia Stoumen—of the International Women's Writing Guild (IWWG), for their untiring efforts to help make many women writers' dreams come true.

And others to whom I am connected through happy karma in this Thousand-Miles-Rest Dust:

Teryle Ciaccia, close friend of two decades and fellow Tai Chi instructor, who never ceases to send me good *qi,* whether by phone or in person.

Elsbeth Reimann, fellow IWWG participant, who always keeps me cheerful at the IWWG's annual conference at Skidmore.

Eugenia Oi Yan Yau, my one-time student, now distinguished professor of music and vocalist, upon whom I have always been able to rely. And, of course, her husband, Jose Santos.

In Chinese fashion, I must also acknowledge the overwhelming debt of a daughter to her parents. Without my parents' vision and selfless support, I would not be who I am today: a happy woman whose dreams have come true.

For my other friends and readers, wherever in this world or another, the same moon shines over us all.

PART ONE

1

The Retreat

Mother choked and spilled her tea. "*Ai-ya,* what evil person has planted this crazy idea into your head?"

I was twenty and had just told her my wish to become a Buddhist nun.

She stooped to wipe the stain from the floor, her waist disappearing into the fold of flesh around her middle. "Remember the daughter of your great-great-grandfather, who entered the nunnery because she was jilted by her fiancé? She had no face left; she had no name, no friends, no hair.

"She just sat the whole day like a statue; the only difference was she had a cushion to sit on. And she called that meditation." Mother looked me in the eye. "Is that the life you want? No freedom, no love, no meat?"

Before I could respond, she plunged on: "Meng Ning, there are only three reasons a girl wants to become a nun: before she meets the right man, after she has met the wrong one, or worse, after the right one has turned out to be the wrong one." Mother clicked her tongue and added, "Not until after you've tasted love, real love, then tell me again you want to be a nun."

That had been ten years ago, but my wish to be a nun had not faltered.

Not until 1987, on a hot summer day in a Buddhist retreat in Hong Kong.

I hopped off the bus on Lantau Island and walked toward the Fragrant Spirit Temple—the oldest in the colony. The path led up a hill beside a maze of crumbling monastery walls over which trees spilled out as if to taste the forbidden world outside.

As I joined the crowd hastening to get under the cool shade of the foliage, a plump, middle-aged woman caught up with me, panting and grinning.

"Miss, is this the route to the Fragrant Spirit Temple for the Seven-Day-Temporary-Leave-Home-Buddhist-Retreat?"

I nodded and gestured toward the throng. Two thick, round pillars flanked the temple's crimson gate. Above its lintel hung a wooden sign with four large, yellow, Chinese characters in ancient seal script: MARVELOUS SCENERY OF GREAT COMPASSION.

My heart raced. Within this gate for the next seven days, I would be tested for my karma to be, or not be, a Buddhist nun. At twenty, I had made up my mind to avoid the harassment of marriage. Now at thirty, I still couldn't decide whether to remain in the dusty world as a single career woman, or to enter the empty world as a career nun.

Why should I feel so nervous? After all, in the absolute sense, is there a difference between a shaved head and one with three-thousand-threads-of-trouble?

Gingerly, I stepped through the crowd into the temple's expansive lobby and a soothing aroma of jasmine incense. Activities were in full swing, with people assembling for the opening ceremony of the retreat. Electronic Buddhist music boomed from different corners of the two-hundred-year-old temple. I listened intently, seeking the music through layers of noise arising from gray-robed monks and nuns, black-robed workers, volunteers, and retreat participants. It was a synthesized version of the traditional Buddhist chant "Precious Incense Offered for Discipline and Meditation." My heart instantly warmed to the familiar tune that I'd heard so many times. However, I still preferred the human voice, even when sung from the wrinkled lips of old monks and nuns. I hurried to the end of a long, slowly moving queue.

A little ahead of me stood a thirtyish man with a robust frame and light hair—a foreigner. Surely a devout Buddhist to have come all the way here to join the retreat.

I flung back my hair, feeling dulled by the heat and hating the sticky feeling of my blouse pasted to my back, unwilling to let go.

Looking around, I saw a gilded Buddha statue on a tall table, hands in the *abhaya* and *dana* mudras—the have-no-fear and wish-granting gestures. Flowers, fruits, and thick incense sticks in bronze burners crowded the rosewood surface encircling the golden figure. Under Buddha's all-seeing gaze, an expensively dressed woman stuffed a pile of banknotes into the capacious belly of the *gongde xiang*—Merit Accumulating Box. How would she look if she shaved her head and wore a Buddhist robe?

"Looks very bad," my mother would say whenever she saw a nun. "Meng Ning, you're a very beautiful woman. Beautiful women deserve nice clothes, nice jewelry, and a nice husband."

Mother was born in the year of the cat. And like a cat, she was snobbish, sensitive, sensuous. In elementary school, she was so cute and petite that her classmates used to call her "Little Sweetie." Then she became "Coca-Cola" in high school. Of course Mother was sweet, bubbly, and as popular as Coke, but she'd told me what her classmates really meant was that her precocious body had the voluptuous shape of the soft-drink bottle.

Mother, beautiful in her youth, had a lot of nice jewelry and, according to her, a nice husband. But a miserable life. My father never bought Mother any of the jewelry; instead, he sold pieces of it so he could go to gambling houses to act like a big spender among the pretty hostesses who'd caress his face with one hand and rummage his pockets with the other. The jewelry came from my grandmother, a businesswoman in Taipei with a chain of jewelry stores.

My grandfather died young, leaving my grandmother with four bony kids and an empty stove. She used the jewelry repair skill she'd learned from Grandfather to obtain work as an apprentice in a small gold store. Later, she was able to start her own business, then expand. She had fourteen stores and more than two hundred employees before she died.

So during those years, the jewelry kept flowing like tap water into my mother's life. But when Grandmother and Father died, they left Mother and me penniless. Grandmother left nearly all her money to her three sons, in accordance with the old Chinese belief that if one left money to daughters, it would eventually be lost to another name. However, she didn't feel right leaving Mother nothing, so over the years she secretly sent Mother money and gave her part of her jewelry. But how would Grandmother feel if she could find out that not only had the jewelry not turned into food on our table, it had paid debts to the loan sharks?

Despite what Father had done, Mother's eyes would moisten and her voice soften when she talked about her first and only love. "Your father was a romantic man. In our age, people had arranged marriages, but we married for love."

Then she told me how Father had hidden a pistol in his pocket the night he proposed.

"Mei Lin"—he'd aimed the gun at his chest—"if you say no, I'll blow my heart out!"

He was gone, and Mother had been the one left with a shattered heart.

That pistol always seemed to me a symbol of my parents' marriage. It had never been fired, but was always there to suggest love, threat, and a bad choice. Their life had constantly shifted between passion and tension, with me squeezed between them like a cushion.

When I was ten, I came home one day and found my parents in a fight.

Mother wagged a finger at Father. "You're a good-for-nothing poet. I can't stand you anymore!"

My heart hurt to hear that. An unhappy marriage makes some women quiet and others garrulous; my mother was definitely among the latter.

"I can't afford you anymore, you spoiled baby!" Father retorted.

"Spoiled? Have you sold your poems or calligraphy to buy me clothes and jewelry?"

Father was speechless for a moment; then he jumped up from the sofa, grabbed me, and shook my arm.

"How did your daughter grow so big if I haven't paid for anything?"

"Do you really think you pay for her—"

Before Mother finished, Father let go of me and snatched my copy of *Dream of the Red Chamber* from the chipped coffee table. "Doesn't this dream cost money?" Then he threw the book down and seized Mother's TV magazines (we couldn't afford a TV). "Doesn't this gossip cost money?" He went on to grab the radio, the cracked teapot, my drawing book, my crayons, the day-old bread, asking the same question until he exhausted both the list and himself.

During their fight, I looked down at my feet so I didn't have to look at their unhappy faces. I imagined my right big toe was my father. The left big one was my mother. The rest were the brothers and sisters I'd never had.

The little toe on the right was chubby, so he was the chubby little brother who'd died three days after he was born. The little left toe was as small as a peanut, and that was me. It always made me sad to look at my two little toes so far from each other, like the unbridgeable distance between us. Would my little brother have lived if Father had stopped gambling?

When Father's and Mother's voices grew angrier, I moved my toes together as if they had stopped quarreling. Married life didn't appeal to me at all, not even when based on love. Perhaps a nun's life would be better. Later I thought so because of a secret I'd never told anyone since the day I fell into the well.

2

The Fall

It was the day after my thirteenth birthday. Father had just lost five thousand dollars in a casino in Macau, forcing our family to move from Tsim Sha Tsui, the bustling commercial district in Kowloon, to a village house in remote Yuen Long. The rent was two hundred Hong Kong dollars, three times cheaper than what we'd paid in the city.

In the communal backyard behind our house was an abandoned well surrounded by tall grass that whispered when the wind blew on winter nights. Older villagers avoided the well because there were rumors that ghosts dwelled in it. A hundred years before, a young concubine, with a stone tied around her neck, had jumped down the well to prove her innocence after being accused of having an affair with a wandering monk. People believed the well was so old that it had absorbed the essence of the sun, moon, stars, water, air, wind, sound, and light until it acquired a spirit of its own. A blind fortune-teller insisted the well was the third eye of an evil goddess who would observe the people above and snatch down the handsome ones—especially children—to feed her jealousy.

While children were warned to stay away from the forbidden opening, the younger adults didn't care about it one way or another. They simply regarded the well in a practical way—as a trash bin.

As for myself, the myth pricked my curiosity during my lonely adolescence. I'd sneak to the well and stare down into the space below. Most of the time what I saw was completely different from the villagers' descriptions. Rather than frightening, I found it fascinating. In the dim light, I could make out all kinds of objects—blankets, books, branches, twigs, papers, clothes—thrown down through a gaping hole in the mesh that covered the well's mouth. I imagined a diary hidden among the piles of refuse, words inscribed on tear-streaked rice paper in vigorous calligraphy by the doomed concubine to bitterly lament her innocence. I also imagined photographs, faded and brownish, of forgotten people. A young bride, a happy family, the sad-faced concubine with her bald lover, a chubby baby with eyes widened as if asking: why was I thrown into this cold world?

During days of heavy rain, water would rise from the bottom and I'd see my own reflection with a small, round piece of blue sky floating behind my head. Sometimes I'd hear noises whispering below when the wind stirred the long grass aboveground. One evening I saw the reflection of the moon, so round and pregnant that I thought she might burst and drop into the well and make a splash so loud it would wake everybody from their dreams.

On other evenings, I saw stars peeking shyly at their own images. I would throw down a stone and watch the reflection split into tiny diamonds, like those that had once sparkled on my mother's pretty fingers. I imagined time itself reflected on the circle of water and, like a kite snapped off from its string, flying away through the opening, carrying away memories of color, smell, and touch.

Whenever I peeked into the well, I felt the evil goddess also staring back at me, her eye hidden. She'd watch my every move and absorb my heart's deepest secrets. She made me see—by linking the earth and the sky together—another world, familiar yet strange. She was the third eye connecting me to a larger, mysterious universe.

I'd always wondered how it would feel to be on the other side of the world.

One hot September afternoon as I studied, my parents began to fight over my father's purchase of a pair of expensive shoes. Mother said he would rather feed his vanity than his family. He argued that a poet must retain his dignity. As my parents' voices began to simmer and boil, I sneaked out to the backyard, went straight to the well and looked down, wondering what I could find this time to cheer me up: a book, a pillow, a doll, a puff of cloud floating in the sky? But in such dry weather I saw nothing except darkness. I looked up and met the angry glare of the sun.

Just when I began to feel uneasy and thought I should go back home, someone bumped me from behind. I lost my balance and plunged into the dark. I didn't know how long I'd been unconscious, but I woke up surrounded by a fresh coolness. Yet my head ached and my body was clammy with a cold, searing pain. My clothes were torn, my knees badly scraped, and my toes swollen like sausages. But I was alive! The trash in the well had cushioned my fall and saved my life. I kept thinking how ridiculous to be saved by a heap of rubbish. I could have laughed, except my joints throbbed as if on fire.

I looked up toward the dim light and saw blurred faces leaning over the well, staring down and howling, "Meng Ning, can you hear us?" "Are you all right?" "Don't be afraid; we'll get you out as quickly as possible!" I could hear my mother crying and see my father holding her tightly in his arms. The world above looked remote and alien. The people, yelling and gesturing wildly, seemed trapped in the circle of clear, blue sky.

But I was the one who was trapped. I tried shouting back, but the darkness, like a witch, snatched away my breath and swallowed my voice. My chest swelled and my heart jumped like ants in a hot wok. My knees were cut and sore. I wrapped some old dirty rags around them to stop the bleeding. I asked myself if it would be my fate to die, rotting with the garbage, in an obscure hole in the earth. The walls around me exuded the smell of decay and rotten fish. I reached out to touch the stone lining of the well, but immediately withdrew my hands when I felt a stickiness like the blood on my knees. I wanted to cry, but no tears came, only gasps.

I looked up again; people were still leaning over the well and looking down at me, with flashlights and kerosene lamps raised high in their hands. Their loud voices carried down to me, but I sensed hopelessness behind their frightened faces. I could almost see them cupping their mouths and whispering, "A doomed child, what can we do?"

Suddenly, I thought of the Guan Yin statue in my neighbor Mrs. Wong's house and of how this plump woman used to ask the Goddess of Mercy to protect her ancestral graves, give her a son, even cure a cold. She'd kneel before the serene ceramic figure in its small shrine surrounded by lighted joss sticks and offerings of flowers and fruit. Then she would press her hands together, kowtow, and pour out fervent prayers. Now, imitating her, I put my hands together and whispered an ardent prayer to Guan Yin, pleading to her to get me safely out of the well.

I kept praying, ignoring the talking, arguing, and crying above, and the strong odor of vegetation, mildew, and rot surrounding me. Then something grazed my head and landed beside me on the ground with a soft plop. I picked it up and held it to the side of the well where the light was brighter. From a thin red string dangled a brightly colored Guan Yin pendant. The Goddess of Mercy wore an orange robe; her hands held a flask with a willow branch and her bare feet rode on a big fish that looked as if it were swimming toward me.

I felt a tinge of warmth.

I looked up and glimpsed my parents' concerned faces. Mother was still sobbing; Father pulled her close to him. Other faces squeezed to lean over the well, looking down while competing with one another to offer comforts and suggestions. I frantically waved the pendant at them, then cupped my mouth with my hands and yelled at the top of my voice toward the opening, "Mama! Baba!" Suddenly hearing that I was very much alive, people got excited all over again. A child clapped. Several old people pressed their hands together and whispered prayers. Teenagers raised their index and middle fingers to show victory. My parents squeezed through the crowd to peek down at me. "Oh, thank heaven, Ning Ning, are you all right?!" Mother hollered and Father kissed her on her forehead, their earlier quarrel forgotten. Then, with my blurred vision, I saw a bald scalp above a pretty face, glistening in the sun. I blinked and strained, but the scalp and the face were no longer there.

The crowd continued to lean over the well, taking turns to keep me company and to throw down a blanket, a sweater, candies, cakes, even several comic books.

Everybody was talking to me to keep my spirits up. One old neighbor yelled, "We've called the firemen; they'll be here any minute!" Another hollered, "We're getting ropes and a basket to get you out!"

So I sat and waited with Guan Yin in my hand and all the people watching from above. The air was dense yet soft. I kept praying to the Goddess of Mercy until I felt my prayers deep underground and my fear dissipated. My hands pressed together and my lips moved as though I'd been practicing the ritual for a thousand years.

It was very strange, but I had begun to like this small world of my own. The rancid smell ceased to bother me. In fact, I felt soothed by the strange coziness of this space, now completely mine. I could almost feel the wall breathing faintly and wrapping close to me, the trash and withered foliage moving gently and warming my body. I listened to the well's pulse beating with mine and felt a stab of gratitude both for my privacy below and for the care of so many people above.

When the villagers were ready to rescue me, they threw down more quilts. Voices shouted, "Meng Ning, spread them out under you!" Then came the long rope and the basket. The voices hollered again, "Get in!" Slowly, I climbed inside and curled up like a baby in the womb. The people above began to pull. The ascent was slow, cautious, wobbly at times, but steady. People kept yelling, "Meng Ning, don't look down!"

But I couldn't resist the temptation. I wanted to take one last look at the little round corner that had unexpectedly given me moments of peace. So I leaned over and looked down. I didn't panic as the villagers had feared. Instead, I felt great tenderness for a larger realm that I couldn't yet name. I recalled the reflection of the floating clouds in the shimmering water, the third eye forever following me when I moved, the pregnant moon, the peeking stars, the murmuring tunes of the grass at night. . . .

Then I was suddenly in daylight again, being pulled out of the basket by my parents, who were crying and shouting, "Oh, Ning Ning! Thank heaven you're okay!" All the neighbors took turns to comfort and greet me. Right then, the firemen arrived. I was immediately rushed to the hospital for a checkup. The doctor said besides a few bruises and cuts, I was fine, and miraculously, not a single bone was broken. He bandaged my knees, gave me a tetanus shot, and said I could go home.

After that, I was considered an extremely lucky child. The blind fortune-teller said any person who had survived such an ordeal could only be a reincarnation of Guan Yin. The villagers held a celebration party for me the next day. They made offerings to the ancestors and gods, then they roasted pigs, butchered chickens, gutted fish, warmed wine, and ignited firecrackers. They also showered me with gifts: lucky money in red envelopes, clothes, toys, books, crayons, my favorite Cadbury Fruit & Nut milk chocolate, first quality tea leaves, wine, even gold and silver ornaments, and small antique statues. My parents' hands were intertwined during the whole evening, their eyes resting tenderly on me.

While I was pampered like a little princess, the two boys who'd knocked me down the well during their game of police-chasing-thieves were severely punished—each had his bottom whacked ten times with a thick stick. My plea that I actually had a good time down in the well landed on deaf ears. The villagers thought I was just being nice and adored me all the more. My neighbor Mrs. Wong gave me the best Iron Goddess of Mercy tea with rose petals, and a roasted chicken like the one she had offered to Guan Yin. Believing that they'd share my good luck, several villagers went to buy lottery tickets. After the banquet, my father took all my lucky money and slipped out to the gambling house.

I almost wished I would fall into the well again, so that Father would stop gambling and fighting with Mother. So I'd always be loved and treated like a goddess. So I could be left alone with just Guan Yin in that quiet place underground.

A few days later, I ran into Mrs. Wong. She told me that near my house was a nunnery dedicated to Guan Yin; she regularly went to pay her respects to the gilded Guan Yin statue sitting on a golden lotus. I soon began to visit the temple after school. Surrounded by glimmering candles and the fragrance of long-burning incense, I'd look up and pour out all my heart's troubles to the Goddess's beautiful image. I'd also watch the nuns' kind faces as they housed and nurtured the orphans, fed the poor, cared for the old, prayed for the dead. Like Guan Yin, the Goddess of Mercy, they plunged into the Ten Thousand Miles of Red Dust—the mortals' field of passion—having sworn never to enter paradise even if only one soul was still left unsaved.

❧ 3 ❧

To Accumulate
More Merit

Now inside the lobby of the Fragrant Spirit Temple, the line continued to move very slowly and people were starting to fidget. Electronic Buddhist music—the "Incantation of Great Compassion"—boomed from every corner of the monastery.

Because I had been too poor to afford it in the past, this was the first time I'd joined a retreat. I had little money, but I thought that at thirty, it was now or never. So I paid with the money I'd saved during my five years of study in Paris as a scholarship student and by doing odd jobs—assisting part-time in a small art gallery, sketching portraits for three francs each in Montmartre, and waitressing.

The temple quickly filled up with people of all ages, including quite a number of children. Some were sitting; others strutted around in their little black robes, their oversized sleeves trailing on the floor, making dry, brushing sounds. A few of the boys exhibited cleanly shaved heads; their pale scalps looked like strangely enlarged eggs under the hot July sun. Groups of men talked animatedly while waiting. I wondered what they were talking about, Buddhism or the stock market? Women whispered and giggled. Were they comparing the charitable deeds of the Goddess of Mercy to those of Princess Diana?

Next to a huge bronze incense burner a young couple gazed

silently into each other's eyes. After a while, the woman pulled out a tissue and wiped the moisture from the man's face. The man gave her a grateful smile and patted her hand. Neither uttered a word. Buddhists say *xinxin xiangyin,* two hearts merge into one. However, their affection made me sad. It reminded me of the many times Mother looked at Father with silent admiration and affection when he was writing poems for her, able to forget for just a moment whatever else she knew about him. Or that our rice vat was almost empty.

It was finally my turn at the registration desk. A sour-faced woman with unruly wisps of black hair stabbed a meaty finger at my name on the thick registration sheet. "Miss Du Meng Ning, your fee for our Summer Buddhist Retreat is two thousand Hong Kong dollars. Have you brought your own Buddhist robe?"

I hadn't. But if I chose to be a nun, I would be wearing the *kasaya,* the gray patchwork vestment. I feared I might miss the color, fabric, taste, and mood of all my other clothes. Especially the dress I was wearing now—purple flowers amid patches of green; whenever I wore it, I imagined myself in a purple dream shimmering with lotuses.

Moreover, I would also be given a Buddhist name. I wondered which would suit me best: Observing Mind, Solitary Light, Enlightened to Suchness, No Dust, or Empty Cloud? I hoped I wouldn't be given the name of my great-great-grandfather's daughter—No Name.

"Miss, have you brought your own Buddhist robe?" the registration woman repeated, waking me from my reverie. "It's fifty dollars."

"Oh, no, I'm sorry, since I've just come back from Paris—"

"All right, you don't have one, no need to explain."

The woman turned to search hastily among a pile of plastic-wrapped packages, pulled one out, tore it open, shook out a robe, scrutinized the inside collar, and handed it to me. Her quick action manifested like the single brush stroke of a Zen painting.

I carefully counted and handed her the money.

She frowned. "Don't worry, miss, even if you pay more; it's a donation to the monastery, and you'll accumulate more merit for yourself."

She emphasized the last word by raising her already loud voice.

Was she trying to amplify the same benefit-nobody-but-yourself message to the people waiting behind me, or was it a self-interested version of the ancient wisdom, "To lose in order to gain"?

I turned and saw in the line behind me a lanky middle-aged man, a young woman talking rapidly with an elderly one, a couple with two bored-looking teenage boys, and two young girls, holding hands and giggling. I smiled at them, but all ignored my cordiality. What should I expect? Buddhist retreat or not, I was in Hong Kong, a city notorious for rudeness, crowding, and money craving. Then why had they come to the retreat? The woman's words clanged like a bell in my ears—To Accumulate Your Own Merit. They saddened me; I'd never thought of joining the retreat to accumulate merit. I had come only to test my karma to be a nun.

Right then, something stirred outside. A shaft of sunlight dappled the temple's rooftop. The amber tiles appeared to be rising and falling, resembling golden dragons in flight. A young nun floated by, her bald scalp glistening under the hot sun, her robe fluttering in the breeze. She looked happy and peaceful.

Had great-great-grandfather's daughter No Name really been unhappy as a nun?

"Of course," Mother had once said. "Since the day she entered the nunnery, she was never seen again. She refused to receive any visitors, not even her parents. They could only communicate with her through other nuns. And she refused to talk about anything but illusion, delusion, and emptiness. No Name died of brain cancer at twenty-eight. On her deathbed, she instructed that her body be cremated. So the nuns took her ashes to a high mountain and scattered them into the air. Her relatives said that was her karma—to have entered the empty gate so she would become emptiness."

Mother had made a face. "But isn't it funny that, if she thought about nothing but emptiness all day, she would die with her brain *full* of tumors?" She paused, widening her eyes. "I know she didn't really die of a brain tumor"—Mother pointed to her chest—"but a broken heart."

I let out a sigh.

The registration woman studied me with a worried look. "Miss, are you not feeling well?"

"Oh, I'm fine, thank you."

"Good. Sorry to inquire, but I don't want any trouble during the retreat. It's already so busy, and we don't have enough workers. You understand?"

I sighed again. This time she ignored me as she scribbled out a receipt, tore it off the pad with a threatening *zeeet!* and handed it to me with the retreat's schedule, then picked up the small pile of money.

I took the receipt and began to peruse the map to find where the meditation classes would be held. Immediately I was interrupted by an angry cry; I looked up and saw her fingers waving like an eagle ready to attack.

"Wait, wait! Miss, one of your five-hundred-dollar bills is fake."

"What?"

She fluttered the note, her face pinched like a bun. "This bill is fake!"

The people behind me now seemed suddenly awake. The lanky man eyed me suspiciously. The young woman stole glances at me, while whispering to her friend. The two young girls, blushing, stared at their feet. The two teenage boys laughed uncontrollably. I imagined—despite the risk of bad karma—smacking their faces with a sharp *thwack!*

In order to get the most from my scanty savings, I'd asked a friend's friend to exchange the Hong Kong dollars on the black market in Paris's Chinatown. But how could I tell this to the registration woman?

Now she threatened to either cancel my registration or inform the temple. She thrust a pudgy finger at the long queue. "As you can see, miss, we can't afford to waste time with this hoax."

"Ma'am, there's no hoax—"

"I mean what I say, and I only tell the truth. Now the truth is that your money is fake."

Just then the foreigner I'd noticed before stepped forward and asked in English, "You need help?"

I looked at him and hesitated.

He asked again, his voice full of concern, "Something wrong? Can I help?"

Before I'd even decided what to do, I blurted out to him in English what had happened, as well as where and why I'd obtained the money.

He pulled out his wallet, fished out a five-hundred-dollar bill and laid it down on the counter, and then, looking very stern, said to the woman, "I think this is just a misunderstanding. This lady was cheated. She's . . . my friend, and I'll pay for her."

Seeing that he was a foreigner, the registration woman flashed an obsequious grin and said in English, her voice now full of warmth, "Thank you, sir." Then she addressed a young nun by the counter in Cantonese. "Shifu, would you please take this miss to the dorm?"

She turned back to me. "This Shifu will take you to your room." Her grin was still stretched wide on her face. "Miss, sorry about the misunderstanding. No hard feelings, eh?"

I ignored her while extending my hand to thank the foreigner, feeling confused yet nevertheless grateful. "I'm Du Meng Ning. Thank you so much for your kindness. I'll pay you back as soon as the retreat is over." I looked at his eyes and noticed they were green.

Five hundred Hong Kong dollars was sixty-five U.S. dollars; why was this green-eyed foreigner so generous?

He smiled. "Don't worry about it, Meng Ning. I'm Michael Fuller from the United States."

I blurted out, "Meng Ning means tranquil dream. . . ." Then my cheeks felt hot. Why had I just offered a piece of such personal information to this stranger?

"Beautiful," he said.

"Thank you." I blushed more. "And I'm glad to meet you, Mr. Fuller."

Probably sensing my embarrassment, he nodded toward the young nun while addressing me. "Meng Ning, why don't you let her take you to the dorm? We can talk later."

"Sure," I said. "And thanks again." While I was turning away to follow the nun, I felt his eyes on my back. I was still wondering, why was this foreigner so generous to a total stranger?

With rapid steps, the young nun led me out of the lobby, then through a back passageway lined with potted plants and flowers.

We passed groups at work: nuns washing vegetables or preparing tea; women dusting; others lighting incense; young girls washing plates in outdoor sinks or doing laundry in large wooden buckets.

An elderly nun loaded down with plastic bags of vegetables and food lumbered toward us. I put my hands together in the prayer gesture and smiled. "Good morning, Shifu." "Shifu" means teacher, or master, the title of respect for Buddhist nuns and monks.

She smiled back. "Good morning, miss. Here for the retreat?"

"Yes," I said, looking at the sunlight reflecting from the big beads of perspiration on her forehead.

"Hope you enjoy it," she said sincerely.

"Thank you, Shifu. I will," I answered respectfully.

Once she had passed by us, the young nun said, "She's Wonderful Voyage Shifu, supervisor of the cooking for the retreat."

"I see." I turned around to look at the elderly nun's receding back.

I always wanted to live a significant life like a nun's. But Mother once asked, when we had just finished dinner, "What kind of success is it if you have no one to share it with? Look at your grandmother. She had cash in her purse and diamonds on her fingers, but no man in her heart to love. You want that kind of life?" Then she threw a big plate of fish bones into the garbage can, where it landed with a thump. "I don't want to see my only daughter die a lonely old woman!" I understood her warning—if I didn't get married, my destiny would be the same as that anonymous collection of fish bones.

The nun and I continued to walk toward the dormitory. We entered a small hall and ascended a broad wooden staircase. The nun climbed fast; I had to take two steps at a time to keep up.

She smiled back at me apologetically. "Do you know you are not allowed to make conversation during the whole retreat?"

"Oh, really?" The steepness of the steps made the climb a physical ordeal.

On the stairs, the nun's cloth slippers thudded softly, like secrets told in whispers. She lowered her voice, her tone didactic. "Unless it's absolutely necessary, talking is not permitted after the retreat has formally started. Also, one is not supposed to make noise during meals, like smacking lips or slurping noodles. Not that we want to be mean, we just try to show respect to the Dharma."

I was amused by the idea of this little "meanness" committed in the name of Buddha's law or, like the registration woman, in the name of knowing the truth.

We arrived at the top of the stairs and the beginning of a long corridor leading into different rooms. She spoke again, her voice high and excited, and her face flushed. "You know, because people come here to meditate, to find peace of mind, it is important to remain silent. Since both the sound and the content of speech can be distracting. Modern people who are under a lot of stress usually talk nonstop, to vent their frustrations and fill up their minds, so they won't feel nervous and restless. But their conversations are mostly about worldly things: TV programs, soap operas, gossip columns . . ."

"I see."

She finally stopped. "Here's your dormitory."

The room was huge and crowded with rows of steel bunks. The walls were empty except for a large photograph of a statue of Guan Yin, the Goddess of Mercy. Her half-closed eyes gazed down at the roomful of women. Under the picture the sweet smell of sandalwood wafted up from a bronze burner.

The nun showed me the location of the bathroom and my bunk bed. Back in the corridor, she continued, "Many people still talk even when they're meditating. They don't talk aloud, they chatter inside. We call this monkey mind, because it's compulsive, like a monkey jumping from tree to tree."

Suddenly she stopped to stick her head inside a doorway. "Ma'am, please don't hang your underwear on the bunk. It's not a very nice sight!"

Tired of her jabbering, I felt relieved that we'd arrived at the rows of stacked lockers. The nun handed me a key, looked at me intently, and instructed me not to lose it.

As she turned to leave, I called, "Shifu, what's your name?"

She turned back. "Miao Ci."

Compassionate Speech.

"Thank you very much, Miao Ci Shifu." I tried my key in the

locker while pondering the contrast between the symbolism of her name and her persistent chatter.

Irritated, I pushed hard on the locker door; it shut with a loud clang.

The nun startled, flashing an embarrassed grin. "Miss, I think you're all set now."

Sorry for my rudeness, I put my hands together and bowed deeply to her.

After she disappeared down the stairs, I sighed with relief—my first moment alone to find peace of mind since I'd entered the temple.

4

The Scarred Nun

At ten o'clock, refreshed from a nap in the dormitory, I ambled back to the Meditation Hall. In the throng ahead of me, a couple gestured in sign language, making *Eh! Eh!* sounds with their throats. I wondered how it would feel to be unable to give voice to thoughts. The mute couple turned around to let an elderly man behind them pass. When I saw their faces, the truth clicked—they were the silently loving couple I'd seen gazing into each other's eyes. It saddened me that they had not voluntarily chosen silence over speech. I felt even sadder that sometimes even seeing and believing could still fail me in trying to find the truth. If I became a nun, would that help me to perceive things better?

At the door, a monk handed out books for chanting and programs for the opening ceremony. Inside, trails of heavy incense paled the peoples' black robes while emitting a sweet, drowsy fragrance. Stripes of red embroidered streamers fluttered in the artificial currents generated by slowly revolving fans. Monks, nuns, workers, and volunteers shuffled here and there, arranging the flowers, the fruit, the cushions, the musical instruments.

I settled down on a cushion a few rows from the front. I looked around and saw a woman whose features reminded me of my longtime nun friend Yi Kong. I'd heard her disciples describe her with a Chinese saying, that the fish sink to the bottom of the pond and the geese descend to the sandbank in despair at competing with her beauty.

Yi Kong was that beautiful. Besides, she was a gifted painter, calligrapher, photographer, and connoisseur of art. No one understood why, at the age of eighteen when most girls' deepest concerns are boyfriends and pimples, she had chosen to shave her head to become a nun. Some said she had been jilted by her childhood sweetheart. Some said she had a rare form of cancer and would have lost all her waist-length hair anyway. Some said she rebelled against her wealthy, overpowering father, who had forced her into an arranged marriage with a crude businessman twenty years older than she. Others said she had a gangster boyfriend who had been killed in a street fight, and she'd become the target of the opposing gang. She had no place to hide but within the empty gate.

Although my mother knew about Yi Kong, she had no idea that the nun was my close friend and guide, nor that she had such a mysterious background. Once, when Mother saw Yi Kong on TV talking about the illusory nature of life and the transience of human passion, she pointed to the scars scorched into Yi Kong's scalp by incense during her initiation into nunhood and exclaimed, "So pretty, what a waste to enter the empty gate!"

I believed Mother had a split personality, for although she disliked nuns, she was fascinated by Yi Kong. Another time she said, her eyes glued to the nun on the screen, "No Name, deserted by her handsome fiancé, was just as pretty." She motioned her head toward Yi Kong. "This one must also have been rejected by someone very handsome."

Mother believed all women's unhappiness was caused by men in one way or another. So she would never have believed the reason I wanted to be a nun had nothing to do with a man, but with a woman. I wanted to be like Yi Kong, to be free of men's crushing power, to attain spirituality, to control my own life and destiny, and most important of all, to push away the ordinary so as to live the life of a poet, a mystic, a goddess.

Mother believed that when people share the same face, they'll share the same fate. This logic scared me, for I had my mother's face, and I didn't want to let a man into my life just to ruin it. A man who would perhaps, like my father, gamble away everything. Even the jade bracelet treasured by Grandmother and Mother and which would have been passed on to me.

Mother had often lamented the loss of the bracelet. "Ah, what a pity! It was made from the finest jade, translucent, spotless, and so green. Your grandmother searched for this piece her whole life. It was not the price she'd paid; many rich people could pay that. It was her eye.

"Your grandmother had a third eye; she could see things most people can't. She knew she'd have no future living in a small town, so she moved from Hualian to the big city of Taipei. Chinese like gold for ornaments and investment, so she opened one gold store after another. People liked to bargain, to pull someone down, so she'd always mark up her prices and give them the pleasure of talking her down. She could see everything; that's why she was so successful. Now I'm sure that, from her grave, she can see you'll fall in love with a nice man, marry, have many children and a good life."

One time I asked her, "Could Grandmother see that Baba would gamble away the jade bracelet?" Mother was speechless. Feeling ashamed of my meanness, I secretly promised myself that I would retrieve the bracelet some day, but I had no idea how. Could Grandmother's ghost foresee this, too?

A nun with a twitch in her eye now stepped forward onto the platform in front of the altar and announced enthusiastically, "I represent the Fragrant Spirit Temple and welcome you to this Seven-Day-Temporary-Leave-Home-Retreat. Before we start our ceremony, let's all stand up and bow to Buddha."

Everyone rose, hands together in the deferential prayer gesture, and bowed to the three figures on the altar: the Historical Buddha; the Medicine Buddha; and Amida Buddha. Next to the three Buddhas stood a small ceramic statue of Guan Yin; her hand held a jar and her eyes looked smilingly at the participants. I was impressed to see several hundred people stand up in one accord as if they were sharing the same body and mind. I could even feel the *qihai,* energy ocean, swell around me.

After the audience resumed their seats, the eye-twitching nun gave her welcoming speech:

"Honorable guests of faith, today I am pleased to welcome you to our retreat to experience the Buddhist Dharma as short-term monks and nuns. I am also very happy to tell you we have an American doctor with us, which shows that the Buddhist Dharma is not only prosperous in the East, it has also spread to the West. It not only attracts ordinary people, it also appeals to the highly educated."

The nun glanced at her notes, then began again in her self-satisfied voice. "We also have a young Chinese doctor with a Ph.D. in Oriental art history from the Sorbonne in France."

I smiled; that was me. But I really hadn't received my degree yet. I still needed to go back to Paris for my oral defense. Hadn't the nun mentioned the Ph.D. in order to make the temple look good? Jet lag made me too sleepy to quibble.

My head jerked and I awoke to the chiming of bells. Now a different nun on the dais announced lunch. Still feeling drowsy, I mechanically shuffled along with the throng moving toward the dining hall.

Tables and chairs were arranged in rows, with men and women seated on opposite sides of the hall. A dense aroma of vegetables, oil, rice, and condiments hung heavily in the air. After everyone had settled into their seats, a malnourished-looking monk came up to the microphone and quiet fell over the hall. He informed us about the etiquette of eating: we should wait until a Shifu, mentor, struck the bell before we began. We should refrain from making noise and from looking around. We should concentrate on our food, not take more than necessary, and eat all of it. We should clean our bowls and plates as well as we possibly could.

A lot of rules for the first day. Did the monks and nuns ever break any of them?

The monk went on to read the menu: steamed tofu with mushrooms, stir-fried lettuce with cashews and chestnuts, and soup with dried dates, seaweed, and lotus root.

The Chinese call the taste of vegetarian dishes "widow's taste"—like the numb feeling of having lost one's beloved. My tongue felt dulled when I heard the menu, despite Yi Kong's teaching that the killing of any sentient being results in very bad karma. You might end up eating your own mother, chewing on the intestines of your brother, sucking the bones of your grandfather, crunching the feet of your daughter, or swallowing the head of your son. Some close relative in a past life may now be a fish, a cow, a chicken, a sheep, a pig.

The monk struck a small bell and we began to chant the "Five Reflections."

I was surprised to hear this frail-looking monk chant in a plummy, sonorous voice:

"I reflect on the work that brings this food before me, let
   me see from where this food comes.
I reflect on my imperfections, on whether I am deserving of
   this offering of food. . . ."

The group chanted more confidently as they continued:

"I take this food as an effective medicine to keep my body
   in good health.
I accept this food so that I will fulfill my task of enlightenment."

The chant ended in a crescendo, with everybody looking spirited; then another monk struck the bell to signal the beginning of lunch.

Although we were not supposed to look around when eating, I still couldn't help but scan the crowd when I lifted up my bowl to eat. Why not—weren't rules made to be broken?

A group of boys looked very cute as they hungrily shoved food into their mouths, forgetting not to smack their lips, nor slurp while drinking their water. The adults ate the mass-produced vegetarian dishes without enthusiasm—here in the renowned eating paradise of Hong Kong.

While scraping rice into my mouth, I saw the American, Michael Fuller, in the front row opposite me. When would I have the chance to repay him the five hundred Hong Kong dollars? Being the only non-Chinese in the retreat, he had to be the doctor whom the nun had mentioned. To my surprise, he ate with a cheerful countenance and a lively rhythm, as if the bland, greasy dish were gourmet food. He manipulated the chopsticks perfectly. Like a conductor wielding his baton to conjure musical notes, he orchestrated the tofu, mushrooms, seaweed, and cashews smoothly into his mouth. Not only that, he also helped to put food into the bowl of the skinny boy beside him, who struggled nervously with his chopsticks.

Fearing that he might look up and see me studying him, I finally looked away. Yet none of the other men opposite me seemed interesting, so I turned to study the children for a while before looking back at Michael Fuller. He ate his rice Japanese style, using the chopsticks to pick up the grains instead of scraping rice into his mouth from the bowl like most Chinese do.

I sighed, impressed by his affection for the flavorless dish, while thinking of how Hong Kong's rich people show off by eating shark's fin soup for breakfast or feeding their children bird's nest soup for supper. Michael Fuller looked up and our eyes met. I immediately looked away.

I turned to watch the stern-faced nuns strolling between the rows to supervise and decided to perform some imaginary improvements to their faces. What if the thin one's eyes were not so pinched— would they look less intimidating? What if the plump one's lips were lifted to a forty-five degree angle instead of drooping like a capsized boat? What if the large mole on the kind-looking one's forehead became her third eye? What if the pretty one relaxed her face muscles just a little bit? She might even show her lovely dimples. What if . . .

Then suddenly I saw a long, red scar. My heart almost jumped to my throat. The nun was moving behind a heavy man in the third row, and I could only see a third of her face. When I noticed her hands, my heart turned over. Parts of fingers were missing from each hand. Who was she? My heart knocked hard against my ribs as I turned away from the disturbing sight to think.

The bell chimed again, signaling the end of lunch. I looked at my bowl and plate; they were still full. Hastily, I scraped mouthfuls of rice and vegetables into my mouth, then swallowed them with big gulps of water. I choked and coughed. A nun turned to look at me. But her hands had five fingers. My eyes swept across the hall; the scarred nun was gone.

I placed my chopsticks on top of my bowl, and seeing the mess I had left, my heart sank.

My eyes wandered back to Michael Fuller. Ah, he was also looking at me, smiling. Before I decided whether to smile back, a monk struck the bell a second time, signifying that lunch was finished.

I went straight back to the dormitory to rest before the meditation session, still feeling disconcerted about the scarred nun. After a while my thoughts suddenly connected. Could she be Wong Dai Nam, a nun friend in Paris? Not likely, for Dai Nam had left the *Sangha,* the Buddhist order. There had been no word of her since she had disappeared into China three years before.

໑ 5 ໑

Depending on Emptiness

After the lunch break, I went back to the Meditation Hall for the lecture and meditation sessions. Inside, men, women, and children sat on brown meditation cushions, waiting silently or squirming to find a comfortable position. Participants continued to stream in; their cloth slippers scraping softly on the clean tiles sounded like leaves rustling in an empty courtyard.

A few minutes later, the nun with the twitching eye stepped forward onto the platform before the altar and tapped lightly on the microphone. Waiting until the vibration subsided, she cleared her throat and announced the venerable nun Yi Kong from the Golden Lotus Temple as the special guest speaker of the retreat.

The audience stirred.

My heart thumped to hear the familiar yet distant name Yi Kong, Depending on Emptiness. She was one of the reasons I came all the way to this temple to join the retreat—after I'd learned that she would be here to lecture on Buddhist Dharma. My head turned with the congregation's to see Yi Kong stride in measured steps to the platform in front of the altar. Her chin was raised, her bald head glistened, her robe trailed behind. She looked like a hairless Guan Yin walking on earth.

Yi Kong was the bald scalp and pretty face I'd glimpsed from the bottom of the well when I was thirteen. At that time she had been a wandering nun who, on her way to visit the Golden Lotus Temple, learned of a girl trapped in a well and went there to throw down Guan Yin's blessing. Yet our friendship didn't develop until two years later, after she had taken residency in the nunnery.

Now Yi Kong still looked handsome as she marched toward the altar. Mother would certainly have been disappointed to see her on TV now, for she had put on some weight, and she didn't look as detached with the extra pounds.

Yi Kong lit incense and led the audience in three deep bows to the three large gilded Buddhas on the altar. Then she seated herself on a cushion and arranged her legs into the full lotus position. With her long, elegant fingers, she drew the gold brocade shawl into a pleasing curve across her tangerine-colored robe and began: "Honorable guests of faith . . ."

I stared at her intense face and concentrated on the rich inflection of her voice. Yi Kong's eyes glowed in the mellow light of the room. I couldn't see whether the corners of her eyes had grown wrinkled, but her speech was as smooth as before.

"I'm so glad all of you are here today. Simply by being here, you've already extended your first step onto the Buddhist path."

Wherever Yi Kong's gaze fell, there seemed to be a face momentarily enlightened, shining with the truth.

"Don't belittle this first step. The journey of a thousand miles begins on the ground under your feet. But neither should you think you'll be enlightened just by attending a seven-day retreat."

Suddenly Yi Kong seemed to notice me, and our eyes met before she glanced away. My heartbeat accelerated to allegro. Had she really seen me? Did she recognize me among the crowd after all these years? Would she, as before, want me to enter her temple as a nun? Now she asked the audience to meditate for five minutes before her Dharma talk. While everyone's head was lowered and their eyes half closed, I carefully studied my nun mentor's face, feeling my mind start to wander. . . .

During my adolescence and into my twenties, years when I disdained and ignored men, Yi Kong really became my only friend.

In the famous novel *Dream of the Red Chamber*, men are compared to mud, but women to water, as they are supple, tender, and nurturing.

When I dreamily turned the pages of the novel, sometimes I'd wonder: Would a man like the hero Jia Baoyu—refined, talented, pure, true, and nice to all the women around him—exist in real life? What about the beautiful nun Miao Yu, Wonderful Jade, who wrote poetry, secretly longed for a man, and gathered snow from plum blossom petals to brew tea for Jia Baoyu instead of fulfilling her passion for him? Oh, how I wished I were like those beautiful, brilliant women in this *Dream of the Red Chamber*!

I had always preferred the company of females. Like the best kind of *yunwu*—cloud and mist—tea leaves picked before the rainy season, women are shapely, delicate, pleasing to look at, intoxicating to smell, enjoyable to savor. And of course, for me, the only female who embodied all this was Yi Kong.

Although Mother knew nothing about my close friendship with the nun, she sensed the infatuation in me. Once I overheard her asking Father, "Our daughter looks dreamy. Do you think she's in love or something?"

I almost chuckled. How could I tell my parents that I was infatuated with a nun?

Yet the relationship between Yi Kong and myself was not without tension, tension that had nothing to do with us, but with the villagers' convictions. Those who worshipped Yi Kong would say, "Look at Yi Kong; she's so beautiful, wise, compassionate, and a nun—how can she not be the reincarnation of Guan Yin?" But another group would argue, "Meng Ning came out alive from the haunted well! Who else could survive this except the reincarnation of Guan Yin?" Once two women broke into a loud quarrel right in front of the statue of Guan Yin inside the nunnery. Another time, two elderly men competed to donate offerings to us until Yi Kong insisted we return all the gifts and money.

Mother, of course, took my side. She pinched her eyes into slits, her voice sharp and intense. "It's easy to shave one's head and put on a robe, but how many, like you, could survive that fall with no injury? I'm sure if she were the one who fell, her bald scalp would have cracked open like an egg hit over a wok and her brain would have splashed like vomit all over her robe!"

I felt terribly sad. How unmerciful to fight so mercilessly over the Goddess of Mercy! Didn't the villagers know it was Yi Kong who'd thrown the Guan Yin pendant down to me? But when I told them this, as before, they just thought I was being nice and adored me more. Sometimes I became confused. If I were really the reincarnation of Guan Yin, why couldn't I stop Father from gambling and fighting with Mother? If Yi Kong and I were both the reincarnations of Guan Yin, why didn't that stop the villagers' childish disputes?

I finally left the villagers' squabble behind when I turned nineteen and received a scholarship to go to college. The same year, Father won seventy thousand dollars at the racetrack, enabling our family to move back to the city of Tsim Sha Tsui. Six months later, he lost all that money, so we had to move again—to a slum in Kowloon city. Then the trip to the temple became long and expensive, forcing me to reduce my visits.

A year later, Yi Kong began to take over the supervision of the Golden Lotus Temple after its chief nun, Wisdom Forest, had become ill and passed away. Whenever I visited her, Yi Kong would express her wish for me to be a nun in her temple. One time she asked, "Meng Ning, do you know you have a perfectly shaped head? I'm sure if it's shaved, it will be an object of admiration for many monks and nuns."

Another time she said, "Meng Ning, you have the rare quiet nature of a high nun. My Shifu, Wisdom Forest, said that if a person has the karma to possess this quality, she should not waste it in the dusty world."

Later, when Yi Kong knew that although my interest in being a nun was serious but I had not quite made up my mind to shave my head, she'd change to a joking tone and ask, "Meng Ning, when are you coming to play with us? There's lots of fun going on here." Of course I understood that by "coming to play with us," she meant when would I become a nun in her temple, and "fun" meant helping with her many ambitious projects.

Being the only child in the family, it was hard for me to tear myself away from my parents and throw myself inside the temple gate. Chinese deem it extremely unfilial for an only child to become a monk or a nun—unless his or her parents have passed away. Otherwise, who would take care of the parents during their old age? Who would carry on the family name? Who would inherit the family's possessions?

6

The Fire

Yi Kong's voice, pealing like temple bells, woke me from my wandering thoughts. She had just begun her Dharma talk on self-centered thinking.

"We all like to judge. And no matter whether we feel superior to what we criticize or feel miserable ourselves, we still like to keep the game going. Because in judging—our spouse, our friends, our partners, even strangers on the street—we can make ourselves the center of things." She paused. "With our mind full of judgments, prejudices, and egotism, we'll always think things like *Why does my sixty-year-old aunt always dress like a young woman? Why does my friend's father date a young girl half his age? I hate my mother-in-law's cooking; it's horrible.*"

Whispers and suppressed laughter scattered among the audience. Yi Kong waited patiently for the noise to subside, then paused to scrutinize the audience in the front rows, then those in the middle, and finally those in back, as if challenging us all to face the truth.

"We also fail to realize that what we need is not this self-centered thinking, but functional thinking—to plan our future, to run our business, to study for examinations, even to prepare a good dinner."

She went on to talk about how meditation could help to rid us of our attachment. "When you meditate, you'll discover self-centered thoughts are like monkeys jumping from tree to tree. Meditation is to help stop this monkey business—"

The audience laughed loudly, cutting off Yi Kong's speech and dispelling the solemn atmosphere. I saw several boys laugh; one arched his back like a cat ready for mischief; an elderly woman giggled, cupping her mouth. I continued to look around and suddenly saw Michael Fuller. He was also looking at me, slightly turning away from a nun who talked intently to him. It was Compassionate Speech, probably now assigned to translate for him.

Yi Kong broke the spell of our stare by speaking again. "We have to empty our self-centered thoughts and learn to let go! Detach!—"

Right then a loud "Fire! Fire!" broke out like a bad dream in the peaceful hall. People looked around and whispered to one another. When more "Fire! Fire!" was heard and the smell of smoke began to fill the air, people sprang up, then pushed and screamed. As swift as a cat, the eye-twitching nun dashed onto the platform and pulled Yi Kong down, knocking over the Goddess of Mercy statue. Yi Kong wanted to say something, but was already being pushed by her captor toward the exit. But it was too late; now everybody—one body and one mind—dashed toward the gate like lunatics chased by lightning. The eye-twitching nun shielded Yi Kong with her plump torso and shouted, "Give way! Let Venerable Yi Kong pass!" The same people whose faces lit up and smiled with ecstasy when they caught sight of her now turned a completely deaf ear to the plea.

Everything happened so quickly that it took me seconds to realize I was squeezed among frightened people pushing in an advancing wave. Part of the ceiling was now ablaze. Splinters of crackling wood plunged onto the floor with startling thumps, shooting sparks in all directions. A man's back caught fire; several people slapped him with meditation cushions. He screamed like a pig being slaughtered. Another woman wailed hysterically when a ball of flame landed on her hair.

The panic was contagious. Everybody cried and yelled—for help, for loved ones, from fear, from pain. My heart raced while my lips frantically muttered prayers. Pressed forward by the mob behind me, I looked toward the platform for Yi Kong and the eye-twitching nun, but they were nowhere to be seen. Exclamations of "Help!" and "Fire!" struck my ears above the cacophony of clanking buckets, clattering footsteps, hysterical pushing, and screaming men, women, and children. More smoke seeped out from the platform and the side walls; its acrid stink tore at my nostrils, stinging my eyes to tears.

My gaze darted around. An old woman trying to squeeze out of the entrance was flung aside by a man. A couple held hands and pushed with one heart. The Merit Accumulating Box fell over; bills and coins spilled across the floor, glittering under the sun angled through the tall windows. Meditation cushions were flattened under the stampede. Slippers and chant books were strewn everywhere on the floor, together with wallets, keys, smashed glasses, gold chains, prayer beads. People cried, squirmed, thrust, tumbled. The air was dense. More splinters of wood fell. Coughing, I covered my mouth tightly so I wouldn't inhale the smoke, or scream. My heart raced. Mother's image kept spinning in my head while tears burned like lava down my cheeks.

Suddenly, I saw the fire devouring the altar and melting Buddha's face. I screamed and pushed as if chased by the King of Hell. Would I survive as I did when I had fallen into the well? Or would I die burning in this hellfire? *Guan Yin, please help me again, I don't want to die! I came here to pursue my spirituality, not my death!* I kept praying, when suddenly I realized the Goddess of Mercy—now a heap of shards on the floor—was even more helpless than I. Another realization hit me like lightning—my fifteen years' cultivation of nonattachment and no self were gone in a second!

Then I noticed a small boy next to me crying his heart out and calling "Mama! Mama!" I picked him up and held him close to me. Right then I felt someone grab my arm. I turned and saw Michael Fuller. He took the child from me and shouted above the din, "Come! Follow me!" Instead of moving with the mob toward the gate, he pushed me away from it. Before I had a chance to protest, he snatched the microphone and used it to smash the window. The boy cried louder. Fresh air rushed in. While I was trying to step out, a flaming beam fell right toward me. Fuller shielded me with his body and pulled me away. The three of us fell hard onto the floor. The boy shrieked. Fuller kicked away the beam, then stood up and gave me his hand. My knee hurt terribly and I was too stunned to respond. He lifted the child through the window and swiftly came back. Then, to my utter shock and surprise, he scooped me up, and before I could protest, he'd already carried me through the broken glass.

"You OK?" he asked in English after putting me down on the floor, unaware of the emotion simmering inside me. I'd never been touched by a man, let alone cuddled in his arms. I was sure now my cheeks were as hot and red as the fire. The child pulled my robe and I stooped to hold him.

Fuller spoke again, his eyes concerned. "Do you think you can take him to the front yard? I need to go in to help other people out."

"I'm fine," I finally said, my lips trembling. "Go ahead."

He stepped back inside and used the microphone to smash more of the glass panes while calling to the people, "Come out through the windows!"

Limping, I led the child to the front yard. In the open air, I could see the fire coming from behind the Meditation Hall. The lapping flames, like hungry ghosts, greedily licked the wooden walls and roofs. I wiped away tears and coughed. The boy next to me cried, "Mama! Mama!" I put my arm around him.

Most people were already outside when two screaming fire engines appeared and halted with squealing tires. Firemen radiated down from the trucks, set up their hoses, and started dousing water onto the leaping fire. Then an ambulance arrived and spat out white-clad men and stretchers. Gray-robed monks and nuns were running around trying to help. Children flooded out from the adjacent orphanage to watch, refusing to be pushed back by two young nuns. The kids' jaws dropped and their eyes shone with a hungry luster, as if watching a Hollywood film. Their curious, innocent faces shone red in the glaring fire.

Now, from a safe distance, my fear gone, I, too, watched with horrified fascination. I knew it was wicked to find the fire beautiful amidst this disaster, but I did. Its rapid motion, intense color, and strong smell reminded me of a vigorous Zen painting, where the artist splashed ink across the paper to bleed his soul and free his spirit. I wished I had my painting tools with me, so I could capture this intense moment. The fire both appalled and appealed. It was like Yi Kong—powerful, alive, and full of energy. It leaped and coiled, flapped and seethed like the Queen of Dance. Buddhism says "To die in order to live." Did this fire carry the same mission? To burn away our ego, desire, attachment, and self-centered thinking?

Yes. But there was more to its beauty. It was passion, pure *yang* energy. Even its crackling sound seemed voluptuous. Suddenly I noticed the sensuous shape of the *stupa,* a tower, in the distance and thought of a woman's curves. How on earth could something be so destructive and yet so powerful in its appeal to the senses? The fire awakened something in me that I couldn't yet name.

In the glaring flame, the stifling heat, the flying cinders, and the choking smoke, my heart became aroused by the splendor of destruction and rebirth. Then I saw that the Sutra Storing Pavilion was right next to the Meditation Hall, and my mood sobered, seeing it being destroyed.

In less than an hour, the fire was under control and had become smoldering ashes. People milled about or sat on the front courtyard's pavement smelling of smoke, their hair unkempt, eyes dazed, faces streaked with tears and soot, slacks ripped, black Buddhist robes torn. They looked as if their souls had been snatched away by some dark, evil force. The deportment of some of the women embarrassed me—legs spread apart, mouths agape, robes still pulled high, exposing bare legs and underpants.

Suddenly I remembered the child. How could I have neglected him while he was right next to me, frightened and helpless? I pulled him close and asked very gently, "Little friend, are you all right?"

To my surprise, he responded by thrusting his tiny body into my arms and rubbing his head hard on my chest. "Mama," he whispered.

My heart melted. I savored his smallness and vulnerability for long moments—I'd never known it would feel so good to have a child nestling against me. "Little friend," I cooed, drawing back so

I could look him in the face. "I'm not your mama, but don't you worry about her. I'm sure she'll soon find you."

He was four or five, his head shaved and his body wrapped in a miniature Buddhist robe. A beautiful child. He stared at me with his big, curious eyes. "Who are you?"

Then I noticed he had no eyelashes; they were all burnt!

Tenderness swelled inside me while I battled tears. Before I could answer him, he reached his small hand to touch my face. "Why are you crying?"

I couldn't hold my tears anymore; they rolled down my cheeks like water flooding a collapsed dam. I pulled him into my arms and caressed his small bald head as motherly feelings rushed up in me. Then this feeling gave way to sadness when I remembered my short-lived little brother, whom I'd never had a chance to hold in my arms.

Right then Michael Fuller materialized out of nowhere. His face and robe were full of dirt, his hair grayed by the dust. He came up to me, removed shards of glass entangled in my hair, and put his hand on my shoulder. "Meng Ning, are you all right?"

I blushed, remembering the warmth of his body as he'd carried me out from the burning hall. Then I blinked back tears; not only had this American stranger remembered my name, he'd just saved my life and many others' as well.

"I don't know how to thank you, Mr.—"

"Michael," he said.

As he patted the child's head, a young woman with disheveled hair and a tear-streaked face dashed toward us and grabbed the child from me. She pinched the kid on the face, arms, and legs until he burst out crying. She laughed. "Oh, my jewel! My heart! Your flesh hurts! You're alive!" Then she grabbed my arm. "Oh, thank you so much, miss."

I pointed to Michael. "Thank him; it's he who smashed the windows and led people out."

The woman's mouth broke into a huge grin. She put her hands together, bowed, and spoke in accented English. "Oh, dank you, dank you, *gweilo* Buddha." Foreign devil Buddha. Then she turned to the child and hollered in Cantonese, "Son-ah, thank this aunty and this *gweilo* uncle, quick!"

The boy plopped down, prostrate, and kowtowed like a little monk. Michael and I laughed despite the recent disaster. The woman laughed, too, then again thanked us profusely as she led her son away. I watched, with sadness, the boy's departing back as he scurried away with his mother on his small, chubby feet.

Michael pointed to the ambulance. "Meng Ning, why don't you come with me to see if they need help?" He took my elbow and we hurried to the white van.

To my surprise, I saw Yi Kong and several other people lying semiconscious on stretchers. My heart flipped. Oh, Goddess of Mercy, please don't let anything bad happen to my teacher!

Although Yi Kong's face looked pale and her lips bloodless, she was whispering to the eye-twitching nun, who knelt next to her. I felt a rush of relief. Then I noticed that her torn robe revealed her smooth-skinned shoulder. It was the first time I'd seen this much of her; my cheeks felt hot. Several other nuns and monks gathered around her, muttering and watching intently. Michael walked up to the van and said to the ambulance men in English, "I'm a doctor. Can I take a look at her?"

After he had checked Yi Kong's breathing and felt her pulse, he said, "She's inhaled a little smoke, but otherwise I think she's fine."

Yi Kong blinked and muttered, "Thank you."

Michael nodded as he walked away to check on the others.

Yi Kong reached out her hand to touch the eye-twitching nun's sleeve. "Make sure everyone is all right. . . ." A tear trickled down from the corner of her eye. "Oh, those books in the Sutra Storing Pavilion!"

Though I'd known her for more than fifteen years, I'd never before seen her face and voice filled with emotion. Despite the tragedy, I felt a secret pleasure at this unexpected revelation.

She spotted me. "Meng Ning, is that you?"

I went to kneel down by her side. "Yes, Yi Kong Shifu."

She muttered, taking my hand. It was also the first time she'd touched me like this—filled with tenderness. My hand brushed against her bare shoulder—so warm and soft.

"You're back—How long have you been away? Five years?" The stressful situation didn't seem to have confused her sharp memory. But as I was about to reply I saw she had already closed her eyes.

As I watched the ambulance carry Yi Kong away, from the corner of my eye I saw a face with a red scar like a snake slithering under the sun. I quickly turned, but saw nothing except the sad-faced nuns with their excited orphans.

$$\approx 7 \approx$$

One Day When
We Were Young

Michael and I stayed in the Fragrant Spirit Temple to help. Fortunately no one was seriously injured, for everybody had gotten out through the windows in time.

By the time everything settled down, we were limp with exhaustion. Then I saw Michael looking at my leg. I followed his eyes and noticed my blood-stained knee and ankle. The bleeding had stopped, but the knee was badly scraped. I burst out crying. He took hold of my shoulders and propped me up. Tears of fear, pain, exhaustion, and pent-up emotion rolled down my cheeks, my Buddhist robe, and spilled onto Michael's. Some young nuns in the front court inspected us with curious eyes.

Finally I stopped crying. "I'm sorry, Michael," I said. He was still holding me; I didn't care anymore about the nuns.

Michael took my hand and led me back to his dormitory. It was embarrassing to be standing in front of him in my torn robe. So when he said I needed to take off my stockings for him to clean the scraped skin, I hesitated.

He seemed amused, then pointed toward the exit. "There's the bathroom."

Although I saw no one in the dormitory besides us, I still didn't want to use a men's room. Finally I backed up against the wall. I lifted up my skirt at the back, found the rim of my panty hose, and pulled them down over my knees and past my shins, feeling the nylon scrape my flesh. Then I peeled the shreds first off one foot and then the other. Now my thighs, legs, and feet were bare; a pool of heat swelled inside me.

I sat while Michael examined my knee and ankle. Then he went to the sink, got a cup of water, and poured it slowly over my leg, rinsing off the gray streaks of dirt. I gasped.

He looked up and touched my arm. "Relax, Meng Ning; you're fine. I won't hurt you. Trust me."

I did. And I was surprised. For I had never thought of trusting a man before. I'd only trusted Yi Kong and Guan Yin, the Goddess of Mercy. But now, although my breath was shallow and my heart raced, I felt secure in front of this man kneeling before me and tending my feet with his skillful doctor's hands. I battled tears and watched him bandage my knee with his clean, white handkerchief. He looked totally focused as if giving full expression to his Buddha mind.

After he had finished bandaging my knee, Michael began to examine my swollen toes. He lifted them and squeezed them lightly one by one, asking me whether they hurt.

I nodded. "Not terribly, just a little."

"Don't worry. Your toes are not broken and the swelling will be gone in a few days."

My knee, ankle, and feet looked much better now and the pain had also stopped. Fortunately, only my robe was torn and stained with blood; my dress underneath was fine. I didn't want to explain about the retreat or the fire to Mother when I got home.

Finally, still dazed, I went back to my dormitory to change, wash, and gather my belongings. Michael and I met later at the main temple gate and we exchanged phone numbers and addresses. He insisted on taking me home; I thought I should refuse—he had already done so much for everyone—but I had no energy—nor desire—to do so.

It took us almost two hours to travel from Lantau Island back to the city. First we took the ferry to Central, then from there took the MTR to Cheung Sha Wan, two blocks from my apartment. When we had climbed up to the street, I politely turned down his offer to walk with me.

"I'll be fine," I said. I didn't want to risk running into Mother with a *gweilo* by my side—I was too tired to explain.

It was almost eleven when I arrived home. Luckily Mother was asleep, and I went straight to my room to change and rest. Unable to unwind, I lay in bed and looked out the window. Suspended in the royal blue sky, the silver moon peeked at me through a few scattered clouds. Su Dongpo's poem popped into my mind. "Even a thousand miles apart, the same moon shines over us all."

What was Michael doing now in the Kowloon Hotel? Sleeping? Watching TV? Or staring at the same moon and thinking of me? I closed my eyes. . . .

> *Under the pearlescent moonlight, the scarred nun wandered around the Golden Lotus Temple where Yi Kong resided. She looked up at the window of Yi Kong's dormitory and wailed, "Shifu, please give me your beautiful face! And your fingers! Those long, elegant fingers!"*
>
> *Yi Kong materialized by the window and threw down a pillow. "Go to sleep, fool!" she said in her silvery voice. "Your scar is your best friend, not your enemy. Let go! Detach! That's what you can learn from it."*
>
> *Just after Yi Kong had snapped shut the window, she threw it wide open again and looked down at the scarred nun with frightened eyes, screaming, "Help! Help! Fire!"*
>
> *Scarred Nun sneered back, "Let go! Detach! The fire is your best friend; you should learn nonattachment from it!" Then she sauntered away, leaving Yi Kong on fire.*

I snapped back into my bedroom, sweating heavily. Mother burst in; her face looked as if the Japanese were again invading Hong Kong.

"Come! Meng Ning, run!"

"What?"

"Didn't you just scream *fire?*"

"Ma, it's just a bad dream. I'm fine." I looked at her concerned face and suddenly felt very tender.

Mother put her plump hand on my forehead. "Meng Ning, you look tired. You need a big, healthy breakfast," she said, then disappeared into the kitchen. Her cheerful whistle pierced through the clanking of pots and pans into my ears.

The tune was "One Day When We were Young."

That was my parents' love song. Before he became a gambler, Father was a poet and scholar who taught school in Hualian, a town in Taiwan. Mother, his student, was nine and Father nineteen when they first met. Mother told me the moment their eyes met, she knew their fates were linked. She always boasted how handsome Father looked with his clean white shirt and thick, cropped hair, how he charmed all his students with his humor and erudition, how all the girls in his class had a crush on him, while his torchlike eyes always sought only hers. "Tall and handsome like a Hollywood star, that's how your father's friends described him."

A year later, Grandmother moved the whole family to Taipei. Grandfather had died, and Grandmother believed that only in a big city would she have a chance to lift herself from poverty and give her children a better future. Mother and Father lost contact with each other.

One day, eight years later, when Mother went as usual to help in Grandmother's store after school, she saw a man chatting with Grandma while choosing gold jewelry from the glass counter. The familiar voice made her heart jump.

"Oh," she muttered to herself, "Goddess of Mercy, let this be *him!*" Then she called on all the gods and goddesses she'd never believed in to grant her wish.

Grandmother chided her. "Mei Lin, what are you mumbling about over there? Come here and help."

The man turned around and their eyes locked.

Mother screamed, "Teacher Du!"

"Ah, so this is the Teacher Du you used to talk about all the time," said her mother. "Now congratulate Teacher Du, for he's getting married in three weeks. He's here to buy gold for his bride."

Instead of congratulating Teacher Du, Mother burst into tears and ran out of the store.

"Mei Lin, let me explain!" Father chased after her out into the street where they fell into each other's arms.

At first they had no idea what to do. Finally, a week later, they thought of an easy way out of Father's engagement to the other girl—they just gathered a few belongings, some cash, and boarded a ship to Hong Kong. A year later, at nineteen, Mother gave birth to me. After that, Father and Mother continued to live together without ever getting married. I'd always thought this was because my parents felt guilty about the jilted girl, for her humiliation, her broken heart. Yet I'd never learned the truth, for whenever I asked what happened to the girl, they'd always avoided my question by talking about something else.

Mother never quite got over the fact that she hadn't had a fancy wedding nor gold-framed wedding pictures. Father, on the other hand, seemed quite proud of the situation. Once, when I was small, he told me, "Ning Ning, since your mother and I were never really married, you're an illegitimate child. But you know what? That's also the reason you're exceptionally handsome and intelligent."

"Baba, I don't understand." I meant my being illegitimate and intelligent and handsome at the same time.

Father smiled mischievously. "Of course you don't. You're still a child. Go ask your mother. I've already explained it to her a hundred times."

Mother's deft hands stopped in the midst of her knitting. She measured the small red sweater against my back, lowering her voice. "Ahhh . . . it's because—because when a couple makes a child in a secret way, so to speak, they're, well . . . ahh, more intense. They give more energy to the child when they do, well . . . *that thing,* you understand? They throw out more *qi,* more everything. That's why you're so beautiful and smart. Lucky child, because you got double what other people have. Double, you understand?"

I didn't.

"Well," Mother snapped, "then go back to your father and ask him!" She resumed her knitting in allegro tempo, lowering her head.

Sometimes I felt glad that the other girl hadn't married Father.

Because not only would she have lost face when Father cheated on her after they were married, she'd probably have also lost all the gold that he would have bought her for the wedding. Could she, like Mother, have survived merely on the memory of a song sung one wonderful morning in May? I knew Father had taught "One Day When We Were Young" to his students in his English class, but Mother said, "Actually, your father wanted to teach it only to me, but he didn't want the others to know of his feelings, so he taught it to the whole class."

Breakfast was finally ready. I sat down to eat and Mother sat opposite me to read her newspaper. On the table, I found three boiled eggs, two thick pieces of ham, and coffee with milk.

"Ma, you seldom cook Western dishes. Why an American breakfast today?"

"Because America is rich, just like its breakfast. You need more energy," she answered without looking up from her paper, then, "*Ai-ya!* Yesterday a monastery was on fire!"

I stopped chewing; she went on reading. "Hmm . . . lucky nobody's hurt . . . because an American and a Chinese doctor helped people leave through windows."

My heart raced. Mother continued, "This *gweilo* doctor graduated from Zhong Hok Kin Si . . . and a Dr. Du . . ."

I snatched the paper from Mother despite her protest. The headline of the article read: "Seven-Day Buddhist Retreat in Fragrant Spirit Temple Canceled Because of Fire. People Saved by an American Buddha, Nobody Killed, Only Slight Injuries."

The article went on to describe the fire, the panic, and the damage. At the end, it said:

> The American doctor, Buddha Michael Fuller, thirty-eight, who saved many lives, is a neurologist graduated from Johns Hopkins University, and currently works in New York Hospital.
>
> A participant at the retreat, Dr. Fuller took refuge as a lay Buddhist in the Shanghai Jade Buddha Temple and was given the lay Buddhist name

Fangxia Zizai. Monks and nuns from the temple expressed immense thanks to Dr. Fuller and Dr. Du, a Chinese lay woman attending the retreat.

I spilled coffee on my name in the newspaper to smear the ink before I handed it back to Mother. Then I gobbled down my breakfast. It must have been the temple that had given the newspaper our names. And it must have been the gossipy newspaper that had put them together.

Memories of Michael holding the child, carrying and lifting me through the temple window, and tending my knee played slowly in my mind. Men had rarely held particular interest for me, but now when I thought of him and his Buddhist name Fangxia Zizai, which means Let-Go-and-Be-Carefree, I felt something stir inside me. And I was afraid. . . .

8

The Same Moon Shines Over Us All

I peeked at Mother, who was still completely immersed in her gossip-column reading. Judging from the cheerful lifting of her lips, I assumed it must be something really juicy. Yet sadness engulfed me, for I knew well this had been the same expression she'd worn when she'd listened to Father's *tianyan miyu*—sugared words and honeyed language. She had willingly let Father cheat her and cheat on her, though she'd always prided herself on being extremely careful.

So careful that she'd spend an extra dollar, an extra half hour, and an extra half mile riding a tram to the particular market where, according to her, not only did the pork cost one dollar less, but also weighed one *liang* more.

"If you're careful, you can steer your ship for ten thousand years."

"But, Ma," I'd argue, "what's the point of steering a ship for ten thousand years when we're even lucky to have eighty years to live?"

Mother's tongue would click away as if it were rolling in oil. "Ah, insolent girl. It's the philosophy, the wisdom behind it." Then she would pour out words while picking up her favorite dish, fatty pork, with her chopsticks. "Let's say your grandmother taught me to be careful, and now I teach you. While in the future you'll teach your daughter, and in the far future my granddaughter will teach my great-granddaughter . . . then all the generations added up together will be ten thousand years of wisdom, or more, right?"

But Mother was careful only in words, not in deeds. While she would warn me not to open doors to strangers, she'd let salesmen into our apartment, serve them tea, and let herself be sweet-talked into buying expensive kitchen equipment that she'd never learn how to use, and which cost her a whole month's food money. While she'd tell me not to drink any beverage offered at a friend's house, she'd happily toss down a dollar onto a street stall and pick up a filthy glass swirling with unidentifiable liquid.

And despite her incessantly cautioning me to beware of handsome, honey-lipped, flower-hearted men, she had blindly loved Father and willingly let herself be cheated by him.

Father had charmed her, not only with his good looks, but also with the numerous love poems he had written her. In his slick calligraphy, he'd write them on fancy rice paper printed with flowers and birds or sprinkled with simulated gold flakes. Occasionally he'd also write them on photographs of himself that he had sent her. Above the poems he would add, "To dear Mei Lin, remembering our eight years' separation"—then below, "Forever yours, Du Wei."

Over the years, Mother carefully pressed the poems in her diary together with the daisies or irises or roses she had bought from wet, smelly, slippery markets or picked from public parks. From time to time, she'd take the poems out to read, or recopy them with brush and ink, imitating Father's calligraphy. Although I was deeply moved by these romantic acts, they also made me sad.

For Father had never written those poems. He had plagiarized them from ancient poets.

I could never pin down Father's real feelings for Mother. One time when I'd asked him how he had courted her, he looked surprised. "I didn't court your mother," he said, lowering his voice, "it's she who chased after me." Then he told me a different version of the gold-store story. There, when they had run into each other, he had not recognized her at all. "How could I?" He frowned and looked surprised. "She was nine years old when we were in Hualian, but when we met again in Taipei she'd grown into a young woman." "Besides," Father added, "how could I remember her puppy love when she was nine and me nineteen?" But then when I asked him why he had dumped his fiancée for Mother, he suddenly changed the subject to talk about the weather. Had he actually been after Grandmother's gold?

One evening, a few weeks after Father's death, Mother decided to bind into a book all the poems he had written her. I helped her work on the project at our dining table.

Although the room was hot, Mother told me not to turn on the fan, for fear the wind would blow off the papers.

I gathered poems from her different diaries; Mother pasted the dried flowers onto a hard board to be used as the cover of the collection. As we were cutting, pasting, and binding, now and then Mother would hum "One Day When We Were Young," then recite the poems Father had written her as if he were still hovering somewhere in the house, meanwhile quietly wiping away a tear or two.

I peeked at her. "Ma, do you understand Baba's poems?"

Mother frowned. "Meng Ning, you don't understand a poem; you feel it."

"Then how do you feel?"

Mother frowned deeper. "If I can tell you how I feel, then your father's poems aren't very good. With good poems you never quite know how you feel. Sometimes sad, sometimes happy, sometimes sweet, sometimes sour, sometimes bitter, sometimes generous. Sometimes you feel and sometimes you don't." She paused, her eyes losing their focus. "When your heart is like a knocked-over shelf of condiments spilling a hundred different flavors and feelings, then the poem is a very good poem. Your father's poems can do just that."

Suddenly Mother stood up, went to the window, opened it, and pointed outside. "Meng Ning, look at the moon, so bright and beautiful tonight. I wonder what your father is doing over there right now." Then she sighed. "*Hai!* He knew this moment would come when he wrote, 'A thousand miles apart, the same moon shines over us all.'"

She meditated awhile on the moon, then came back to sit down by me. "Your father was such a great poet, and he was psychic. He knew that the moon would bring him and me together."

I swallowed hard. Didn't she know this was not Father's poem, but Su Dongpo's?

Mother took a picture on top of the pile of papers and handed it to me, her eyes misted. "Your father when we met again after our eight years' separation."

The brownish, hand-tinted photograph showed a very young and handsome Father. His hair was pomaded and slicked back in the fashion of the forties, while his eyes, large, sparkling, and dreamy, seemed to radiate pleasure and passion. He looked eager to show off, with his generous smile, his sensuous lips, and gleaming white teeth. Mother had told me, repeatedly, he was so handsome that many people had mistaken him for a movie star. A Hollywood, American movie star. "Kar Gay Bo," she said proudly. Clark Gable. Looking at Father's picture, I could understand why, despite his dishonesty, Mother could never gather enough strength to resist him.

Although my parents had lived together for more than twenty years, Mother had never really captured Father, for he was as slippery as a snake—just when you thought you might get a hold of him, he had already vanished into the depth of the bush. Sometimes this made me think that maybe in life you should never try to capture what you really want. For at the moment when you're holding the conquest in your hands, your victory only signifies the beginning of the end. Maybe only the ignorant will hold on. The wise will either let go or simply live with imperfection as it is. Or, maybe, in her own way, Mother truly felt happy with Father. For this romantic love was the only dream she had in life; without it, she'd be like a flower without the sun, a beauty without a mirror. Softly, Mother began to recite the poem written on the picture:

"Eight years blurred between life and death;
Even as I try not to think, I can't forget.
A solitary grave a thousand miles away has no way to
    express its melancholy.
I fear, when we meet, my face will be dusty and my hair
    white."

"That's how he wrote to express his grief for our eight years' separation," Mother said. Then she looked lost in thought. "Your father was such a genius; he had such deep feelings. If people could appreciate poetry today . . . he'd be famous, very famous. . . ."

It saddened me to see how the years had caused Mother's lips to droop helplessly at the corners and her eyes to lose their luster. Too, it saddened me to know the truth that, again, this poem was not written by Father but by Su Dongpo, the great Song dynasty poet. Worse, Father had changed the original "ten years" of Su's poem to suit his eight years' separation from Mother. It broke my heart that Mother could not see the truth, even when it was bared right in front of her eyes. To her, believing *is* seeing, rather than the reverse. Or did she deliberately choose to be blind?

Suddenly, a strong wind blew from the window and the rice papers scattered on the floor in a flurry. Mother stooped to pick them up, embarrassing me with her plump torso and her awkward pose.

"Quick, Meng Ning, close the windows! And be careful not to trample on your father's poems!"

I went up to the windows and saw, to my surprise, that what brightly shone outside the window was not the moon, but a streetlamp.

The phone's trilling jolted me awake from my reverie; I snatched it up. "Hello."

"Can I speak to Meng Ning, please."

"Michael?" My heart raced.

"Yes. Meng Ning." A pause, then, "Are you all right? I called last night, but nobody answered the phone. I was worried about you."

"Oh, I'm so sorry, Michael. I didn't hear anything. Mother must have turned off the phone. Sometimes she doesn't want to be bothered. I'm fine."

"Your knee and ankle . . . you want me to come over and change the bandages for you?"

"No thanks. I think I can manage," I said, feeling a tug at my heart and suppressing it.

He asked whether I would like to go to the hospital with him to visit Yi Kong and other patients from the fire.

I was glad he'd asked, and suddenly ashamed. How could I have forgotten to think of my mentor, who not only had taught me Buddhism and Zen painting, but also had given me free meals and even lent me money for my father's funeral?

Michael was waiting for me by the entrance of Kwong Wah Hospital when I arrived at five-thirty in the afternoon. We bought some fruit and juice at a street stall outside, then walked into the lobby.

Yi Kong slept, with two nuns sitting at her bedside—the eye-twitching nun and a young novice. Once I'd put the gift on the chest beside the bed, they signaled us to go outside.

When we were in the corridor, they both exclaimed, "*A Mi Tuo Fo!* Praise to the Merciful Buddha! Thank you so much for what you two have done." Although I remembered them from the retreat, I'd never asked their names. The eye-twitching nun was Lonely Journey and the young nun No Dust. Lonely Journey told us Yi Kong was only exhausted from the fire and worried about the damage caused, but she was otherwise fine.

Michael asked how the fire started. No Dust frowned. "An eight-year-old boy did it." Her voice grew angry. "He is the naughtiest in our orphanage, can never be disciplined. Yesterday he stole some meat from who knows where and tried to cook it behind the Meditation Hall, but he fell asleep. We only learned about the cause this morning when another orphan came to tell us. He hasn't come himself to apologize."

No Dust paused. "This boy came to our orphanage after his father stabbed his mother to death and none of his relatives were willing to take him, fearing he'd bring bad luck into their houses. We took him, and now see what he's done to us." Then she widened her eyes. "Bad boy! The fire could have killed the Venerable Yi Kong!"

Michael spoke, his voice sad. "He's just a boy. It's just his ignorance, and . . . it's hard to be an orphan."

The two nuns smiled, looking embarrassed, then began to talk about other things. Toward the end of our conversation, Lonely Journey told me that Yi Kong wished to see me after she was out of the hospital.

Michael and I headed toward the Yau Ma Tei MTR station on Waterloo Road. The broad street was crowded with hurrying people and speeding cars. As we passed the YMCA, I saw our reflections in the glass door. Michael looked spirited in his green shirt and khaki pants, his hair slightly mussed by the breeze. While I, in my white blouse and long skirt (to cover my scraped knee), looked like a child beside him. Then I noticed we were holding hands. Feeling my color rise, I immediately withdrew mine. Michael seemed not to notice. "Meng Ning, would you like to have dinner with me tonight?"

❦ 9 ❦

The Peak

Michael suggested the Peak Restaurant, so we walked to the station, took the MTR to Tsim Sha Tsui, then walked to the pier to board the Star Ferry to Central. On the ferry, I felt the teeming life of the harbor with its buzzing noises and its smells of salt, seaweed, and fish, while I watched the imposing skyline draw near. In the twilight, outlines of the many-layered buildings seemed to undulate like contrapuntal music. I pondered which was real, which illusory: Central District, where the world's most frenzied speculators meet to invest their billions, or the Fragrant Spirit Temple, where thousands of disciples flood to accumulate merit? But wasn't their merit now all gone in the blaze? In my mind, once again the fire, like a fierce goddess, danced, glared, and radiated spidery fingers through my imagination, to mock my fascination and fear.

I shivered.

Michael put his arm around me. "Meng Ning, are you OK?"

I looked at his face and remembered Yi Kong had once said, *Detach from human love; it's illusory.*

But what about her compassion and Michael's kindness—were they equally illusory?

"I'm fine, Michael," I said. "Just a bit confused."

"You're still thinking about the fire?"

I remained silent. How could I tell him I was, in fact, less troubled by the fire than by my aroused feelings about men—about him?

He pulled me closer to him. "It's over, and we're fine."

We got off the ferry and began to stroll. The walk took five minutes, during which we didn't talk much except about the fire.

It was almost eight when we arrived at the Garden Road tram station. We stood with a few tourists and local Chinese in the small waiting area. Trams ran every ten minutes, so it wasn't long before we boarded.

With a jerk and a crisp *ting!* the tram began to climb the steep hill. Inside, tourists squirmed excitedly on wooden seats or clutched nervously at leather straps. Three Chinese women with teenage daughters, all carrying small cameras over their small breasts, giggled and screamed whenever there was another jerk or *ting!*

Michael and I leaned by the window, gazing outside. The sky had just blushed into fuchsia, anticipating the rising of Goddess Moon. It was hot, but the sea breeze felt fresh on my face.

After a while, I saw Victoria Harbor appear in ellipses between crowded buildings. Across the harbor, the emerald water reached lazily to embrace the ragged coastline of Kowloon. I found myself seeing Hong Kong through fresh eyes. After the fire, now everything—even the familiar—looked acute and interesting: the harbor, the sea, the meditating boats, the shimmering neon lights blinking like sweet dreams. As a solitary cloud drifted across the moon, I nudged closer to Michael.

He pointed outside. "Meng Ning, look at the airport runway." His long finger directed my eyes to Kowloon.

The brightly lit runway stretched out into the royal blue sea like a fiery tongue, quietly lapping up a plane. My heart stirred at Michael's physical presence. The air around me seemed to be filled with his cologne and his body heat.

He said, "I think Hong Kong is the only city in the world where the plane lands right in the middle of things. I like that. It's Zen, right here and now."

The tram strained toward the top of the hill and all the buildings outside looked slanted, as if they were falling down. I felt a jolt inside. Was it an omen that I'd also soon be falling . . . in love?

Just then the tram passed a thicket of bamboo and fir trees and jerked to its stop—the upper Peak Tram station.

It took us less than five minutes to walk to the Peak Restaurant. A pretty hostess in a tight black skirt, with a flirtatious smile aimed solely at Michael, told us that since someone had just called to cancel their reservation, we were fortunate to have the last table by the window.

Wriggling her hips to the lively rhythm of the background jazz, she led us to the table by a floor-length window with tall, tropical plants. As the hostess clicked away on her narrow high heels, Michael stepped to my side of the table to pull out the chair for me.

I looked around and remembered once reading that during the colonial period, this site had been a resting place for sedan carriers who brought the very rich and privileged to the top of Victoria Peak. Now it was a restaurant for all. I liked its English medieval pointed vaults, cozy stone fireplace, dark paintings of English landscapes—and, of course, the mouthwatering aroma of food permeating the entire place: roast beef, grilled shrimp, lamb in curry sauce. . . .

A tuxedoed waiter handed us large menus. Silence fell as we looked over the long list of dishes.

"Well, Meng Ning, have you decided?" Michael finally asked.

"Not quite, what about you?"

"I'm vegetarian, so I'll have sun-dried tomato pasta and Perrier."

Feeling embarrassed at being carnivorous, I said I'd have the same, suppressing my craving for a lamb chop. When the waiter left, Michael asked, "Are you also vegetarian?"

"Not really," I said, then quickly added, "Are you vegetarian because you're a Buddhist or because you're a doctor?"

"Both." He nodded toward a neighboring table where a rotund Chinese man was attacking a pork steak, clanking his knife and fork like a warrior, and gobbling heroically. "That battered pork over there used to be a healthy pig, who sunbathed on the meadow, flirted with his girlfriend, told jokes to his children, dreamt sweet dreams under shaded trees, played, laughed."

I blushed.

Michael leaned forward to pat my hand. "Don't worry, the Buddha was also carnivorous, since he had to eat whatever he found in his begging bowl, meat or vegetables."

Not knowing what to say, I looked out the window. The revolving restaurant inched on in largo, taking in the skyline of City Hall, the Conrad Hong Kong hotel, the Hong Kong Bank, the Mandarin Oriental Hotel, the needle-like Bank of China tower designed by I. M. Pei.

My gaze continued to wander until it alighted on the dim outline of the mountains of the Kowloon Peninsula, the presence of China looming behind them.

Yi Kong once said *If our hearts are not centered, even living in the remotest mountain is like living in a prison.* She tapped her heart. *Our home is where our hearts settle, and as monks and nuns, our hearts settle anywhere. Whether Hong Kong, the United States, China, even in prison, that shouldn't make any difference.*

If there was no difference, why then did she want me to enter her temple to become a nun?

Michael's voice broke in on my thoughts. "Amazing that I find Hong Kong so beautiful, since I mainly like simple things . . . I mean simple, yet beautiful things, like Chinese art." He paused for a second, then said, "Meng Ning, you have a Ph.D. in Asian art history from the Sorbonne?"

"Yes and no. I still need to go back to Paris for my oral defense."

"I love Chinese art."

"You do?" I studied Michael's green eyes and high nose.

Just then the waiter arrived with our Perrier. When he'd poured our drinks and left, Michael raised his glass to touch mine with a crisp *clink!*

"Cheers, Meng Ning. To our having met."

"Cheers," I echoed, feeling a little breathless.

Between sips, I explained how I'd learned to appreciate Zen art from my nun friend Yi Kong, also a collector. Michael said he liked Song and Yuan dynasty art for its simplicity and elegance, but disliked ornate Qing dynasty art because it was created to show off rather than to give private pleasure.

"It doesn't inspire the same feelings of solitude and meditation." He looked into my eyes. "Things might not last forever, but affections can, and that's what we cherish in life."

I felt both stirred and uneasy. "Sometimes," I said, avoiding his gaze, "I do like busy art, though."

Michael ignored my remark. He leaned forward to gaze at me, a smile blossoming on his face. "Meng Ning, I like to forget my troubles with beautiful things. Chinese art does that for me."

I turned raw and tender inside. Few Chinese can understand the subtlety, deep vision, and the deceptive plainness of Chinese art, let alone Americans.

He went on. "I like its sense of nature. It's still hard for me to understand why something so simple can be so beautiful . . . and so comforting."

"Because when feelings are too fully expressed," I said, being very careful to sound casual and not to look at him directly, "no room is left for the unknown and the mysterious."

Right then the waiter came back with our dinners. After he'd served us and left, Michael watched me start to eat before he dug his fork into his spaghetti. The pasta tasted much better than I'd expected. The cooking and seasoning were just right, and the slight bite of the parmesan cheese was pleasing.

"Michael"—I watched him twirl long strands of pasta around his fork—"how long have you been interested in Chinese art?"

Michael finished chewing the noodles, then put down his fork and dabbed his mouth with the napkin. "Since medical school. One day I received a package in the mail and opened it, not realizing it was for someone else. Inside I found a book on Chinese painting; I glanced through it, not paying much attention at first. Then I became captivated. Those paintings had the kind of beauty I'd been looking for my entire life.

"It's the sense of tranquility—the way a whole landscape is built up from simple brushstrokes. Opening that package changed my life. I believe what happens is the result of karma. The package was addressed to a Professor Michael Fulton in the Fine Arts department. I received it by mistake. Fulton, Fuller—a simple mix-up that awakened me to Chinese culture and led me to become a Buddhist.

"Later, I took the book to Professor Fulton's office and ended up spending more than an hour discussing paintings with him. The next year I managed to sneak away from some of my medical school lectures to attend his class on Chinese art. He's now one of my best friends. His collection of Chinese art is small, but all are masterpieces. He jokes that he could never marry because he needs the space for his art collection."

"Michael, you must be Professor Fulton's favorite student."

Michael's expression changed slightly. "Michael Fulton and I are very close; he's . . . like a father to me."

"Oh . . . and your own parents?"

"I've been an orphan since I was a teenager," Michael said matter-of-factly, yet I saw a glimmer of sadness flash across his eyes.

"I'm really sorry. . . ."

"It's all right."

The green in his eyes softened; his voice became a whisper. I wondered if he had transcended sorrow and spoken from wisdom.

Suddenly a strange emotion caught me by surprise—I felt a strong desire to comfort him with a touch, or even . . . a hug. Like what I had given to the little boy after the fire. I bit my lip and suppressed my feelings. I wanted to know more about his life, but since I'd just met him, I didn't think I should be too inquisitive.

Michael changed the subject, his voice cheerful again. "Why don't you tell me about your family?"

I did.

Michael seemed very interested in my life. "You're a very unusual woman, Meng Ning."

Just then the waiter came back and asked, "Is everything OK?" at the sight of our almost untouched plates.

As Michael reached for the check, I said, "Michael, I still owe you money; can you let me pay?"

He held my hand under his. "Please, I hope I'm Buddhist enough not to be too attached to money." Then he asked me whether I would take him to see more of Hong Kong the next day.

"I'd love to." The words stumbled out of my mouth before I could stop them.

After leaving the restaurant, we took a short walk on the peak along Harlech Road, then rode down in the tram in silence, absorbing each other's thoughts and presence.

Later, when we got off at the Cheung Sha Wan subway station, I declined his offer to walk me home.

"It was a wonderful evening, Meng Ning," Michael said, his face looking pale and dreamlike under the fluorescent light. I felt him squeeze my hand. "And thank you so much for your company." His hand was large, warm, and comforting. So comforting that it was disturbing. He bent close to scan my face. "May I call you tomorrow morning?"

"Yes."

"I'll call around nine then. Good-bye."

"Good-bye," I echoed, unwilling to detach from him while not quite knowing what else to do. Then, to my utter surprise—with several teenagers and other people standing around us in the lobby—Michael drew me into his arms and brushed his lips against mine. After that, he smiled at me one more time, turned, and was gone.

∽10∽

Decadent Pleasure

Michael invited me out each day for the remaining days of the canceled retreat. We spent time near the Kowloon Star Ferry terminal—going to the art museum to look at Chinese paintings and the Space Theatre to see a film on black holes. I felt pleased yet befuddled. After the fire, my life suddenly seemed to have switched onto a completely different track. It had always been my desire to become a nun—if not, then at least a single career woman. Now not only had the fire burned away this ambition, it had also fired my passion for a man, an American! What would my life turn out to be? And . . . what did Michael want from me? Did he really like me or was he just having fun?

One evening I took Michael to the night market in Temple Street in Yau Ma Tei. The noisy alleys were crammed with people shopping at open-air street stalls illuminated by the yellow glow of kerosene lamps. Vendors' and buyers' heated haggling rose above the strollers' chatter and laughter. Western pop music blared from boom boxes and competed with raucous live Cantonese operatic singing. We squeezed through the crowd and saw a heavily made-up sixtyish woman singing in a high-pitched falsetto, "Flowers falling from the sky . . ." She gestured prettily with her embroidered handkerchief as the audience hummed the popular Cantonese opera aria to accompany her.

Michael's face glowed as he listened intently. Then he whispered into my ears, "Meng Ning, I'd love to see a Chinese opera. Would you take me to see one someday?"

"Sure," I said. Then I told him this aria is from *The Royal Beauty,* based on the tragic love between Princess Chang Ping and her fiancé during the Ming dynasty—they committed suicide, refusing to surrender to the new emperor of the foreign Qing dynasty.

After I finished, Michael looked deeply into my eyes. "Meng Ning," he said, "when you take me to see a Chinese opera, I want something with a happy ending."

His remark embarrassed, but pleased me. A silence, then we continued to walk and look around. Goods for sale were either spread on top of wooden planks propped on cross-legged tables, or strewn on large blankets on the ground: used books, pornographic magazines, electronic gadgets, leather goods, T-shirts, plastic toys, combs, eating utensils, buckets, stools, flip-flops, chopping boards. Chinese medicines ran the gamut. Michael asked me to translate the package labels: aromatic white flower oil for headache, dog-skin pomade for chill, earthworm and toad for circulation of blood and relaxation of joints, black snake for arthritis and rheumatism, wine-pickled baby sea horse for lumbago and sexual weakness. I passed over tiger's penis and Golden Gun Never Droop Pills. Grimy stacks of pirated CDs and videos ranged from Cantonese pop to Mozart, Madonna, Michael Jackson.

Used trinkets were labeled as antiques, ranging from dark red *yixing* teapots to opium pipes, bamboo birdcages, Guan Yin statues, clay figures of Tai Chi masters and Bruce Lee, tin biscuit cans from the fifties with oil paintings (Fragonard's *The Reader,* Ingres's *Valpinçon Bather*) reproduced on the lids, coins strung together in the shape of a sword to cast away evil spirits. Tables of jewelry held jade, amber, marcasite, coral, crystal, even plastic. But there was always a chance one might acquire something valuable discarded by ignorant heirs and sold by more ignorant vendors.

Michael bought the coin sword.

When I asked him why, he said, "Because it never hurts to keep evil spirits away."

Food carts emanated tantalizing aromas as Michael and I squeezed forward through the crowd. We saw steaming sticky rice, smoldering sweet potatoes wrapped in aluminum foil, marinated chicken innards, shiny red sausages, grilled barbecue beef impaled on thin bamboo sticks, boiling ruby porridge made with cubes of coagulated chicken blood, smoked duck's liver, stewed ox tongue, fried pig rind, squid dyed fluorescent orange.

A stray dog appeared around a corner and began to sniff among the tidbits of food underneath the stalls. Michael watched it with tenderness in his eyes. "Poor dog. I used to have a spaniel, really big and beautiful, then he got cancer and suffered so much that I had to put him to sleep. After that, I didn't want a dog again. I just don't have the heart." He turned to me. "You like dogs, Meng Ning?"

"Of course," I teased, "they're delicious!"

Just then, a young girl of high school age was walking toward us. The English words on her T-shirt caught my attention: THIS SUM- MER I COULDN'T FIND A JOB, SO I HAD TO TAKE THIS BLOW JOB.

I pointed at her T-shirt and asked, "Michael, what kind of job is this?"

He seemed unable to speak. Laughter spilled out.

He wasn't answering, so I pressed. "Michael, what kind of job—"

"Meng Ning, quiet, please." Michael was still laughing. "I don't think this girl understands . . . I'll explain it to you later when I . . . have a chance."

"But I'm giving you the chance right here and now."

"No, I'm sorry. I really can't explain—"

"Michael, you're a doctor. Is this blow job so hard to explain?"

"Shhhh . . . Meng Ning, plee-eeze!"

He became boneless with laughter and that ended our conver- sation.

The night before his departure, Michael suggested we imitate the Chinese literati of the past—discuss and appreciate the four decadent pleasures: wind, flower, snow, moon. Since there's never any snow in Hong Kong, we decided to go to an outlying island—Cheung Chau—to appreciate the other three. We took the ferry from Central and spent an hour amid boisterous people atop the sapphire sea, before we arrived at the fishing village.

Now at eight o'clock in the evening, the sky turned steel blue with streaks of clouds; behind a chubby one shone the moon. While walking off the ferry, Michael stopped to study the silver disc for a while and then, to my surprise, recited a line from a Chinese poem: "A crescent moon induces melancholy, but a full moon makes one amorous."

I immediately responded with another. "Under the moon in Chang An, the sound of a thousand clothes beaten on stones; the autumnal wind carries the women's never-ending love."

Michael took my hand and I let him. After looking at the moon in silence for a few moments, we resumed walking. It pleased me to see that the small island, although now adorned with modernized buildings and vendors in Western clothes, was clear of cars and retained its ambiance. A few sampans and junks rested contentedly on the shimmering water by the port; others were busy loading or unloading passengers or goods. Thick vegetation, rarely seen in the city, thrived everywhere. A sea breeze wafted onto the shore to ease the heat. In the distance, bits of the turquoise roof tile of the Heavenly Goddess Temple glistened between the laced foliage of ancient trees.

In a store facing the harbor, Michael bought sandwiches, fruit, and drinks for our picnic. Then we headed toward the beach in the company of the moon.

He found a small hill overlooking the sea, but hidden from the beach by thickets of trees, plants, and exotic flowers.

"Perfect for our decadent talk," he said, while spreading out a cloth and arranging the food.

We sat side by side and quietly ate our sandwiches, sipped mineral water, and nibbled apples while feeling our bodies touch each other, watched silently by the moon. In the distance the sea roared, sending white-capped waves to break on the shore. Faint snatches of Cantonese opera tunes carried from the village. I saw the silhouette of a young couple holding tightly onto one another as if fearing even the slightest breeze would blow them apart. Were they walking before love, or after? Not far away, a young man arched his back to hurl something into the sea. A wish to be picked up? Or a hurt to be washed away?

We finished eating and I hugged my knees, listening to the cicadas' small, persistent call until I felt my whole body ache with a longing I'd never known. Then suddenly I realized my dress had slid up to reveal my thighs, which glowed pearlescent under the moonlight. I quickly pulled my dress down, then took several deep breaths, taking in the fragrance of the vegetation, all the while conscious of Michael's intent eyes. Our hips touched. I peeked at his legs, warm and tanned, outstretched as if waiting to be caressed. I noticed their golden hairs glimmering faintly in the moonlight and resisted the urge to touch. I closed my eyes, aware of his body and its pleasant fragrance of mint and the sea.

Michael slowly turned my face toward his, cupped my chin with his hands, and began to search my lips with his. After a long time, he opened my mouth with his tongue, which began to indulge itself in all sorts of decadent pleasures. His hands, large, warm, and eager, moved under my blouse, then my bra. Feeling a rush of desire, I clutched his strong torso.

I felt small under him. Behind him the big, round moon glistened like an enlarged pearl. A star drifted close by. Like me, she wouldn't feel lonely tonight. I held Michael tighter.

My knees weakened and my heart thrashed like a trapped bird. I felt caught and free, wretched and blissful all at once. Until somehow my awareness lifted. In this game between a man and a woman, I suddenly glimpsed the jeweled flowers of the Western Paradise and felt oddly at home. The sea droned in the distance, echoing Michael's breathing. I imagined other lovers also exploring and enjoying each other somewhere on the island, under the watch of the same moon.

And then I covered my face and wiped away a tear. I did like men. I was also upset that Michael, now holding me in his arms and caressing my damp hair, remained so calm and silent. It frightened me that this man seemed gentler than I, yet stronger; that so close to me, he seemed so distant; that he was so kind, and yet so unknown. Let-Go-and-Be-Carefree, his face now serene under the moonlight, was the only man I'd ever let into my life. Suddenly I wondered about his life. What other women had he kissed? Whose sighs had he heard? Whose breasts had he caressed? His hands were large, with fingers as expressive as if they were able to breathe. Men's hands had seemed monstrous and belligerent to me before, but his held comfort and gentleness.

I went home late that evening, feeling dazed. Mother came up to sniff at me. "Ah, Meng Ning, I don't smell alcohol, but you look drunk. Is something wrong?"

"No, Ma, I'm fine." I headed straight to my bedroom.

Mother muttered as I was closing the door. "Oh yes," she said emphatically, "it's a man I smell!"

I locked the door and didn't turn on the light; I had no heart to keep the moon out. Then I went to the mirror, took off all my clothes, and looked at my naked reflection under the moonlight. I stared at the thirty-year-old body that until tonight had never been so touched, nor so aroused. I searched the still-smooth face, narrow shoulders, small breasts, flat stomach, spindly legs, and the small area of black hair that, in the past, I had avoided looking at. But tonight I reached my hand to touch . . .

Slowly, like a cat, I felt my way into bed and inhaled deeply at the silky texture of the sheets against my naked body. I ran my hand over my breasts, remembering Michael's warm, luxurious touch. While my body was serene in the darkness, disturbing memories weaved a confusing tapestry: images of the powerful Yi Kong, of the scarred nun at the retreat, my ex-nun friend Dai Nam, No Name and her fiancé, my father and my mother's ruined life. . . .

At three in the afternoon I awakened with a terrible headache. Mother slammed down a steaming bowl of chicken rice soup. "Some *gweilo* called early this morning, so I said wrong number!"

I burned my tongue on the hot liquid. "Ma, why didn't you wake me up? Maybe it was for me!"

Mother snapped, "Then why did you lock your door when you slept?"

∽ 11 ∽

The Proposal

I called the Kowloon Hotel and asked for Michael several times, but each time the syrupy, professional voice of the receptionist told me he was out. Finally Michael called back at five, but I was quite upset because now we'd only have a few hours together before he had to fly back to New York tomorrow.

I could hear the tension in his voice. "Meng Ning, I called several times in the morning, but a woman kept telling me that I dialed the wrong number."

"That's my mother."

"Hope she's not offended."

"I don't think so. She's just overprotective of me."

Our conversation was brief and somewhat strained; however, toward the end, it started to brighten up when Michael invited me to dinner, then asked if I'd like to go to the Cultural Centre to see a Chinese opera performance.

We went to Tsim Sha Tsui and dined at the Merit Forest Vegetarian Restaurant. After dinner, Michael and I strolled down Nathan Road toward the Cultural Centre. Neither of us mentioned what had happened between us the previous night.

As we were window-shopping, enveloped by the heat and noise of the boulevard, I noticed our reflections in the glass. Michael's arm encircled my waist; I nestled my head on his shoulder. Bathed in the shimmering neon light, he looked cheerful, as usual. His beige suit hung well on his broad shoulders, and his flowered tie in burgundy, brass, and amber complemented my floral dress in Chinese imperial yellow. My face was flushed and my hair tumbled loosely around my shoulders. Mother was right; I looked drunk—in a man's aura.

Once inside the Cultural Centre, Michael excused himself to get us drinks. I looked around and saw that on the pink-tiled walls, colorful banners advertised upcoming performances. One, advertising a Beijing opera, showed a heavily made-up figure in a pearl-tasseled crown and a many-layered, sequined costume. But "she" was a man. Beneath the banner a group of expensively dressed *tai tais,* society women, were discussing this impersonator. One—her plump, goldbangled hand gesturing in big movements—spoke shrilly: "He can play a young widow so well because he's a man, so he's not inhibited. That's why he can express a woman's frustrated sexual desire so openly."

Her friend in a pink suit nodded. "But if a woman acted like that, could she have face to go home to her husband?"

A pretty one in an embroidered Chinese dress chimed in, her diamond teardrop earrings swaying erotically in the air. "Ah, Mrs. Chan, you don't have to worry." She winked. "If she acted like that I bet her husband would find her even more desirable!"

They all giggled, covering their mouths with their brightly manicured, many-ringed fingers.

Michael returned with orange juice in tall glasses. I told him about the ladies' conversation.

"That's an interesting theory." He handed me the glass and a neatly folded napkin, and looked at me curiously. "But don't you think a man will also lose face by acting like a *real* woman?"

"No, on the contrary. He'll gain face." When I tried to drink, the rim of the tall glass hit my nose. "Chinese used to think that because men are free of the impurities of the female body, they can portray feminine beauty from a distance—and render a more gripping performance."

Michael touched my hair. "Meng Ning, you really know a lot about Chinese opera."

"My mother is a Chinese opera fan. She used to take me to performances when I was a kid."

He searched my eyes. "You think I'll have the chance to meet her someday?"

Right then the bell chimed. Michael cupped my elbow and eased me through the throng into the concert hall. A young Chinese woman in a tight dress and spiked heels moved rhythmically ahead of us. Her ponytail kept pecking her buttocks while her arm held tightly onto a foreigner.

Discreetly, I freed myself from Michael's grasp. Hadn't I promised myself I'd never be attached to a man?

Inside the concert hall, the mostly middle-aged and elderly audience settled into their seats. At the right-hand corner of the stage, a small orchestra gathered, its musicians carrying drums, gongs, clappers, cymbals, two-stringed fiddles, flutes, and a wooden fish.

After Michael and I had exchanged more small talk, we began to read the program notes amid the crescendoed ambush of the tuning. There were two performances tonight: "Longing for the Pleasures of the World" and "Seduction of the Zither."

"Longing for the Pleasures of the World" told about a beautiful young nun forced by sickness and poverty to enter a nunnery as a child. Reaching womanhood and bored by the daily routine of *sutra*-reciting among lifeless statues, she decided—after many months of inner turmoil—to taste the forbidden splendors of the floating world outside. "Seduction of the Zither" told how a young scholar seduced a Daoist nun by skillfully playing the *qin*—the seven-stringed zither.

A strange feeling crept over me. Could it be coincidence that Michael and I came to see two operas about the love stories of nuns? Was Michael—like the scholar—a messenger of some mysterious destiny, sent to lure me further away from the empty gate? Were the two operas to tell me that the world outside, not the one inside the temple, was my true calling in life? Or were they warning me against its temptation?

I turned to look at Michael; he squeezed my hand, then continued to read his program notes.

The orchestra began with ear-splitting sounds of drums and

gongs, and the lights dimmed to the audience's enthusiastic applause. Next to the orchestra, English subtitles were projected on a screen.

Slowly, the curtain rose to reveal a temple scene with a nun in a loose robe, her bald head simulated by a pink plastic wrap. The flute began to play a mournful tune in the background, and the nun, her eyes flitting among the various objects on the altar—a bell, a drum, a roll of *sutra,* a big-bellied Buddha—recited in a melancholic tone, "A pity that my head was shaved to become a nun. Time spins fast and spins people old. I don't want to sacrifice my youth for nothing!"

Stroking her "bald" head, she declared, "My name is Form Is Emptiness. In my youth, my mistress shaved my head to make me a nun." She frowned, her delicate finger pointing to an embroidered pillow. "Every day I burn incense and recite the *sutra,* while every night I sleep alone with only this pillow!"

The music changed to a passionate outpouring of fiddles, flutes, gongs, and cymbals, with the nun singing in a high-pitched voice full of sweet innocence. "What a pity that my cushion is not a wife's pillow." She pouted her lips. "I am a woman, not a man, so why should I shave my head and wear a loose robe?"

She strode to the imaginary temple gate, made a butterfly stroke with her white-powdered hands, and delicately extended a step. Her expression turned mischievous. "Every morning when I burn incense, I see a lad idling on the mountain behind the temple. He keeps peeking at me and I keep peeking back. Ah, how we long for each other, my destined love! My destined love!"

She turned to look directly at the audience, her tone decisive. "I don't care if the King of Hell is going to punish me by throwing me into a boiling wok or sawing me in two. Let him do whatever he wants." Suddenly the music increased in speed and volume; she wildly beat her chest. "We always see the living souls suffer. When do we see the dead despair? Ah, I don't care! I don't care! I'm going to tear my robe and bury my *sutras,* throw away my wooden fish and give up my cymbal. I don't care what the King of Hell will do to me when I'm dead!"

Both the music and the nun's singing shot to an extremely high register. "Honestly, I don't want to be enlightened! I don't want to recite the Heart Sutra!" She yanked her robe, her eyes glowing with passion. "Whenever I see husband and wife wearing silk and brocade, drinking wine and making merry, my heart burns with desire! Burns with desire!"

This bold declaration from a Buddhist nun took me aback, even though it was only a play. I peeked at Michael; he looked thoughtful. I turned around and looked at the audience. Some men cackled. The foreigner looked thrilled, while Ponytail next to him smiled a dimpled smile. Several rows behind them the three *tai tais* giggled, this time without covering their mouths and so revealing all their gleaming teeth.

I turned back to the stage to find the nun now singing with a lingering voice, as if unwilling to let go. "I wish I might soon give birth to a baby boy, and joy is awaiting! Joy is awaiting!" Then the curtain closed on this unabashed pronouncement, to the audience's thunderous applause.

It was intermission and when the cheers died down, Michael turned to me, his face vivid. "Wonderful, Meng Ning." Then he asked me how I liked it, but I was still too disturbed to give any opinion. Finally I managed to comment on the actress's supple body movements, her rich falsetto, and the orchestra's lively playing . . . all to avoid talking about the story.

But not Michael. He said, "I think the nun looks like you."

"What do you mean?"

"She's so pretty and lively. She just . . . makes me think of you." He smiled suggestively, then said, "I think people shouldn't stay inside the empty gate if it's against their nature to be monks or nuns."

His words sent a tremor across my chest. Had he realized that I'd always wanted to be a nun? But before I could respond, he eyed me askance and said, "When I first got seriously interested in Buddhism, I thought of becoming a monk. But I realized that it's not for me."

I felt myself starting to blush. He went on: "I once read a Japanese legend about an immortal. One day when he flew above a river, he happened to look down and see a pretty woman washing clothes by stamping her feet on the garments. Her beautiful legs dazzled him so much that he instantly lost his magical power and fell to earth. But he had no regrets about becoming mortal—he'd realized that if a man has no taste for women, he has no life." Michael's expression turned mischievous. "So, if I'd become a monk I'd have been like him."

As I wondered what to say to this, the light dimmed and the curtain began to rise. Michael turned back to look at the stage.

The flute led the other instruments in a lyrical melody as the second play opened. In a garden, the Daoist nun Wonderful Eternity played the *qin* under the moonlight, her hair wrapped up in a tight bun and tied with a long, flowing white ribbon. A handsome but effete-looking scholar hid behind the imaginary temple gate and listened intently to her playing. A smile bloomed on his face as he watched her fingers glide on the strings like butterflies drifting from flower to flower.

When the nun had finished, the scholar stepped forward and bowed, introducing himself as a poet and *qin* player. They exchanged small talk about music and poetry, then the nun invited him to play. The scholar seated himself, paused in meditation, put his fingers on the strings, and began to sing, "In the clear morning, the turtledove flies home by himself, feeling lonesome because he has no wife. Single for such a long time, I feel lonely, oh so lonely. . . ."

While I concentrated on the scholar's quivering voice and the vibrato of the fiddle imitating the subtle inflection of the *qin,* I felt my stomach whipped by some delicate emotions. Onstage, the scholar stole a glance at the nun to see her reaction.

I peeked at Michael; he was also looking at me. I lost myself in his face for a few moments, battling an urge to kiss his intense, searching eyes. The wailing of a flute broke the spell of our stares and I turned my attention back to the events onstage.

Now the scholar stepped out of the nun's garden as she sang to herself, "I deliberately put on a harsh expression, and talked as if I didn't understand his insinuation of love. How can I, being a nun, accept his love?" Her voice turned anxious. "But, while pretending not to understand his love, my heart aches with desire for his tenderness!"

The nun bent her slim torso to watch the scholar's departing back, her eyes flickering with longing and melancholy. "Ah, look at the moon, casting a lonely shadow on him, as well as on me. . . ."

My mind began to drift. Was a nun's life that lonely? Yes, according to Mother's description of No Name's existence. No Name had passed endless nights in her bare room inside the walled nunnery, with only the faint glow of a solitary lamp, the echoes of her own monotonous chanting, the tedious beating of the wooden fish . . . and emptiness. Endless emptiness, which had become so haunting and overwhelming that it had finally taken her last breath on earth.

Yet my mentor Yi Kong's life seemed to me quite the opposite of No Name's. Yi Kong meditated and chanted, but she also lectured and traveled extensively, painted, took photographs, collected art—and large donations. A celebrity surrounded by admirers and followers, she was never lonely.

Which nun's life painted a truer picture of life within the empty gate—Yi Kong's or No Name's?

I couldn't be sure. I was only sure that as a woman, Yi Kong had a higher vision of her life than just to let a man in, get married, and have children.

But Mother said, "Higher vision? Nonsense! What kind of vision can be higher for a woman than to get married and raise children? That's her heavenly duty!"

But heavenly duty can turn to hell, as when Mother lost her baby— my chubby little brother—who'd died at three days old. Mother told me little brother had looked perfectly healthy with bright eyes, ruddy cheeks, and a full head of hair, even when his tiny body, the size of a small thermos, lay motionless in an equally tiny crib. He was sick, of what nobody knew. In the column for cause of death on his death certificate, the doctor only put down one character: Unknown. As if little brother's life, and death, were not worth any deeper concern beyond this one word.

As a child, I thought maybe my little brother just didn't want to be born into the world. This thought made me sad, because, had he lived, he would have enjoyed my tenderest love. I'd have sung him lullabies to sweeten his dreams; told him heroic tales to strengthen his character; knitted him warm sweaters when cold wind began to blow from the north; cooked him hot, tonic soup and wholesome meals when his stomach rumbled hungrily; loved him with all my being and soul and shared with him my heart's deepest secrets.

I guessed that Mother secretly thought little brother's death came as a punishment for her love with Father. Other times she'd think that little brother had actually died of malnutrition because she didn't have enough milk to feed him. Because Father, his money lost to the gambling house, hadn't brought enough food home to feed her in the first place. However, this didn't keep Mother from questioning all the gods and goddesses about why they'd planted such a beautiful seed on earth, but had crushed its chance to grow, flower, and bear fruit.

But Father thought about another kind of chance, as in gambling: sometimes you win, sometimes you lose. He even wrote a poem. "I call it chance":

Sometimes you win
Sometimes you lose.
My baby boy born and gone.
Like the gold on the gambling table.
In life there's no take two.
Gambling has a different rule:
Nobody knows if luck's up or down.
Today I lose; tomorrow I'll win
Keep going; there's always another round.

When I was small, Father would whisper this poem into my ear. "Ning Ning, this is a secret between you and me only." Then he'd hold my hand, whirl me around and around, and begin to sing, "Sometimes you win, sometimes you lose . . ." Toward the end, his voice would trickle like water dripping from the tap—"So just keep going, there's another round, another round"—until I collapsed in his arms in giggles. I couldn't believe that I used to be so happy to hear Father sing this poem. Now I felt sick. . . .

And a touch on my thigh. Michael slipped me a piece of paper—a handwritten haiku:

These thirty-eight years
All empty now.
Can the rest be full?

Followed by:

I love you. Meng Ning, will you marry me?

Startled, I didn't know how to react. As if sensing my emotions, the music now suddenly became stormy with a cacophony of drums, cymbals, flutes, fiddles, and a frantic beating of the wooden fish. Michael took my hand in his; I felt its warmth, but also my own confusion. Slowly I withdrew myself, feeling sad, guilty, and uncertain.

A long pause.

I lowered my head and whispered a soft, "No."

Right then the curtain fell and the opera ended amid waves of applause crashing out at the performers. When the crowd began to disperse, Michael excused himself to go to the men's room. Although he looked calm and poised when he came back, I noticed the red in his eyes and his wet hair.

"Meng Ning, you want to go back to the hotel with me to have something to eat before I take you home?" he asked awkwardly, our bodies pressing against each other in the lobby swarming with people.

We walked back to the Kowloon Hotel in Tsim Sha Tsui in silence. Once inside the lobby, Michael led me to the counter to check whether he had messages.

He did.

"Damn!"

"What's wrong, Michael?"

"I don't know, but it's urgent. I need to return the call immediately."

"I'll take a taxi home then."

"No . . ."

"Don't worry, Michael. It's just a ten-minute ride."

"No. I can't let you go home by yourself," he said, his voice full of concern and tenderness, breaking my heart.

But I insisted repeatedly until he gave in.

Michael hailed a taxi in front of the hotel and helped me get in. The door closed with a disheartening thump. I turned to him and our eyes locked.

When the taxi started to take off, he mouthed, "Take care. I love you."

His face was lost among a crowd thronging toward the entrance. My heart hurt with such a swelling emptiness that I wanted to cry, but no tears came.

Did I really want the life of the empty gate?

12

The Nun
and the Prostitute

I didn't hear from Michael the next morning. Finally, just before eleven (his flight was scheduled to leave at two-thirty), I called the Kowloon Hotel, but the receptionist told me that he had already checked out. However, a letter had been left for me.

I got out of the taxi at the entrance to the Kowloon Hotel, hurried to the counter, took the letter from the receptionist, tore it open, and stood in the lobby to read.

> Dear Meng Ning,
>   Professor Fulton has suddenly fallen very sick while visiting a temple in Lhasa. I had to take a flight to Sichuan at six AM, the only way I can connect to Lhasa today. I believe things will turn out fine, so please don't worry. I'll call you as soon as I can.
> Love,
> Michael

By myself in the lobby, I tried very hard to stifle tears as I watched tourists—faces beaming and laughing as if mocking my misery—whirling in and out of the hotel's glass door.

* * *

A week had gone by and I still hadn't heard anything from Michael. I thought again of Yi Kong and realized I had not inquired about her since my visit to her in the hospital. I decided to make a trip to the Golden Lotus Temple.

Walking down the sunny corridor lined with potted plants leading to Yi Kong's office, I ran into a young nun clasping a stack of files in her arms and asked her about Yi Kong. She told me, with chin pressed to the folders to keep them from falling, that her mistress had flown to Shanxi to invite high monks to come to bless the Fragrant Spirit Temple after the fire.

I asked about the damage caused.

"Everything's fine," she said, her tone casual. "Except that the whole five thousand three hundred and twenty *sutras* of the Tripitaka were burnt to ashes."

"I'm so sorry!"

A meaningful smile flashed on the nun's face. "But doesn't Yi Kong Shifu always teach us that everything in this world is transient?"

An awkward pause, then she said, "Miss, before you leave, please take a look at our new Tang dynasty–style temple complex, which took Yi Kong Shifu five years to achieve." After that, she lumbered down the corridor and disappeared down the stairs.

I wandered about the temple complex, stopping here and there to try to figure out the locations of the old places I'd been familiar with before I'd left to study in Paris. Construction was going on all over the place. Half-finished buildings, surrounded by bamboo scaffoldings and green mesh, looked imposing but vulnerable, like huge bandaged animals. Thick-torsoed workmen in yellow hard hats, shorts, and soaked T-shirts or bodies bared to the waist, toiled with intense concentration—cementing a foundation, plastering a wall, hammering a beam, pushing a cart piled with bricks. Sweat dripped down their deeply tanned faces; their tightly muscled arms flexed and gleamed under the scorching sun. Judging from their solemn expressions, they must have felt honored to work for the most influential temple in Hong Kong.

The new sites under construction did not really interest me. I wanted to go to the old stone garden, hoping to see the carp in the fishpond. Before I went to Paris, I'd spent many days reading in the garden, perched on my favorite stone bench overlooking the pond. When tired, I'd walk up close and stare at the carp to abstract my spirit. Sometimes Yi Kong would join me to discourse on Buddhism, the arts, or her many charitable projects while we sat shaded from the sun, or under the bright moon and twinkling stars.

I felt relieved that the garden was not under construction, and pleased to see that the bamboo, evergreens, ferns, and moss looked more spirited than before. The air still held their fragrance and *qi* still flowed through plants and the pond as I stepped along the pebbles set in contrived random patterns on the ground. I smiled, remembering Yi Kong explaining to me how the spontaneity of most stone gardens is really the result of a deliberate scheme. She'd also reminded me that we should not only raise our heads to admire the trees; we should also lower our heads to appreciate the moss below. I thought she said this to remind me of the lesson of nonduality that I should have learned from my fall into the well— spirituality can be attained low down as well as high up.

Across the pond I saw an elderly woman doing *qigong,* energy exercise, under the shade of the bamboo trees. She was the only other person in the spacious garden, except for the occasional nun who'd pass with a straight back, quickened pace, and an I-know-what-I'm-doing expression.

Carps lazily wagged their tails amidst the entwined water plants. One with patches of gold among white scales broke the surface into concentric circles of ripples before disappearing into the murky depths of the water. Was it my favorite one that I used to feed five years ago?

A girlish voice chimed, "Good morning, miss."

I looked up and saw *Ah-po,* the old woman, her face heavily wrinkled with a grin. She swayed her arms in the form of the Chinese character "eight."

"Good morning, *Ah-po*." I smiled. "What kind of exercise are you practicing?"

"Aromatic intelligence awakening *qigong.*" Ah-po's breath whistled through her nearly toothless mouth, her tone parodying a master's authoritative utterance.

"Ah, very good for your health." I studied her leathery face and wondered how old she was.

"You bet. I'm one hundred," she said, now flapping her ears with her puny hands.

"Wow! Is that true? Congratulations! You only look eighty."

All the creases on *Ah-po*'s face deepened; she looked pleased. "Thank you. You look eighteen." Her toothless smile stretched so wide that the distance between her nose and her lips seemed to be dissolving.

"Oh, thank you, but I'm thirty," I said, then peeked in the pond and was startled that my reflection—among the fish, the seaweed, and the ripples—was as wrinkled as *Ah-po*'s. I suddenly felt very old.

Ah-po's eyes glowed with interest. "How many children do you have?"

"I'm still single." I stared at the empty space next to my reflection in the pond and thought of Michael. What was he doing now in Tibet? Was he used to the thin air there? Was Professor Michael Fulton all right? Why hadn't Michael called me?

Ah-po's tone turned disapproving, but her smile still stretched big. "Ah, single at thirty, no good. Better get a man and get married fast." She narrowed her eyes. "Miss, any man is better than no man!"

"Why?" I asked. Of course I knew why she thought so, but I still wanted to hear it from her.

"Because even when you're old, you'll have someone to quarrel with. It's still better than talking to the four bare walls!"

"How's that?"

"At least you get some response!" *Ah-po* laughed, then she began to swing her elbow from left to right.

I counted the wrinkles on her face. "How many children do you have?"

"One daughter, but she died a long time ago."

"I'm so sorry . . . and your husband?" I immediately regretted asking. Since she was one hundred, her husband must have already been dead a long time.

But her answer surprised me. "No husband." She kept smiling, but her smile was now lopsided.

I wondered why, because during her generation it was inconceivable to bear a child without a husband. Right then, from the corner of my eye I saw, at the other end of the garden near a stone lantern, a cheek with a red scar gleaming under the sun. The scar belonged to a nun approaching the dormitory, her bald head shining like a bright mirror.

"Nice to talk to you, *Ah-po*." I waved good-bye to the centenarian as I hurried past her to follow the nun. Behind me I heard *Ah-po*'s cheerful voice echo like the many ripples of the pond. "Get married soon and have children! Many, many!"

Now the nun quickened her pace, passing doors and windows as her cloth slippers scraped harshly against the pavement. As I again noticed the two mutilated fingers, my heart pounded within my chest. In order not to miss her, I dashed to the parallel path on the other side of the garden, scurried a short distance ahead, then cut across another path perpendicular to the one that the nun had taken.

We stopped, face-to-face. I tried not to stare at her scar. "Dai Nam!"

She halted. Her face had the expression of a frightened cat.

"Dai Nam, don't you recognize me? I'm Meng Ning, your friend from Paris."

The nun's face showed no recognition. "I am Miao Rong."

Wonderful Countenance.

"I'm sorry . . . Miao Rong Shifu," I said, looking at her scar and feeling ridiculous. Why did the temple give her this name? To remind her of her past karma? And what karma was that?

An awkward pause, then I said, "Can we find a place to talk? . . . I've been thinking about you since you left for China. . . ."

"What do you want from me?" the nun asked flatly. I could almost see her scar writhe like a trapped snake.

"I don't want anything. I just want to talk, to know how you are."

"I'm fine." Her eyes flickered suspiciously under her oversized, black-rimmed glasses.

"Yes . . . but that's not what I mean. . . ." I hated my stammer. "Can we talk? Dai . . . Miao Rong Shifu." I moved close to her to let her know that I would not give up. That although she was bigger and older than I, and now had the status of a nun, I was not intimidated.

Her eyes looked impenetrable.

"Please, I won't take up too much of your time." I felt embarrassed to be pleading, but stood firm on the ground in front of her.

"All right . . . follow me."

Once we arrived in her room, Dai Nam excused herself. "Please sit and wait for a moment."

I was suspicious. Would she just disappear as she had done three years before in China?

Her room was small and neat; the air conditioning seemed almost noiseless. Outside buzzed the distant noises of construction; inside floated the scent of fresh flowers and incense. Along one wall rested a cot; beside it stood a wooden chest as tightly closed as if stoutly guarding its mistress's secrets. A bronze incense burner and a bowl with fresh lotuses sat before a small altar with a ceramic Buddha. Framed pictures and documents hung conspicuously over her desk.

I stepped closer to inspect the pictures: Dai Nam as a nun in Thailand, holding a begging bowl, in front of strangely shaped stone ruins. Dai Nam in front of the Arc de Triomphe, her full head of black hair fluttering in the wind. Dai Nam with her French professor at the entrance of the Université de Paris VII. Her doctoral certificate in a gold frame. The pictures hung in chronological order, but none showed her stay in China. Why had she left out this part of her past?

I slumped down into the chair. Did Dai Nam really think she could settle her mind by shaving her head, putting on a robe, and strenuously tidying up her room? I wondered what torrents flowed under her emotionless face and the tidy appearance of her room. And what demons knocked around within her.

I remembered that one evening as we were sipping tea in her attic in Paris, Dai Nam told me how she'd run away from her alcoholic-gambling-womanizing father and money-thirsty stepmother, and had swum across the shark-infested Mirs Bay to Hong Kong. She had tried and failed seven times. She said, "During Daruma's nine years sitting in Zen meditation, his legs were nibbled away by rats, withered, and fell off. Yet after that, he remained upright because he had found his center through meditation. You know the proverb, 'Fall down seven times; get up eight.' The limbless Daruma doll always rights itself when knocked over. That was also how I came to Hong Kong."

After she had arrived in the Fragrant Harbor, Dai Nam's great-aunt took her in, bought her a Hong Kong identity card, and enrolled her in a charity Buddhist middle school. Later, she sent Dai Nam to a Buddhist college. When we met in Paris, Dai Nam had just spent two years in Thailand experiencing the life of a lay nun, begging for her food—the experience she had turned into her Ph.D. dissertation.

Dai Nam and I became friends because of our shared interest in Buddhism. Her eccentricity, her loneliness, and her obsessive cultivation of nonattachment intrigued me. Yet her withdrawn personality had always made our friendship tense and difficult. She rarely looked me in the eye when she talked, and when she did, her eyes were bottomless holes revealing nothing. Although her face never showed definite emotion, her gaze betrayed agitation and restlessness. Silent most of the time, she could also be talkative. When she talked she seemed more withdrawn—her eyes would turn abstract and her mind seemed to be at some far-off place.

One day when we were still living in Paris, she'd invited me to her home and told me she had to leave for China immediately. Her long-estranged father was dying from lung cancer. That was the last time I, or anyone else I knew, saw her. Until now, when suddenly she had resurfaced in Hong Kong as a nun.

The door's click woke me from my musing. Dai Nam entered with a tray laden with a pot of tea, two cups, and a plate of fruits. She put the tray onto the desk, pulled up another chair, and poured tea.

"Please," she said.

I watched her closely as she held the teapot with her mutilated fingers. How had this happened?

I took the cup she handed me with both hands to show my respect for her new status as a nun. "Thank you . . . Miao Rong Shifu," I said. It still felt odd to call her by the preposterous name of Wonderful Countenance.

I quietly sipped my tea and struggled to think of something appropriate to begin the conversation. Dai Nam picked up a couple of grapes, popped them into her mouth, and chewed noisily. Despite the small wrinkles around her eyes, her thick-rimmed glasses, her disturbing scar, and the worn-out clothes she wore, this enigmatic woman in front of me might have been attractive in this life. Did she deliberately hide her charm? Why this radical effort at nonattachment? What really resided in her mind and in her heart?

Finally, I could only think to say, "How have you been?"

"I'm fine. Thank you."

"When did you come back to Hong Kong?"

"A couple of months ago."

"Oh . . . did you ordain as a nun in this temple?"

"Yes."

"So you plan to stay?"

"Yi Kong Shifu has asked me to be her assistant to take charge of the temple's affairs."

My cheeks felt hot. Hadn't Yi Kong always implied that she wanted *me* to be her successor?

Dai Nam, as though reading my mind, said, "It's only temporary. And she asked me only last week." She paused, her gaze resting on her tea cup.

"Oh." I put my cup down with a sharp *clank*. What had I done to my life? I'd turned down Michael's proposal, neglected Yi Kong, and so far had no news about any interviews I'd applied for.

I squeezed out a smile. "Do you plan to take the position?"

Dai Nam stared at the construction outside for long seconds before she returned her gaze to me. "Do you think anyone could turn down such a call from Yi Kong Shifu?"

I could not think how to answer.

She changed the subject. "How was your talk with Chan Lan?"

Why was she suddenly asking about something totally irrelevant? "You mean the old lady in the garden?"

Dai Nam nodded and I said, "Interesting but sad . . . she told me she had a child but no husband. I wonder why."

"She was a comfort woman in the thirties." Noticing the shock on my face, Dai Nam sighed. "In 1932, the Japanese Navy set up comfort houses in Shanghai where more than a hundred Chinese women were forced to work. Chan Lan, even though already in her fifties, was one of them. A year later, she escaped from the comfort house and managed to board a ship to Hong Kong. There she washed dishes at a restaurant for twenty years. She'd saved some money and used it to open a small noodle shop. When she was too old to run her restaurant, she came to the nursing home in this temple."

"Oh, I see . . . and her child died of some sickness?"

"No, her child didn't just die. Chan Lan had an abortion."

Dai Nam's face now transformed into something indescribable, like images frozen in a distant dream; the scar was inert, in hibernation. She spoke as if talking to herself. "The father was one of the Japanese sailors, so she had to end her pregnancy. Otherwise the child would just grow up to be an object of humiliation. . . ." Dai Nam's voice trailed off and the uncomfortable silence returned.

Since Dai Nam had only been in this temple for a few months, I wondered how she knew all this about Chan Lan.

My friend's face stirred as if awakened from a trance. She sipped her tea and again changed the subject. "I heard you've got your Ph.D."

"Hmmm . . . not quite. I still have to go back to Paris for my oral defense. I think the Fragrant Spirit Temple made a mistake about the information. . . ." I paused. "Were you also at the retreat?"

"Yes."

"Then you saw me there?"

"Yes."

"And you also saw me in the garden just now?"

"Yes."

Suddenly I realized Dai Nam had been avoiding me all along, which explained my spotting the red scar several times in the Fragrant Spirit Temple without getting a clear view of her. Why was she hiding from me?

After a pause, I mustered all my courage. "Dai . . . Miao Rong Shifu . . . what happened . . . to your fingers?"

"I burned them off."

"What?" I gasped and spilled my tea on the floor. "But why?"

"To show that I'm not attached, not even to my own body." She stared intently at the stain on the glossy floor. "I also burned them as offerings to Buddha."

"But . . . Miao Rong Shifu, did you really have to do that?"

"Yes. If you really want to show your devotion and detachment."

I tried to feel her mind with mine, but was lost in its unreadable remoteness. I wanted to argue, but nothing came out when I parted my lips. I could not understand how someone could do this to her own body.

Isn't the desire for detachment an attachment in itself?

Dai Nam continued calmly, "I didn't feel terrible pain when I was burning them."

"But how can that be possible?"

"I was in deep meditation. Anyway, I chose the pain as an ordeal."

I thought to remind her of the first line of Confucius's *Ode to Filial Piety*: "My body and hair are inherited from my father and mother; therefore, I would not harm nor damage them. This is the beginning of filial piety." But looking at her emotionless face, I finally swallowed my words.

After a pause, I asked, "You did this here in this temple?"

"No, in China."

I had been dying to know about her disappearance in China, but now had no courage to ask, fearing that another nightmare revelation would writhe out from her mouth to assault me.

Dai Nam stood abruptly from her chair. "Nice to see you again, Miss Du. Now I have to get ready for the temple meeting."

Before, in Paris, she hadn't called me Miss Du. I knew it was now meant to stretch a distance between us. Or, between her and what I knew of her past.

Feeling restless and uneasy after my meeting with Dai Nam, I went to the Meditation Hall to try to meditate, but snakes kept popping from every cranny of my mind, spitting out fiery tongues at me. I went to the library and tried to read, but all I could see in the words of the *sutras* was Dai Nam's inscrutable face behind her thick-lensed glasses, challenging me with her nonattachment and her mutilated fingers.

Unable to relax, I decided to go back to the garden. Maybe *Ah-po* was still there, and I could find some relief in her cheerfulness.

But *Ah-po,* the old woman, was with someone else. So I stopped at the entrance to watch as a nun helped her walk back to the nursing home.

It was Dai Nam. She asked Chan Lan, "Great-Aunt, how are you feeling today?"

I was startled—so this old woman was Dai Nam's comfort woman great-aunt, who'd helped her stay in Hong Kong. I moved behind a hibiscus hedge to stay out of sight.

Chan Lan smiled widely. "Very happy. I talked to a pretty girl. She's thirty but still single. So I told her that's no good, better get married soon and have children, many, many."

She poked Dai Nam's arm with her shriveled, clawlike fingers. "You too, grand niece, get married soon and have children! Many, many!"

I went softly to sit on a bench, to ponder the revelation and to gather my thoughts. However, stray thoughts sleepwalked through my mind, bringing me back to my encounter with Dai Nam in Paris five years before. . . .

❧ 13 ❧

The Non-Nun Nun

I had first met Dai Nam in the library of L'Institut des Hautes Études Chinoises. It happened not long after I'd arrived in Paris when I went to the library to borrow a rare version of the Heart Sutra. When the librarian told me that someone had already checked it out, I became curious about this stranger who shared my interest not only in Buddhism, but also in rare texts. I asked the librarian to introduce us.

She arranged for us to meet in her office on a Saturday morning, a time when the library was mostly empty. Dai Nam was already there when I arrived. The first thing I noticed about her were her eyebrows—a weak and flattened Chinese character "eight," as if executed when the calligrapher was depressed. Then, as I sat down opposite her, a shaft of sunlight entered through a tree-lined window to land on her face. My heart jumped. A large maroon scar, resembling a frightened baby snake, crawled down her right cheek. How had her face been ruined? What kind of accident could have caused this? A car crash? The result of some inexplicable karma? An act of revenge from a spurned love? It must have hurt terribly. As I was wondering how this had happened, suddenly my cheek flared with an itch as I watched the shadow of a many-branched twig, like a witch's broom, sweep the blood-dark stripe. Dai Nam said, "Hello" in a raspy voice.

Our conversation didn't last long; Dai Nam said that she had come to the library to study and did not have time to talk. When I suggested we meet another day in a café, she would set no definite time. I was curious to get to know her better, so when I ran into her again in the institute I suggested we meet at the Café de Flore on Boulevard Saint-Germain. This time she agreed.

Dai Nam had been in Paris longer than I, so I imagined she'd have been to this famous place before. It would be my first time. I hoped I'd have the luck to sit at the same table where Jean-Paul Sartre and Simone de Beauvoir used to sit many decades ago!

Yet on Saturday evening when I arrived at the famous café, I felt disappointed. Except for the prices on the menu by the entrance, it didn't look particularly special. Maybe it had been when Sartre and de Beauvoir set up literary shop here during World War II. Then I suddenly remembered my guidebook's comment: "As with all historic cafés, beware of the prices!"

I took a seat on the front row of the terrace. It was one of those days in Paris when people looked as if merely breathing the Parisian air was the greatest blessing in life. Near me sat two giggling young Japanese women with expensive suits and handbags. Two French women lounged and smoked, hurrying sips of espresso amidst ceaseless talk.

I turned to look at the busy boulevard. A taxi pulled to a stop in front of me and spat out a veiled and gloved old woman in a hat and coat. After she'd paid the driver with her shaking hands, she began to wobble along with the support of a crooked cane. Three chattering young women in four-inch heels and miniskirts strode past her, almost knocking her over, but not noticing. The old woman raised her cane to swing at their bared backs. She missed, but was not discouraged. In the middle of the street, she kept waving her cane in threatening arcs and mouthing obscenities at the departing figures. *Bravo,* I almost shouted to her. Where did she get her strength? Surely not from her arthritic hands nor her crooked cane. Was it from jealousy aroused by the aura of youth and beauty that had once shone on her, but had now passed on to the girls? I was lost in this scene when Dai Nam's voice rang like a broken bell in my ears. "Meng Ning."

I looked up and saw my friend in a plain white cotton shirt, loose dark blue slacks, and sandals. Her hair seemed shorter than the last time I had seen her. Her large, thick-lensed glasses perched low on her nose, blurring her otherwise quite delicate features. She had a large green canvas bag slung across her sturdy shoulders.

Dai Nam sat down and immediately asked me about my life in Paris.

"I love it," I said.

"Why?"

Both her tone and question surprised me, so I pondered for a while before I said, "The whole city has so much energy, like a piece of calligraphy saturated with *qi*." Then I looked at her pale, chapped lips, wondering how they'd look if painted a seductive red. "What about you? Do you love Paris?"

Dai Nam's eyes followed a passing young woman who was fondling her terrier. "I like it OK, but I wouldn't use the word 'love'."

Right then a waiter came to take our order. Dai Nam read the menu very carefully before she whispered into my ear, "There's almost nothing for me in this café . . . either too expensive or too strong."

"Oh, I'm sorry. I picked it because Sartre and de Beauvoir used to come here. So I thought you would like it."

She adjusted her glasses and looked around; her gaze flickered suspiciously. "I've never been here before, never even heard about it."

"None of your friends have ever mentioned the famous Café de Flore to you?"

"I don't have friends."

An awkward pause. Finally I ordered espresso and she Orangina. After the waiter had left, I said, "Dai Nam, next time you can order espresso like me; it's the cheapest. Other drinks cost double."

"I don't drink anything with caffeine—except Chinese tea."

"You can't sleep at night?"

"No, not that . . ."

"You don't like the taste?"

"No, not that either."

The waiter returned with our order. *"Espresso et Orangina."*

After he left, Dai Nam took a long sip. Her gaze looked abstract while her face seemed to relax a little. "I was a nun in the past."

The revelation took me by surprise. "Oh, then . . ." I looked at her full head of hair. "Why did you quit the *Sangha*?" I asked, referring to the Buddhist order of monks and nuns.

"Because my mission had ended."

"Your mission? What was that?"

Dai Nam took another noisy sip of her Orangina. "To gather materials to write about my experience as a nun."

I tried but failed to think of a comment on this peculiar reason for becoming a nun.

Dai Nam's voice was a monotone amid the high-pitched chatters and giggles of the two Japanese women to our right, the earthy, asthmatic voices of the two French women to our left, and the busy traffic in front. "I chose to shave my head in Thailand because in that country nuns are discriminated against within the Buddhist order. I wanted to understand the situation based on firsthand experience."

Before I had a chance to ask whether she was a feminist, Dai Nam said, her gaze darting between several teenage girls giggling as they walked past the café, "Since women cannot be ordained there, I wanted to break that tradition. Maybe 'break' is not the word; 'break through' is more appropriate."

"Did you succeed?"

"No. I completely failed," she said. "During my four years in Thailand, not a single monk was willing to ordain me."

"Why?"

"Because the tradition of ordaining nuns had long been abandoned. And no monk is willing to revive it. No one has the courage to shave a woman's head."

"But what's the big fuss about shaving a woman's head?" Like a mountaineer, my voice climbed higher and higher.

"Monks are not supposed to touch women—not even their heads."

"But we're living in the twentieth century!"

"Yes, you are, but not those monks. Inside the temple walls things are pretty much the same as they were a thousand years ago. The monks don't feel they have any grounds to change the rules that have been the same since the Buddha's time. So finally I shaved my own head, put on a nun's robe, rented a small hut, and practiced on my own. Besides meditating, I begged; sometimes I also sat in the back of a temple and joined in the chanting. The Thai monks were very uneasy about what I did." Dai Nam went on after some consideration. "I looked and lived like a nun, but at the same time I was not a nun."

"Then how do you feel about being . . . a non-nun nun?"

She frowned. "The Chinese say, 'being disappointed by the secular world, one puts on a Buddhist robe. Being more disappointed by the Buddhist regime, one puts it off.' That's how I felt."

I tried to digest what she'd said. "Then are you . . . content with your life now?"

"I am disappointed both by being a nun and by not being a nun."

"Then what are you going to do with your life? I mean . . . what will you do?"

"I'm still looking for the true Dharma and I won't give up until I find it."

"What is this truth you want?"

Dai Nam picked up her cup and swallowed the last drop of her drink. The neon lights cast colors of red, yellow, blue, and green on her face. It was like the tension in a theater before the show begins. While everything is ready—music blaring and lights criss-crossing—something is still missing.

Dai Nam's voice again sounded disturbingly harsh. "An intense spiritual life. Having visions, opening my third eye, being at one with things and beings, and most important, achieving nonattachment."

I almost chuckled. Although I didn't know her well enough to judge, Dai Nam gave me the impression more of an escapist than a seeker. She rarely even looked at me when she talked, so how could she think she could achieve all these spiritual goals?

I studied her in the twilight. What exactly was the intense spiritual life she so eagerly sought? Perversely, I thought of the Tibetan statue in the Guimet Museum showing the god and his consort in the *yab-yum* posture of copulation. But of course I shouldn't imagine Dai Nam in that situation.

Now, accented by a shaft of fading sunlight, suddenly her scar seemed to come alive, struggling to tell an intense story I could not grasp.

Dai Nam's throaty voice piped up again in the cool Parisian air. "The strange thing is, while nuns are not allowed to be ordained in Thailand, temples are scattered everywhere side by side with prostitution houses."

I thought: The house for "selling smiling lips" and the temple work together: one saves your soul; the other saves your body. Why shouldn't they exist side by side?

"Do you know whether the prostitutes and the monks—"

Before I finished my question, with "have any social interactions?" Dai Nam's eyes suddenly glowed. "Look, someone is going to perform."

I followed her gaze and saw a street performer in front of us, smiling and bowing to the clientele in the café.

Dai Nam's voice now turned into a child's shrill. "See, Meng Ning, he's smiling and winking at us."

Right then a young couple strolled by, arms around each other's waists. The girl's eyes looked dreamy and her lips slightly parted in a half smile. The mime winked at the people in the café, then dashed behind the couple to imitate their gait and the girl's intoxicated expression. Laughter scattered here and there; the lovers turned and spotted the pursuer. They looked puzzled for a few seconds before big smiles blossomed on their young faces. The performer saluted them as they walked away happily.

Next came a lanky old man clutching a bag tightly to the chest of his expensive suit jacket. The sober, defeated expression on his wrinkled face made it appear longer than it was, like those in Modigliani's paintings.

The mime quickly went up behind him to imitate his long face and dejected gait. Again, laughter sprinkled the air. Encouraged, the mime pressed closer to the man until his body brushed against the other's suit. His imitation was now so exaggerated that the audience burst into loud laughter, and, to my utter surprise, among them Dai Nam's was the loudest.

The old man turned and soon realized what was going on. Anger broke out on his face like the eruption of a volcano. All his wrinkles seemed to flush a flaming red. He yelled and shook his bag at the performer, *"Allez-y, vous merde!"* Go away, shithead! He waved so hard that the bag finally fell and spilled its contents onto the ground—a pink-laced half-bra and bikini pants, garters, a corset, fishnet stockings. Now his whole face seemed to be on fire; then, like a mouse scurrying across a busy street chased by drunks waving broken bottles, he sped away.

Men in the café burst out laughing while the women gave out disgusted sighs. The two Japanese girls lowered their heads to stare at their hundred-dollar shoes. The two French women killed their cigarettes in the ash tray and spat a wet *"Salaud!"* Scumbag!

The mime, probably deciding that as a professional he should finish his show with dignity, began to pick up the underwear piece by piece from the ground. More laughs from the men and disgusted exclamations from the women. When finished, he chased after the old man, waving bras and bikinis and stockings over his head and screeching like the Queen of the Night in Mozart's *The Magic Flute:* *"Monsieur, attendez! Vous avez oublié vos trucs!"* Wait, sir, you've forgotten your things!

Dai Nam, her face blushing a deep purple and her scar an angry black, shot up from her chair and barked at me, "Meng Ning, let's go!"

Later, while I thought on and off of telephoning Dai Nam, one day she called me up to invite me to her home for dinner. Her friendliness surprised me, for as far as I knew, she'd never invited anybody to her room, let alone to have dinner. At the end of our short telephone conversation, she said, "It's also a farewell dinner. I'll be leaving for China in two weeks."

Dai Nam lived in the Septième Arrondissement, a relatively expensive area in the vicinity of the Eiffel Tower. However, like most students, she didn't live on one of the main floors but in the attic. I wondered whether she had to clean house in exchange for rent.

Light seeped out from her slightly open door, tinting the gloomy corridor pale yellow, like a moldy lemon. I knocked gently, careful not to wake her from any of her visions. "It's me, Meng Ning."

Dai Nam's voice boomed from inside. "Come in!"

I pushed open the door and was startled by what I saw. Right by the entrance, she was squatting with legs far apart and stirring some broth in a pot on a small stove. I apologized for almost knocking her over; she looked up at me. "Meng Ning, go and sit wherever you like."

I looked around the room and was startled again—the four walls were all painted black. In the darkness, desk, chairs, lamp, books, piles of papers, and trails of incense appeared to be floating like wandering ghosts. A sense of oppression closed around my throat, forcing out a gasp.

Dai Nam cast me a sidelong glance. "I should get a stronger lightbulb."

"But why didn't you . . ."

"Paint it white? It was white originally; it took me a whole day and cost me one hundred francs to paint it all black."

"But why?" The incense's strong aroma tore at my nostrils. "Don't you find it a bit—"

"Oppressive? That's the point." Dai Nam's hand kept vigorously stirring the pot. "I want to force open my third eye."

Startled at this declaration, I almost saw a black-haired, yellow-skinned witch in front of me, mocking my ignorance. Yes, it's sometimes in darkness that we obtain the light of wisdom. But painting a room black? Did she want to see ghosts?

Dai Nam looked at me from the corner of her eye past the thick rim of her glasses. "I can teach you how to do it, too, if you want."

"Oh, no. Thank you very much," I said, feeling perspiration break out on my forehead.

After looking around the eerie room, I finally sat down on a cushion on the floor next to bookshelves made of stacked crates. The strong-smelling incense wafted from an altar with a small ceramic Buddha. Next to it stood a writing desk, its surface piled with books and manuscripts; on it a solitary lamp gave out a faint beam of light. Above the desk was, more to my liking, a narrow window looking out over the Left Bank with the tip of the Eiffel Tower visible in the distance. Nearer to us, past rows of light green rooftops, lines of traffic moved like glimmering, meandering dragons. Only the window linked Dai Nam's vision to the bigger, more cheerful world outside.

"I didn't have time to clean up, for I have to finish my dissertation before I leave." Dai Nam stood up, releasing herself from her awkward squat, and then walked to the sink. She still wore the same white blouse, loose blue pants, and sandals. Did she have different sets of the same style, or was she wearing the same clothes over and over? Staring at her back, I felt distaste slowly crawl up my skin, but suppressed it.

She began filling the pot with water and said, her voice loud to compete with the noisy tap, "Rest for a while, Meng Ning. Dinner will be ready soon. Now I'll fix tea."

She spoke again when she returned from the sink. "My father is dying." Her tone sounded so casual she could have been telling me that the water was boiling.

"I am terribly sorry. What happened?"

"Lung cancer. He smokes too much."

"Oh, I am so sorry."

"You don't have to be sorry; it's his karma," she said flatly. Then, to my slight disgust and fascination, she squatted down once again to prepare tea.

The "kitchen" was a small area with several bricks on top of which rested a few cooking utensils, bottles of sauces and condiments, and two gas burners. The soup now emitted an aroma of mixed vegetables and herbs. The water for tea began to boil, uttering a deep guttural sound, like a wise old man trying to give advice. I started to feel more relaxed.

After a while, Dai Nam went to the wooden table, cleared space among the manuscripts, and motioned me to sit down opposite her. She began to arrange a ceramic tea canister, a teapot, and four tea bowls on a lacquer tray. To my surprise, the bowls were as tiny as soy-sauce dishes. Was she not thirsty, or was her tea that precious? She lifted the kettle and began to pour hot water over the outside of the pot and the bowls.

I asked, "Dai Nam, shouldn't you pour water *inside* the pot?"

"I'm performing tea ceremony for you." She looked at me chidingly. "It takes time. This is only the first step, called warming the utensils."

Feeling embarrassed, I remained silent while intently watching her next move. With her strong, thick fingers, she took tea leaves from the canister and dropped them into the pot, then added water until it rose to the top. "Now let the tea enjoy a quick spa," she said, closing the lid. Then she repeatedly poured hot water over the pot and bowls. "This is to warm the pot and bowls. Otherwise the taste will be spoiled."

Moments later, she lifted the lid and told me to appreciate the leaves. "Before we taste it with our mouths, we should first savor it with our eyes. Now look at how the leaves blossom into different shapes when they unfold in the water."

After we'd taken a quiet moment to appreciate the leaves, she poured tea into the four bowls. "I laid them in a straight line so that when I pour water into the bowls, the tea's strength will be the same. " She handed me a cup. "Now appreciate the color."

"Beautiful," I said. "Looks like champagne."

"No, it doesn't." Dai Nam cast me another chiding glance. "Ancient connoisseurs said that wine emboldens heroes' guts while tea inspires scholars' thoughts. So the two are completely different."

I nodded; she continued, adopting the tone a teacher uses when directing her student. "Now smell." She brought the cup to her nose, deeply inhaling. Immediately I did the same.

"Good!" She lowered her cup, her eyes closed.

Indeed, the fragrance seemed pure to the point of intoxication.

With her thumb and index fingers holding the upper rim of the cup and her middle finger its bottom, Dai Nam lifted the cup to her mouth and took a sip. I did the same, but burned my tongue; I let out a small cry.

She squinted at me. "Meng Ning, you don't drink good tea in one big gulp—that's considered to be very crude, not to mention that you've wasted it."

My ears felt hot. "Then what am I supposed to do?"

"You hold the tea in your mouth for a few seconds to savor its sweet, pure taste before you swallow it." She demonstrated with another cup and I followed suit.

"Now do you feel a cool breeze in your armpits?"

Of course she didn't mean it literally, but symbolically—that I should feel as light as a spirit.

"Thanks, it's great tea."

She contradicted me again. "It's good, but not great. It's not just the leaves that matter. In Paris, it's impossible to get good water to brew tea. I only use bottled spring water."

"That's not good enough?"

"Of course not. The best is water from a mountain, second is water from a river, third is water from a well." She paused, then spoke again meditatively. "Melted snow gathered from petals of plum blossoms and stored over years in tightly sealed ceramic jars is also supposed to be very good."

She must have read about the nun Wonderful Jade in *Dream of the Red Chamber*. Like the nun who'd brewed tea from snow, had Dai Nam also been longing for a man? I was wondering, but I said instead, "I never knew there was so much scholarship behind tea drinking."

"There's always more to things than what meets the eye."

Meaning what—that there was a poignant love story behind that scar of hers?

She was now busy preparing another round. I asked, "Why is the cup so small that we have to drink so many to quench our thirst?"

"Meng Ning, you've completely missed the point."

"What is it?"

"The point is not to quench thirst, but to quench one's restlessness and arrogance. Preparing and tasting tea is a process of self-pursuit and cultivation."

As I listened to Dai Nam's rough voice speak of the philosophy of tea and watched her calloused fingers deftly maneuvering the tea utensils, I was intrigued by this newly revealed side of her character. I wondered what other sentiments lay concealed under her emotionless face.

She went on. "I learned tea ceremony from a nun I met in the Buddhist college I attended in Hong Kong. I have to drink a lot of tea to keep me from falling asleep when I meditate." She broke off, then began again. "Also, the ritual of preparing tea pacifies me. The ancients said that tea drinking could dissolve loneliness, dissipate troubles through one's pores, purify one's heart, and lead one to enlightenment."

I nodded in agreement while she slowly wiped the pot with a clean towel. "This is to nurture the heart as well as the pot."

Watching Dai Nam's practiced fingers, I suddenly realized that the warmth and fragrance of tea and the order of tea ceremony must be a source of sanity in her life, and the stylized ritual a means to channel her trapped emotions.

Dai Nam picked up a handful of leaves and put them under my nose. "Smell—this is the best oolong tea."

I inhaled deeply. "Very good indeed. Where did you get it?"

I wondered how, as a student, she could afford these luxuries for the tea ceremony.

She said, "It was a gift. Almost all my possessions are gifts. My school fees and living expenses here are all sponsored by a nunnery in Hong Kong."

"You're so lucky, Dai Nam."

"Hmm . . . yes and no." She pondered. "People back home are nice to me, but my professors here are not giving me enough help with my research. I have a feeling that since I am Chinese and my French is no good, they just don't want to bother." Dai Nam went on to complain about how all the courses on Buddhism in the Université de Paris VII were too elementary for her and a waste of her time, how people snubbed her in the Cité Universitaire dormitory so she'd had to move here, how the library of L'Institut des Hautes Études Chinoises didn't have the books she needed for her dissertation. . . .

She had finished preparing the second round of tea and handed me another cup. This time I had learned my lesson and sipped the tea carefully.

Her raw, intense voice filled up the room. "I've always liked tea as my father liked cigarettes," she said. "But I'm disgusted by his smoking, the rotten addiction and attachment behind it." Finally she took a long, noisy sip, then added matter-of-factly, "Anyway, I don't like my father, smoking or not."

This open criticism of her father shocked me; I put down my tea. "What makes you dislike your father?"

Taking another noisy sip, Dai Nam said, her eyes half closed and her voice distant, "Because he never liked me. I'm a girl, his first born." She broke off, put down her cup with a hard thud, then went on as if talking from a dream. "In Canton where we lived, my father worked as a waiter. Every night after the restaurant was closed and the owner had finished calculating the bill and paid everyone, my father would dash off to a prostitution house owned by a middle-aged widow. My father went crazy over her and spent almost everything he earned buying her clothes, jewelry, perfume, and food, and then gambled what was left in her prostitution house.

"My father had always wanted a son, but for a long time didn't have the luck. Like a typical Chinese man, he blamed my mother for failing to give him one, and me for bringing him ill fortune. He still cherished hope for a son; that's why he named me Dai Nam— Bringing a Boy. In fact, I did bring him a boy later. When I turned eleven—my mother gave birth to a son, but this good luck left us as quickly as it had come. My brother died at four."

"Oh, Dai Nam, I'm so sorry." I looked at her directly to show my concern.

But Dai Nam avoided my gaze. She went on: "My mother was always sick, so it was I who actually raised and took care of my brother. When he was a baby, I carried him on my back in a red cloth embroidered with the characters 'lucky child, one hundred years long life.' I carried him everywhere: when I was cooking, sweeping the floor, washing clothes in the river, shopping in the market. Whenever he had a bad dream and cried, I'd rock him and stick a piece of sweetmeat in his mouth. When he got older and too heavy to carry, he'd follow me everywhere, hanging on to the hem of my clothes. That's why my clothes were quickly torn, so my father constantly scolded me. He said I was a boor and wasted his money because he had to buy me new clothes. Actually he hardly bought me any. I mended the old ones and wore them again and again until the village kids followed me around calling me 'beggar' and snatched my brother away."

"What do you mean?"

Ignoring my question, Dai Nam continued. "One day, as usual, I took my brother with me to wash clothes at the river. He had been happy catching small crabs and playing by the bank, then got tired and fell asleep. Fearing that he might fall into the river, I carried him on my back. Then suddenly three village kids materialized a few feet in front of me and began to sing 'beggar girl, beggar girl, why don't you go to hell?' I felt so angry that I splashed water onto them and cursed. They cursed back, then picked up stones to throw at me. One sharp rock hit my bare foot; I slipped and dropped my brother into the river."

"Oh! What happened?"

Dai Nam waved her hand as if to dispel an ugly thought; her voice trembled a little. "The kids quickly disappeared while I ran and cried for help until I bumped into two villagers on their way home from work. They rushed back with me to the river to search for my brother. By the time they pulled him out, he lay unconscious and his breathing was like a thread breaking on the threshold of death."

"I'm so sorry," I said.

A long, uncomfortable pause, then Dai Nam spoke again. "My brother cried to me, 'Mama!' before he took his last breath. This broke my mother's heart, for she felt she'd lost her son twice. At the funeral, when I looked at his small body lying lifeless in the tiny coffin, I suddenly realized the brevity of life, remembering how happy I'd felt when I was carrying him on my back, and how fast my happiness fled!

"Then my mother found out she was sterile due to an infection in her tubes that she'd caught from my father. This convinced my father even more that I was his curse—his all-destroying star—and that I had not only cut off his offspring, but his family name. He began to abuse me more. Whenever my mother tried to stop me from overworking, my father would yell at her, 'Stupid woman, let this creature do what her fate allots her! Don't you know she has to labor for our family to redeem the evil deeds accumulated in her past lives, or else she will be doomed even more in her next?'

"When he uttered the word 'doomed,' he'd roll his eyes as large, and open his mouth as wide, as if he were actually witnessing my doom. Then he would hit me with whatever he could lay his hand on—a shoe, a pan, a broom, even a chair. And I would burst out crying. 'What are you crying for?' he once yelled. 'Is your father dead? Of course you wish me dead, don't you? You've already destroyed your brother and now you want to destroy me so that you can have more graves to kowtow to. But I won't let that happen! You hear me?' He slapped my face. 'I don't know what I did in my past life to have you as my punishment!'

"After the death of my brother, my mother slept by herself every night. My father rarely came home. We both knew that he spent his nights in the whorehouse. He also stopped bringing money back for the family. He said he'd rather throw his money into the gutter than squander it on me—a money-losing shrew, or my sickly mother—a medicine cauldron. Then my mother had to work as an *amah* to support me and herself. She died when I turned fourteen.

"Then my father had to take me back with him, and by that time he had already been living with the widow for more than two years. Of course the widow didn't like me, so she made me do all the chores, not only at her house but also at her prostitution house—cooking, cleaning, scrubbing the floors, washing clothes, waiting on her favorite money-bringing prostitutes, everything except shopping, for fear that I'd cheat her of her money. I only got one meal a day of cold leftover soup or thin, meatless congee made from broken grains. She wouldn't let my father live in her house for free either; she made him work as a guard at the prostitution house.

"Finally when I reached nineteen and thought myself strong enough, I planned my escape—to swim to Hong Kong, my dreamland of freedom. I failed seven times before I made it on the eighth attempt. In Hong Kong, I also succeeded in finding my great-aunt, who took me in, bought me a Hong Kong identity card, and enrolled me in a charitable Buddhist school. Later I attended a Buddhist college, then went to beg in Thailand. When I returned to

Hong Kong, a nunnery learned about my ordeal and offered to sponsor me to write a dissertation based on my experience. That's how I'm here."

After she finished her account, Dai Nam's spirit seemed to come back to the room. She sipped her tea and said after some silence, "I still have nightmares of my escape to Hong Kong . . . one time I was almost drowned and another time almost eaten by sharks. . . ."

I gasped, then blurted out, "Then is . . . the scar on your face—"

"No, that has nothing to do with my escape; it was cut by a little boy, a neighbor's son."

"Why?"

"I don't know." She paused.

And I was surprised, for the first time in this terrible narration, to see sadness flicker in her eyes.

"I was ten, playing by myself in front of our house, when a neighbor boy came over, picked up a piece of broken glass from the floor and cut my face, just like that."

"You mean you were not in a fight?"

"No, not at all. I was playing by myself, and so was he. Then he just came up and slashed me. You may not believe it. It sounds so strange, but that's exactly what happened. His parents rushed me to the hospital, where I had a tetanus shot and eighteen stitches. Later when his parents asked him why he did this to me, he said he didn't remember the event at all. They beat him severely anyway. Since he was only six, everyone wondered where his strength came from. As you can see, my wound was long and deep. It should have been the work of someone much older. Some neighbors said he must be possessed by a demon. So the parents hired a professional exorcist to fix him. He made the boy drink water boiled with magic figures, he scribbled *sutras* on the boy's face with red ink, and chanted incantations for him for hours—with the result of giving him a high fever for a week.

"As Buddhism says, his deed was merely *wuming,* no reason. There's no reason for a little boy of six . . . nor for an adult like my father."

Dai Nam paused to study the submerged tea leaves. "But it seems now that my father regrets what he did to me. I received a letter a week ago written for him by his old neighbor. He said he's in his terminal stage of lung cancer and probably won't make it through Double Nine Festival. He wants to see me before he dies. That's why I have to go back right away." Dai Nam turned to look at me. "Meng Ning, if you don't mind, can you come over here once a week to take care of the altar and make offerings to the Buddha while I'm away?"

"Of course I will."

Dai Nam refilled my cup. Savoring the bittersweet taste of the newly brewed tea, I began to tell her about my family, the death of my little brother, and my father, who had gambled away everything. When concluding my story, I said that, unlike her father, my father had never abused me.

Dai Nam surprised me by saying, "Maybe we were sisters in our past life. It's just that our father liked you because you're beautiful and talented, but hated me because I'm a boor."

Chan Lan's loud and comical "Have children, many many!" jolted me back to the nunnery—the here and now. Now the sun had vanished and the street lights cast deep shadows. Nuns or not nuns, I thought, our lives are like shadows fleeting past the splendors of this floating world.

14

Under the Paris Sun

A few days after my visit to Dai Nam in the Golden Lotus Temple, I received a call from the French consulate, asking me if I was ready to go back to the Sorbonne for my oral defense. I was. Besides, if I went to Paris now, I could at least leave behind my confusion for a while. As I packed, I felt pangs of sadness that Michael had never called. Maybe Yi Kong was right after all—men are not trustworthy. Nor would they feel magnanimous after being turned down and their egos wounded.

The next day, with an uneasy mind, I boarded the plane.

Paris looked as if I'd never been away. I felt a little strange that it had not changed, because I had. I had been at one time innocent, curious, and eager for life. But now I felt as if I'd been holding a lamp that had lighted many paths, but missed the one home.

It was six-thirty when I stepped from the taxi and walked to the entrance of La Maison d'Asie. The sense of strangeness grew because this was where I'd first lived when I came here to study. In the twilight, I climbed up the stairs to the entrance, silently greeted by the two stone lions standing guard before the building.

I took the key from the man at the reception desk, went to my room on the third floor, put down my luggage, then headed straight to the communal bathroom to take a shower. After fifteen minutes, refreshed from the scalding water, hot steam, and the pleasant smell of sandalwood soap, I went back to my room, changed into my pajamas, and sat in bed to prepare for my oral defense the next afternoon. I could study only halfheartedly, distracted by thoughts about Dai Nam. While I tried to imagine what had happened to her, I also could not keep from thinking about Michael and his *haiku* proposal:

> *These thirty-eight years*
> *All empty now.*
> *Can the rest be full?*

I felt a rush of feelings. Did I want to fill this man's life? I stared at my Ph.D. dissertation and could not come up with an answer.

The next morning the ringing of my alarm clock startled me awake. It was seven-thirty and my oral defense was scheduled at two. I bathed and dressed, then glanced through my dissertation one last time. At eleven, I walked to the Cité canteen and ate a small lunch of cheese, fruit, and coffee, then took the Metro to the Sorbonne.

Since my purple floral dress had survived the fire, I deemed it very lucky. So I wore it again today to bring me more luck. And it did. Not only did I pass the exam, my dissertation got an unanimous "très honorable" from the three professors. After the hour-long ordeal, they all came to shake my hand and wished me the best of luck. My supervisor, always cool, distant, and too busy to grant me more than five meetings during my five years of study with him, hugged me and whispered pleasantries. After more felicitations and small talk, they all went back to their seats to get ready to interrogate the next candidate.

Outside the exam hall, I felt sad that none of my friends had been there. In fact, I had not told any of them. Because except for Dai Nam, the others were really only casual acquaintances, and most of them had left Paris before I did.

Feeling a bit sad, nostalgic, and sentimental, I went straight to the café a few blocks from the Sorbonne's main entrance—the same one where I'd had my first meal on my first day in Paris.

I sat down in the front row and a gray-haired waiter came to take my order. Wondering if he'd waited on me on that first day, I smiled generously and asked for an espresso and a *croque madame*—exactly what I'd had during my first visit here five years ago.

A few minutes later, the waiter came back with my order. Waiting until he'd left, I raised my glass and whispered to myself, "Congratulations, Dr. Du."

Then I softly recited the Song dynasty poet Su Dongpo's poem:

A cup of wine amidst colorful blossoms,
Sipping all by myself,
I raise my cup and invite the moon to join me.
With my shadow,
There are finally three parties here!"

As I was enjoying my espresso and my *croque madame,* I looked about. There was always something magical simmering in the air of Paris. Even the smallest corner seemed to wink at me and whisper, "Come, take a look; it's fun in here." The shop windows of the clothing stores opposite the café were decked with the colors of fall—chocolate brown, khaki, camel, cadet blue, navy, black, gravel black. As always, I was impressed by the refined French eye, which selects colors that compete and complement all at once. I watched a shapely, red-attired woman dash across the street to hail a taxi; her silver scarf lifting in the wind resembled a wisp of incense or cursive calligraphy.

I dropped two sugars into my espresso and slowly stirred it with a spoon. With pleasure, I listened to the sound of metal hitting against the rim of the ceramic cup. Then I took a lingering sip, savoring the coffee's bittersweet taste. After that, I cut a big piece of *croque madame* and put it, slowly and sensuously, into my mouth.

Pedestrians walked, talked animatedly with friends, or window-shopped while munching crepes, nibbling sandwiches, or licking ice creams. I watched leaves shiver in the early autumnal breeze and the intense but blasé expressions of the Parisians, somehow feeling a Zen-like tranquility amidst the hustle and bustle of the city.

Scenes of my first day in Paris five years ago flashed across my mind. . . .

The morning after my arrival, I had awakened in the dormitory of La Maison d'Asie with the sun gently touching a corner of my bed. I flicked and warmed my toes in the patch of light, then stretched, yawned, jumped off the bed, and went to look out the window. Although there was nothing much to see outside except other dormitory buildings, I still felt thrilled to be in Paris.

Bonjour, Paris! Comment allez-vous?

I took several deep breaths, inhaling as much of the Parisian morning air as my small lungs could take. Then, when I saw a young couple pass under a tree munching crepes, pangs of hunger stabbed my stomach. I flounced into my sweater, slipped on my jeans, and went out.

My feet thudded eagerly on the cobblestone street as I twisted my neck, looking in all directions, trying to take in all the scenes: a gray stone building covered with crawling vines; a window with an intricately patterned decoration in the shape of lilies; a young girl with a lavender scarf and violet boots. After passing a cigarette store, a florist, and a newspaper stand, I spotted a supermarket and plunged in.

Walking around and looking at the huge varieties of produce, I felt impelled to look for a simple meal—something cheap. With my mother back in Hong Kong for me to somehow support, plus unknown years ahead in Paris, I had to stretch my small scholarship as far as possible. I looked at the rows and rows of food arranged neatly on the shelves, until my eyes landed on a package of *craquelin*. I did not know exactly what was inside, but the cover picture looked very appetizing, with a colorful display of biscuits with shrimp, ham, cheese, sausage, lettuce, tomato, olive, pepper, onion. My eyes caressed the different items of food while my mouth watered. The price—one franc fifty—seemed unusually cheap for a hearty meal like this. I grabbed two packages, hurried to the beverage section to get some instant cocoa, then went to pay at checkout.

Back in my dormitory room, I cooked myself a cup of hot chocolate to go with the *craquelin*. I sucked back the saliva flooding my mouth. Then, with great anticipation and affection, I opened the package.

Alas! As if struck by an anti-magic wand, all the shrimp, ham, cheese, sausage, tomato, and onion were gone! What lay in front of my eyes were a few stacks of wrinkled, paperlike biscuits, completely bare, like the miserable and weathered face of an octogenarian. Anger welled up into my throat.

I was cheated by the supermarket! Or, I almost cried out in despair, somebody had opened the package and ate all the delicious toppings!

But what should I do? I didn't think I could go back to the supermarket and complain to the checkout person. Anyway, who would care? Making a fuss over one-and-a-half francs, I would be the one who would become the laughing stock, not the checkout person nor the owner. Stuttering in my insufficient French, I would sound pathetic and ridiculous.

After a long mental struggle, I finally sat down submissively and started to nibble my first Sunday brunch in Paris, à la Zen.

Not to my surprise, the so-called *craquelin* tasted terrible. I felt like an old woman chewing on tree bark during a famine. How I missed my mother's delicious cooking: soy-sauce chicken, steaming fish with black bean sauce, sweet and sour pork, crispy salt-and-pepper shrimp. . . .

Then, as I was about to throw away the rest of the biscuits, I suddenly spotted a line of small letters at the bottom of the package, hidden among the pictures of shrimp, ham, cheese, sausage, tomato, and onion: *"Proposer de servir"*—serving suggestion. A joke at my expense!

Still hungry, I began to unpack.

As I was pulling out items one by one, a cockroach crawled out from the suitcase. How incredible that this little ugly thing had traveled with me six thousand miles—all the way across the Pacific Ocean from Hong Kong to Paris! Poor creature! I studied the dazed-looking brown bug for long moments. Was he starved after all these long hours in the airless dark trunk? Was he now lonely and miserable like me? Would he be able to make friends in the future? Then suddenly I realized he was at this moment my only companion in the whole world. A gust of loneliness swelled up in me.

I broke off a piece of the leftover *craquelin* and threw the crumbs onto the floor. To my surprise, he didn't eat. Even a Hong Kong cockroach was too well fed and spoiled to have any appetite for the tasteless biscuits! Finally I used one *craquelin* to scoop him up, then went to the communal kitchen and put him on the counter. What would his fate be? Maybe he could find some better food here, or, his death. It'd all depend on his karma, his fate. . . .

I decided to go out and get a real meal, even though it would deplete my tiny budget. I took the Metro to the Sorbonne and finally settled in a café in the little plaza in front of the university.

Barely did I have time to look around when the waiter plopped down a menu and demanded, *"Que voulez-vous manger?"*

While I couldn't answer a simple question about what I wanted to eat, he urged, *"Croque monsieur, croque madame, sandwich avec jambon et fromage?"*

"Croque madame, s'il vous plaît." I had no idea what that was, but, feeling rushed, ordered it because the word "madame" made it sound like something special for women. The only flaw was it cost one franc more than the croque monsieur.

"Bien, quelque chose à boire?"

I hastily glanced at the menu. "Es . . . pres . . . so." It was the cheapest kind of beverage, but the hardest to pronounce.

When the waiter put down the coffee cup, I was surprised at its diminutive size—not much bigger than the toy cup I used for pretend drinking as a child. Don't the French get thirsty? I took a sip and involuntarily spat out the liquid, shocked by the bitterness. *Mon Dieu!* Isn't life bitter enough for the French? Fortunately the *madame*—French toast topped with fried egg over a thick piece of ham and melted cheese—was filling and delicious.

Ah, I imagined how wonderful to be rich; even one franc could make such a big difference in life. . . .

*   *   *

Some car horns snapped me back from my reverie. The café looked exactly the same as five years before, but my karma now seemed different—though just as uncertain. I had my Ph.D., but was still unsure of my future—would I take refuge as a nun or get a job in the secular world, remain single or get married? But I'd already turned down Michael's proposal! I let out a sigh.

PART TWO

PART TWO

∽ 15 ∽

New York, New York

Back in Hong Kong, right after Mother had helped me bring in the luggage and closed the door, she lowered her voice as if to divulge a secret. "While you were away, some *gweilo* has called several times."

My heart started to pound. "Oh, what's his name?"

"Mic Ko something. He said he called from the United States." Mother eyed me suspiciously. "Who is this foreign devil?"

"Nothing, Ma—"

"You mean this man is nothing, or he wants nothing from you?"

"Ma!"

"If a man's mouth says he wants nothing, that always means he does want something, you understand?" She paused. "I don't like foreign devils—they always want more, more, more!" Now she stared at me through her pinched eyes. "But then when you want to get married, they don't want you anymore!"

"Ma, no one is talking anything about getting married!"

"Oh, if you react so strongly, that means you're thinking about it, right?!"

"Ma!" I decided to lie to save myself from more motherly harassment. "I think it must be the Asia Society in New York, which might be interested in my application for a position."

Mother looked happy. "Good. Now let me fix some tonic soup to invigorate you after the plane ride," she said, then whistled "One Day When We Were Young" all the way to the kitchen.

Although I was dying to call Michael right back, I decided to wait a little.

Mother prepared a big dinner. "This is to celebrate your Ph.D." she said, then started to pile fish, chicken, shrimp, and vegetables onto my plate.

Starved from the unsatisfying airplane meals, I was hungry for my mother's delicious cooking and ate with great relish. As I was raking rice into my mouth with my chopsticks, I noticed that she was not eating.

"Ma, are you not hungry?"

"Ah"—she looked at me as if I were her first love, then rolled her eyes heavenward—"I don't know how an ignorant woman like me can give birth to a doctor daughter like you!"

I reached to pat her hand. Just then the phone rang and Mother dashed to pick it up.

She cupped the receiver and made a face. "It's that same *gweilo!*"

I went up to snatch the receiver from Mother and waved her away. "Michael?"

"Meng Ning?"

A silence. Then Michael's voice again. "Meng Ning, where have you been? I was worried about you!"

He sounded so upset that I didn't have the heart to blame him for not calling me earlier. "I was . . . in Paris."

"Your mother told me that, but she wouldn't give me your phone number."

"I'm sorry, Michael. She doesn't trust strangers."

"It's all right. So you've gotten your Ph.D.?"

"Yes."

"Congratulations, Meng Ning. I'm so happy for you!"

"Thanks."

Another pause. His voice now sounded low and edgy, as if he hadn't slept for days. "I'm so sorry I didn't call you earlier. The operator tried many times, but couldn't connect from Tibet to Hong

Kong. Then when I tried from the States, you'd already left for Paris."

"Michael, I'm sorry about all that . . . but anyway, I'm talking to you now." A pause, then I asked, "How's Professor Fulton?"

"He had a stroke while collecting antique *thangkas* in Lhasa. When I arrived, the local doctors were treating him with Tibetan medicine, which I didn't understand at all. I immediately booked a flight, brought him back, and put him in New York Hospital."

Michael went on to tell me that fortunately it was only a mild stroke, so the Professor's partial loss of memory and motor function would only be temporary. Already he could eat on his own and move around, though with a walker.

"You don't have to worry, Meng Ning. He's fine now," Michael said, sounding more relaxed. Then he changed the subject. "Will you come to the States to see me?"

I didn't know how to respond to this for several seconds. Then I felt his anticipation rolling toward me from the other side of the world.

"Meng Ning, you there?"

"Yes."

"Will you come? Please . . ."

I didn't know what to say. Wasn't he angry with me? If I went to see him in the States, what would happen? Would he still be serious about me, even though I'd turned him down?

I covered my chest, fearing that my heart would flutter out of me. In the intimate silence stretching across the Pacific Ocean, I imagined myself listening to his breathing and touching his eyebrows, which resembled the Chinese character "one" saturated with *qi*. . . .

"Meng Ning, please." Michael's urgent voice rose again. "Please say yes."

A moment later I looked at the telephone receiver, now back on the table. I had agreed.

I went back to finish my celebration dinner. I decided not to tell Mother about Michael—not yet.

So, when she asked about my long-distance telephone conversation, I said, "Ma, it's the Asia Society in New York. So I'm going to the United States for a job interview."

"Wow, Meng Ning." A big smile bloomed on her face. "Now good luck finally pours into our house one after another!" she enthused, beginning again to pile food on my plate until it'd become a miniature meat mountain.

So barely two weeks after I'd come back from Paris I was packing again. My hands were busy smoothing the tiny red flower on a pair of black lace bikini panties, from which Mother's suspicious eyes seemed unwilling to part.

Then my mother, who'd never been to New York, but who had her opinion about any city, told me emphatically, "Meng Ning, when you take a taxi in New York, you have to make sure you never take your eyes off the meter, because the driver has fixed it to jump faster."

"Ma!" I cast her an annoyed glance, stuffing the panties in the suitcase. The flower now looked like a drop of blood on the black spider-web pattern.

Mother plunged on. "I was told in New York passersby will just stand and watch while people are being robbed, or even murdered. But this is not the worst. The most disgusting is that when passengers push and shove to get onto the subway, they'll thrust others onto the rail and the train will just keep going and nobody cares. So this is New York! Be careful!

"Oh, I also remember there is a place called something like Sentro Bark which is famous, not for its scenic spots, but because it is packed with drug addicts, murderers, whores, child molesters, gigolos, rapists, and vampires at night. So promise me you'll never go there, will you?"

On September third, near the end of the six-hour flight to New York from San Francisco, the captain's cheerful voice announcing the plane's arrival at JFK awoke me from a nap. I looked out the window and saw the 747's wing bank low over the water and turn back toward the sandy beach. Inland, miniature buildings, cars, highways, skyways, and a few patches of green angled away from me. When the plane finally struck the runway, I realized I'd be seeing Michael in a few minutes. My heart started to pound. I took out the painting I'd made for him and looked at it one last time as the plane taxied down the runway. It was a white-robed Guan Yin riding on a huge lotus leaf, holding the Heart Sutra. Since I couldn't afford to buy him anything expensive and did not want to bring him anything cheap, I hoped the Bodhisattva I had brushed onto gold-speckled rice paper would find her way into his heart.

The moment I walked into the waiting area I spotted Michael leaning against a pillar. I was startled by the sadness on his face and by the leanness of his once robust frame. A pain stabbed inside me. Then our eyes met. The air had reincarnated. Michael swiftly came to me and, without a word, pulled me into his arms. After long moments of silence, he whispered into my ear, "Meng Ning, I've missed you so much." Then more hugs and kisses before he released me, grabbed my suitcase, and led me to the cab stand.

Beside me in the confines of the cab, Michael looked very appealing in his black turtleneck and gray corduroy pants. I felt happy feeling his shoulder against mine as the nearness of his body soothed my heart. My eyes busily played a tug-of-war between the passing scene outside and his long-missed face within. Michael put his hand on my thigh as the car sped along Grand Central Parkway toward Manhattan.

Michael held my hand during the trip, until our taxi pulled to a stop at a nondescript apartment building. "We're on the Upper East Side," he told me as he paid the driver. A blue-uniformed doorman came to open the door for us and carried my baggage into the lobby.

"Good evening, Doctor," he said to Michael.

Michael introduced me and told Frank, the doorman, that I would be staying for a few weeks. Should I need any help, his assistance would be appreciated. Frank nodded while he held open the elevator door and punched the button for the twenty-eighth floor. "Nice to meet you, Miss Du. Enjoy your stay."

I smiled back and saw Michael stick a twenty-dollar bill into his hand.

After we entered his apartment, Michael set down my luggage, took my arms, and tilted back to study me. I felt his lips warming my forehead and my brows. Moments had passed before he released me to look me in the eye. "Meng Ning, how come each time I see you you're more beautiful than before?"

With his fingers, he slipped the band from my ponytail so that my hair tumbled over my neck and shoulders. He smoothed it back and began to search my lips with slow, gentle kisses.

"I missed you," he whispered, his breath light and ticklish in my ear.

Feeling myself stir, I pulled him to me and ruffled his soft hair. "I missed you, too, Michael."

We collapsed in the chaise longue in the foyer. His caresses started to alleviate my body's stiffness from the twenty-two-hour trip. When I was about to rest my head on his shoulder, I noticed the door was still left half open.

"Michael, the door . . ."

But he murmured, "Forget the door," then kicked it shut and pulled me closer to him. . . .

With my first glance I could see that Michael's home was full of books, paintings, and works of art. The residue of incense permeated the air. I suddenly remembered something and broke away from him.

"Meng Ning, stay with me. I haven't seen you for weeks."

I ignored him, went to open my carryon, took out the Guan Yin painting, then returned. "Michael"—I handed him the framed miniature painting—"I did this for you."

Michael scrutinized the Goddess, his eyes like those of a child who has just discovered a treasure chest. Moments passed and his gaze was still glued to the white-robed image riding a lotus on the turquoise waves.

Finally I asked, "You like it, Michael? The Goddess will protect you—"

"Like it? Oh, Meng Ning, it's wonderful." He turned to look at me hard and long, as if this were our first encounter. "How come you didn't tell me that you're also so talented?"

I blushed.

"And so seductive," he said, tilting up my chin so that he could press his lips hard on mine.

Ten minutes later, Michael stuck his head out of the kitchen and asked, "Is tea OK?" his spiked hair sending a tinge of warmth to my heart.

"No," I said. "I want Coke. Since I'm now in America, I want something American."

"Then Coke it is." His voice sounded cheerful and the sound of his energy filled the kitchen.

I walked around to appreciate the apartment. Illumination from two blue-and-white porcelain lamps warmed the cozy living room. Several pieces of antique Chinese furniture glowed in the soft light. On a low table stood a delicately crafted and subtly glazed *blanc de chine* Buddha statue.

Bookcases lined two walls; the others were covered with Chinese paintings. A very simple brush painting caught my eye: Han Shan and Shi De—the two legendary lunatic-poet-monks of the Tang dynasty— swept the floor of the temple gate with straw brooms, and laughed as if everything in this Ten Thousand Miles of Red Dust is but a joke.

One of Han Shan's poems was written in cursive calligraphy in a corner of the painting:

Unknown
I live on the mountain
Enjoying the solitude among white clouds

Michael's apartment possessed a lonely quality. Was this what drew him to Zen? Was I feeling the loneliness of someone orphaned at a young age, or something more philosophical—or both?

Again I looked at the two hermits in the painting. Han Shan— Cold Mountain—got his name because he'd lived a secluded life on a remote mountain where, even in the hottest summer, its snowcap never melted. His friend Shi De—Picked Up—got his name because he was an orphan dumped on the street and found by a Zen master who went about riding on a tiger. Since the boy had no name, no parents, no possessions, the Zen master simply called him by the way he'd found him—Picked Up. Picked Up lived a carefree and detached existence. His eyes always shone clear and bright, and his smile was penetrating. Day in and day out, he and Cold Mountain swept leaves, scrawled poems on rocks, played with the village children, and appreciated the moon. They are honored in Chinese legend because they lived their lives according to the Dao—The Great Way.

A strange feeling crept over me. Michael's life, in a certain respect, resembled that of the two monks. He'd been orphaned (I hadn't yet had the chance to ask how). He seemed detached; he wrote poems and appreciated the moon. . . . However, instead of an isolated mountain monastery, Michael lived in a nice apartment in one of the busiest cities in the world. But hadn't some of the old Chinese sages taught that the true hermit feels free of the dusty world while dwelling in the clamorous city?

I walked to the kitchen and asked Michael whether he needed help. He was arranging crackers in a bowl. "No, Meng Ning. You must be tired from the trip; why don't you relax in the living room? I'll join you in a minute."

I went back into the living room, not because I wanted to relax, but because I had to suppress an urge to cry. I was confused. If I was so attracted to Michael, why had I turned down his proposal in Hong Kong? But then what about Yi Kong, and the Goddess of Mercy? What about my calling since my fall into the well seventeen years before? What about my dream to be part of the nuns' carefree life?

I leaned against one of the bookcases, and to distract myself began to read the titles. There were many volumes of Chinese philosophy and literature, all in English translations: the *Book of Changes, Dream of the Red Chamber, Six Records of a Floating Life, Journey to the West.* . . . But I also found *The Plum in the Golden Vase*—China's most notorious erotic novel. I pulled it out from the shelf, flipped through the pages, and ran into:

> The moment the young monks saw the wife of Wu Dai, their Buddha nature and Zen mind were lost. Their hearts were like unleashed monkeys and their spirits un-

tamed horses. In disarrayed groups of seven and eight, they collapsed in her sensual aura. . . .

When they were supposed to strike the stone chimes, their minds were so bewitched that they wrongly smashed the elder monks' scalps. All the efforts of their meditation in the past drained into the gutter; even the Buddha's ten thousand warrior attendants could do nothing to guard them against their desire for this woman. . . .

This was followed by a woodblock print graphically portraying the beautiful woman coupling with a monk.

My cheeks felt hot, yet my eyes wouldn't detach themselves. I was fascinated by the forthright description, written three hundred odd years ago, of the monks' sexual craving for an attractive woman. The author's courage to express the yearning of his heart without fear of condemnation by Confucian hypocrites deeply moved me. I felt a heat rising gradually in my groin. I was sure my cheeks were now the color of a monkey's butt, but that didn't stop my hands from impatiently turning the page to read more.

Just then I heard Michael coming from the kitchen. I pushed the book back onto the shelf.

"Meng Ning, what are you reading?"

"Oh . . . nothing special." While I felt the burning sensation in my cheeks, my mind raced with scenes of our first night together behind the mound in Cheung Chau, the bold declaration of the two nuns in the Kun opera, Michael's poem, our resumed intimacy not long ago. . . .

Michael put the tray onto the low Chinese table, then came to embrace me from behind. I heard playfulness in his voice.

"But you look so absorbed—something sexy? Tell me."

"I can't."

He reached toward the shelf for the book, but I pushed his hand away.

"Must be some kind of love story between a monk and a nun, right?" He nibbled my neck. "If you entered the empty gate to be a nun, I'd also become a monk."

There was a long, pregnant pause. Then he released me and led me to sit down on the sofa. "Let's have something to eat."

Then he offered me his white-glazed cup with Iron Goddess of Mercy tea. "Want to try?"

"No. Thanks. I have my Coke." I decided to be stubborn, like an American woman. Then I said, "Michael, I envy you living in such a lovely apartment," expecting he'd finish the sentence with the "but no bachelor's house is complete without a hostess" cliché I'd detested so much in the past.

Then I sensed something discordant. The *qi* in his apartment was unbalanced—almost all *yang* energy. Suddenly I felt an itch to add something *yin:* a vase of roses or daisies or carnations next to the Buddha; frilly white-laced curtains against which dangled a tinkling wind chime; lilac, cedarwood, and bay leaf potpourri on the coffee table.

But Michael was busy buttering the crackers. He handed me one and said, absentmindedly, "Oh, thank you." Then he refreshed my Coke, which made bright, tinkling noises with the ice.

At seven-thirty, after I'd had a nap and a shower, Michael took me to La Côte Basque in midtown for dinner. The restaurant was decorated with colorful murals depicting groves of trees and cozy eighteenth-century buildings beside the Mediterranean Sea. The bold brushstrokes and vivid colors invigorated my senses, which had been dulled by jet lag. I could feel the *qi* circulating everywhere.

After we were seated, I found out that the prices on the menu were as rich in *qi* as the surroundings. Michael and I ordered Perrier, salad, then vegetarian pasta for him and bouillabaisse and lobster for me.

In a few minutes the waiter returned with our drinks, a basket of assorted bread, and spheres of butter nestled with ice in a small silver bowl. He poured us the Perrier and left. Sipping the mineral water, I looked around. The customers were all attired tastefully, men in suits and women in evening dresses, as if about to attend a concert or an elegant private party. Bathed in the pleasant aroma of gourmet food, they chatted, smiled, ate, drank deeply, and looked satisfied. The tuxedoed and silent-footed waiters moved around the white-clad tables, making delicious clinking sounds. Off in a quiet corner I noticed a distinguished-looking couple—a white man with an Asian woman—both with graying hair and elegant clothes.

Michael pointed toward them. "Meng Ning, see the couple over there? They're a trustee at the Met and his wife."

"You know them?"

"Yes." Then, to my surprise, Michael rose from his chair. "Excuse me, Meng Ning, I need to say hello," he said, then walked to the couple.

Michael shook hands with the man and engaged in a brief conversation with him. He looked eager to please; the two responded with faint smiles and slightly nodding heads.

As I was wondering what they were talking about, Michael had already come back. "Sorry to keep you waiting." I nearly asked, *Then why didn't you introduce me to them?* but Michael was already speaking. "Benjamin Hill has one of the best collections of Chinese paintings in the West. I'd have introduced you, but I didn't want to interrupt their dinner. Hope you don't mind." He buttered a bread stick and handed it to me.

Feeling my upset wane, I asked, "You know a lot of people in the arts?"

"Just a few. Michael Fulton knows most of them, in Oriental art anyway. It's through him that I've met a few. I enjoy talking about art, but most of the art collectors are not very nice unless you are at least as rich as they are."

No wonder he hadn't looked entirely at home when he'd talked with the trustee.

Just then the waiter came back with our food.

Michael reached to squeeze my hand. "Let's enjoy ourselves, Meng Ning. It's so good to have you here."

I started to eat my soup and Michael dug his fork into his greens. He looked happy and ate with great relish. I felt touched, while also wondering: why wasn't he acting upset that I'd turned down his proposal?

After we had finished our appetizers and were waiting for the next course, a very handsome man in a silvery gray suit and matching silk tie came over to greet Michael. Michael introduced him as Philip Noble, a dear friend, and invited him to sit with us. "Enchanté," the stranger said—then to my surprise, bowed and brought my hand to his lips.

Michael put his hand on my shoulder. "Meng Ning, Philip has been my best friend since high school. Nice guy and a great theater talent. Used to play Romeo in our school drama club, so be prepared for his theatricality."

Philip slapped Michael's shoulder amicably, flicked his thatch of thick blond hair, rolled his long-lashed eyes, and flashed his perfect white teeth. "Oh, no. Michael is the genius. We used to call him 'the professor.' Actually he liked that. He knew he was good." He winked. "And now, of course, he's the best."

Michael smiled, looking almost boyish. After the two men had exchanged a few more pleasantries, they told me bad jokes from their training at Johns Hopkins.

I could see the bond between them despite their different temperaments and physiques. Noble cut a striking figure—well over six feet, broad-shouldered and athletic, like Achilles stepping from Greek mythology into the twentieth century in a tailored suit. Next to him, Michael, quieter, with a medium build, more resembled an artist or a scholar. I didn't understand the affinity between them, but there were surely many corners in Michael's life still waiting for me to explore.

Watching Philip Noble's glamorous features and manners, I almost felt I was interviewing a movie star. I was conscious of his curious, fresh blue eyes on me.

When Michael went to answer his beeper, Philip asked, "Meng Ning, how long are you going to stay in New York?"

"A few weeks," I said, feeling a little dazed. "Can you suggest places to go?"

"Fifth Avenue, the Met, SoHo, Central Park—" He paused. "I think you'd better ask Michael. He knows all the cultural places, though he's always so busy."

"Are you also a neurologist?"

"Oh, no. That's Michael's field, takes a lot of brains. I'm a cosmetic surgeon."

"That's interesting." No wonder he was so flashy.

"Oh, yes. I love it. I like to make people look beautiful. Vanity, isn't it?" he said, then tossed his blond hair again and shot me a young Paul Newman stare.

"But if that makes people happy, why not?" I smiled.

"Exactly. God gives a woman a face, but she wants a different one—that's where I come in. People care about themselves so much that they don't want to be themselves. But I shouldn't complain." He shrugged. "I live off people's vanity."

"Or taste," I added. "If faces are works of art that reflect the taste of their owners, then we should appreciate their efforts to enhance."

Noble looked at me deeply with his sparkling, fathomless eyes. "Good. I like that, Meng Ning. But I'm afraid I'll never see you as a patient. Not only do you not need a different face, but I'm sure many of my patients would want one as naturally beautiful as yours."

Embarrassed by this flattery, I sipped my water, then uttered a shy "Thank you, Philip, but you're overpraising me."

Noble signaled with his head to an elegant, fortyish woman at the table across from us. "See the lady over there? You find her beautiful?"

I looked and exclaimed, "Oh, yes!"

He shook his head, his silky hair shifting like waves under the moonlight. "To be blunt, I find her look totally repulsive."

I was horrified to hear this. "But why?"

"Because there's nothing natural about her. It's all work under a skillful knife."

"How can you tell?"

"I'm the expert. Too bad she didn't come to me. I could have taken another ten years off her original fiftyish face."

"Oh, heavens!"

Philip reached to pat my hand. I noticed his gold cuff links—miniature sculptures of that Egyptian queen who may be the most beautiful and mysterious woman in history.

"Meng Ning, your naïveté is very charming."

I studied Noble's perfectly chiseled features. Was this beautiful Romeo's face also the masterpiece of an adroit knife?

As if he were a mind reader, Philip smiled. "While I'm a plastic surgeon myself, I don't trust any colleagues in my specialty. So I'd never put my face at risk in their hands, not even twenty years from now."

I didn't know how to respond to this.

Philip cast another glance at the fiftyish woman who looked forty before he resumed the conversation—in a different thread. "How long have you known Michael?"

"A few weeks," I said, feeling a little tense. "And you've known Michael for much longer."

"Almost twenty years," he went on, creasing his thick brows. "Since high school, Michael has never failed to amaze me. When we all went out to movies or a bar, he'd stay in the dorm burying himself in all kinds of books. He always said life is too short to learn about all the things he's interested in. This guy never wastes a minute and works like a dog to get what he wants. Back at Johns Hopkins, often he didn't even bother to eat, so I'd bring him back pizzas or Chinese takeout."

I enjoyed watching Philip's facial expressions swim effortlessly from one emotional zone to another. How many more faces did this Romeo have?

He continued. "Michael went to Hopkins on scholarships, you know, because his parents died when he was a teenager. It was very hard for him—"

Right then Michael returned as the gray-haired waiter came with our entrees.

"Enjoying a good conversation?" Michael asked. I felt his hand warming the nape of my neck.

"Is everything OK?" Philip shifted sideways for the waiter to put down our plates.

"Fine, it was just a patient asking for a prescription."

I smiled up at Michael. "Philip was telling me how smart you are," I said, feeling stirred by his soft, caring touch.

Just then Philip Noble excused himself and went back to his table.

I smiled at Michael before I dug my fork into the lobster. Still so fresh and alive, it looked as if he (I liked to think the lobster was a he and the shrimp a she) was just out of the ocean. Bad karma. Both for myself and for "him," I thought, while spearing a juicy piece and putting it into my mouth.

Was it my mother or my father?

"Good?" Michael asked.

"Couldn't be better." I licked my lips.

⇜ 16 ⇝

The Fortune-Teller

We arrived home at eleven. Riding up in the elevator with our bodies touching, I was aware of Michael's desire. The floor indicator seemed to blink forever. When it finally read twenty-eight, Michael took my hand and we walked out. He found his key, opened the door, and let us in. Soundlessly he closed the door, and, without a word, led me straight into the bedroom. Knowing what he was going to do to me in a while, my heart flipped to allegro tempo.

He took off his tie and jacket and tossed them over a chair, then came over to embrace me. He nibbled my earlobe and kissed my neck while his arms closed around me, his hands reaching to unzip my dress.

"Michael"—I was still not used to being so intimate with a man—"please turn off the light."

"But, Meng Ning—"

"Michael, please." I insisted until he gave in.

Instantly, dimness fell over the room, with only the moonlight illuminating one side of his face. Eyes intent in the dim light, his hands worked to take off my dress and peel off my stockings. When he tried to unhook my bra, I pulled his hands away. The disappointment on his face pained me, but I felt too shy to be naked—I wasn't even used to looking at my own nude reflection in the mirror.

"Meng Ning, let me—"

"Maybe later," I said, disentangling from his grasp, then swiftly jumping into bed and pulling the sheet over me.

Michael's eyes never left me while he was unbuttoning his shirt, pulling off his pants, and slipping off his underpants. Though fully covered, I felt completely exposed by his stare.

It was the first time I had seen him, or any other man, totally naked. I almost let out a cry—he had so much hair! Like a teenager scrutinizing the painting of a nude for the first time, I anxiously studied his body. My gaze consumed his profile, his broad chest, the long stretch of his thighs and legs, the pleasing curve of his hips, until it finally fell on that which I'd been avoiding looking at. Did he feel pain that it swelled so much? What would happen if it kept ballooning? I remembered the unspeakable sensation I'd experienced from this swelling under the watchful moon on the remote island of Cheung Chau. I felt my color rising and pulled my eyes away.

Bathed in the moonlight streaming in from the window, Michael's skin appeared ivory, while his face glowed. He came toward me as if his movements were connected to roots deep under the earth. Then, swiftly, he slipped into bed next to me. I felt his cologne and body warmth filling up the air underneath the bedsheet when the honking of a car slashed the air outside the window.

I immediately turned my back to him.

"Meng Ning . . ." Michael's voice was filled with desire as he again reached to unhook my bra.

A vortex of heat stirred inside me. It grew as his large hand slowly peeled off my panties.

I was now completely naked, lying in bed with my body cupping against a man's. His hair pricked my skin while his hand sent nervous impulses from my shoulders down my hips. As he nibbled me, I could feel his lashes tickling my neck.

If Mother touched my forehead now, she'd certainly scream, "Watch out, Meng Ning! You have a high fever!"

Michael tried to pull down the bedsheet; I immediately pulled it back. "No, Michael—"

"Please." Slowly he turned me over to face him, his voice painfully pleading and seductive, his eyes glowing like emeralds under a search light. "Let me see your body."

"Then you have to close the blinds."

"No. I want to see you under the moon."

Neither did I want to keep out the moon, but I felt too shy. I begged repeatedly until he unwillingly slipped out of bed and went to the window. While my eyes traced the curves of his back and hips outlined against the moonlight, my body was subsumed with a burning sensation—almost as I'd felt when watching the fire in the Fragrant Spirit Temple.

He swiftly climbed back in. Now in the dark, with his strong body curling against mine, his invisible hands and lips went free in their adventures. I felt him cup and caress my breasts, hold my lips with his, kiss, suck, and tease my nipples. His lips were soft yet burning. His hands made me feel beautiful and sexy under their touch. Seemingly understanding well the desire of my body, they made me moan and squirm. I felt flustered, scared, pained, happy, and fascinated all at once. My mother's comment about my father's poems arose in my mind:

> *With good poems you never quite know how you feel. Sometimes sad, sometimes happy, sometimes sweet, sometimes sour, sometimes bitter, sometimes generous. Sometimes you feel and sometimes you don't. . . . When your heart is like a knocked-over shelf of condiments spilling a hundred different flavors and feelings, then the poem is a very good poem. Your father's poems can do just that.*

This was exactly how I felt now. If this lovemaking could be translated into a poem, I was sure it would surpass those put together by Father.

Now, while my body descended into agony from the overwhelming sensations, Michael seemed not the least in a hurry to further satisfy me. He savored every bit of my body, including the small area covered by black hair that I had been scared of and avoided looking at before.

"You," he whispered while kissing ardently, "my moon enchantress."

He took my hand, spread it open, laid himself in my small palm, then gently closed my fingers one by one. I felt it keep growing under my touch like a fluffy chick, until suddenly it fell from my hand and, as effortlessly as a fish, slipped inside me—shattering my world of nuns and goddesses and *sutras* and temples.

The sunlight was sprinkling in the room when I woke up. Lying comfortably under the covers of Michael's bed, I watched him as he still slept. His lashes trembled slightly and his eyes fidgeted under his lids. Was he having a sweet dream or an erotic one? As I listened to him breathe and watched his chest rise and fall, my heart was filled with a tenderness and warmth I'd never felt.

I tried to touch him, but my hand stopped in midair. *Let him sleep more,* a voice at the back of my mind said. Right then, a shaft of sunlight broke through the cracks of the blind and splashed his face. Slowly he opened his eyes and reached for me; I felt my body melt like a burning candle.

Later, I sat on a stool in Michael's small kitchen and watched his practiced fingers stir-fry eggs with mushrooms, butter toast, squeeze oranges, boil water. Many men's hands seemed hideous and unfeeling to me, but Michael's were graceful, like fish in water. I felt something stir inside—perhaps a sort of recognition. Surely we had met somewhere before. In a past life. Or lives. Was he the fish, and I the water?

Michael carefully planned out our first two days together in New York: today we'd go to the Asia Society, the Metropolitan Museum, walk for a while, and have dinner in Chinatown. Later in the week he'd take me to a reception at the Met and I would at last meet Professor Fulton, who, Michael told me, was recovering rapidly from his stroke.

We started by appreciating the Buddhist art at the Asia Society, but I suddenly felt very hungry from the jet lag and suggested to Michael that we skip the Met and go straight to Chinatown for dinner. When the taxi pulled to a stop at Canal Street, the distinctive Chinese cooking smells began to waft into my nostrils. After less than five minutes' walking, I spotted a sign in Chinese: DUMPLING HOUSE—ALL THE DUMPLINGS YOU WANT. A poster in the window listed them all: mixed vegetable, pork and vegetable, shrimp and cabbage, shredded beef and scallion. Steamed, panfried, in soup, in all kinds of sauce . . . Feeling an irresistible pull, I grabbed Michael's elbow and steered him inside.

Dinner was wonderful. We finished everything, scraping clean our plates until they looked like round, wisdom-reflecting mirrors. After he'd paid and we'd stepped out of the little restaurant, cool air rushed to greet us. With my satisfied stomach, all looked appealing to me: housewives bargaining with potbellied shop owners; round-cheeked children begging for Chinese pastries; girls flipping through trinkets piled into small mountains in front of a sign, EVERYTHING HAS TO GO; open street stalls whose crates spilled over with herbs, dried scallops, preserved fruits, candies, vegetables.

As Michael and I walked along the bustling street heading toward the subway station, I spotted a signboard in Chinese hanging from a dingy building:

INTERNATIONALLY RENOWNED MASTER LIVING BUDDHA
ALL REQUESTS GRANTED
PHYSIOGNOMY, PALMISTRY, NUMEROLOGY, ASTROLOGY,
NAMING AND NAME CHANGING, WORD ANALYSIS,
FENG SHUI, I CHING

I told Michael what it was and asked him to come with me to have our fortunes told. To my surprise, he suddenly looked tense and uncomfortable, his earlier humor gone. "No, Meng Ning. I'm a scientist and I'm not going to let some charlatan tell me about my fate."

"Why not try it? It'll be fun."

"No, let's go." He tried to steer me past the building.

But I didn't budge. "Michael, in China, fortune-tellers are considered doctors, too. That's why Chinese rarely need to see psychiatrists. Besides, they charge only one-tenth of what psychiatrists do."

"Meng Ning, fortune-telling is superstition."

"No, it's five thousand years of Chinese wisdom!" I paused. "What about your buying the coin sword to drive away evil spirits? Wasn't that superstition? Come on, Michael! Stop being rational for a few minutes!" Without losing a beat, I dragged him into the building—past the curious stares of several old women sitting and fanning themselves in front of a discount clothing store.

The long, steep staircase was lit only by a bare, grimy bulb swinging shakily on its thin wire. I heard my high heels clicking eerily on the scuffed wooden surface, syncopating with Michael's heavy footsteps dragging behind. After a long climb and some twists and turns, we finally reached the third floor, found the Master Living Buddha's office, and rang the bell.

From within, a saccharine voice piped in Cantonese, "Please come in."

Michael yanked my sleeve. "Meng Ning, let's go now!"

"No, let's face our fate."

I pushed and the door swung open with a long squeak, like a bird crunched underneath a slow truck. The unexpected blast of chilled air made me shiver as the pungent smell of Chinese medicinal soup choked my nose.

A very young and voluptuous Chinese girl came up to us and asked whether we had an appointment. When I told her no, she flashed an obsequious grin. "It's all right," she said, sizing up Michael and me from head to toe and then back from toe to head. "Since you're tourists, Master will squeeze you in. Please wait." After she'd asked our dates of birth and I'd told her that we wanted *kanxiang*, physiognomy, she went toward a corner and disappeared.

I looked around. There were no other people in the room, but its four walls were cluttered with photographs. Michael and I stepped close to look. A shriveled, sixtyish man wearing a goatee and a loose Chinese robe appeared in every picture: painting the eyes of a lion to bring the beast to life before its dance performance; making offerings to a huge Buddha; performing *feng shui* for the Hong Kong Bank in Chinatown.

Michael said, "Meng Ning, do you trust these people?"

"Michael, relax—"

Just then the voluptuous girl appeared again and asked us to follow her. My heart thudded as we passed rooms and turned corners. What would our fates be—Michael's? Mine? Ours?

The master looked older, yet handsomer, than in the pictures. He waved the white-cuffed sleeve of his Chinese suit to signal Michael and me to sit in the chairs across from his large desk. Then, like a connoisseur examining rare art objects with a magnifying glass, he carefully studied us through his thick, tortoiseshell glasses. Michael turned to smile at me nervously and squeezed my hand underneath the desk. I smiled back, feeling the moistness of his palm.

The master asked me in Chinese who'd go first. After I told him I would, he plunged right in. "You were a nun in your past life."

That startled me. Yet before I had the chance to say anything, he went on. "But because you hadn't meditated enough to extinguish your worldly desires and pacify your six senses, you fell in love with a man and broke the monastic rule. That's why you were cast out from the religious order and become a lay person in this life." He paused to look me in the eyes. "Since you have to pay back this love debt you owed in your previous life, your love life in this incarnation will not be smooth."

As I opened my mouth, he waved his bony, jade-bangled hand to stop me from talking. "You have a smooth and high forehead, which shows you're very intelligent. Your big, glistening eyes are considered beautiful, but they're not a good sign for your love life."

"What do you mean?"

"You attract men, but . . ."

When I asked him to explain more, he said, stroking his white beard with his long-nailed fingers, "There's some confusion along your path of romance, but it's a mystery that heaven will not divulge to me." Then he smiled. "Don't worry too much, miss, just remember the Chinese saying: 'With absolute sincerity of the heart, even stone and metal can be opened.'" I knew this old Chinese saying that means lovers will break any barriers and overcome any obstacles to be together if their love is sincere and undying.

Toward the end, he summed up my life as long, auspicious, and full of adventures. "Soon very favorable to cross the great water," he said.

Did it mean crossing the Pacific Ocean? To be with Michael? Or going back to stay in Hong Kong?

Overall, even if some pronouncements were still obscure, I was quite happy with the reading.

But not Michael. While listening to our conversation and not understanding a word of Cantonese, he had the anxious look of someone watching a foreign movie with no subtitles. Barely had the master finished with me when Michael asked me to translate, but the fortune-teller had already gone on to start his reading.

He scrutinized Michael's face while addressing me. "Good physiognomy." He paused to lean closer to Michael; Michael pulled back, his cheeks flushed. But the master seemed unperturbed. "Your friend has a good face: full, straight, smooth, and lustrous. His three powers—heaven, earth, and man—are well balanced. Broad forehead which signifies honor, long and straight nose which signifies wealth, and full chin which signifies a long life. In a word, his face has the features of high-ranked people, such as emperors or ministers of state."

I nudged and smiled to Michael, silently expressing to him the master's praise. But Michael, curiously, looked like a boy who had done something mischievous and was now waiting to accept his karma—whatever punishments were going to fall on him.

Then, to my disappointment, the master added, "Yet your friend's physiognomy is not without deficiency. His eyebrows are far from each other, showing that he has no karmic relationship with his relatives. Not only that, he could even be . . . unfavorable to them—"

"Master, what do you mean by unfavorable?"

"Meaning that some of his relatives, like his mother, father, or even son, will sacrifice their lives for him so that he can live a good life in this incarnation."

Michael was an orphan. But what about . . . his son? I felt a chill down my spine.

Right then the master spoke again in his composed tone. "But that's in the past; no blame now."

In the past—what did he mean? Was Michael hiding a son somewhere?

Just then I felt Michael's hand on my thigh. "What did he say?"

But I had no chance to translate, for the master pointed to his forehead and continued. "See, the pale shadow hanging over your friend's forehead also shows that he had a difficult youth. Something happened to him when he was . . . I think fifteen, or sixteen." He tilted his head to get a better look at Michael under the light. "As you can see, his eyes are long and deep and his gaze spirited, signifying wealth and honor. But because sometimes his eyes are also fathomless, his love life will not be smooth." He paused. "In fact, it's rather troubled. He might have more than one marriage. Anyway, when he was a rich and eminent Chinese in his past life, he kept several concubines. He needed their *yin* energy." Then he paused to scrutinize me. "Your friend also needs to build his *yin* energy, which he let run down. Too many negative *yin*"—he meant "dead"—"people in his life. They drain away his positive *yin* energy."

I remembered the décor in Michael's apartment, which desperately needed some positive *yin* touch—sources of female energy like crawling plants, flowers, wind chimes, colorful pictures.

"Although he's orderly and well organized on the surface, his spirit underneath is restless. He needs more earth and water in his life to balance his fire and metal. Miss, inside you there's a spring of young *yin* energy that you should put to good use by helping your friend. Remember: when man and woman occupy their correct places it is the great righteousness of heaven." He paused, then added, "Your friend is starving for your *yin* energy."

Before I had the time to absorb what he'd said, the master went on to praise Michael's strong fingers with conical tips, which indicated intelligence and moral rectitude. And Michael's voice, deep and sonorous like bells, signified longevity. But, he added, if a person has a bell-like voice and also a deformity like a mole underneath the eyebrow, he can still risk dying young. Like my father, I suddenly realized—and squirmed.

As if reading my mind, the master stroked his beard meditatively. "Our faces are formed by our hearts, and we can always change our hearts by accumulating merit." He concluded his reading by motioning to Michael. "His beginning has not been good. But as long as your friend is steadfast to face his loss, his life will be long and righteous."

He stopped, then asked, "Are you his girlfriend?"

I lowered my head and felt color rising to my cheeks.

He smiled. "Good. Then listen carefully, miss. He not only needs you, he needs the *woman* in you, not the little girl."

"Master, what do you mean?" As I tried to make him explain more, he waved a dismissive hand. "I've already revealed enough of heaven's secrets."

The girl came and took us out of the room. After we'd paid, she walked us to the door. "*A Mi Tuo Fo*—Hail to the Merciful Buddha—and good luck." Then she winked at me. "Your boyfriend is too thin; you should cook him more tonic soup, like I do for Master."

I smiled, wondering what her relationship was with the fortune-teller. Then I turned to look at Michael and felt a tenderness swell in my chest.

During our taxi ride home, I told Michael about the fortune-teller's readings: my previous incarnation as a nun, my love debt, his good physiognomy, fortune, longevity, and his bad karmic relationship with his relatives.

As I wondered whether I should tell him what had been said about his troubled love life and his lack of *yin* energy, Michael asked, his eyes intense, "Meng Ning, is that what he really said?"

"Yes."

"Did he really say my parents, or even my . . . son, sacrificed for me?"

"Yes . . . but, Michael, this is just for fun." I looked at his creased brows. "You're not going to take his words seriously, are you?"

Michael's face flushed; he didn't respond.

"Michael, you were not"—I swallowed the words—"married before?"

Michael had already guessed my question. "Meng Ning, I've never been married."

"Then the fortune-teller is wrong and you shouldn't worry—"

"But didn't he say anything at all about my love life?"

"He said . . . you might have two marriages—"

"Damn!"

"Michael, relax! Didn't you say this is superstition?"

Right then the taxi jerked to a stop in front of a red light. A very tall truck pulled up right next to us. Michael looked up; the truck driver, his muscular, tattooed arm dangling outside the window, looked down and hollered, "What are you, some kind of asshole?"

Michael shot back, "Why don't you go fuck yourself!"

"Why don't you bite my ass!"

Michael yelled, "You jerk off, asshole!" and gave him the finger.

The truck driver's eyes read murder. Then, just as he opened the door to get out, the light changed and our cab shot ahead.

Shocked, I threw him a sharp glance. "Michael!"

He didn't respond.

"Michael, you all right?"

"I'm sorry." His face reddened and his voice cracked. "I'm so ashamed of myself. . . . I . . . I guess I'm just tense."

Something was troubling Michael. What was it? Were there still things that the fortune-teller had deliberately left out for fear of revealing too many secrets of heaven? As I wondered, the taxi pulled to a stop in front of his apartment building.

❦ 17 ❦

The Teenage Orphan

Back home, Michael brewed coffee and prepared some snacks. When we were sipping and munching, the fortune-teller's reading kept spinning in my mind. I eyed Michael. There was much I wanted to ask him about, but his forlorn expression made me swallow my questions.

The crunching of chips seemed to be the only sound punctuating the silence between us. Finally Michael looked up and smiled wryly. He tried to say something but stopped before he began.

"Michael"—I reached to touch his face—"please tell me what's on your mind."

"I've been thinking about my parents."

I remembered the fortune-teller's words:

The pale shadow hanging over your friend's forehead also shows that he had a difficult youth. Something happened to him when he was fifteen, or sixteen.

Knowing that this was a difficult subject for him, I asked very softly, "You mind telling me about them?"

"Only briefly, for I really don't want to bore you with the details."

"I understand. Go ahead."

"When I was fourteen, my mother had an unexpected pregnancy and died giving birth to my younger sister. A year later, my father remarried. The woman was his gold-digger secretary and a monster. The marriage lasted less than two years because my father died seven months after being diagnosed with cancer. After the funeral, I never heard from my stepmother again, and I'm actually very glad about that. However, my father left all his money to her and I was penniless."

"I'm so sorry, Michael. Then how did you survive?"

"Philip Noble. Philip's father was an ophthalmologist and comfortably off. He invited me to live with them."

"What about your other relatives?"

"My grandparents were gone. My mother had sometimes mentioned a black-sheep uncle who owned a small bar in New Jersey. But when I finally tracked down his phone number and talked to him, he was furious that I'd found him. Not only did he refuse to help, he hollered, 'Who gave a shit about me when I was poor?'

"I spent some time with the Nobles, but I couldn't ask for too much from them—after all, they are not my parents. So it was really my discovery of Chinese art that changed things for me. Somehow it brought me back to life again. Both the art and Professor Fulton. I became closer to him than to Philip's father because we shared more interests. Professor Fulton should be at the Met tomorrow; I'll introduce him to you. He was very kind to me. I owe him a lot."

I reached to hold Michael's hand. "Michael, I'm so sorry about what happened, but you're fine now."

"Thanks." Some silence, then Michael said, "Now tell me more about yourself."

I sipped my coffee, then told him how my father, a disillusioned poet and scholar, had become a gambler, how he had stolen the bracelet from my mother, and how he had gambled it away on my twentieth birthday.

My mother meant to give the bracelet to me as a birthday present—the last piece of jewelry her mother had given her. When I asked Mother whether I was too young to receive Grandmother's heirloom, she said, "Silly girl, of course I don't expect you to flaunt it around. It's just when it's under your name, hopefully your father won't gloat over it like a monk over enlightenment."

One morning, to prepare for my longevity birthday dinner, Mother had gone to the market to buy a live chicken and a fish, butchered and gutted on the spot. We rarely dined out in those days, for Father had been jobless for years, and we mainly lived on Grandmother's money, which had almost all fled across the gambling table.

Dinner was ready and Father was still nowhere to be found. After waiting for an hour, Mother decided we'd go ahead without him. On the red-clothed table, Mother carefully set down five dishes: steamed fish in scallion and black bean sauce, soy-sauce chicken, stir-fried bok choy in crushed garlic, and—a must for a longevity dinner—hard-boiled eggs dyed a cheerful red, and noodles symbolizing long life. We savored the fish, relished the chicken, and chewed the noodles in silence. Although neither of us mentioned Father, we both knew he must be at that moment drowning himself in the gambling sea of *samsara*.

After dinner, Mother set out a cake with two candles. She lighted them, smiling. "I'll go get the bracelet."

Almost immediately, Mother screamed like the chicken slaughtered for my birthday. I dashed into the bedroom and saw her clutching the empty jewelry box on her lap. "Your father has stolen your grandmother's bracelet!"

Father didn't come home that night. That piece of jade, worth ten thousand Hong Kong dollars, could maintain his gambling habit for a long time—long enough that he'd completely forgotten the day when his only daughter was born.

Father came home the next morning with bloodshot eyes and breath smelling of alcohol. Mother started to scream at him for his gambling away the household money.

Suddenly Father began to sing, "Sometimes you win, sometimes you lose . . ."

I almost burst into tears. "Baba, that's a secret only between you and me!"

Mother cast me a questioning glance. "What secret?"

Father laughed. "Oh, don't you remember we lost our baby boy on the gambling table?"

Mother went up to Father and slapped his face.

The air in the apartment suddenly became like that in a mortuary.

A long silence.

"Sorry," Father finally said, "it's my fault. I've lost everything." His voice rang with heroic defeat.

"Where's the money my mother sent us last month for the Mid-Autumn Festival, before she died?" Mother demanded. "There was two thousand dollars."

"Gone" was Father's reply.

"And the other jewelry in the bank safe? Then what about the stock my mother bought me several years ago?"

"Long gone," Father said, avoiding our eyes.

It was then that we found out Father owed a loan shark ten thousand dollars. And if he couldn't pay tomorrow, it would rise to fifteen thousand.

The next evening, when Father, Mother, and I came home together from a cheap dinner at a street stall, we found both our apartment door and the wall next to it splashed with characters in red paint dripping like blood.

My parents' mouths dropped open.

"The Big Ear Hole!" Father exclaimed. The loan shark.

The huge, evil characters forced themselves onto my eyes:

WARNING:
IF WE CAN'T GET THE MONEY,
WE'LL GET THE THROAT

Mother pushed Father on the shoulder. "Hurry! Let's get inside the house! Quick!"

Father fumbled in his pants pocket for several moments before he pulled out a string of keys, singled out the right one, and pushed it into the keyhole with trembling hands. "Damn!"

"What's wrong?" Mother yelled.

"They glued the keyhole!"

Just then, a thirtyish man with a boy passed by our apartment in the long corridor. The bespectacled man peered at the graffiti, then lowered his head and dragged the boy away.

Hurrying his steps to follow his father, the little boy looked back at us and asked, "Baba, will they die?"

The man smacked his son's scalp. "Shut up and mind your own business!" After that, the two disappeared around a corner.

It took Father almost ten minutes to scrape clear the glue with the Swiss Army knife he always carried. Then we entered the house and locked the door. In less than five minutes, the bell rang. Father jolted up from the sofa, but Mother pushed him down.

"Let me get it," she hushed.

Mother looked through the peephole, then cleared her throat, her voice determined. "Who is it?"

"We're looking for Du Wei," said a raucous male voice. I pictured him standing right outside the thin door, his bulging muscles tattooed with a monstrous dragon and his eyes screaming murder.

Mother yelled, "No such person!"

Raucous Voice roared back, "Hey, bitch, don't fool with me. I know Du Wei lives here. Get him out!"

Father and I listened with our ears pressed tightly to the door. I tipped my head to peek at him and saw big beads of perspiration oozing from his forehead.

Mother hollered again through the firmly closed door, "I'm not fooling with anyone, and I've told you already there's no such person here!"

Silence—then another scratchy male voice said, "Hey, listen, bitch, the earlier Du Wei shows us his face the better—you understand?"

My heart plunged into a frenzied flip-flop when I heard Mother shout at the top of her voice, "Mister, I'll call the police right now if you continue to harass me!" Then she almost paralyzed me by threatening, "I'll also sue you for damaging my apartment wall!"

Yet, miraculously, after Mother's threat, the scratchy voice dropped an octave. "All right, bitch, I'll leave you alone now, but be careful if I find out the truth."

Some heavy breathing, followed by loud footsteps. We pressed our ears against the door and listened until they faded like the dissolving of a nightmare.

Mother, Father, and I stood holding our breath for long moments. When we were sure that the two messengers from hell were gone, the three of us went to sit down on the sofa.

To my surprise, Mother didn't scold Father, but instead said in a whisper, "Now we have to find a way to either put the Big Ear Holes off or to avoid them."

"But how?"

Mother's voice came out low, yet firm. "I don't know, but we've got to figure out a way."

But we didn't.

A week later, I was walking back from school with my parents. As we were nearing our building, we smelled smoke. Then we saw a fire engine parked right by the entrance. A group of pedestrians, a few policemen, and firemen milled around. We immediately sensed it must be our apartment. Father, Mother, and I spat out simultaneously, "The Big Ear Hole!" The three of us pushed through the crowd and dashed up to the fourth floor, which smelled strongly of smoke. Once we jostled through our neighbors and saw our apartment, I burst out crying. Our whole home was gone! Literally. Past the door was only a black hole. Tangled bunches of wires hung down, the ceiling had fallen, and our furniture was only a few smoldering sticks. Seeing that my mother and I were crying, a policeman went up and asked whether we lived here. We said yes; then he went through the procedure of asking for our identity cards, names, and who did we think would do this. Father told him it must be the loan shark.

The government put us in a temporary house, and two weeks later Father went into the hospital and never came back. They told us that he died of a heart attack.

To make ends meet, I tutored school kids every afternoon after I finished my classes at college. My mother worked at home, supplying meals. One time Mother had her biggest source of business ruined. The order was for a twelve-person birthday banquet for an octogenarian. His son, who'd heard from a relative about my mother's delicious home cooking, had canceled a restaurant reservation in order to place an order with her.

The twelve-course banquet was a big thing for us, both for the money and the opportunity for my mother to show off her culinary skill. Mother spent three days planning the menu and purchasing the ingredients. She even bought a new wok. "This is a banquet dish, so I have to use a banquet wok." She smiled, weighing the huge, shiny utensil in her hand.

That day, in order to finish the dishes in time for delivery that evening, Mother woke up at five-thirty in the morning, washed, dressed, put on her new apron, then burned incense to whatever gods and goddesses she could conjure up in her mind to get their blessings. The whole day I stood by to help—cutting up meats and vegetables, mixing ingredients and sauces, passing mixing bowls, oil, condiments, knives, chopsticks.

Finally, we had everything finished by six-thirty, half an hour before the old man's servant was to come to pick up the dishes. We kept staring at the clock and waiting anxiously while relishing the praise and the thought of the five hundred dollars that would mean so much to us.

The servant was an angry-looking young man with a crude face and rude manner. One by one, my mother handed him the dishes for him to put into two big baskets. Right after Mother had given him the shark fin soup, he turned around, lifted off the lid, and spat into the velvety liquid.

I caught sight of him.

"What are you doing?" I shouted, then turned to Mother. "Ma, he spat into your soup!"

"*What?*" Mother's eyes shot daggers.

The young man made a face. "That's none of your business! This is for the old man. I hate him!"

"But that's my soup!" Mother yelled.

"So what?" he shot back. "He's the one who'll eat it, so why don't you mind your own business!"

"That's just what I'm doing right now!" Mother yanked his sleeve. "You dead boy, give me back my soup!"

"No! Now this is the old man's birthday soup. Ha, ha!"

Mother kept yanking his sleeve until some of the soup spilled on the floor and she slipped and fell, knocking over the young man and the baskets of food. All the dishes splashed and shattered on the floor.

"Oh, Meng Ning, " Michael exclaimed. "That's terrible."

I went on. "I helped Mother up and immediately we began to clean up the mess. When we finished, we realized the young man had already gone."

"Then what happened?" Michael asked.

"The old man's son called and we told him the truth. Furious, he hung up the phone. Three appetizers had not been packed, but we couldn't even eat them for dinner, for Mother said to eat someone else's ruined birthday meal would bring bad luck for years—not that we didn't have enough as it was. So although we felt exhausted and our stomachs ached with hunger, we threw the food away. Worse, we lost a lot of money in preparing the food and buying the wok, for the young man had left without paying us. That evening we deliberately went to bed early so as to ignore the complaints of our empty stomachs. To comfort me, Mother said, 'Maybe we'll have a wonderful dinner in our dreams.'"

After I finished, Michael reached to touch my face. "I'm sorry you had to go through that." He took my hand, kissed my palm, and ran the tip of his tongue along it. "And I'll make it all up to you, if you're willing to be my—Meng Ning, can you be my refuge, my temple?"

Yes. And I, the reincarnation of Guan Yin, would be his guardian goddess. But I swallowed my thoughts.

"Michael," I asked, "you're not upset at me that I . . . turned you down?"

"I was devastated. But deep down I believed you love me. I just thought something was bothering you, maybe another man in your life."

"Not a man, but a woman."

He looked at me curiously. "A woman?"

"I've always wanted to be a nun like my idol Yi Kong, and swore I wouldn't let any man into my life! Not until you . . . found your way there."

"How could I help falling in love with you?"

"But you looked calm when . . ."

"That evening after the concert, I only excused myself to the men's room to get ahold of myself. When I came out to meet you again in the lobby, I forced myself to act normal—I didn't want to feel or act like a failure."

"Is that true?" I felt tenderness rising in me.

"Meng Ning, then why did you—"

"Because I thought you were not serious about me."

"Oh, of course I am serious about you! I hope someday you'll realize how deeply I love you." Michael's eyes glistened. "Meng Ning, you looked so beautiful, so full of life when you hurried to line up at the registration counter."

I was glad to hear that, but I was pretty sure that I had also been sweating, and my hair was unkempt. Hadn't he noticed that?

"I asked you to come see me in New York because I wanted to have you near me. I also needed to do whatever I could to make you change your mind about turning me down."

Michael must have assumed I'd already said yes, because we were soon settled in the comfort of the bedroom. Then, to my surprise, he pulled out a pink jacket from a bag and wrapped it around my body, very carefully, as if I were made of fine porcelain. The silk—which felt voluptuous on my skin—was finely decorated in satin stitches depicting butterflies, bats, and floral sprays. To enhance its beauty even more, its cuffs were embroidered with flowering chrysanthemums done in bright green, purple, and gold and silver threads. With my fingertips, I traced the texture of its embroidery while blinking back tears.

I had never been treated so nicely by a man. Though I believed my father loved me, he had never brought me gifts. Instead, he would steal things from me—gold, silver, antique statues given by the villagers who thought I was the reincarnation of Guan Yin—to pawn them for money to gamble.

Now I wanted to say something to Michael, but swelling in my throat stifled my voice.

Finally I said, running my hands over the jacket he had just given me, "Michael, this must be very expensive?"

He ignored my question. "I know what it's like to be deprived—I don't want you to be anymore." He looked sad for a moment, then, "Meng Ning, I want you to be happy."

A long silence, then he pulled me to him, tilted my face, and looked deeply into my eyes. "Meng Ning, will you marry me?"

Pushing my doubt about trusting a man and marriage to the back of my mind, I uttered a soft, "Yes."

Not long after, we made love in his bed, playing hide-and-seek with my naked body under the embroidered jacket.

Two days later, my left hand looked different—adorned with a solitary diamond the size of a lentil. Walking hand in hand with Michael on Fifth Avenue, I kept moving my hand, marveling how such a small surface could give out so many sparkles, like the shimmering of ships' lights on the sea.

"This diamond is flawless," the saleswoman at Tiffany had said, shifting it under the light. "Look at its fire, so brilliant that it'd blind your eyes!"

When Michael had been paying with his credit card, another saleswoman nudged my elbow while motioning to him. "Hey, lucky girl, this man must really fucking love you to buy you this."

✎ 18 ✎

Reception at the Met

It was a cool evening and the Metropolitan Museum of Art had already closed to the public. Alongside the curb, luxury sedans and yellow taxis disgorged elegant couples—men in impeccable suits or tuxedos and women in gowns or designer suits—carefully walking up the wide flight of steps. Although not heavily bejeweled like some of the ladies, I was at least clad in the elegant Chinese jacket that Michael had bought me, and got a few approving stares.

Michael took my arm and led me across the Great Hall, then down past the Egyptian exhibits into the Temple of Dendur where the reception was starting. After Michael had gotten our drinks, we stood under the sloping glass wall to watch the scene. The temple was at the center of a spacious area with a high ceiling and sloping, floor-to-ceiling glass windows. Central Park was now cloaked in pink twilight. But at this moment even this magnificent sight failed to attract attention. People, looking dignified yet cheery, engaged in hushed conversation in this respectful zone of taste and class. Diamonds, emeralds, sapphires, rubies, and gold glittered, echoing here and there the glint of crystal glasses and silver bowls. To complete this picture of elegance, a small orchestra in a corner was playing classical music that I could not identify.

Michael asked, "Beautiful, isn't it?" He wore a proud expression, as if by just being here he had already fathomed the mystery and prestige of the art world.

Looking around, I caught sight of a slender sixtyish woman with platinum blond hair tied into a smooth bun, and a necklace of large diamonds—each bigger than my engagement ring. She was talking to a taller woman who instead of diamonds wore a string of pearls as big as my knuckles. Behind them stood two black tie, well-established, gray-haired gentlemen waiting patiently in the registration line.

"Michael"—I nudged his elbow—"these people all seem very distinguished."

"Meng Ning"—he lowered his voice, now also eyeing the blonde and the tall woman—"this is the Met, so I can tell you these are the richest and most powerful people in New York, including the mayor and the chairman of the Rockefeller Foundation.

"Now look at the couple talking to the mayor. Do they look familiar?"

This couple definitely had the appearance of the privileged. "Hmmm . . . no, nothing special," I said with a deliberately nonchalant air.

"They are Kennedys. And the couple to their far right is the Met's trustee Benjamin Hill and his Chinese wife."

Although my eyes were now scrutinizing the handsome couples with relish, nevertheless I felt annoyed that Michael was so taken with these social elite. I wanted to say, *Oh, so . . . what's the big deal?* but swallowed my words.

We sipped our champagne while continuing to watch the rich and famous, before Michael excused himself to the men's room. I went to look inside the temple. Once I stepped into the sandstone area, I heard two women's voices, one shrill, the other husky, rise in excited tones. I walked farther inside and saw the duo—a big, fiftyish woman in a silver gown and black pearls; the other, equally big but with more delicate bones, in a red evening dress with matching rubies. Seeing that now the three of us were the only people in the small temple chamber, I smiled at them. Instead of returning my cordiality, they cast me sharp, scrutinizing glances. Feeling embarrassed, I pretended to look at the mural while trying my best to suppress a rising resentment.

As if I were invisible, the two continued their conversation.

Black Pearl—the bigger woman with a husky voice—asked, "So have you heard about the Dunns' divorce?"

"Oh, yes," Red Dress replied in her shrill voice, "I'd known from the start it wouldn't work out." She paused to wet her lips. "The girl's nobody, all she's got are her boobs—but just like old Dunn's Song dynasty painting collection, half are fakes."

The two burst into laughter.

Then Red Dress, her big eyes darting around, added, "Besides, there are rumors that she's wild."

"You mean—" Black Pearl's high-cheek-boned face lit up.

"Oh, come on, don't tell me you haven't heard about her and that actor."

Black Pearl nodded knowingly. "You mean the one who does independent films and commercials?" She winked. "He's cute, though."

"That's why. Besides, she's had enough of old Dunn. I doubt he even had sex with her during their honeymoon."

"You sure?"

"He's seventy, so maybe he's already used up . . ."

The two exchanged meaningful glances, then malicious smiles.

Black Pearl spoke again. "The girl's not as lucky as she thinks. Dunn's ex-wife got the better end of things. Now they say he's going to have to auction off his collection of jewelry."

Right then I heard Michael's voice calling me softly from outside the temple. I hurried past glittering pearls and rubies and cold glances and stepped out of the gossip zone.

Michael slipped his arm around mine. "You like the temple?"

"Oh, yes," I said, faking enthusiasm, while wondering whether I should tell him about my temple experience.

After we'd had our glasses refilled at the bar, we went to a corner to sip our drinks. I continued to watch the people, feeling self-conscious. Then my eyes caught an elegant-looking man walking toward us, smiling. It took a moment before I recognized him—

Philip Noble, Michael's glamorous buddy whom I'd met at La Côte Basque.

He shook hands with Michael. Then, like last time, he lifted and kissed my hand. "It's such a pleasure to see you again, Meng Ning. How have you been? Enjoying yourself?"

"Yes." I looked into his sapphire eyes. "I'm also starting to let the famous names and faces sink in."

Philip mocked disapproval by tossing his thick blond mane. "Nah, big deal, they're just common people like us—eat, sleep, work, play, and you-know-what."

He leaned forward and looked deeply into my eyes. "I hear that Michael and you are engaged. Congratulations."

"Thanks." I smiled, then blurted out, "Philip, then when is your turn?"

He threw back his head and laughed. "I'm different from Michael; he's the thinker and I'm the hedonist. Since he was a teenager, he's known what he wanted. Now he's gotten it, while I'm still living the floating life and enjoying it. Difference is, I'm just not interested in finding a center—unless someday when I meet someone as lovely as you." He slapped Michael's shoulder. "If I'm as lucky as him."

Michael said, "Meng Ning, just wait. Philip will be married with kids and living in Scarsdale in a few years."

We all laughed. Although I had no idea where Scarsdale was.

A shaft of light landed on Philip's face, bringing out more blue in his eyes. How would it feel to be so handsome, to be able to charm all the women in the world?

Then, taking me by surprise, he leaned down to plant a kiss on my lips. I felt my blood cascading like a waterfall. After that, he said, "Michael's a very nice guy; take good care of him."

I blushed, then nestled against Michael's chest.

He sighed. "Why is Michael always the one who gets the best?"

Michael laughed. "It's because you never look in the right direction."

Philip smiled, then saw a friend and excused himself. He winked at me as he walked away. I felt my heart skip a beat.

Michael took my hand. "Let's go find Professor Fulton."

As I was looking around, I saw a silver-haired gentleman in his sixties with a lofty air and a no-nonsense look. I nudged Michael. "Michael, this man looks so pompous. . . ."

He cast me a chiding glance. "Meng Ning, he's Professor Fulton."

I blushed and muttered an apology. Michael took my hand. "Let's go and greet him."

The professor was now talking intimately to a very tall and handsome young woman.

"Michael, who's that beautiful tall woman next to Professor Fulton?"

Michael looked uneasy. He said awkwardly, "She's . . . Lisa Fulton, Professor Fulton's daughter."

Just then the woman spotted us and smiled. Michael forced a smile back. We finally waded through the crowd and went up to them. The professor greeted Michael warmly. I was impressed that although the professor's frame was frail and lean after his stroke, he nevertheless had a commanding bearing.

Michael put his arm around my shoulder. "Professor Fulton, this is Meng Ning from Hong Kong. Meng Ning has just gotten her Ph.D. in Chinese art history from the Sorbonne." Then he turned to the woman and introduced us.

The professor smiled down at me, exchanged a few pleasantries, then turned right back to chat with Michael.

Lisa Fulton moved to my side and smiled warmly. "So you are Michael's fiancée?"

I nodded, appreciating this very tall, striking beauty in front of me in a turquoise gown decorated with sequins.

To my surprise, she abruptly lifted up my hand and squinted, her voice sharp. "Wow, the rock is huge! Michael must really love you."

Before I could respond, she asked, "When are you getting married?"

"Oh, I have no idea. You better ask Michael."

She imitated my tone. " 'You better ask Michael.' Lucky little woman! Everything is being taken care of."

I didn't know how to respond to that.

While Michael and the professor were engaged in a deep conversation on the arts and the art world, his daughter and I went on learning more about each other. Lisa told me that she was a painter of mainly abstract works and had a gallery representation in SoHo. I was only half listening, for my eyes were busy studying this turquoised goddess in front of me.

Then in the middle of our conversation on New York's art galleries, she suddenly said, "Oh, excuse me, I need to greet someone," and hurried toward a white-haired, heavily jeweled, and lavishly dressed couple.

The clickings of her high heels on the floor sounded uneven to my sensitive ears. The perfect-looking goddess was limping. Did she just hurt her leg?

Now I was standing beside Michael and Fulton, feeling like a child bumped into an adult's party. The professor was still completely immersed in his conversation with Michael, ignoring me. Michael squeezed my hand from time to time to show that he hadn't forgotten me.

When he finished talking to Michael, Fulton finally smiled down at me. "You enjoying the reception so far?" He didn't say my name; maybe he'd already forgotten it.

"Yes. I'm impressed; I've never been to anything so grand," I said, swallowing the following words: *or so pompous.*

We exchanged some more abstract social babble. I listened and responded, yet was aware that his words were directed mainly toward Michael. I sensed a strong affinity between the two, forming a glass wall through which I could only be a spectator peeking in. Suddenly I decided that I didn't like Professor Fulton, no matter how important he was in the art circle and to Michael. Maybe it was jealousy; I didn't feel that I'd ever have a place in this world of the rich and powerful.

Finally Michael said to Fulton, "Meng Ning is also a painter. She learned Buddhist ink painting from a very influential nun in Hong Kong."

Now the professor's face glowed slightly. "Oh, please tell me more."

Eager to draw his attention to me, I pushed away any vestige of Confucian modesty and plunged on to tell him about Yi Kong: how her temple had become the most influential in the colony; how she had acquired a priceless collection of Buddhist art from all over China; how she was now building a multimillion-dollar museum in cooperation with the Hong Kong government.

"But the point is, only my mentor has the connections to take her priceless art out of China," I said, feeling my face flush.

The professor's attitude toward me was obviously changing. Now he looked at me intently, asked many detailed questions about Yi Kong's art collection, and seemed to be very satisfied with all my answers. I tried not to show how much I was enjoying this.

"Next week"—now his smile was reaching high to his ears— "when I'm not as busy with the exhibit, you'll have to let me take you two to dinner."

❦ 19 ❧

Beauty with a Limp

The next day I slept late and Michael had already left for work. After I washed, I brewed tea, then cooked myself a simple brunch of instant noodles with cabbage and a pinch of chili. The engagement ring spread its sparkles everywhere—in the mirror, on the glaze of the ceramic tea cup, the silverware. I felt happy, both for the ring and my scalding spicy noodles.

While I was wondering where I should spend the afternoon exploring Manhattan by myself, the phone rang.

I picked up the receiver and cooed into it flirtatiously, "Hi, Michael."

"Little woman, is that all you have on your mind?"

"Who's this?"

"Lisa Fulton, Michael Fulton's daughter. We met at the Met yesterday."

"Hi, Lisa. How did you get my phone number?"

"You mean Michael's phone number? Ha, I knew him long before you did. He's an old friend." Before I could respond, she went on. "I'm calling to invite you to see the Pollock show at MoMA in the afternoon. I'm sure you have time and you're interested?"

"Pollock? Yes, I'd like to go."

"Good. I'll find you inside the exhibit around three," she said, then hung up.

It had begun to drizzle in the afternoon, and the Museum of Modern Art was relatively quiet when I arrived. In the lobby, there were only a few people—milling around, waiting, or inquiring at the membership service counter. An intense-looking man, hands locked behind his back and head tilted high, scrutinized the bold-stroked Motherwell painting spanning the wall to the left.

The Jackson Pollock exhibit was a huge show with more than two hundred works on display, beginning with Pollock's early drawings, and even a few by his teacher, Thomas Hart Benton. I wandered in front of the many canvasses and drawings, trying to look for possible secret codes hidden within the labyrinths of lines and splashes. I was staring at the intricately choreographed energy of *Number 32* when a woman's alto voice rose to my ears, sweet and mellow like a ripe papaya.

"Beautiful lines, aren't they?"

I turned and saw a very tall and beautiful woman with a smile like a crescent moon across her tanned face. Her long hair was a matching color; the curls splashed down her shoulders in Pollockian lines. On her neck, several gold chains glittered flirtatiously. Her eyes were dark amber. A Pollock black and bronze scarf with frenzied lines was draped casually across her breasts, and a tight black top slithered around her torso.

I blurted out, "Lisa Fulton! You're beautiful."

"Thank you." Her eyes shot out sparks like Pollack's dots. Her bronze eye shadow and lipstick enhanced her strong features.

"Pollock is one of my favorite painters." She smiled. Her teeth, catching the reflection of the light, glowed like fine Chinese porcelain. Her long tapering nails were painted with bronze polish, the color of her hair and lips. Gold bangles jingled on her wrist; one, heavier than the rest, was a panther biting its own tail.

She turned to look at me. "I like the spontaneity, the splashing, and the wildness!" Then she threw back her head and laughed a rich alto laugh, like temple chimes in the wind. A ponytailed guy stared at us. She winked back.

We both turned to look at the painting. But I couldn't concentrate. Lisa's presence seemed to fill the space around me; I could almost feel the air next to me move in curves and splashes. She smelled of wild ginger flowers, my favorite. What kind of perfume was scented like this?

Half an hour later, Lisa and I were sitting at the museum café munching sandwiches and sipping drinks. I looked out at the garden; the drizzle had stopped and the air shimmered with a fresh, clean look. A young couple sat on a bench eating pastries. In front of them, giggling Asian teenagers scrutinized a Henry Moore statue; their slim fingers wagged at the swelling surfaces. Farther on stood a tree; its interlacing branches now looked exactly like Pollock's lines.

As I wondered what to make of my new acquaintance, she said, "You want to see my paintings someday? I'll invite you to my studio, just you and me, a girl thing."

I nodded.

"I heard that you're an artist, too?"

"Hmm . . . yes and no," I said, then I told her about myself.

"I'm impressed. A Ph.D. and Zen paintings, these are my dreams."

We continued to talk more about paintings, Oriental philosophies, the art world, the art scene in New York. Not only was I surprised that Professor Fulton's daughter and I had so many interests in common, I was also impressed she knew about Chinese philosophy. Our conversation carried on until we noticed that the museum was about to close.

Outside, Lisa and I said good-bye. Then, after she had walked a few steps, she suddenly turned and came back to me—to invite me out again tomorrow night.

I didn't know whether to accept or not, though I was tempted. Not only by her beauty and cordiality, but also by an urge for revenge on Professor Fulton—he didn't give a damn about me, but his daughter did!

"I'd like to, but Michael may want to do something with me tomorrow night."

She smiled mischievously. "Oh, forget Michael for a moment. He's too serious and busy. Let's have some fun together for one night!"

"All right then, but let me ask him first."

As she started to walk away, I noticed her limp again. That startled me. Such a beautiful woman—how could this have happened? I realized that because she was conscious of her limp, she deliberately walked with an overly dignified bearing. Her pride made me sad. The limp was not very obvious, but, like a grain of sand in the eye—however small—it hurts. Or, like a crack on an otherwise immaculate antique vase—however thin—it mars. Then I thought of Dai Nam and her scar and felt sympathy swell up inside.

Back home, I couldn't sleep, being too excited by the afternoon's encounter. I decided to read in the living room and wait for Michael; it was not until nine-thirty in the evening when I heard the lock click.

I dashed to kiss Michael as he closed the door behind him. "Michael, you want me to fix you something to eat?"

"No thanks." Michael looked exhausted. "I'm too tired. Let's just go to bed."

Although I knew he was too tired to listen, I still couldn't help blurting out the news about my meeting with Lisa.

Now he looked completely awake. "Meng Ning, I don't think it's a good idea for you to see her."

"But why?"

"Just stay away from her, OK?"

I was surprised; Michael had never talked to me like this before.

"But I had a good time. I think we may become good friends."

"Friends?" Michael widened his eyes. "She's more trouble than you realize. I just don't want you to get—"

"But I find her very interesting and intelligent, let alone beautiful."

"Meng Ning, she fools a lot of people." Now Michael looked at me with concern. "You're a very sweet and innocent person. I just don't want you to be—"

"To be what?"

"Please just take my word for this."

"Michael! She's your professor's daughter, and I'm sure you know her well. . . ."

"Yes, only too well."

"What do you mean?"

"Can't we just drop this now?" Then he pulled me into his arms and started to kiss me.

The next day, when I woke up, Michael had already gone to work. When I turned on the bedside lamp, I found his message.

> Dear Meng Ning,
> Tonight I have to work late again and probably won't be home till midnight. Sorry about this. It's completely unexpected—there is an emergency patient with a very complicated case. You can get takeout or go out and have fun. Last night you made me the happiest man in the world.
> Love,
> Michael

When I was wondering if I should contact Lisa, the phone rang and Lisa's voice floated from the other end of the line. She said tonight she would like to invite me to a new experience—but she wouldn't say what.

"Just meet me downtown, between Spring and Twenty-third Street, in front of the only green building."

Before I could agree—or disagree—she had already hung up.

Lisa looked as tall and striking as she had at the museum. Again, she had dressed all in black—high-heeled ankle boots, loose silk pants, tight top. But this time the Pollock scarf was black and silver, and wandered down her neck to her supple waist. Under the twilight, her bronze hair hung loosely like crawling vines.

"I hope you haven't been waiting too long," I said, feeling the pull of her aura.

"Oh, not at all. I've been watching people go in and out. Interesting."

She stood almost a head taller than I, so when she looked down at me, her eyes seemed half closed. This reminded me of Guan Yin—head lowered and eyes half closed to manifest modesty and compassion.

"Meng Ning, let's go now. I'll take you to a bar."

"A bar? I don't think Michael would like the idea."

"Forgive my bluntness, but I think Michael has too much influence over you. You're an independent woman, not his little sister."

I didn't know what to say to this, so I muttered, "But I neither smoke nor drink."

"Then you can watch me. Come on, let's go!" she said, then half pushed me inside the building. "It's in the penthouse." Lisa motioned me to the elevator.

As I followed her into the elevator, someone hollered behind, "Please wait!" We turned and saw a man dragging a little boy and hastening toward us.

Lisa held open the elevator door.

"Thank you," the man said when the two plunged in.

There were a few moments of silence while we all meditated on the numbers blinking above. A moment later, Lisa suddenly stooped down to tousle the boy's blond mane. "Oh, darling, you're so beautiful. How old are you?"

The kid didn't respond. He glowered at the friendly and beautiful creature whose face was now almost touching his. But my friend didn't give up. She kept mussing his hair, caressing his cheeks, and flashing her porcelain teeth.

"You're so cute, honey. Tell me your name." She tilted her head, raised her voice, and stretched a Minnie Mouse smile.

The kid stuck out his tongue. "You dumb cookoo head!"

Lisa looked shocked, then annoyed; her face flushed a deep crimson. The man looked stunned. I was amused.

"Jason! That's very rude! Say sorry to the nice lady."

"No!" The boy hid his face behind the man's back.

The man got down on his knees. "Jason, be a good boy. Will you say sorry to the lady?"

Jason shook his head violently, then buried his face deeper into the man.

"I'm sorry." The man looked up at us. "My son never behaves like this; he must be really tired."

Right then, the elevator arrived at the fourteenth floor and the boy's father led him out. When the door was closing, the boy pulled up his head and made a face toward Lisa. "You dumb cookoo limp!" he said, and was slapped by his father behind the closing doors.

I peeked at my friend. Her face was twitching with anger, and that suppressed my urge to ask what a "dumb cookoo limp/head" is.

"That kid's a total brat. His father should have smacked his head against the wall and shattered his skull!" Lisa spat.

That was quite a violent curse toward a small boy.

Soon we arrived at a door decorated with a huge reptile. Then we passed through a glass door enameled with big red letters: THE WINKING LIZARD. We entered a room filled with smoke, the odor of spilled beer, and shouted conversations. Loud jazz made me itch all over as if my whole body were crawling with squirming lizards. I looked around in the dim light. The décor was minimalist and monochromatic, with leather, steel, and glass furniture. Men wore ponytails and earrings while women had shaved heads with lips and brows pierced by small silver rings. The hurrying waitresses all wore black leather. Suddenly I felt very self-conscious. My hair was long and my dress floral, with lace around the lapel. I must have looked like someone who had just walked out of an all-girls school!

A very tall waitress led us to a corner table in the rear of the bar. I wouldn't say she was beautiful, but she was definitely striking, with her white-chalked face and crimson lips. Her eyelashes fluttered over her blue-shadowed eyelids. Above the leather miniskirt a Bruce Lee–style top exposed muscular arms.

Once seated, Lisa ordered a martini on the rocks and when Muscular asked me what I wanted, I said, "Regular Coca-Cola."

My friend chuckled. "Oh, Meng Ning, forget the regular. I'll order you something more sophisticated." Then she turned to Muscular to reveal an expanse of porcelain teeth. "Give her a Cuba libre, light on the Coke and heavy on the rum, please." She winked at the waitress.

In almost no time, Muscular came back with our drinks and a

bowl of nuts. When she walked away, I saw she had muscular calves covered with veins like a brood of baby snakes. "Coolie's calves," the Chinese would call these. Then I soon noticed that most of the waitresses here were tall, athletic, and had coolie's calves.

Lisa clinked her glass with mine. "Cheers."

"Cheers," I echoed. The drink scorched my throat; I grimaced.

"You like it?" Lisa smiled prettily.

"It's . . . interesting." I hadn't really lied. Since it tasted like kitten's urine mixed with spicy chili oil.

She asked, "You like this place?"

"Hmmm . . . I can't tell yet; it's strange." My gaze fell on another brood of "snakes." "Lisa, have you noticed the waitresses here are all very tall and muscular?"

She patted my shoulder. "You're so innocent." She leaned close to me and whispered, "They're all men."

"Are you kidding?"

"Shhh . . . not too loud. Of course not."

"With makeup, earrings, miniskirts, and even lace tops?" My voice adamantly remained in the high register.

"They're transvestites. . . . Meng Ning, please lower your voice."

"You mean they're men with breasts?"

"Shhh . . . some are, but they're mostly men who like to dress like women."

"So they're gay?"

"Meng Ning, would you please lower your voice?" Lisa squeezed my elbow.

Right then, our "waitress" came back to ask whether we wanted anything more. As I was thinking, I noticed her nails were long, tapered, and painted crimson. I tried to look at her neck to see whether she had an Adam's apple. But no luck. She was wearing a spiked leather choker.

Her husky, high-pitched voice slithered its way into my ears. "Honey, anything more I can get you?"

"Hmm . . ." I didn't want anything else; I only wanted to study "her."

She flashed a derisive grin that emphasized her bloodred, full lips, her long-lashed eyes ping-ponging between Lisa and me. "Let me help you. Hmm . . . what about some dessert? We have cheese-cake, Sacher torte, tiramisu. . . ." She kissed her fingers and made a loud smack; the gloss of her fingernails gave out a few sparks in the faint light. "So, sweetie"—she turned to me—"what d'you want?"

"Hmm . . ." I looked at Lisa, then back at the "waitress," speechless.

She knelt down, put her elbow on our table, then rested her chin on her hand. She blinked several times as if her eyes were really itchy now. Anxiously, I half expected her lashes to drop into my Cuba libre.

"So, my China doll?" She winked at Lisa, then stared at me. "You want a minute? I can wait."

Finally Lisa came to my rescue. "Give her a chocolate mousse, please."

"Gotcha." She wagged a finger at Lisa and chuckled flirta-tiously. Her silver hippie earrings trembled like virgin breasts sav-agely squeezed.

She pushed herself up, and her leather-wrapped, narrow bot-tom wriggled away. I noticed a few holes, big and small, in her fish-net stockings.

I felt an army of ants crawling up my spine. "Lisa, you don't find this place . . . weird?"

"Oh, no, I'm an artist, Meng Ning. Nothing surprises me."

"Even men with breasts who wear dresses and flirt with you?"

"If you look at a thing as it is, it just is. "

"You like men dressed up like women?"

She squinted at me with a curious expression. "I thought I'd ex-pand your horizons. You know, Michael won't bring you to a place like this. He's too serious—and too protective of you. I know him well. Sorry, Meng Ning. If you don't like it here, I can take you somewhere else."

"No, Lisa. I also like expanding my horizons." It surprised me that suddenly my voice sounded so loud and vehement.

After more drinks and more talk, I began to feel at ease and got into the rhythm of the bar. Waitresses floated between tables like fish in water; men drank, smoked, cracked jokes, turned heads at passing buttocks, and threw glances at us.

Under the warm light of our table's gilt brass lamp, Lisa's skin took on a golden sheen, looking almost translucent. I felt her body emit waves of energy toward me. During our conversations, her eyes sometimes focused intently on me and sometimes far in the distance—darting between men in tight jeans, bomber jackets, and cowboy boots. Judging from the few wrinkles making their debut around her eyes, she was like a flower at its ripest moment of perfection, which was also perilously close to wilting.

Lisa turned back to look at me. "You know, Meng Ning, I'm actually part Chinese. My grandfather was a missionary and met my grandmother in Shanghai. My mother spent her childhood there."

Now Lisa's eyes were unreadable, like a cat's. "I never lived in China, but Mom used to tell me strange tales about her life there."

"Tell me her tales."

She made a face. "OK, but don't blame me if they're too weird."

"Go ahead." I took a big gulp of my Cuba libre.

"One time her parents took her to a zoo where she saw a man talking to a flower—"

"That's not very strange—"

"Meng Ning, there're more to the story; would you let me finish?" Lisa feigned annoyance, then continued. "The man was a street performer. He told the audience that every day he had to feed and wash the flower like a person. Just when he was about to demonstrate how, the flower opened up to reveal a pretty girl's head—"

"Oh."

"While everyone was exclaiming in wonder, the man stuck a lighted cigarette in her mouth. The girl's head started to smoke, blowing out clouds of smoke in circles, triangles, squares, even a heart. After that, she went on to perform other tricks, like singing, eating, and making funny faces. Of course everybody tried to look and see whether she was hiding her body somewhere. But all they could see under her head was a stem."

Mesmerized, I asked, "Is this true?"

She shrugged. "So I was told by my mother."

"What other things did she tell you?"

"She also saw a baby's head with a dog's body. It could perform all kinds of tricks, like somersaulting, walking on two legs, chasing his own tail—"

"Oh, no! Lisa, your mother must have made this up."

"No, she didn't. But . . . it's a horrible story."

"What is it? Tell me."

"The dog was skinned alive and right afterwards, its skin was wrapped onto the newborn baby until the two grew together."

"Yuck, that's really sick. . . ."

"I told you it was horrible."

"These stories are true?"

"What do you think?" She winked.

A pause before we both burst out laughing.

A long silence fell between us, then Lisa took out a pack of cigarettes, shook one out, tapped it on the pack, and handed it to me.

"No, Lisa, I don't smoke."

"Have you ever?"

"No."

"It doesn't hurt to try."

"No thanks."

"All right then." She lit the cigarette, slid it between her lips with a slick movement of her hand, then took a deep drag. She released a mouthful of smoke, her lips still in the shape of a perfect O—or a chicken's ass, as my mother would say; or a Zen circle, as Yi Kong would.

My eyes were smarting from the smoke.

Lisa asked, "So Michael is your boyfriend?"

The question took me by surprise. I carefully sipped my rum-soaked Coke, lowered my voice, and changed to a whispery tone, as if I were about to reveal the deepest secret. "Fiancé."

She didn't say anything, but kept squinting at me and blowing more clouds of smoke. "How did you meet?"

I sipped more of my rum and Coke, and before I'd decided what to say, began blurting out everything: how Michael and I had met in the Fragrant Spirit Temple; how he'd saved my life in the fire; my fall into the well when I was thirteen; my earlier contempt for men as well as my aspiration to be a nun; my friendship with Yi Kong and Dai Nam.

After I'd told her about myself, it seemed a new intimacy of sorts existed between us.

Lisa listened with a fascinated expression. "Incredible," she said at last, raising her eyes to the ceiling and releasing a long, slow stream of smoke, then dropping her head and looking me in the eyes. "You called men 'stupid piece of meat,' 'monk head,' 'four-eyed monster,' 'stinking testosterone,' 'walking garbage'? I love that!"

As if pulled by some magnetic force, I found myself shifting closer to her. She asked our "waitress" for another round of drinks.

Delicately she sipped her fresh martini, leaving a ring of her silvery lipstick on the glass. "Michael must be very fond of you."

I nodded.

"Wonderful," Lisa said, then she took a deep gulp of her drink and soundlessly laid down her glass. Next she picked up a few nuts and popped them into her mouth, chewing noisily with lips closed.

Suddenly the warmth in her eyes was gone and her voice was cold. "So when are you getting married?"

"He wants to soon, but I'm not sure I want it so quickly."

"So you're still not sure whether you want to marry him?"

"Not that—I love Michael. But I've spent most of my life hanging around nuns, so theirs is the world I'm comfortable in. Also, when you're told over and over for fifteen years how human passion is illusory and how men are untrustworthy, it's confusing. And I'm even more confused since I don't feel that way with Michael. He seems as centered as a rock, and never bothered—"

"Nobody is not bothered by anything, Meng Ning."

She sipped more of her martini and inhaled deeply her cigarette. "Now let me tell you another story. It's Japanese, about a lighthouse watchman living on an island. He fell in love with a beautiful pearl diver who lived on the island opposite his. Every evening he turned on the light so his lover could see the way when she swam across the sea to meet him. Then he fell in love with another girl. One stormy night, when the pearl diver was swimming toward his lighthouse, he put out the light—"

"So what happened?"

"She drowned. Of course." Lisa squashed her cigarette in the ash tray.

"Why do you tell such a terrible story?"

"That man was my fiancé."

"Oh . . ."

Lisa seemed to wrestle with her emotions. "I use the story as a metaphor." She paused, then said, "He dumped me . . . for someone else." She bit her lips, her eyes darting around. "But I'm still in love with him." She paused to stare into her glass, now quite empty. "You can't analyze love, can you?"

Yi Kong could. Love is illusory. It's the cause of suffering.

Lisa's voice, mingled with the tobacco, wafted bittersweet toward me. "That fiancé was Michael. We were engaged."

Back home, I felt dizzy and had a terrible headache. I paced back and forth in Michael's apartment, waiting for the *click* of the door to bring his face.

Michael finally came home at 11:00 PM. Before he even had a chance to take off his jacket, I told him that I had spent the evening with Lisa and that we needed to talk—right here and now.

"All right. I'll explain. Let's sit down." He led me to sit on the sofa. "Meng Ning, yes, Lisa and I were engaged—a few years ago."

"For how long?"

He hesitated, then said, "Five."

"Five years? You were engaged for so many years and didn't marry her?"

Michael didn't answer my question. He continued on a different track. "After I'd become Professor Fulton's student and gotten to know Lisa, he'd take us together to museums and concerts. In the beginning I did feel affection for her . . . she seemed interesting and intelligent." He paused. "But then it turned out she has a personality disorder—"

"What do you mean?"

"She has frequent nervous breakdowns. When I told her I was going to break the engagement, she tried to slash her wrists. . . . Meng Ning, this was all in the past—can we just not talk about it now?"

Then the fortune-teller's reading poured into my mind:

Some of his relatives, like his mother, father, or even son, will sacrifice their lives for him so that he can live a good life in this incarnation . . . his love life will not be smooth. In fact, it's rather troubled. He might have more than one marriage.

I blurted, "So you also have a son with Lisa?"

Michael looked stunned. "Did she tell you that?"

"No. Remember, the Master of Living Buddha said you'll have two marriages, and your son—" Now I understood Michael's nervousness about his reading.

"Did you have a son with her?"

"Yes."

"Oh, heavens, then where is he now?"

"He never lived. She aborted him during her fourth month of pregnancy."

"You didn't try to stop her?"

"She only told me after the abortion."

"Is it because of your guilt that you stayed with her for so long?"

"Meng Ning, I'm too exhausted to go into this and I have another very hectic day tomorrow. Can we talk about this some other time?"

Through the night, though Michael slept as if comatose, I flipped and tossed by his side, imagining his wild past with Lisa. I also couldn't help but imagine how he'd done it with *her*. Had he cupped her breasts as tenderly as he cupped mine? Had he whispered into her ears the same endearing phrases he whispered into mine? Had he slipped his tongue into her mouth and let it indulge itself in all kinds of decadent pleasures as it did in mine?

Philip Noble

Michael's busy schedule kept him at the hospital for long hours and we didn't have much chance to talk. Two days later, before I could bring up the issue of Lisa again, he had to go to Boston for two days, to attend a meeting about one of his research projects. He'd already told me about this and apologized when he'd invited me to visit him in the States.

Although I was still very upset by what had happened, without Michael's presence the apartment suddenly seemed quiet, as if a veil had fallen over it. Pangs stabbed my chest as I saw the empty space by my side in the foyer mirror. I went to lie on the sofa, but the fabric felt cold under me.

Finally I went to the study, flipped on the desk lamp, and braced myself to do some reading. When I was picking my books, I noticed a folded card leaning against the lamp. On the side of the card was a gold phoenix, and next to it was Michael's handwriting: "To Meng Ning." I snatched it up and opened it. It read:

Dearest Meng Ning,
　　I'm so sorry I have to leave you on your own during your stay here. In case you need cash, there is some in the top desk drawer. The fridge is still stocked, but

please also go out and have some nice meals. In case
there is any problem, call Philip Noble, or for small
matters, ask Frank the doorman. Take care. Sorry that
we quarreled. I'll talk more after I've come back. I love
you.
    Michael

I pulled out the drawer and found a pile of bills—fifties, twenties, tens, and ones. I counted; there was about five hundred dollars altogether. A surge of warmth rose inside me as I dropped the money back into the drawer, muttering, "*Hai,* Michael, I love you, too. But . . ."

Still feeling very confused and upset, I went to the kitchen and imitated a Cantonese café in Hong Kong by fixing myself a "fatty jumps into the sea"—a raw egg dropped into sugared hot water. Stirring the water and looking at the egg dissolve into surrealistic yellow-orange ribbons soothed my nerves. I nursed the glass to warm my hand, then sipped the scalding liquid and let out a sigh.

The phone startled me. I almost knocked over "fatty" as I reached to grab the receiver.

Steadying the glass, I said into the phone in a loving tone, "Hi, Michael, you miss me?"

To my shock, what came from the other end of the line was a vaguely familiar male voice. "Of course I miss you, Meng Ning."

"Who is it?"

"Philip. Philip Noble."

"Oh, Philip, how are you?" Michael's glamorous buddy's achingly handsome face quickly crept its way into my mind.

Then his rich baritone voice breathed into my ear. "Meng Ning, since Michael is away, I'm calling to ask if you need any help, like . . . my company?"

"Hmm . . ." I couldn't really say *I don't want your company,* could I? So I remained silent.

"Come on, Meng Ning, don't be stuck at home by yourself—that's not healthy. Come out and see the world." Now his voice was like heavily sweetened hot cocoa, or my "fatty." "You don't have to be like Michael, who works so hard all the time. Anyway, Michael asked me to tend to you while he's away. So, would you let me teach you how to relax and have fun?"

"Hmm . . . but I'd rather stay home . . ."

"Please, you should go out and let other people see how beautiful you are. Nice things should not be hidden from the world."

"But, Philip . . ."

"No more 'buts,' Meng Ning. Michael will be away for two days. Can you just forget him for forty-eight hours? I'll take you to a real nice restaurant and then a café that brews the best coffee you've ever tasted. Please, humor me."

In spite of my uncertainty, I found myself chuckling at his language and heard myself mutter an "all right," while the handsome face refused to vanish from my mind.

"Wonderful. I'll pick you up at six this evening."

At the door, I was surprised to see Philip holding a dozen elegantly wrapped, long-stemmed pink roses.

"For you, my Chinese Goddess."

"Oh, Philip, you don't have to do this."

"But I can't help it."

A few minutes later, Philip was opening his car's door for me. Although the car looked small and very uncomfortable with its extremely low seats, a few passersby threw us envious stares.

A thirtyish black man rushed toward us from the adjacent building, exclaiming, "Wow, a silver Lotus!"

Philip pointed a finger at him and split a white-toothed smile. "You bet."

The black man winked. "Beautiful Chinese girl, too. Man, your luck's up. You have it all!"

"Sure thing, pal."

"You like the car?" Philip asked when the car hit the road. Despite the heavy Manhattan traffic, he managed the steering wheel like a performance artist.

"Not really. You're so tall, don't you find it uncomfortable with such low, plunge-and-hit-your-bottom-hard seats?"

He gave out a hearty laugh, silvery like his moving toy. "Then I must be a fool, paying a fortune to be uncomfortable. Meng Ning, that's why I really like you. You're so different from all my exes. A breath of fresh air among suffocating perfume."

I didn't know what to say to that. Then, in less than five minutes, Philip pulled to a stop in front of an elegant entrance. Out of nowhere, a young man arrived and took Philip's key with extended hand, into which Philip stuffed a few bills.

"This is the very famous Russian Tea Room," Philip said as he held my elbow and gently steered me into the lobby filled with elegantly dressed people, milling around or occupying thick, red leather seats amidst Tiffany lamps and luscious oil paintings of flowers and landscapes.

"We're not dining here, but on the higher floor in the Palace." He cast me a conceited, mysterious glance.

I understood right away why this was called the Palace the moment I stepped inside the dining hall. The ceiling was almost two stories high with a huge chandelier hanging low like an old womb. Crystals, like diamonds, shot their dazzle in all directions, not missing a soul. Everything seemed to be floating in gold, silver, and vibrant red.

A tuxedoed waiter led us to a seat at the corner under a floral oil painting and took our orders for drinks. In no time, he came back with a bottle of red wine and a glass for Philip and a Coke for me. Since I had had my "fatty" earlier and was not hungry, I decided to skip the appetizer and Philip said he would do the same to keep me company.

After the waiter scribbled down our orders and left, Philip clinked his glass against mine. "Welcome to the Big Apple, Meng Ning."

"Thank you," I said, feeling a little breathless in the company of such a gorgeous man.

Now I noticed that Philip was wearing a perfectly tailored beige suit and a gold silk tie. His thick mop of blond hair swayed to his fluid movements as if it had a life of its own. When he talked, he gestured a lot with his delicate hands and sensuous fingers. His eyes, blue and unfathomable as the night sky, possessed a dreamy expression as if he were forever enamored with this floating world.

"You like Coke a lot?"

"Yes, it's my favorite Western beverage."

"You want to try my fifty-year-*very-old* Château Lafite-Rothschild?"

"What's that? No thanks." Then I felt I had to challenge his emphasis on the *very-old* drink. "Philip, things have to be at least three to four hundred years old to be considered *very* old."

He chuckled; sparks flicked in his blue eyes like twinkling stars. He changed the subject. "Since you dismiss my silver Lotus, hope you like this gold Palace?"

What should I say? The whole place smelled of money—old or nouveau—but to get rich was not my goal in life. Besides, as Yi Kong always pointed out, riches are transient and illusory.

However, I put on a stunning smile to match the stunning face across from me. "I think anyone would be impressed by the Louvre or Buckingham Palace. Only I would never live in such a place—too uncomfortable to inhabit, just like your Lotus."

"Meng Ning, what secret formula do you possess to make yourself so likeable? " Philip stared straight at me, his voice sincere; his expressive blue eyes were now the color of Van Gogh's starry sky. "Can I have the pleasure of knowing you better?"

Before I could respond, he continued. "How come I'm always a step behind Michael?" He let out a chuckle. Now his hair glistened like Van Gogh's sunflower under the restaurant's golden light. "Otherwise you could have been *my* fiancée. Why is he always so lucky to get the best?"

"Philip, don't you already have all the best in life? Your Lotus, your practice . . ." I wanted to say *your movie-star good looks,* but stopped myself just in time. I definitely didn't want him to think that I was attracted to him romantically. . . . Then my heart started to pound. Was I?

He squeezed my hand with his perfectly manicured one. "Maybe, Meng Ning, but I haven't gotten the best woman." He sipped his fifty-year-old drink meditatively, then said, "I've been with lots of women in my thirty-six years, but none as beautiful nor unique as you."

"Philip, you barely know me." Although I was flattered by what he said, he also made me feel uncomfortable. *Hai,* that's exactly what Yi Kong told me over and over—never trust men, handsome or ugly, rich or poor, Oriental or Occidental.

"You're definitely an old soul. I had this gut feeling the moment Michael introduced you to me." He paused, his expression turning very tender and his voice intoxicating. "Meng Ning, allow me to be bold . . . I think maybe we were soul mates in our past lives."

Before I knew how to respond, he went on. "To be honest, I've never known any woman who can bring out so much tenderness in my whole being. Right now, my heart is aching."

"Philip, please . . ." While not knowing what to say, I felt a heat growing inside me and radiating through my whole body. I downed some more icy Coke while my eyes devoured the face of this Hollywood-handsome man, seemingly so approachable, and yet so distant.

Just then the waiter returned with our food. "Scampi with pasta for madame and steak tartare for the gentleman. Enjoy."

The food was delicious, the drink soothing, and the setting romantic. Under the dazzling, yellowish light, Philip's strong cheekbones and sharp jaw looked like they were chiseled from a sculpture. He looked very manly in a slightly disreputable way—a completely different kind of man from Michael. He was so excessively handsome that he seemed impossible to reach—even though he was sitting right across from me. But then why would he want to reach me so eagerly? Did he want me to be his next toy, a China doll, like his Lotus? Or just because Michael had asked him to tend to me while he was away?

We ate in silence for a while. The only sound was the pleasant clinking of the forks, knives, glasses, and dishes. I also noticed a few women—young and old—shooting envious glances toward me. The young girl across from our table accompanied a wrinkle-faced, richly dressed old man. The sexy girl at the table next to her seemed to draw away from her horse-faced nerd companion.

I tried but failed to suppress the corners of my lips from rising.

Philip looked at me curiously. "Hope you at least like your food. Good?"

The scampi melted inside my mouth. "It tastes like it was cooked by an imperial chef in an ancient palace where if the emperor took only one bite instead of two, the cook would be executed."

"Wow, that's really dramatic! I like that." Philip smiled, showing his perfect white teeth. "There are two things I really love in life—good food and beautiful, intelligent women."

"Me, too," I said, spearing another scampi, "especially women. That's why I am so close to my Buddhist nun mentor. She is beautiful, like a film star."

"But Buddhist nuns have to shave their heads, right?" Philip took a hearty bite of his raw steak. "I can't imagine a bald woman being attractive."

"Not until you see my mentor."

He was now sipping his wine thoughtfully. "But why would you have a nun as a mentor?"

I blurted out, "Because I wanted to be a nun, and it's Michael who . . ." I stopped.

"You did? Michael never told me that!" He scrutinized me intensely. The blue of his eyes shone like a sapphire under the mysterious full moon. "That would be such a waste. Meng Ning, promise me, never try again to be a nun. Anyway, I don't like nuns."

"Why? These women are very nice, compassionate people," I said, picking at my vegetables.

"Because they don't like men! That really irks me, especially those pretty ones. They deprive men who deserve good women."

I'd never thought of it that way.

He cut off another chunk of meat and put it into his mouth. I noticed the color of his sensuously moving lips matched exactly his blood-streaked steak. "Your naïveté makes you so appealing," he said.

"Thanks, but I'm already thirty, so I don't think I'm that naïve." I tried but failed to twirl the pasta onto the fork.

He eyed my awkwardness with amusement for a while, then said, "That makes you even more naïve. OK, now tell me about your past with the nuns." He put down his fork, then delicately dabbed his lips with the white napkin.

So I did.

After I'd finished, Philip held my hand for a long time before he finally released it. "Meng Ning, let's go home."

I was surprised that the place where he pulled up was not Michael's apartment building. "Philip, but this is not where Michael lives."

"I know. It's where I live."

Although I wanted very much to say I needed to go home, my body involuntarily followed his.

Philip's apartment looked very different from Michael's. While Michael's was decorated with Chinese objects, Philip's was, like him, glamorous and sumptuous. Richly colored abstract oil paintings and glass bookcases covered the walls. Antiques of various shapes and sizes struck elegant poses in ornate cabinets. The carpet was thick, lush, with Occidental motifs of mystical animals in vermillion, green, and purple.

"Very nice apartment," I exclaimed. "But I think I really should go home. Michael may call anytime."

"Meng Ning, would you compassionately grant a lonely chap the pleasure and honor just to have an after-dinner drink with you?"

Feeling completely powerless, I muttered a weak, "Yes, of course."

After he led me to sit down on his huge ivory leather sofa covered with colorful pillows, he went inside the kitchen and soon returned with a lacquer tray. He put down the tray and handed me a glass. After that, he sat next to me on the sofa, took off his jacket and tie, then started to sip his drink thoughtfully. Although he was not very near to me, instinctively I moved away a bit.

We started to chat about various things—music, films, art, museums, and his practice. I was surprised when he told me that some of his patients were Hollywood stars.

"I'm very tempted to tell you who they are, but I can't." He took another sip of his drink and looked at me with eyes soft and tender like blue silk. "But you know what? None of these stars can compete with your beauty."

"Thank you for your kindness, Philip, but please don't exaggerate."

His expression turned serious. "No, not a bit. Their beauty is all skin-deep. I'm the one who fixes their skin so I know. Meng Ning, none of them can compete with your natural beauty, your naturalness, your mystery. It must be because of your Zen study."

"Oh, Philip, you're overpraising me." Now my face must be the same color as his blood-streaked steak!

"With you, I only speak from my heart. I'd never have the heart to lie to this innocent face of yours," he said, reaching to touch my cheek.

"Philip . . ." My cheek was hot, and so was his hand.

He murmured, his voice soaked in alcohol, "Meng Ning, I can't help it; I just can't. I'm in love with you, helplessly and desperately."

"But this is only the third time you have seen me." I tried to act calm, but my heart was beating like a door frantically knocked upon by a debt collector.

"Time is irrelevant," he said, then pulled me close to him.

"Philip, please don't . . ."

"Shhh . . . be quiet." In no time, he sealed my lips with his. His hands held my waist tight. Then he pulled my whole body against his, warm like an oven.

I felt his body heat gradually penetrating my clothes, my skin, then trying to grope its way into my heart. His kisses, like the lava of a volcano, melted my lips. I felt my body plunging right into this dark, fiery pit of passion and danger.

Suddenly a sadness hit me so hard that I pushed him away. I started to weep, then sobbed involuntarily. My whole body shook like a tiny boat in a merciless storm.

Finally Philip let go of me. "Meng Ning, I'm so sorry. Are you all right?"

I shook my head.

"Did I . . . offend you?"

"I don't know. Philip, I'm just engaged to Michael and now I feel strongly attracted to you. That's not right!"

"Love has nothing to do with being right or wrong." He tilted my chin and his penetrating eyes peered into mine; their expansiveness reminded me of the vast blue sky, the fathomless ocean. His voice was soft and tender like a feather. "Do you love Michael?"

I remained silent, overwhelmed by his mere presence and desire.

"If you don't, feel free to love me. I'm all yours." He kissed my hand, then pressed it against his chest. "Feel my heart, Meng Ning. It's beating for you."

"Philip, just let me go home."

He kept staring at me, but didn't say a word.

"Please, Philip."

He pulled my face close to his. "Meng Ning, look me in the eyes and tell me you don't love me."

"Sorry, but I . . . can't. I'm very confused. I should've stayed with Yi Kong and been a nun!"

"No, you're not going to be a nun," Philip said, starting to kiss me again.

I had to use sheer willpower to push him and my desire away. "Please, Philip, I really have to go home."

"All right, if that's what you *really* want." He planted a kiss on my forehead, stood up abruptly, and held his hand out to help me up.

The next day I woke up late with a splitting headache, dry lips, and aching all over my body. Scenes from last night with Philip kept spinning in my head. I tried to listen to music, read, and meditate. But nothing worked. Philip's hot kisses still seemed to linger on my lips, melting my heart and my body. Was I betraying Michael? Did I make the right choice to be his fiancée, or should I return to Hong Kong to take refuge with Yi Kong? How could I be attracted to another man so quickly? Was I becoming a slut?

The air felt a bit chilly and I rubbed my arms. The Guan Yin pendant that I'd laid down on the sofa now seemed to be smiling at me, whether at my misgivings or ignorance I could not tell. This was the amulet that Yi Kong had dropped down to me in the well seventeen years before. Then the Goddess of Mercy had come toward me in the subterranean darkness, riding on a fish. I had found peace of mind for the first time in her spiritual presence, amidst the stink of rotten vegetation and mildew. Later in Golden Lotus Temple, I had admired the nuns' kind faces and compassionate deeds. . . .

I felt an impulse to bare my thoughts and pour my soul out to a female. Since the Goddess of Mercy was, after all, but a gold-plated miniature painting, I needed a woman friend to turn to, but I had none here except . . .

❦ 21 ❦

Why Don't You Try It with a Woman?

When Lisa opened the door, I felt instantly soothed by the fragrance of wild ginger flower. Her face, framed by the half-closed door with the light flooding at her back, looked soft and inviting. I followed her inside her apartment as if in a trance.

"Make yourself at home, Meng Ning. I'm going to get us something to drink."

I looked around. The walls were painted white and the floor partly covered by dark green, intricately patterned rugs. The furniture included two bookshelves, a coffee table, and a reddish-brown wooden chest with bronze drawer handles. The feeling of simplicity and cleanliness pleased me. But what caught my attention were the paintings covering the main wall. They were huge, and I could now feel the strong yet disturbing energy emanating from the many circles and lines. Though impressive, somehow the whole effect still didn't look quite right to me. Was Lisa deliberately striving for confusion?

"Lisa, your paintings are very . . . powerful," I said, lowering myself onto the sofa next to a large window.

"Thanks." She was busy with the refrigerator in the small kitchen, her dress straining at her hips. Then she came to put down on the coffee table a tray with two glasses and handed me one.

"It's your Coke—with a squirt of rum in it."

She sat down on the sofa opposite me and crossed her legs. Her toenails, painted a phosphorescent bronze, gave out a few sparks as she flicked her toes. The silver filigreed ankle bracelets twinkled in response.

It had started to rain outside. We sipped our drinks in silence while I studied her—the tawny motes flickering in her dark amber eyes, the curves of her long lashes matching those of her nose. I had always been fascinated by women, though my feelings were not at all erotic.

The beautiful female sex.

I never have thought that beauty is merely skin deep. I was sure even Yi Kong, as a nun, agreed. The novices she'd picked to be around her were all pretty. Not to mention her exquisite art collection. Beauty always whispers mystery, and how can mystery just be on the surface? Maybe that was the reason I was now attracted to Philip?

Lisa looked at me curiously. "Meng Ning, what is it? Please tell me."

"Hmmm . . . just a bit confused, so I need someone to talk to."

"So, what's your problem, a fight with Michael because of me?"

I remained silent.

"Meng Ning, you should open yourself more to the world. And to men, too."

Did she already know what had happened between me and Philip last night?

"Are you mad that I was Michael's fiancée?"

I shook my head. "No, there's something else on my mind."

"You've been sheltered too long by the nuns, and now by Michael. That's not healthy."

"What do you mean?"

She stood up and came to sit down next to me. Then her hand started to stroke my hair, tenderly, as if I were her little sister. The rhythmic touches were soothing, almost hypnotic.

"You're a very attractive woman, so I think maybe you should date other men besides Michael. You know, now Asian women are hot among American men. What do you think about Philip?"

My heart started to pound. I blurted out, "Do you already know what happened yesterday?"

"You mean you already had sex with Philip?" She didn't look surprised, but amused.

"Oh no, not like that, but . . ." I took a big gulp of my drink.

Suddenly I noticed Lisa's hand had already moved from my hair down to my collar bone, then shoulder. Now she leaned her face very close to mine, staring at me long and hard. "Tell me, Meng Ning, do you think sex is bad?"

"No, hmmm . . ." I put down the glass.

"It's nothing wrong, right?" She tapped her head. "It's only wrong in people's heads."

Seeing that I didn't respond, she continued. "Even Buddhism teaches that sex is good. For Tibetans, sex is the way to enlightenment."

She refilled my drink. "When you come, there's no place for the mind, only the experiencing of the moment. There's no separation—you become truly one with your partner." She went on, a mischievous smile on her face. "The guy is famous for seducing reluctant women and giving them unprecedented pleasure."

"Lisa—" I was slowly absorbing the shock. "Do you think what I did was wrong? Being engaged to Michael and attracted to Philip?" I took another gulp of my Coke.

"So what? That doesn't mean you can't have a little fun, does it? Meng Ning, you're taking things too seriously. Relax. Life should be a party!"

"Then does it mean that when you were engaged to Michael you also had a little fun?"

"Sure." She didn't bat an eyelid. "That's why we split up. Michael's just like you; he can't relax."

"But I think you told me he left you for someone else."

"Take it easy, Meng Ning." She was playing with my hair. "You know Michael's past. That's why he's always starving for affection."

I didn't know how to respond. Then suddenly I noticed her hand, like a predator, was now perching on my breast.

I felt blood rush to my cheeks. "Lisa, what are you—"

"Meng Ning, relax, it's no big deal."

"But—" I realized that it was already the umpteenth time that I'd used the word "but."

"You're a Buddhist, right? So let go of your inhibition, detach from your puritanical rules and live in the moment. Rules are not made by God, but people, and most of them are pricks anyway." Now she studied me as if I were an elementary school student. "For Christ's sake, Meng Ning, I'm just trying to educate you!" Then her tone softened. "Believe me, it doesn't hurt to give it a try."

"Try what?"

She handed me my glass. "Have more; it'll help to relax you."

I took a long swig under her scrutinizing eyes.

"Every woman should try it at least once with another woman. I'm sure you'll like it. It'll feel much more open and free than with a man—"

"Lisa, stop that. I'm not a lesbian!"

"You don't have to be. Are you an American, because you speak English?"

I was speechless.

"Me neither," she said, then, as if I didn't understand, added, "I'm not a dyke."

"Then why do you want—"

"There shouldn't be any distinctions. I like both."

"Both what?" I felt my vision blur and a headache coming.

She lowered her voice as if to tell a secret. "Both sexes. As long as I find them attractive." She paused to sip her drink, then added, "You know what, Meng Ning? I had a crush on you the instant I saw you at the Met. Do you know when you leaned your delicate head against Michael's broad shoulder, you looked so damn cute and vulnerable? I already imagined making love to you—"

"Lisa!"

Oblivious of my reaction, she went on, searching my eyes, "Ahhh . . . Meng Ning, you're still like a little girl. That's why I'm here for you." She paused for a few moments before she went on. "Innocence is irresistible . . ." she almost sang, while her hand lightly pressed my nipple.

"Lisa, please stop—"

"Don't worry. I'll be very gentle." She drew close to me and began to lick my neck; her voice sounded as if it were coming from a deep, delirious dream.

I was trying to resist, but her kissing was becoming ardent. She shifted her weight and moved her leg to lock mine. It was then that her loose cotton slacks slid up, revealing her legs—one muscular and the other shriveled. While tears stung my eyes at the pathetic sight, somehow I also felt strangely moved.

"It's OK, Meng Ning. Feels good, doesn't it?" she purred, misunderstanding my tears of compassion for something else.

Quickly she peeled off my blouse, then slipped her hand under my bra. I was still staring at her leg, feeling both too intrigued and appalled to respond. Then I felt her unhook my bra, and her fingers slowly traced around my nipples.

Now seemingly in a state of complete intoxication, her eyes closed; she began to lick the inside of my ears. This time the tickling became so unbearable that I involuntarily jerked.

"Feels wonderful, eh? I know you like it."

I tried but failed to speak, or think. Her moist, ginger-flowered breath was all over my face. The sight of her shriveled leg struck something deep inside me that I had not known existed. Then the tickle became so intense that I involuntarily closed my eyes, letting shudders escape me like a fish released back to the sea.

Lisa became more aggressive in her advances. She moved her burning lips all over me. When she was pressing her tongue on my collarbone, I opened my eyes and saw her full breasts, now completely bare, pressing against mine. This was the first time I had actually seen another woman's breasts naked, except, of course, my mother's when I was a child. In Golden Lotus Temple, any contours would be either hidden under loose, thick robes as if they didn't exist, or flattened under layers of cloth as if they were diseases trying to break out.

I couldn't take my eyes off Lisa's swelling flesh tipped with large nipples like embroidered plum-blossoms. Bits of perspiration glowed there like pink dew.

Suddenly she squirmed; my hand jerked and brushed against the plum-blossom. Wisps of her hair touched my face; her warm skin sent a tremor down my spine. I remembered after the fire when I'd accidentally stroked Yi Kong's shoulder. But the touch felt different, because Yi Kong was a nun, while Lisa was a worldly woman, who now shifted and moaned breathlessly, her hair spilling over her shoulders and her head falling to the side.

I snapped, "Lisa, stop it—"

But I was not able to finish my sentence, for she had already sealed my lips with hers. The wild ginger flower fragrance coiled around me like a heavy net into which I helplessly plunged. . . .

22

The Dying Kitten

After I'd left Lisa's apartment feeling totally confused, angry, and sorry for myself, I was not in a mood to go back to the empty apartment and so I headed for the comforting aromas of Chinatown.

The rain had nearly abated as I strolled along Mott Street. I walked past an eatery where an oily-faced man was cooking dumplings with a pair of long, thick, wooden chopsticks. The dumplings looked fat and juicy in the bubbling broth, but they didn't rouse my appetite. I passed a noodle shop from which wafted the fragrance of meat, ginger, garlic, and Chinese scallion, then a café window hung with roasted baby pigs, soy-sauce chickens, and crispy ducks glistening with oil. The animals' clouded eyes stared at me as if hungry for life. Just then I heard a loud *chuuup!* I turned and saw a chicken's head fly off from a blood-stained chopping block.

I continued walking aimlessly, trying to clear—or maybe numb—my mind. I walked past a café, an open street market with fish squirming in wooden buckets, then a grocery where Cantonese opera tunes blared from the sound system. A teenager kicked away a crushed can; a greasy-haired man flicked a lighted cigarette butt right into the middle of the street. Cartons, crates, Styrofoam containers, scraps of newspaper lay strewn all along the curb.

Still feeling sick, I jostled my way through the pedestrians and passed a narrow opening from which a sad, feeble cry startled me. My senses were awakened at once and I traced the sound into a back alley.

It was a kitten. Her hair was matted to her bony body and her eyes had the look of a person dying an unexpected death. Beside her lay a piece of rotten-looking meat. As I approached her, two Chinese boys around eight years old appeared from nowhere. One, heavy, wearing a stained T-shirt and torn blue jeans, held a bamboo stick. The skinnier one, in shorts frayed at the hem and sandals that revealed mud-caked toenails, cheered the other on as he tried to snap the kitten's tail.

Right then a back door swung open and a Chinese man, wearing a blood-stained apron and with a cigarette dangling from his mouth, strode out to dump a huge plastic garbage bag onto the curb. When he saw the kids and the kitten, a hateful grin split his face. He took a deep drag of his cigarette and flicked the lighted butt onto the kitten. "Dead cat!" he spat, then stalked back, slamming the door with a loud bang that seemed to make the ground shiver. The kids roared with laughter; the kitten jerked. The rotund kid dropped his bamboo stick and picked up the cigarette butt while his comrade cheered him on. "Yes! Poke it in the eyes, the eyes . . ."

"Stop that and leave her alone!" I shouted. My voice sounded surprisingly intimidating to my own ears. Both kids halted, the fat one's hand hanging in midair. They looked up and studied me with eyes full of spite. Fat Boy gave me a dirty look and spat, "Bitch!" while Skinny made a gargoyle face by stretching his mouth with his filthy fingers and dropping his tongue. He shouted to Fat Boy "Let's go!" and the gang of two dispersed noisily, feet splashing in puddles.

I knelt down by the kitten. She lay on the debris-littered sidewalk beside several huge garbage bins with rotten meat and vegetables spilling from the lids. The piece of maroon meat next to her gave off a sickening stench. I stooped nearer and murmured, "Meow, meow" as gently as I could while holding my breath. She struggled to open her eyes. "Meow, meow," I cooed again, rubbing my finger against her nose, still cool. Then to my utter surprise, she raised her paw to grab. Instinctively I jerked back. But when she mustered all her strength to reach again, a revelation hit me. She was trying to play with the gold-plated Guan Yin pendant swinging from my neck! Deeply moved by this act of innocent desire, I took off the chain and swung the trinket in front of her. She must have found the sparkling gold fascinating, for despite her weakness, she managed to get up and wobble two steps toward me. She grabbed at my pendant several times, making languid arches with her puny paws. After that, she uttered a feeble "meow" and slowly plopped down, her eyelids dropping. Dying—I supposed—from food poisoning.

A sadness climbed up my spine. I stooped there to let the drizzle wet my face, not knowing what to do. Finally, I recited the Heart Sutra and said a short prayer to Guan Yin, asking the Goddess of Mercy to take her soul to the Western Paradise, so that when she was reborn in this world, she would be reincarnated as a human and lead a happier life.

After I finished my prayer I covered the kitten with some newspaper, then hurried out from the back alley. My head ached as I continued to wander along Mott Street, trying to forget what had happened in Lisa's apartment while the kitten's image lingered. When she saw my pendant she had wanted to play with it. Even a kitten facing death had not had her desire quenched. Let alone we humans! Dai Nam—hadn't she spent her whole life hanging on fiercely to the very idea of letting go?

I began to walk fast, and the rain, resuming, trickled like tears down my face. Through my blurred vision, I noticed something green and red in the wet mist—a temple. I dashed across Canal Street, hurried toward the crimson gate, and plunged in.

Inside, I found myself in a large foyer with an unattended reception desk, then a smaller hallway leading to a room painted bright yellow. I stepped across the threshold into the huge deserted chamber, and started to walk around below the large dome. An elaborately carved table, decorated with offerings of flowers and incense, stood before the altar. Behind it, on the altar itself, stood images of Buddhas and Guan Yins. I made a quick bow and turned around toward the exit.

Along the hallway hung rows of pieces of silk, all dyed bright yellow. Fastened to each were pictures of men, women, children, even babies. Curious, I paused to scrutinize them for a few moments until a realization hit me—these were tablets for the dead!

Then my eyes met a baby's. He was about seven or eight months old, with thick, spiky hair, a round face, and a dimpled smile. On the right-hand side of the tablet was a small row of Chinese characters:

To our dear baby boy Guo Wang
(Country's Hope),
who passed away on July 10, 1930

The left side read:

With great sadness in heart, your loving parents,
Chan Yan and Lu Feng

I turned away, having no heart to stare any longer at that innocent face. Had he lived, he would have transformed first into a handsome young fellow and by now into . . . a middle-aged man! I imagined his sad, wrinkled eyes staring at me, as if saying: "Since my parents are long gone, now no one comes to pay homage to me anymore."

For a moment, I was overcome with sadness. Who knew when it would be my turn to have my picture on a little yellow tablet? Sooner or later we would all join my father, my little brother, the little Country's Hope, and even the little kitten.

Feeling despondent at the thought, I dragged my feet back to the foyer. Wanting to look for solace and maybe even some answers for my life at present, I walked and looked into several rooms to try to find someone—a monk, a nun, a lay Buddhist volunteer.

Then I heard faint noises emitting from a room. I hastened there, peeked in, and saw a small TV running a Hong Kong soap opera.

"Hello!" I yelled, despite myself.

The door was pulled open and a huge head thrust in front of me. The man's eyes, big, bulging, and bloodshot, scrutinized me with annoyance. "What's the matter?" he asked in accented English.

"I . . ."

"Do you want to burn some fragrant oil and ask for your fortune?"

"To burn fragrant oil" is a euphemism for a donation, since one has to pay both for the fragrance and the oil.

"Hmmm . . . yes."

He asked me to pay for a prepackaged offering, then pointed to small bundles of rolled-up rice paper on a tray. "Now pick your fortune."

When I hesitated, he said, "Don't worry, miss, all good ones."

With a pounding heart, I picked up a paper scroll, untied the ribbon, and let my fortune unroll in my palm:

Chances of success: Good
Thunder awakens one who's in a cocoon.
The butterfly flies off under the evening sun.
What's within and without combines.
The phoenix finally takes off to meet the dragon.

Confusion together with a bittersweet feeling overwhelmed me as I dragged my feet away from the temple. Was I the butterfly to be awakened from a cocoon and then fly off toward the sun? Was I the phoenix and Michael the dragon? So this was the message from Guan Yin?

After I got out of the taxi from Chinatown and was walking toward Michael's apartment building, I saw, to my utter surprise, Philip Noble's tall frame leaning against the wall next to the apartment's entrance. Wearing a T-shirt, blue jeans, and running shoes instead of his Italian suit and leather shoes, he took on another image—casual, down-to-earth, approachable. He looked tired and depressed, his face gaunt and his eyes sunken. An unspeakable feeling swelled inside me as I stepped toward him.

Spotting me, Philip dashed forward and pulled me into his arms.

When he tried to kiss me, I disentangled myself from his eager arms, then looked up at his pathetically handsome face. "Philip, why didn't you call?"

"I meant to, but thought I should come and see you in person."

There was an awkward silence before I asked, "Philip, anything special you want to see me for?" Although I knew exactly the reason.

"Meng Ning, I just want to apologize to you for what happened last night."

"It's all right."

"Can I . . . come up to your place?"

"You mean Michael's place."

"I need to talk."

"Philip, why don't you just go home and let's forget what happened?" I was feeling overwhelmed by this man's beauty and sadness.

"I can't . . . can you? Please, Meng Ning, let me go up—or would you like to come to my place?"

"No, I don't . . ."

"Please, I really need to talk."

Just then the doorman Frank appeared outside the building, holding open the door for an elderly resident. He spotted me and smiled. "Hi, Miss Du," he said, then searched me and Philip with curious eyes.

I quickly slipped away from Philip and entered Michael's building.

Back in the apartment, I went straight to the bedroom, threw myself onto the bed, and cried my heart out. What had I done to my life? How could I possibly turn from a potential nun to a slut in less than two months? No, only two days! Now I desperately needed Michael's strong arms around my shaking body, his large hands to wipe away my tears, his gentle voice to whisper comforting words, steering my life back onto the right track. Or maybe Yi

Kong would be the only one who could guide me in life, and her temple my only refuge.

The sharp ringing of the telephone jolted me upright. I picked up the receiver and heard Michael's tender voice from the other end of the line. "Meng Ning, you had a good time today? What are you doing right now?"

23

Vegetable Root Zen Center

The following day, Saturday, Michael returned from Boston. I feigned a headache and slept most of the time to avoid conversation. He tended to me tenderly, our two-day-old quarrel forgotten. On Sunday, sensing my distress, he insisted on taking me to a temple in Flushing where, he told me, I could meditate and feel better. I had no energy to say no. Besides, my conscience told me that I should please him.

While we were lining up for lunch with other lay Buddhists in the Vegetable Root Zen Center, Michael told me that he would like me to meet some of the monks.

A yellow-robed Chinese monk came up to greet us. I could not help finding his face very ugly, with its bulging eyes, buckteeth, and sharp chin. Bones seemed to stick out of his tattered robe.

Michael put his hands together and bowed respectfully. "*Nan Mo A Mi Tuo Fo,* Master Hidden Virtue." Then he gestured toward me. "This is Du Meng Ning, my fiancée."

The monk grinned so widely that I feared his teeth were going to fall out. He pointed to my tray. "Eat more, Miss Du."

While exchanging bows with him, I tried my best to use my Zen mind to suppress my aversion.

Before he left, he said cordially to Michael, "Please eat more,

Doctor Fuller. Then stay for our performance of martial arts by monks from the famous Shaolin temple in China."

As he walked away under the overhead fans, the fluttering of his robe somehow seemed to show detachment from the dusty world— so far the only redeeming feature I could find.

This center was quite unlike the temples I had known in Hong Kong. Everything seemed depressing—the bare, paint-peeled walls; the bare, gray stone floor. What appeal did Michael find in this place where there were no pretty nuns, no tender *yin* energy, but only monks like bundles of dried-up sticks? I let out a long breath.

"See, Meng Ning, " Michael, oblivious of my mood, said jokingly. "Master Hidden Virtue is not interested in the fact that you're my fiancée and that we're getting married."

I didn't respond.

Michael continued on a different track. "He must think that, as a *gweilo,* I'd like martial arts, but I don't."

"I do." I deliberately contradicted him to vent my frustration.

"Do you?" He raised an eyebrow. "You've never told me that."

"You never asked."

But Michael looked at me tenderly. "I'm sure there're still lots of things I'll learn about you, Meng Ning. I look forward to that." He took my hand in his and whispered into my ear, "I love you."

Again I didn't respond, but kept inching forward with the crowd. Ahead of me stood a Chinese boy whining to his mother that he hated vegetarian food and wanted a hamburger from McDonald's.

The mother lowered her voice, widened her eyes, and chided, "Son, I warn you, no more complaining! Now it's only one more week before you can eat meat again. Can't you wait just one more week? When your grandfather recovers from his operation, he'll give you big lucky money for the merit you accumulated for him by eating no meat. You understand? So stop fussing right now and think about your karma!"

The boy, though he stopped complaining, continued to sulk, his face a wrinkled tangerine. His mother pinched him on the ear.

"Aiii-ya!" He made an animal-being-slaughtered sound.

Michael and I got our food, then sat down on a bench to eat. The food was tasty and balanced in *qi*—cooked with the right proportion of sugar and salt, wine and vinegar, water and oil. A mindful preparation, but even that didn't arouse my appetite. For now, things in my life seemed—like the smell of the food and the pained *"aiii-ya!"*—suspended in midair.

Michael put some of his fungus and mushrooms onto my plate. "I'm so happy we can be together in this temple." He began to eat ravenously. "Reminds me of how we met in the Fragrant Spirit Monastery."

"I hope there won't be another fire."

Michael squinted at me curiously, then returned to his food. In this modest temple, Michael seemed transformed, especially in comparison to his bearing at the Met the other night. Then and there he'd acted and talked fastidiously, while here he seemed happy and relaxed, like someone in his natural habitat.

When most had finished eating, Master Hidden Virtue walked to the center of the hall and announced, "Gud afternun, evibody. I hope you all enjoyed your lunch. Before we start our meditation sexssions, the monks from the Shaolin Temple of the Henan province of China will perform for us their famous marso arts." Now I was even more annoyed by this bony monk's thick accent.

He motioned to the fourteen gray-clad monks standing behind him by the altar. The monks smiled back, showing fourteen rows of teeth against darkly tanned faces.

Master Hidden Virtue pushed his glasses up and, bulging-eyed and bucktoothed, went on. "Shaolin kung fu has been handed dan drough seventy generations—over one dousand years—from the northern Wei dynasty to the present day. This heart and mind boxing, which mimics the actions of animals and men, is known to be as swift as lightning, as ferocious as a taiger, and as elusive as qinging clouds. All the Shaolin Shifus are renowned for their airlegant posture—sitting crossed-legged like a bell, standing steadfastly like a pine, woking speedily like the wind, sliping with bodies curved like a bow.

"Shaolin kung fu specializes in boxing, cudgeling, and internal exercises that embody a deep Zen philosophy. Combining soft and hard strategy, the monks defend like a virgin and attack like a tiger."

Amidst waves of applause, the Shaolin monks now strode to the center. I felt a little happier that they looked young, muscular, and full of confidence. One with an angular face and torchlike eyes walked in front and led the others to bow deeply to the audience, hands in the prayer gesture. Fleetingly, fourteen bald heads caught the reflection of the bulbs hanging from the ceiling. Another round of applause exploded in the hall.

When the cheers finally died down, the monks stepped aside. Then, out of nowhere, four young child monks dashed to the front. Pink-cheeked and robust, their eyes darted like dark marbles on a cloudless sky. From the side, their clean-shaven heads resembled big question marks. They giggled and bowed; the audience clapped halfheartedly.

But then, like flashes of lightning, they thrust their fists and jolted their legs in a series of graceful movements—kicking one leg to the side, squatting on one leg with arms punching, stretching hands like a dragon's claw, kicking while standing on their heads, back-somersaulting . . .

The audience was silent for a beat, then broke into thunderous applause.

The next performance was *qigong*. The head monk, all muscles and fierce eyes, firmly planted his feet apart on the ground and looked quite still, when in fact, Master Hidden Virtue told the audience, he was moving his *qi*—internal energy.

Michael said into my ear, "I like this, motion in stillness, or vice versa."

Still upset, I didn't respond. Now the head monk finally finished moving his *qi* and was ready for actual kung fu. Four younger, twentyish monks tested their broad knives by rubbing their blades back and forth on the head monk's abdomen. Then, before I knew what was going to happen, the novices let out a sharp "Ahhh!" and stabbed him in the stomach with full force.

I screamed; Michael pressed my shoulder against his. "Meng Ning, you all right?"

"I'm fine."

And so was the monk's abdomen. It was not even lightly injured. There was no gash, no blood, nothing.

"I don't like this, Meng Ning. Why don't we leave?"

"No, I want to see," I said stubbornly.

The next performance began with the head monk moving his energy while the novices brandished spears by his side. The audience sent waves of applause to the center of the hall as the blades swished in the air and light glinted off them in myriad directions. Then, barely had the master finished when one novice thrust forward with an upward tilt of his spear and pressed its needle-sharp point against the master's throat.

"Nooo!!!" the audience blurted out collectively, only to discover that the master remained unscathed. The hall was now completely packed, and the audience looked high, as if they were on drugs—or attaining enlightenment. I clapped until my palms turned red.

More seemingly impossible martial feats followed. One teenage monk performed One Finger Zen by "standing" on only one finger. Another, after he'd moved his energy, defied gravity by leaping up to the ceiling in one bound. Toward the end, a white-haired, leather-skinned monk appeared out of nowhere, and concluded the show by licking a burning-hot iron shovel while maintaining perfect composure—the most difficult and masochistic of all stunts.

I was flabbergasted by the feats, the agility of the human body, and the monks' perfect self-control achieved through *kulian*, bitter practice. But the little monks—how could they have acquired an adult's perseverance and discipline? I knew that not only do the monks carry out year-round training with no rest, they also have to abstain from sex. The Shaolin Temple allows wine-imbibing monks and even carnivorous monks, but not sex-indulging monks. They believe sex will disperse their energy, distract their spirit, and so destroy their kung fu. Just as the nuns in Golden Lotus Temple believe that human passion, illusory as it is, will destroy their concentration for higher deeds. Since I'd fallen in love with Michael and had sex with him, was I also losing my *qi,* my focus in life?

The performance ended with everybody clapping enthusiastically.

As Michael and I were heading with the crowd toward the meditation hall for *zazen,* sitting meditation, he asked, "Did you enjoy the show?"

I nodded. It was cathartic for my present state of mind.

"But I didn't. It's militaristic, not peaceful." He frowned. "I'm not impressed by Buddhist acrobats."

"I disagree." My voice rose, and I felt combative, like the monks. "That's what Hidden Virtue said during his introduction. Shaolin kung fu is more than fighting. It's art, philosophy, mysticism. Each routine has a symbolic meaning—a dragon leaving its cave, a golden cock spreading its wings, a warrior embracing the moon, a hungry tiger climbing up the mountain . . ." My tone was getting tenser and tenser. "So Michael, how can you just dismiss them as Buddhist acrobats?"

"Why do you sound unhappy?" Michael looked surprised. "You've been acting strange ever since I got home. Is something wrong?" He paused, then asked tentatively, "Are you still upset about my past with Lisa?"

"No, Michael, I'm fine." I tried to appear calm, but my cheeks felt hot.

Right then Master Hidden Virtue came up to us and proudly asked, "Dr. Fuller and Miss Du, how did you like our kung fu?"

Michael said, "We loved it. It's wonderful."

The Master said, "This way, please, Doctor Fuller and Miss Du, meditation is about to begin."

The meditation session was led by an octogenarian monk whose emaciated body and hollow-cheeked, coppery face made me think of a pile of dry sticks.

We sat down on meditation cushions amidst the other participants, and Michael, seemingly having forgotten our bickering earlier, leaned close to me. "Meng Ning, this is Master Silent Thunder. Don't let his decrepit look deceive you; he has the sharpest mind I've ever known."

I didn't care whether Silent Thunder's mind was sharp or blunt; I only knew that mine was now a killing field where all the monkeys were let loose—fighting against each other, slashing stomachs, spearing throats, burning tongues. My head ached, my legs cramped, my body fidgeted on the cushion as if it were a bed of nails. I could hardly breathe, let alone concentrate. I peeked at Michael, but he looked as stable as a rock. Then I peered at Silent Thunder. With legs locked in the full lotus position like the roots of a heavily gnarled ancient tree, he looked as light and detached as a cloud. A tide of envy rose inside me.

I was still fidgeting until I felt my elbow poked. Michael cast me a chiding glance, then he said in a heated whisper, "Meng Ning, you should stop that and concentrate on your breathing."

The session seemed to last forever. Finally when it ended, Silent Thunder started to "open a revelation"—lecture on Zen.

The old monk's eyes swept across the room like a peal of silent thunder. When they fell on me, I felt as if my body were being brushed by the cool blade of a sharp knife. I shuddered.

He spoke. "One time, the great Song dynasty poet Su Dongpo went to visit his monk friend Buddhist Seal. After they'd finished meditating, Su Dongpo asked his friend, 'What did I look like during meditation?'

"The monk said, 'A statue of Buddha.'

"Then the monk asked Su Dongpo, 'Then what do you think I looked like?'

"Deciding to tease his friend as well as to test his cultivation, Su Dongpo said, 'A piece of shit,' expecting the monk to be boiling with anger.

"'Ah, what a pity!' Buddhist Seal said, smiling gently. 'In Buddha's eyes everyone is pure and possesses Buddha's nature. But if one's eyes are smeared by shit then he can see nothing but shit.'"

Barely had Silent Thunder finished when the participants burst into laughter, breaking up the solemn atmosphere. The octogenarian's deeply tanned face remained as dry as a stick.

I was still chewing on Silent Thunder's "shitty" revelation when Michael and I stepped outside the Zen center and started walking toward the subway station. It was five in the afternoon and the street was crowded. Ahead of us, a young Chinese couple held hands and talked intimately between giggles. Michael and I held hands, but we neither talked nor laughed. Our minds seemed to be on opposite sides of the Pacific Ocean.

When we were waiting for the light to change, he said, sounding upset, "What is it, Meng Ning? I don't understand."

"Understand what?" My voice was as sharp as the monks' knives.

His eyes looked wounded. "I've tried to be nice, but you're acting like a stranger. You haven't shown any affection since I came back last night. I can't read your mind. Won't you tell me what this is all about?"

"It's because my mind is full of shit!"

The light turned green and we started to walk. When the crowd thinned, I pulled forward. Michael let go of my hand. He had to be really angry now. Afraid, I hurried back to him and took his hand. "Michael . . . I'm sorry."

He looked at me, his gaze intent but wary. "Please, tell me what's bothering you."

But I remained stubbornly uncommunicative, bottling up all my feelings.

24

Men Are Nothing but Trouble

Back home, Michael led me to sit down on the sofa. "Meng Ning"—he looked concerned—"what is it? Please tell me."

I surprised myself by uttering a bitterness I'd never known, nor experienced. "Maybe I should. But I don't know whether I can trust you, Michael, or your professor, or . . . your monks." I knew I was venting the anger caused by my encounters with Lisa and Philip on Michael. I knew I was being absurd. But I couldn't help it.

Michael looked startled. "Have I been doing something wrong? I thought you enjoyed the martial arts at the Zen center, so now why suddenly bitter? That's not like you."

"Maybe from now on it is," I snapped, then blurted out in spite of myself, "and I should have known it's dangerous to be too close to the heart of a man, for it spurts nothing but trouble."

But Michael didn't get angry; he looked worried instead. "Why are you suddenly angry with men? I've never heard you talk like that before. What's bothering you?"

"I think I should have entered the empty gate to be a nun. . . ."

"What are you talking about? Can you shake yourself out of this?"

"No," I said bitterly, blaming all my recent disillusionments and confusion and guilt on him. "Michael, I always wanted to be a nun. I never intended to love men, but to avoid them. Then you come along and toss my world upside down . . ."

He remained silent while staring at me, looking puzzled.

Though feeling powerless and knowing I was being unfair, I couldn't stop my bitter talk. "Michael, it was never my intention to fall in love with you. I've always thought I'd be a nun like Yi Kong, or maybe a single career woman, instead of ending up being a jobless and penniless thirty-year-old spinster."

Now Michael seemed really stung by my words. "Meng Ning, would you stop all this nonsense?!"

I hugged my knees and buried my face between them, ashamed of my attachment to Michael, my weakness, my meanness to him, my childish attack on men. And, of course, my near-betrayal of him with his ex-fiancée and his best friend.

But then when I looked up and met Michael's penetrating eyes, my irrationality was fueled anew. "Michael, you have your professor and your meditation and the rich and famous in the art world."

He swallowed hard, willing himself to calm down. "Why are you talking like this? You know I care about you. Besides, I don't know why you hold a grudge against Professor Fulton."

I retorted, "Because he acted cold to me. He hardly even glanced in my direction. He's a snob."

"Maybe he's a bit of a snob, but he helped me through my difficult years after my parents' deaths. It was he who introduced me to Buddhism and Chinese art, which is what brought us together.

"Whatever his faults, Professor Fulton has done a lot for me. Be honest, Meng Ning. Who wouldn't jump at the chance to go to a VIP reception at the Met and get a glimpse of a Kennedy and the mayor of New York?"

I held my tongue, realizing what Michael had said was true.

He went on. "I'm not a social climber, if that's what you think. But I do want to be a part of this art world. Because it gives meaning to my life. Not to mention the privilege of getting close to objects that outsiders wouldn't even dream of having the chance to see. Meng Ning, it wasn't easy for me to get myself accepted into this world." He cast me a meaningful glance. "Professor Fulton has just met you twice. I'm sure he'll like you; just give him a chance, OK?"

I nodded.

"Now tell me what you don't like about the monks."

Because Master Hidden Virtue was bulge-eyed and bucktoothed and his English was heavily accented. I wanted to say this aloud but knew how it would sound.

"Because they are boring." That was all I could mutter.

Michael dismissed my opinion with a laugh.

Before he could say anything, I blurted out, "Besides, that Zen center is an eyesore. And it's a bad influence on you—too much meditation."

"Meng Ning, meditation is the core of Buddhism. It is what really trains your mind. How can you dismiss it like this?"

"You know what? I think you overwork your intellect with those monks. That's why you're so guarded and serious." I was repeating what Lisa and Philip had told me.

Michael frowned. "What do you mean? I'm not withdrawn. Have I been neglecting you? Don't I show my affection for you?"

"It's not that, it's . . ." Suddenly I remembered the fortune-teller's saying:

Your friend also needs to build his yin *energy, which he let run down. Although he's orderly and well organized on the surface, his spirit underneath is restless. He needs more earth and water in his life to balance his fire and metal.*

"You're losing touch with your feminine side."

"My feminine side?" He looked completely puzzled.

"Michael, you're always in control." Seeing that he didn't respond, I ventured on. "Your life is arranged so perfectly that I don't see any place for me."

Michael seemed to be thinking deeply, then he said, his voice pained, "Why are you telling me these things? That's not like you."

He'd never sounded like this before and it made me worry. I knew I was being mean and unfair to him to cover my guilt. I'd never talked like this to anyone, but then I'd never even had a boyfriend. "Michael, I'm sorry. I don't mean to hurt your feelings."

"But you just did."

"I'm so sorry."

"Art has been my great solace in life. That is, until I met you. So how can you say that you don't see a place for you in my life? You realize how that hurts me?"

"Oh, Michael . . ."

"Please understand." Michael's voice turned gentle. "Besides Professor Fulton, I'm also very grateful for the monks in the Vegetable Root Zen Center. Their meditation teaching helped me through a lot of the stresses in my life."

"Like what?"

"Problems at work, when I broke up with Lisa, after she'd aborted our son, the car accident . . ." As if realizing something, he suddenly stopped in midsentence.

"What car accident?"

"I don't want to talk about it now."

"Now is the only time, Michael. What car accident?"

His face looked pained. "The one that caused Lisa's limp."

Before I had time to absorb the shock, Michael said, "I was driving."

"Oh heavens, what happened?"

"We were on the way to a gallery opening, quarrelling over her abortion. Then I missed a red light and the car crashed. Miraculously I was not even scratched, but poor Lisa . . ."

Jealousy swelled inside me like a dam about to burst. "Michael, do you still love her?"

"No! What kind of a question is this? I'm in love with you!" He paused to smooth back his hair. "Do you know how it feels to make someone—someone you care about—a cripple? You have no idea!" He paused, then said, "Anyway, I do feel I owe her because of the accident."

"Was that the reason you stayed with her for so long?"

"Yes, partly, and maybe to pacify Professor Fulton."

"Did he blame you for that?"

"Yes and no. But of course he was heartbroken."

"But the whole thing is not entirely your fault!"

"This is not a question of whose fault it was, Meng Ning. The result is that it cost Lisa her leg."

"Then what made you finally decide to leave?"

"Enough is enough. After that, she went back to Philip Noble."

"What?" I could hear my voice, sharp like a thrusting Zen knife.

"Philip and Lisa were high school sweethearts. The most handsome couple, they were chosen by the school's drama club to play Romeo and Juliet over and over. But she only went back to him for a short time. After that, she started sleeping with lots of people, both men and women, so I hear."

My ears felt on fire while I remained silent, completely shocked and drained by this unexpected and unwelcome revelation.

Michael changed the subject. "Meng Ning, I believe it's good karma that Lisa finally left. Otherwise I would never have met you. Now you know my past, and please, let's just leave it at that. Will you?"

I nodded, still too shocked to say anything.

Michael looked more relaxed now. "And you're not going to be a nun, Meng Ning. Sorry, but I just don't see a nun in you, except in your head. Time now to wake up from this nun dream. Besides, just as you think that the monks are not a very good influence on me, I'd tell you neither is Yi Kong an entirely good influence on you."

"Why?"

"All these prejudices against men."

"But she's guided me since I was thirteen."

"I'm just telling you things you've been choosing to ignore. Yi Kong may be a good nun, but her calling is completely different from yours. You could have become a nun years ago, but you didn't. Besides, being a nun won't get rid of men, if that's what you think."

"No, Michael, Yi Kong doesn't care about men!"

"You really believe that?"

"Of course!"

"Maybe she doesn't," Michael said matter-of-factly, "but I'm sure that won't stop her from wanting their money. If Yi Kong is as successful as you say, I'm sure she has to deal with men all the time, helping her with her projects or donating to her temple—"

"Michael, you don't know her, so don't criticize her!"

"You really believe she got all her donations to build a school, an orphanage, a nursing home, a museum, and to reconstruct the whole nunnery only from women?"

I was speechless.

Michael went on. "Instead of just letting you worship Guan Yin and recite the Heart Sutra, I think your mentor should have encouraged you to meditate more."

"She did. But I don't care about it."

"But that's the only way to free yourself from your prejudices. I don't say your devotional feelings are bad, Meng Ning. But, after all, Guan Yin is just a symbol."

A long pause. Then Michael's voice turned gentler. "Meng Ning, you don't know what Yi Kong really had gone through before she entered the empty gate. If she has no idea what it's like to be loved by a man, then how can she be so sure that that kind of love is illusory?

"We're all going to die someday, whether inside or outside the empty gate. We cannot avoid death, but no one should die filled with regret over denying one's heart. And don't judge all men by your experience with your father. Nobody has two Buddhas as parents."

Suddenly I felt mortified and eager for physical intimacy. Yet Michael, sitting easily beside me, didn't seem to have any idea what to do.

Finally he asked, "What do you want me to do, Meng Ning?"

I remained silent.

He reached toward me, pulling me to him, and kissed me. Then, as if suddenly thinking of something, he stood up, walked to his briefcase, took something out, and returned to hand me an embroidered Chinese pouch. "I bought this for you in Boston."

"What is it?" I asked, unzipping the pouch.

It was a jade bracelet.

I felt tears stinging my eyes and a pebble stuck in my throat so I couldn't talk.

Michael looked at me tenderly. "You like it?" His eyes were green, translucent, and flawless like my grandmother's jade bracelet.

I nodded.

"I'm sorry you lost your jade bracelet. I hope this can cheer you up a bit." He cupped my face; my heart pounded at his soft breaths.

"You break my heart when you look so sad," he said, then kissed me again.

He went on: "I know your father gambled away the bracelet you meant to inherit. I'd love you to have another one." Lovingly, Michael slipped the bracelet onto my hand. But it hung pathetically loose on my wrist.

"Can we size it?" he asked, now looking extremely dejected.

"I'm sorry, but I don't think so, Michael."

"I feel so bad. What . . . are we going to do with it?"

Silence, then I said, "Why don't we give it to my mother as a gift?"

Michael's face seemed shrunk, his voice sad. "If that's what you want—"

"Michael, I'm sorry . . ."

He looked completely crushed.

My heart, like a knocked-over shelf of condiments, spilled a hundred different feelings and flavors.

❧ 25 ❧

The Funeral

The next morning, the air between Michael and me was still tense. We ate our breakfast quietly, without much talking. After that, he planted a kiss on my forehead. "Meng Ning, I'll be coming home a little early tonight, around six." Then he left like a breeze.

Toward four in the afternoon, I suddenly realized I needed to go grocery shopping to replenish the almost empty fridge. By the time I arrived home, it was five. After I'd closed the door behind me I saw, to my surprise, Michael. He was sitting on the sofa and looking very pale. My heart started to pound. Something must have gone wrong; otherwise he wouldn't be home so early. Had he found out what happened between me and Philip, or me and Lisa?

I put down the groceries by the door, then hurried to sit next to him on the sofa, feigning calm. "Michael, you all right?"

"Some very bad news," he said, looking pained and on the verge of tears.

My heart flipped. "What is it?"

"Professor Fulton died this afternoon. I tried to call you, but there was no answer."

"Oh, my God . . . I'm sorry . . . so sorry. How . . . did it happen?"

A shadow fell across Michael's kind face. "Massive heart attack. They tried to resuscitate him but it didn't work."

My initial shock was now replaced by a flood of guilt. I had spoken ill of the man, Michael's substitute father! Why had I been so insensitive?

"The funeral will be held in three days," Michael said darkly.

"Michael"—I took his hand—"I'll be there with you."

"Thank you," he said, then nestled his head against my chest. I thought I could feel a sob, but could not see his face.

Later as we made love, I was aware of Michael's sadness. His fiery passion and hunger for affection, instead of pleasing me, made me think of him being with Lisa. I couldn't help but imagine how he had made it with her, or she with him. Had she led Michael on as she had me? Then a new jealousy hit me. Her shriveled leg—caused by the car accident when Michael was driving. Although it marred her beauty, paradoxically it also enhanced it. Perfection tires the eyes, but a little flaw can be an opening into something more exciting. Was Michael still enticed by that vulnerability, that perfect imperfection?

After lovemaking, Michael lay silently next to me. I suddenly realized that, instead of sharing his grief, I'd been absorbed in my own jealousy and confusion.

"Michael . . ." I heard the guilt in my voice as I reached to touch him. But he'd already fallen asleep.

On Thursday, Michael and I arrived early at the funeral home.

Inside its grand but gloomy and depressing lobby, Michael shook hands with the funeral director and chatted with him for a moment.

When we were alone, he said, "Do you mind coming with me while I see Professor Fulton this last time?"

I nodded. He took my hand and led me to kneel before the casket. I always felt uneasy looking at the dead. But Professor Fulton actually looked calm and dignified. His high forehead, together with the thatch of white hair, made me think of a snowcapped mountain where high monks and nuns would live a secluded life far from earthly foulness. I closed my eyes and whispered a short prayer to wish him happiness and entry into Amida Buddha's Western Paradise.

I continued to stare at the professor as I felt tears in my eyes—
for his death, for his life, for Michael, for my guilty conscience, for
some other submerged yearnings I had yet to name.

I turned and saw Michael's face damp with tears.

"Oh, Michael . . ." I reached to take his hand.

"Meng Ning, you're all I have now," he said without looking at
me. "Please . . . always be with me."

"I will," I whispered back, feeling his sadness and helplessness
in my grasp, and touched by both.

I thought of the dying kitten. Had it been a premonition of Fulton's death?

Then I turned to look at the encoffined professor and mused
that no matter how much rouge they had applied to his face to give
him the illusion of life, he was still but a corpse. A breathless, emotionless, souless object on display.

An installation art.

Now where was this man who, only a few days ago, had extended an invitation to Michael and me for dinner, not knowing
that he'd never be able to show up?

Feeling ridiculous and a bit unbearable, I said to Michael, "I'll
go look at Professor Fulton's pictures."

"All right, but don't be long. If you come back and I'm not here,
just look around. I'll be greeting people."

"I won't be long," I said, then stood up and walked to the desk
in a far corner, on top of which were several albums. I turned the
pages of one album and saw pictures of Professor Fulton—talking
to some important-looking people in a meeting, giving a lecture,
appreciating a Chinese scroll painting, standing in front of a huge
ceramic vase. I continued to turn pages and saw Fulton and Lisa
and Michael in various settings: a room tastefully decorated with
antiques and paintings and filled with books; in an open-air café; in
front of museums, statues, ruins . . . until my eyes fell on something
that made my heart knock hard against my chest. In a fancy restaurant, arms linked and eyes locked, Michael and Lisa were giving
each other champagne to sip from tall glasses while Professor Fulton looked on, smiling. Then the next one showed Michael and
Lisa kissing on a mountain top, the amber setting sun glowing be-

hind them. Yet another one was taken on a beach. Clad in swim-
suits, they were holding each other by the waist, their foreheads
touching, their eyes devouring each other's souls. Clad in a revealing bikini, Lisa's tanned, near-perfect body could be the object of
bitter envy of any woman and the determined goal of all men. In
this picture, her two long legs, symmetrical and healthy, would stir
the lust of all beings.

Had Lisa deliberately included the photos of her with Michael
so that I would see them? I set down the album—more loudly than
I had intended—and turned to walk away. But the place was now
very crowded and there was not a trace of Michael. My heart fluttered like a bird struggling to fly out of its cage. Dying for some
fresh air, I hurriedly moved toward the exit. Then, when nearing
the gate, my feet halted. Michael was chatting with an important-
looking couple. And next to them stood Lisa, tall and imposing like
a bronze statue. Engaged in a very deep conversation, the four
seemed to have known one another for a long time. The sixtyish
Asian woman in a finely tailored black suit gestured nervously and
looked almost anorexic. I recognized them—the trustee of the Met
and his wife—from La Côte Basque, where I had been upset because Michael hadn't introduced me to them.

Michael turned and spotted me. Lisa also spotted me and our
eyes met; she cast me a knowing smile as if we'd been sharing the
profoundest secrets under heaven. I imagined her saying, "You
liked what we did the other day, didn't you? Admit it." And now
she smiled as if suggesting we were allies performing tricks behind Michael's back.

My heart clutched and I disliked her bitterly at this moment. I
pretended not to see them and quickly walked behind a crowd.

Then I heard a familiar voice emanating from this small gathering of tall, expensively dressed men. I looked up and saw a familiar
face—Philip Noble.

Oh heavens, my heart started to beat hard and loud like a battle
drum. Would he see me? When I tried to move away stealthily I
bumped right into the man next to Philip.

The man turned and looked; I had no choice but to mutter a
soft "Sorry," and hurry away.

From the corner of my eye, I think I saw Philip turn and look. But then he turned right back to talk. Did he see me? Or did he feign not seeing me?

Just then the funeral director asked the crowd to move into the next room and be seated.

The ceremony was very well organized, with many speeches by celebrities in the art world, collectors, deans and professors from the most prestigious universities, directors from Sotheby's and Christie's, the president of the Met . . .

After that, it was Lisa's turn. Even though I sat in the third row, I still craned my neck to follow her as she approached the podium. Several men's eyes widened as they watched her black silhouette, like a gilded *devi,* glide by in the eerie funeral light. She had not relinquished jewelry, but pared it to a mere bracelet—the ruby-eyed panther biting its tail. Silence fell in the hall as people, mesmerized, intently watched her limp her way onto the podium. Then, breaking their voyeuristic trance, a cry arose. Lisa had stumbled. Michael and one dignitary onstage dashed to her rescue. They helped her up, steadied her, and held her by the waist and shoulders. As a pang of jealousy seized my heart, Lisa regained her balance. She thanked the two men with a nod, then limped—now very noticeably—to the microphone.

"Don't worry"—she smiled a little shyly—"this may be my way to be enlightened."

Nervous laughter exploded in the audience. It seemed that people liked the daughter as much as they had liked the father. Clearly the fall had brought out an affecting vulnerability that set off her fierce beauty and strong physique. Moreover, Lisa's speech turned out to be vivid and touching. Instead of praising Michael Fulton directly, like the others had, she told us anecdotes about him that made him seem very human and appealing.

When Lisa finished, tears glistened in her eyes. I looked around. In the front row, the curators and professors and the art dealers looked at her appreciatively. The middle-aged woman behind me wiped her tears and sighed. Then, to my unease, Philip Noble's alluring face entered my vision. Head lowered and expression tender, he was listening intensely to an elegant woman of indeterminate age. Then he looked up and smiled a little. Did he see me? Heart beating quickly, I quickly turned back to the stage and saw Michael's warm, sad eyes keenly searching for mine.

Michael's speech, though a little less eloquent than Lisa's, was equally moving. He recounted how Fulton had "adopted" him as a son and generously shared with him his knowledge of Buddhism and art. And how, without the professor's teaching and sharing, he, as an American, would have never aspired to the refinements of a Chinese scholar-gentleman: lighting incense, sipping fragrant tea, appreciating delicate scroll paintings, reciting Zen poems. Toward the end, he said, "I believe the karma of knowing Professor Fulton will continue for the rest of my life. I am forever indebted to his kindness."

I also felt stirred. Not only by all the powerful speeches and the rich and powerful, but also by the whole drama of life and death condensed in this cool, polished parlor. Michael and Lisa looked so sad and beautiful onstage, the important guests so dignified. And Professor Fulton, alive in their words, and yet so dead in his coffin. Even Michael, sitting onstage among them, seemed altered to me. I wondered: would he someday become one of these dignified, arrogant, silver-haired gentlemen?

Pondering all these matters, I was surprised when the audience started stirring and realized that the formal part of the ceremony was over. People were standing up, some making their way toward the lobby, others grouped together and talking in restrained tones.

Michael came to me right away and asked how I'd thought it went.

"You spoke very well." I studied his face. "Professor Fulton must be very proud of you."

"Yes, he was." He looked at me fully. "Meng Ning, please come with me while I talk to people."

"No, Michael," I said, suddenly feeling defensive, "it's awkward for me. I don't know any of these people here." I wanted to add *I just don't belong to this circle of the rich and famous,* but stopped myself.

Michael's eyes were pleading and his voice a little tired. "But please, Meng Ning."

"No, Michael."

"Meng Ning—"

"Why don't you go talk now while I use the restroom. I'll join you later."

"All right."

Inside the ladies' room, I stared at my reflection in the mirror, my heart no more at peace than before. While images of the stylish Lisa, Philip, and the elegant guests flashed across my mind, suddenly a voice broke into my thoughts, startling me. "I'm worried about you, Meng Ning. You look pale. Are you all right?"

It was Lisa towering over me in the mirror.

I did not know how to reply. I simply stared.

"You're not going to talk to me—even at my father's funeral?" She was smoothing her bronze hair with a small hawksbill-turtle comb.

"I'm fine," I said at last, darkly.

"But you're not, Meng Ning. Don't fool yourself."

My throat felt choked and I couldn't utter a word.

"Can I do something?" She stared at me with concern.

Haven't you done enough?

"No thanks, I don't think so." Although I still found it hard to be angry at those eyes, I managed to say, "Please leave me alone."

"All right then, take care," she said, dropping the comb inside her pocketbook and snapping it shut like a small explosion. "Thanks for coming to my father's funeral." Then, "Have you seen Philip and his very rich lady friend?"

Witch, I mouthed. Then I watched until the door closed behind her before I went inside a stall at the far end to quiet my clamoring mind. All these complicated relationships in the dusty world— were they worth it? Maybe I should have listened to Yi Kong all along.

My mentor's words rang loud in my ears:

There is no real life other than that inside the temple gate.
Life in the dusty world would only get people more tangled
up, causing endless suffering. But life inside the empty gate
would free you from karma.

And finally:

When are you coming to play with us? There's lots of fun going on here.

I made up my mind—to go back home to Hong Kong.

Once outside the ladies' room, I spotted Michael. He hurried up to drape his arm around me. "I'm tired. Let's go home now."

The day after Professor Fulton's funeral, I told Michael I had decided to go back to Hong Kong.

To my surprise, he agreed. "I know it's hard for you in a new environment, and you must have missed your mother, Yi Kong, and Golden Lotus Temple. So maybe it's good for you to go back for a while."

"Thanks for your understanding, Michael," I said, feeling truly grateful as well as disappointed.

"Meng Ning, while you're in Hong Kong"—he looked at me, eyes full of tenderness—"also think about our wedding. If you don't have another suggestion, I'd like us to be married in Hong Kong. So I think maybe you can start asking around about where we can have our wedding."

That was not what I'd expected to hear. Marriage? My purpose in going back to Hong Kong was exactly the opposite—to give myself some time and space to think over carefully whether I really wanted to be married.

Michael spoke again, twiddling my engagement ring as if to remind me of our pledge. "I'll miss you terribly while you're in Hong Kong. So please come back soon."

PART THREE

PART THREE

Form Is Emptiness

Yi Kong's smooth, beautiful face hangs over mine. Naked under the fiery redness of the setting sun, her head's gentle curve appears unmistakably sensuous. Its luminous gold reminds me of the halos on the heads of Christian saints. But this is a halo around the finely shaved head of a Buddhist nun.

I knew this handsome image before me was as illusory as it was powerful. For I was but daydreaming in Yi Kong's office in the Golden Lotus Temple. Although I'd visited her in the hospital, this would be the first time I'd seen her in this new place since the fire in the Fragrant Spirit Temple. Though it felt like coming home, my heart was so much changed that the temple seemed like my home in another life. In the past, coming to visit her nunnery had always been soothing; now it was unsettling.

A nun had told me earlier that Yi Kong was in a meeting and wouldn't be back until after five-thirty. It was now only five, so I slipped out of her room to take a look at her new office compound. As I passed along corridors and peered in through partially open doors, I noticed that in the five years I'd been away in Paris, the Golden Lotus Temple had been expanded and transformed from an old, shabby eyesore into a grand complex with a Tang dynasty–style temple building as well as this modernized one. I had mixed feelings about the change. Of course I liked the comfort of air conditioning, elevators, clean restrooms. But the omnipresent computer terminals and the stark reception room with polished reproductions of antique Chinese furniture seemed unsuitable for a monastery. Besides, I also missed paper lanterns, peeling paint, rain-furrowed windows, long-burning candles, sun-bleached gateposts, and crumbling walls covered with intricately patterned ivy. From my early visits these had always been an entryway to a world of quiet imaginings and aesthetic associations.

After fifteen minutes, I went back to Yi Kong's office, but she was still nowhere to be seen. So I strolled around the spacious room to look at her art collection, which had also grown bigger and better. The contemporary ceramic Guan Yin statue was replaced by a Ming dynasty one, exquisitely molded. On the altar, a gilded antique Buddha statue took the place of a wooden one. Other new acquisitions included two antique bronze incense burners, one in the shape of a lotus and the other a *qin*—seven-stringed zither. There were also antique altar cabinets, Pure Land paintings, Song dynasty vases, Ming dynasty furniture. The lively grain of the *huanghua li,* flowering pear hardwood, glowed reddish brown in the warm twilight. I ran my fingers over its smooth surface.

How hard had Yi Kong worked to achieve all this in five years? Wondering, I was soothed by the beauty of the art and the wisps of sweet incense mingling with the fresh scent of flowers.

This world had felt like home to me for so long. I let out a long sigh.

Then I saw the looming presence of a huge photograph of a statue of a seated Guan Yin. It faced a large window overlooking the train station and towering high-rises of Yuen Long. The photo, which I recognized as Yi Kong's work, took up nearly the entire wall except for the space underneath where a *zitan*—red sandalwood—altar was placed. On this sumptuous shrine, abundant offerings of fruit were tastefully arranged in subtly contrasting yet complementary colors: bananas, papayas, mangos, oranges, pineapples, green apples, green grapes, melons—all set on high-legged silver plates. Ginger flowers, lilacs, lilies, irises, azaleas, and other flowers competed quietly in white vases.

Resting in the "royal ease" pose, the Goddess of Mercy's right arm extended in a graceful curve with the delicate point of her elbow poised on her raised right knee; her left leg dangled. Patches of pink revealed themselves beneath her gilded crimson robe. I could almost see the multilayered drapery rise and fall, as if she were breathing with life and feeling, excited to be seen.

When Yi Kong saw me, would she ask me again the same question—*Meng Ning, when are you coming to play with us?*

For ten years she'd been expecting me to become a nun in her temple. How should I respond this time?

I didn't want to lose Yi Kong's friendship, nor Michael's love. I wanted both the fish and the bear's paw. But how would I have the luck, or the wisdom, to keep both?

Feeling a slight headache coming, I stepped closer to the enormous picture, made a deep bow to the Observer of Worldly Sound—the name given to Guan Yin because she always listens for cries of help—then put my palms together and whispered a prayer.

Another half hour had passed. With a lacquer tray in hand, a very young nun timidly peeped through the half-closed door. I beckoned her to enter. She smiled carefully, so as not to reveal her teeth. Soundlessly, she set the tray on the table and placed the objects one by one onto its shiny surface: two lidded teacups, a teapot with steam escaping from the lid, a small, pale blue ceramic plate filled with an assortment of nuts and a larger one with fresh fruits.

I watched this young novice with pleasure.

While every personal relationship now seemed impermanent and fragile to me, youth suggested a contrasting picture of life as simple and everlasting.

She possessed a native grace; things bloomed in natural order and charm under her slender, pale fingers. I was quite sure she was also conscious of her poise and took pride in doing things in adagio, so that she, as well as her guest, could watch her delicate fingers' choreography.

Why hurry? There is no time limit in a temple, just living in the bare moment, the here and now.

The table now displayed a lush spread of food. Concluding her delicate ritual, the young nun took a white handkerchief from her loose gray robe and dabbed her well-shaped bald head.

She addressed me respectfully. "Yi Kong Shifu said she would be with you in a minute and apologized for the long wait."

I smiled. "Oh! Not at all. Tell Shifu to take her time."

Still standing, she smoothed her long robe with elongated fingers. "Shifu is in a meeting to discuss the art work of the temple."

"Ah, that's a huge project."

"Yes, she's also organizing her painting and photography exhibition, a Buddhist art festival, a Zen play, and a retreat."

I widened my eyes to show amazement.

The young nun gushed with pride. "But don't worry, Shifu is always full of energy." She bowed to me before she left. "Please have some tea and fruit."

"Thank you. What's your name?" Seeing that she was so young, the word *Shifu,* teacher, just refused to come out of my mouth.

"Wu Kong." Enlightened to Emptiness.

"Just like the Monkey King in *Journey to the West?*"

"I'm afraid so."

We both laughed. Like her mistress, she had perfect, white teeth.

I made a slight bow to her. "Thank you very much, Wu Kong Shifu." I hoped she was too innocent to notice that this time the word finally slipped out from my mouth with a bantering tone.

Still smiling, Enlightened to Emptiness closed the door with a crisp click and disappeared.

How wonderful to be so young, even as a nun.

Then I saw Yi Kong saunter toward the office building, face flushed, gray robe swaying in the summer breeze and shaved head gleaming under the sun. My heart kept knocking hard. Was my true karma to be a nun in her temple? Or was I just confused about the world?

You could have become a nun years ago, but you didn't. Michael's words rang loud in my ears.

Yi Kong looked tired yet cheerful. Unexpectedly, her presence filled my body with the happiness of the Dharma, as it had so many times before in my long years of visits to her temple. But the last five years had affected her perhaps as much as they had me. I was sad to notice that her skin looked weathered and her gait was slower. I hated to recognize that my mentor was, like us all, yielding to the passage of time.

Yi Kong, Depending on Emptiness.

A woman.

A nun.

A celebrity nun.

A celebrity nun running the biggest Buddhist temple in the last British colony.

Had she been content living behind the heavy temple gate for twenty-nine years? But wasn't her beaming countenance the proof of a positive answer? Besides, if everything in this world is but an illusion, what is real happiness after all?

She entered the room, saw me, and smiled. "Meng Ning, sorry to keep you waiting."

"Yi Kong Shifu, don't worry. I've been enjoying your exquisite art objects."

"The temple's art objects," Yi Kong corrected me as she seated herself behind the enormous black wood desk adorned with curios. Gingerly, I sat facing her—and the Guan Yin posed in royal ease.

"I'm glad you like them. I'll show you more later. Now let's have tea." She picked up the teapot with three of her tapered fingers and poured us both full cups. "How's everything?" she asked, then set the teapot down with a delicate sound.

"Fine, thank you." The scalding tea tasted slightly bitter, yet pure. I lifted the cup to my nose and inhaled the stimulating fragrance. Floating in the apple green water, the emerald leaves joined and parted to form intricate patterns. Was there a sign of my fate hiding among these pretty shapes? Was it the right choice to forsake the empty gate and plunge into the Ten Thousand Miles of Red Dust? A married life over enlightenment? I closed my eyes to absorb the sensations of the steam moistening my face and warming my heart.

"Very good tea," I said.

"The best," Yi Kong corrected me again.

"What kind?"

"*Yunwu,* from the Lu Mountain of Jiangxi province."

Yunwu, cloud and mist. Didn't she have any idea that *yunwu* is a subtle variation of another word, *yunyu,* cloud and rain, meaning lovemaking?

Suddenly, I could feel the weight of Michael's perspiring body, followed by a vision of Lisa's heavy bosom and her atrophied leg, then Philip's helplessly handsome face and pained expression. . . . I shuddered.

"Meng Ning, are you all right?" My mentor cast me a look of concern mixed with suspicion.

"I'm fine," I said, feeling the heat on my cheeks. Quickly I changed the subject. "How are you?"

Now I looked at her composed face, feeling both guilty and sad. Why didn't she act more affectionately toward me—as she had when she lay on the stretcher after the fire?

"I'm fine as long as the Fragrant Spirit Temple is fine. I'm relieved that nobody got hurt in the fire." Yi Kong sighed. "*Hai!* But the five thousand three hundred twenty volumes of the Tripitaka . . . anyway, thanks for your help." Then she changed the subject. "How was Paris?"

"Good." I condensed my answer to one word for I knew she was not really interested in anybody's business in Paris.

"What's your plan now?"

"Nothing special yet." I really didn't know how to respond.

"Good." She paused, then went on. "Since you've gotten your Ph.D. and we are going to add a lot of artwork to our temple after its reconstruction, you can help us as our consultant. Think about it."

"Thank you. I definitely will." Married or not, I needed something to get my career started. Still, I felt disheartened. Why had she given the post of assistant to Dai Nam? Why hadn't she waited for me? Had she already known that I wouldn't need it anymore?

Yi Kong studied me intently. "You look good."

Her eyes rested on my cup. I followed her glance to the discovery of a lipstick mark, moist and tender as in the memory of a sensuous kiss. My cheeks felt hot as I remembered how Michael's lips had pressed on mine, sending ripples all over my body. Yi Kong had never seen me with makeup before. How could I have forgotten to not put it on today?

"Thank you. You, too. Are you still as busy as ever?" Anxiously, I tried to distract her; she liked to talk about the temple and her projects.

Her face glowed. "Yes, but as you know, work in the temple never ends. People always tell me to relax and do things slowly, but how can I? So many Buddhist treasures either vanish or are damaged in China every day.

"That picture of the monks chanting in a temple in Tibet that I photographed six years ago—do you remember? When I went back last year, the temple was all gone, mysteriously burnt, not a trace left behind.

"As I planned to leave for Shanxi to record the chanting of a ninety-year-old monk—the last one who knew a particular style—I learned that he had just died from choking while taking some Chinese herbal soup for longevity. The news arrived two days before I was to leave. So how can I slow down when I see these precious traditions disappearing before my eyes? On the contrary, I have to work faster."

Yi Kong stopped. "Oh, I've been all immersed in my own talk. Are you hungry? I'll ask the chef to cook something for you. Today we have very fresh tofu, bamboo shoots, and mushrooms."

"Thank you very much, but I had lunch before I came."

She squinted at me. "Do you still eat meat?"

"I'm a part-time vegetarian now," I said, avoiding her gaze.

"Ah, part-time!" Yi Kong exclaimed.

I blurted out, "Shifu, although my mouth is not completely vegetarian, my heart is."

Yi Kong smiled, then spoke jokingly. "Ah, that I don't know, but I'm sure you have a tongue rolled not in vegetable oil, but in pig fat."

I felt my ears on fire.

Sensing my embarrassment, she picked up from her desk a round clay incense burner and changed the subject. "Let me show you my little treasures here. This one is a rare Ming piece from an antique store in Kyoto. See how the lid has several small holes? When you burn incense inside, the smoke coming out through them smells exceptionally good, since it is the essence extracted from all the fragrance inside.

"Besides, the meandering smoke is such a pleasure to look at, like cursive calligraphy forming in the air. If you meditate on its ever changing lines, you'll gain more insight into the transience and impermanence of life."

Yes, like Professor Fulton's death, and even the kitten's. Was the professor now contentedly stroking the kitten in Amida Buddha's Western Paradise?

Yi Kong went on. "You'll also feel calm just by looking at the graceful shape of the burner."

She handed me the container. "Feel the smooth and subtle cracks on the surface; it's very soothing."

True. It felt like her creamy skin, which I'd once touched after the fire. I felt embarrassed, but my hands refused to leave its comfortable form.

Next Yi Kong showed me a small ceramic teapot made to resemble a Buddha's Hand citron, the shape and deep purple color of which reminded me of eggplant, a favorite dish in the monastery. Two rows of calligraphy on its round belly read:

FLOWERS CAN LISTEN AND UNDERSTAND,
AND STONES CAN BE AMIABLE.

"Very nice—a stone can be likable. I love the idea," I murmured while peeking at my engagement ring. I'd meant to leave it at home before I left for the nunnery, but had completely forgotten to do so.

"Stones are indeed charming," Yi Kong said. "But not just the idea. I would also like to collect stones, you know, like those in a scholar's study. Besides being appreciated as objects of art, do you know that stones can also be served as food?"

"Oh, really? No, how?" I was still peeking at my stone.

"Ah, a modern girl who rarely enters the kitchen." Yi Kong eyed me disapprovingly. "It's quite sad, though, since the stone dish is only for the poor. In the past, poor people could rarely afford to eat

meat, so sometimes when they wanted it so much or when they had
a guest, they'd cook stones. There were different ways to prepare
the dish: stir-fry with black bean sauce, quick fry with Chinese scallion, or fry and then stew with wine. Of course, you couldn't eat the
stone. The idea was to pretend, so you'd flip your chopsticks into
the dish and pick up the scallion, or the black bean, or mix the
sauce with your rice. The whole thing aimed to boost your appetite,
so you'd end up finishing the big bowl of rice in a happy mood."

Amazed at her account, I thought for a while before I asked,
"It's sad and not very Buddhist, is it? Pretend instead of facing the
truth."

"But that's their truth, to be happy and eat one more bowl of
rice. Besides, people in poverty usually don't think much about the
truth one way or the other."

"It's sad then, the truth."

"If it's the truth, it's just a truth, nothing sad nor happy about it,
just the plain truth." Caressing the teapot, Yi Kong remained silent
for a while.

Was this meant for me?

"When we choose to accept or reject, we do not see the true nature of things."

This did seem meant for me. The great Zen teachers always
knew what their disciples needed to hear. I'd once thought I saw
the true nature of things; now I did not know what to accept or reject.

Yi Kong looked up at me for a fleeting moment and spoke again,
this time staring at my hand. "Our temple welcomes any form of
donation, including nice stones."

Involuntarily I moved my right hand to cover my ring.

"Well . . ." Not knowing how to respond otherwise, I laughed,
though harder than I would have liked.

Yi Kong went on calmly: "All right, enough of stones and truth.
Now let's look at musical instruments."

She turned to a wooden fish and a bronze bowl resting on two
cushions identically embroidered with red, gold, and blue lotuses.
Then, picking up a wooden mallet, she gently struck the bowl's
belly with its cloth-padded head. It vibrated softly yet sonorously,

reverberating in the cabinet, expanding into the room, then lingering for a while before departing into silence.

Pleased by my bemusement, Yi Kong eagerly showed me her other collections. She pulled open a drawer in her desk from which she took out a small wooden box. "Smell . . . this is a very precious kind of eaglewood incense, which you can only get in China, not in Hong Kong."

Yi Kong lowered her head to scoop the incense. I could clearly see the twelve scars on her scalp's bald surface.

So round and so bare.

A guarantee that no hair can grow again in these spots.

A proof of faith through the willingness to be marred.

A symbol of a path of no return.

What is it like—this path of no return? How much did it hurt when the burning incense scorched this flesh? What had she been thinking when her master did this to her? Did she hesitate even a tiny, tiny bit, upon leaving this mundane world? Now, when she scorched her disciples' scalps, what would she think about? I wanted to know all but didn't have the courage to ask. After all these years, Yi Kong still remained an enigma to me.

I felt a pull inside; I still wanted to learn all the mysteries along this esoteric route.

Now Yi Kong carefully put the incense into a small silk bag and handed it to me. "Take this and offer it to Buddha every day." Then changing into a joking tone, she asked, "By the way, are you still very busy with your writing and research? When are you coming to play with us? There's always lots of fun going on here."

As I would never learn the mysteries along the forbidden path of a nun, Yi Kong, similarly, would never taste the pleasure of a man's warming hand on her breast, his tender eyes eagerly finding their resting place in hers.

I hoped she didn't see the hot pink crawling up my cheeks. I'd thought she'd guessed already. How could I face disappointing her, telling her that instead of forsaking the world and striving for Buddhahood, I had fallen in love with a man, flirted dangerously with another one, and even . . . had sex with a woman? I hesitated, inhaled the piquant incense, and said, also in a half-joking way to cover up my guilt and embarrassment, "I know there's lots of fun going on here, but I . . . I . . ." I paused, then involuntarily blurted out, "Someone . . . is waiting for me." Was I so sure of marrying Michael?

At that moment, I felt like a school girl waiting for the principal to find out I had misbehaved.

Yi Kong picked up and fondled the incense burner in her hands, head lowered, not speaking. The only audible sound was the restive pounding of my heart against my ribs like the rattling of bars shaken by a prisoner.

I watched her intently, for the first time with guilt instead of pleasure.

Minutes passed. Yi Kong still caressed the burner with her elegant fingers, appreciating it from different angles. She grasped the burner firmly, as if fearing it would slip from her hand. Although I couldn't see her expression, I knew well she would prevent things from breaking rather than have to pick up pieces later.

Finally she looked up, with a smile struggling on her face. "Too bad! I've always thought you have the most nicely shaped head, and what a shame to hide it under your three-thousand-threads-of-trouble."

She paused, then asked, "Is he the American doctor I saw in the Fragrant Spirit Temple during the fire?"

"Hmm . . . I think so." As at other times in the past, her acute power of observation impressed me. Back then, did it already show that I was in love?

She started to straighten things up on her desk and said, without looking at me, "Don't forget to tell him we are impoverished here because he takes you away from us."

She turned around to pull a thin book from the shelf and handed it to me. "A gift from our temple."

Two characters on the cover shimmered with embossed gold: *Heart Sutra*.

I opened the slender volume and my eyes alighted on:

Guan Yin, the Bodhisattva of Observing Ease, undertook a spiritual practice called *prajna paramita*. Realizing, from the practice, that the five elements are nothing but emptiness, she enabled all beings to transcend suffering. Form is not different from emptiness nor emptiness from form. Form is emptiness and emptiness is form. . . .

After I thanked her and took leave, Yi Kong said, "It's getting late, Meng Ning. So I think you'd better take the shortcut through the bushes behind the Hall of Guan Yin."

"Thank you, Yi Kong Shifu." I bowed to her and gently closed the door behind me.

✄ 27 ✄

The Golden Body

After I'd left Yi Kong's office, I didn't go home directly, but headed into the stone garden. As I walked along the bamboo grove leading toward the entrance, I kept thinking about the phrase, "the five elements are nothing but emptiness." Although I'd read the Heart Sutra more times than I could remember, I still couldn't completely grasp the meaning of its first paragraph. If all the five elements—form, feelings, perceptions, tendencies, and consciousness are emptiness, then Yi Kong's compassion and achievements must also be empty, and so was the beauty of art, and the love between Michael and me. But then why, each time I thought of Michael—especially after my betrayals of him—did the tender aching of my heart feel so deep?

Although I didn't want to believe that all the five elements are nothing but emptiness, I felt happy to find the garden empty. Under the bluish white brilliance of the moon, the bodhi trees and bamboo groves were clearly visible. In the pond the stone bridge cast a dark shadow; the stone lanterns and rocks blended into one mysterious blur of cobalt blue. The frogs' croaking, the crickets' chirping, and the occasional flop of a fish's tail wove a contrapuntal heartbeat in the evening's sensuous silence.

I went to sit down on my favorite carp-viewing bench. The

fishes' scales, in the shadowy world of water and lacy weeds, glinted in the silvery moonlight; they made me think of the endless birth and cessation of the wheel of karma.

After a while, I stood up from the bench and followed the frogs' croakings to the separate lotus pond. The large, wavy-frilled lotus leaves trembling in the air reminded me of flamenco dancers' whirling dresses. I counted the dewdrops gleaming in the moonlight on the lotus pads until I felt my own tears. Were there other mysterious universes embedded in these glimmering beads? Could I just walk in and leave my confusion behind? Then one fat, wide-eyed frog, who I'd thought to be a stone ornament, suddenly rolled his eyes at me and croaked loudly, as if he were a sage who'd been waiting for ages for a fool like me to air his wisdom to. I reached out my hand to touch him, but he'd already jumped into the water with a splash— dismissing my sentimentality.

I looked up at the sky and came face-to-face with the moon. Through my eyes, the succulent disc resembled a teardrop smeared on rice paper. I imagined that it was about to drip, and stretched out my palms to receive the silvery sprinkle. I thought of Michael and wondered what he was doing now in New York, whether he was also looking at the lonely moon and thinking of me.

I held up my hand. The moon beams alighted on the solitary diamond, splintering it into a thousand shards of light. If I married Michael, would it be a mistake, as it had been when Mother decided to elope with Father? She always boasted how Father had brought a gun with him to propose. How finally it was not the gun that exploded, but Father's passion.

The truth was, my father's gun did explode—not on the night he'd proposed, but twenty years later—on my twentieth birthday when he gambled away Mother's jade bangle.

After Father had failed to stop Mother's suicide threat, he took out his gun and pointed it at his chest, as he'd done so many years ago. "Mei Lin, stop this, or I'll blow my heart out!"

Mother dashed toward him and tried to snatch away the weapon. During their struggle, it went off. The bullet didn't blow Father's heart out, but made a small hole in the wall. Mother and I felt so relieved he hadn't hurt himself that we had no idea that the end of this nightmare signaled the beginning of another. After this, Father was rushed to the hospital with a heart attack and before he recovered, died of another.

To save face, Mother didn't tell any friends or relatives of Father's attempted suicide, nor even his death. "I don't want to be treated as a widow and you a half orphan," she said.

Therefore, since my father's death, Mother and I avoided friends and relatives, until we completely stopped seeing any. The only exception was, of course, my continued friendship with Yi Kong. Besides teaching me meditation and Zen painting, she would soothe my sadness and listen to my troubles with compassionate smiles, discreet lips, and generous hands, attracting me more and more by her charitable deeds and her rich, mysterious life behind the empty gate. Therefore, whenever I heard people say that temples are only for escapists and losers, I'd chuckle. Ha, nothing could be further from the truth!

Now the moon was beginning to set; I stood up and walked out of the garden. Still unwilling to go home, I wandered listlessly in the huge, silent temple complex. Then I looked for the shortcut that Yi Kong had told me about.

I strolled down a long, winding path that, I began to suspect, led nowhere. Curious, I kept walking until I bumped into a weather-beaten door in a small structure hidden by heavily gnarled and foliaged ancient trees. Why had I never found this place before? Hesitantly, I pushed the door and to my surprise, it swung open into a small hall lit by one tiny bulb near the floor. In the air floated the scent of flowers and the residue of incense. The room looked empty except for an imposing glass shrine in the center, inside of which sat a life-size, gilded Buddha. Offerings of fresh flowers and fruits surrounded the shrine.

I stepped up to scrutinize. The statue's gilded face gleamed faintly in the nearly dark room. The legs were locked in the full lotus position. Beautiful image. But it was not a Buddha or Bodhisattva that I could recognize. A plaque attached to the bottom of the glass shrine caught the light of the small bulb.

Open the Shrine and Realize the Master's
Whole Body Does Not Decompose
Enlightenment to Nonattachment of Body and Mind
Eternal Transmission of Truth

As I was racking my mind to figure out what this all meant, I discovered another row of small characters:

I pay respect to her Golden Body,
revealing Mystery Shifu,
the Teacher of My Teacher,
the Venerable Wisdom Forest.

Disciple in the Dharma,
Yi Kong

I let out a gasp and took a step back. Suddenly the gilded face lit up for a few seconds. From the corner of my eye I saw a candle in the doorway before a sudden breeze blew it out.

Then the door creaked like sharp nails grating on metal. I felt my blood curdle inside and sweat break out on my forehead. As I desperately looked for a place to hide, a sonorous voice echoed in the hall: "Is that you, Meng Ning?"

Goose bumps shot down my arms and splashed over my body. My heart thudded violently and my armpits felt wet. I turned to find, like a hairless ghost, Yi Kong's face flickering ominously over candlelight. It took me seconds to regain my senses. Then I stared intently at the figure in front of me to make sure she was not an apparition.

I finally got hold of myself and muttered, "Yes, Yi Kong Shifu."

A long pause.

"How did you get in here?" She had relit the candle in her hand; the flame, raging and flashing under her, threw her face out of proportion.

"You told me about the shortcut."

"Except for a few Shifus who work closely with me, no one else knows about this place." Yi Kong eyed me reflectively. "It must be your good karma to be here. . . ."

Yi Kong led me in lighting incense and making three deep bows to the statue. Her voice, deep and respectful, began to resonate in the hall like an ancient chant. "This is the Golden Body of Revealing Mystery Shifu, the teacher of my teacher, the Venerable Wisdom Forest. . . ."

Instinctively I took a step back, then turned to look at her. "Yi Kong Shifu, what do you mean by the Golden Body . . . how is it possible that—"

"Be patient, Meng Ning. Listen carefully to what I'm going to tell you."

Her voice filled the empty hall with voluptuous reverberation. "This phenomenon is called flesh-bodied Bodhisattva. That is, when a monk or a nun has achieved profound meditation practice, after they die, their bodies will not decompose—"

Feeling a chill, I again cut in: "Yi Kong Shifu, do you mean that this is actually the nun's . . . mummy?"

Yi Kong shot me a chiding look and ignored my question. "Only one in a million will attain the state of a golden body, and this phenomenon will happen only once every few hundred years."

She made another deep bow to the shrine; I immediately did the same. "Revealing Mystery Shifu passed away on March eighteenth, nineteen fifty-eight, at age eighty-eight. In February, she'd recognized that her worldly life was about to end, so every day she drank ten bowls of a medicinal soup. This was made from one hundred different kinds of herbs, with the result that she perspired and urinated profusely. A month later, although she'd lost a lot of weight, her face was flushed and her eyes blazed like torches. Ten days before she'd attained her circular tranquility, she entered this shrine. Then she instructed her disciples to seal it up, and after that, she meditated and recited *sutras* all the way to *nirvana*.

"On the day she entered the shrine, she also instructed her disciples to open it eight months after her death, then take her desiccated body out to be lacquered and gilded, and then put back in the shrine. As they had been instructed, my teacher Wisdom Forest and other Shifus opened the shrine on October eighth, and found that not only was the Dharma body of their mistress intact, but her head had grown hair, and she emanated a faint, sweet fragrance and a pale gold aura. According to Buddhism, this resulted from her profound practice, strict vegan diet, and asceticism."

I asked, "How?"

"Because monks and nuns with a long, strenuous practice of sitting meditation will have their arteries and veins opened up. And if half a month before they enter *nirvana* they also stop eating completely—so that only a minimal amount of fat and water will remain in their bodies—then their bodies will be mummified after they die. There are many ways to preserve the body. Some put it in an arid cave to let it air dry. Others leave it in an earthenware jar stuffed with wood scraps and straw papers. Then the jar will be sealed to keep out air and stored in a cool, dry place to dehydrate the body."

I began to feel disgusted, but also fascinated to learn about all these methods of preserving dead bodies.

Yi Kong went on: "Revealing Mystery Shifu was a very special teacher. In the last fifteen years of her life, she didn't eat anything, speak a word, or step out of this monastery."

"But how can this be possible?!" I exclaimed, the air suddenly feeling stale in my mouth.

But Yi Kong again ignored me and continued: "Revealing Mystery Shifu hid herself in this small hut behind the Hall of Guan Yin. That's why, after her death, we converted it to a relic hall for her body's storage. During her long years of closed-door meditation, she consumed nothing except water, herb soup, or juice. Neither did she talk to anybody. If for a specific reason she really had to open her mouth, she'd just say 'yes' or 'no.' Later, she stopped talking completely. To communicate in case of emergency, she used a sign language that only Wisdom Forest Shifu, my teacher, could understand. Similarly, except for very specific reasons, she would not receive visitors. Every day for the last fifteen years of her life, all she did was meditate and silently recite *sutras*."

Yi Kong stared into my eyes and added, "Only due to Revealing Mystery Shifu's strenuous practice could her body attain this imperishable state."

As my initial fright waned, I felt myself becoming entranced by this dead nun and suddenly revealed aspect of the monastic life. Could my body attain the same imperishability if I started to meditate strenuously tomorrow?

But before I had a chance to ask, Yi Kong spoke again. "Every day I come here to pay my respect to Revealing Mystery Shifu and never run into anybody. So today must be a very meaningful karmic day that I see you here. Anyway, it's late now and we shouldn't disturb Shifu's Golden Body anymore. Let's go outside and I'll tell you more about this if you want to know."

Hands pressed together, Yi Kong and I bowed deeply to the Golden Body three times before she led me out of the hall. As I turned back to the golden face, I felt as if she were looking at me with something to tell me, if only she could speak.

In silence, Yi Kong and I walked meditatively on the winding path leading back toward the stone garden. The air outside was balmy and scented by the healthy vegetation; the sky burned with stars. Was my encounter with the flesh-bodied Bodhisattva in the relic hall a dream, a nightmare, a hallucination, a revelation . . . or a calling?

We finally arrived at the stone garden and sat down on a bench next to the waterfall. Amid the sound of rippling water and the deep-throated croaking of the frogs, I asked Yi Kong if my body could also attain the same imperishability as Revealing Mystery Shifu's.

"No," she said, "unless . . ." She caught herself in midsentence.

"Unless what?"

She didn't answer my question, but steered the subject in a different track. "Meng Ning, this only happens to monks and nuns." She stared deeply into my eyes. "I should say this is a rare karmic result for only a few very special high monks and nuns."

In the silence that followed, suddenly I realized her implication: if I wanted my body to attain imperishability like Revealing Mystery's, I also had to be a nun. I shuddered.

Yi Kong looked up at the starry sky, then looked down around the moonlit garden before she continued. "What Revealing Mystery Shifu did certainly deserves the greatest respect. But we also need active, 'entering the world' nuns and monks to spread the

Dharma and to carry out compassionate deeds." She turned to search my eyes. "Our temple needs more open-minded, outgoing women to become nuns."

Feeling an awkwardness crawling inside me, I looked down at the ground to avoid her gaze. A beat or two passed before I asked, "Shifu, why can't lay people's bodies attain imperishability after they die?"

Under the moonlight, Yi Kong's nicely shaped bald head seemed to glow with enlightenment. "Because lay people are constantly bothered by worldly affairs. They can never concentrate as deeply in meditation as do people who belong to the religious order."

I blurted out, "What about . . . someone like me? If I were to become a nun, could my body be imperishable after I die?"

Yi Kong shot me an intense look. "Possibly . . . but only if you become—"

Just then, a shout pierced the quiet of the garden like the twang of an arrow shooting through the air. "Shifu! Shifu! Oh, *A Mi Tuo Fo!*" It was the young nun Enlightened to Emptiness. She dashed into the garden, gasping, sobbing, and wiping her tears with her sleeve. She tripped over the stone lantern a few feet in front of us, and fell.

"What's the matter?" Yi Kong dashed to her and helped her up. I hurried to both of them.

"Yi Kong Shifu . . . no good . . . no good . . ." She kept swallowing her own words. Yi Kong lightly touched her shoulder and said, her voice that of a concerned nurse, "Calm down and tell us what happened."

Her face flushed, with some blotches of white, Enlightened to Emptiness spat out in one breath, "Wonderful Countenance Shifu tried to kill herself!"

Although Yi Kong's voice sounded loud and sharp, her face stayed calm. "How did this happen?"

"I don't know . . ."

"Let's go to her now!" Yi Kong took my arm and the three of us dashed out of the garden and sped to Wonderful Countenance's— Dai Nam's—dormitory.

Nuns crowded the small room—milling around, talking, crying, yelling, passing Chinese medicinal oil, towels, a glass of water. Yi Kong spoke authoritatively: "Please step away and give Wonderful Countenance Shifu fresh air." She turned to Enlightened to Emptiness. "Call the ambulance, quick!"

Dai Nam was lying on the floor. Next to her lay a rope, numb and stagnant like a lifeless snake. Shards, like miniature mountain snowcaps, were scattered everywhere. It was the ceramic Buddha knocked over from her altar. Dai Nam had tried to hang herself. The realization hit me so hard that I felt my heart lose balance and plunge over a precipice.

I jerked back, then asked a young novice, "How did this happen?"

She said, "A Shifu was passing Wonderful Countenance Shifu's dormitory and heard a loud shattering sound. She knocked to ask what happened, but nobody answered, so she broke in. She found Wonderful Countenance Shifu hanging herself, so she immediately took her down."

The young novice pointed to the heaps of shards on the floor and whispered into my ear, "Buddha sacrificed himself to save Shifu's life."

Yi Kong knelt beside Dai Nam. I went over to kneel next to them.

"Wonderful Countenance Shifu," Yi Kong asked very gently, "are you all right?"

Dai Nam opened her mouth, but no words came, only the sound of forced air. The red, snakelike scar on her face writhed painfully as if it were freshly gutted.

"It's all right now, and you'll be fine." Yi Kong pondered for a few moments before she asked, very softly, "But why?"

Dai Nam repeatedly shook her head while lifting her hand to wave us away, then she closed her eyes.

A nun found a piece of paper on the altar and handed it to Yi Kong. I craned over her shoulder to read.

Shifus,
  At twenty-five, I took my vow to be vegetarian so as not to harm any sentient being nor consume any stimu-

lant to hinder my cultivation. But today I broke the
vow I'd kept for twenty years. A lay woman offered me
a turnip cake, which I gladly accepted and ate. Later I
found out there was garlic, one of the five stimulants,
sprinkled in the cake.

In my whole life, I have tried very carefully to keep
my vows and I am very proud that they have never
been broken for twenty long years. Now I am ashamed
of myself. My contaminated body should not continue
in this life.

Your servant in the Dharma,
Wonderful Countenance

Yi Kong whispered into Dai Nam's ear, "But, Wonderful Countenance Shifu, you didn't know there was garlic in the cake. . . ."

Right then the ambulance arrived. When the two ambulance men
tried to take Dai Nam onto the stretcher, she frantically pushed them
away. So finally several nuns had to take hold of the stretcher and
move her into the ambulance. Then we all followed the van to the
hospital. Except for Yi Kong, we were all made to wait outside the
emergency room. After a long time, Yi Kong finally came out with
a doctor. We all felt relieved when the doctor told us that Dai Nam's
life was not in danger. But to make sure that everything would be
OK, she would have to stay in the hospital for observation.

The next day, I went early to Kwong Wah Hospital to see Dai Nam.
Enlightened to Emptiness was feeding her from a bowl of congee
when I entered the medicinal-smelling room.

Dai Nam spotted me instantly; a faint smile came over her face.
I put down the fruit basket I'd brought her on the bedside chest
and said very softly, as if she were now my child, "Shifu, I've
brought you some grapes and juice."

She nodded. Enlightened to Emptiness put down the bowl and
came to whisper into my ear, "Miss Du, the doctor says due to
Shifu's throat constriction, she shouldn't talk for a while."

The young nun went back to feeding her. When finished, she

helped Dai Nam lie down on the bed. None of us said anything until Dai Nam closed her eyes and fell asleep.

Enlightened to Emptiness lowered her voice. "Miss Du, you've missed Yi Kong Shifu. She and the others have just left."

Just when I was about to inquire about Dai Nam's condition, the doctor came in. He examined Dai Nam's neck, listened to her breathe, then read and signed the chart. When we followed him outside the room, he said, "The patient has hemorrhage and edema of the larynx, so she shouldn't talk or eat anything solid for a while." He paused to adjust his glasses. "Besides, she's still emotionally unstable, so watch out for her and avoid saying anything she has to answer."

After the doctor had left, I asked the young nun, "Is Shifu still upset over eating that cake?"

"I suppose so."

After a pause, I said, "I'm sure you must be very tired looking after Shifu, so why don't you go outside to get some fresh air, food, and take a rest? I'll stay with her."

"You're so nice, Miss Du. Thank you." The young nun smiled and turned to walk out. I watched until her back disappeared down the stairs before I went back to Dai Nam's room. The real reason I had told the young novice I would take her place was that I wanted to share some tranquil time alone with my friend.

But Dai Nam remained deeply asleep and so, when Enlightened to Emptiness returned, I left the hospital and took a bus to Golden Lotus Temple. I wanted to continue my unfinished discussion of the Golden Body with Yi Kong.

Yi Kong had just finished lunch and was looking at some pictures.

"Have some tea, Meng Ning," she said after I'd sat down opposite her.

I took the cup she offered, then told her about my visit to Dai Nam. Yi Kong told me not to worry, for the doctor had assured her that Dai Nam would be fine.

After that, Yi Kong continued to scrutinize the pictures for a few moments before she handed them to me. "These are photographs of the Buddhist stone statues and cliff sculptures I took in Sichuan a few years ago."

I carefully studied the numerous Buddhas, Guan Yins, wrathful warriors, Buddhist attendants. "They're beautiful. And very powerful, too. Even now I'm only looking at the pictures, but I can feel their *qi* emanating."

Yi Kong nodded while she quietly sipped her tea. "It's a shame that I don't have time to go back to take more pictures and do more documentation. You see"—she handed me another one with a Buddha whose face was completely weathered away—"if we don't do anything, in the future not only the face, but the whole Buddha will be gone." She shook her head. "What a shame."

"But there must be other people who are saving all these?" I asked.

"Of course." She stared at me intently. "But they are either scholars whose perspective is purely academic, or Buddhists whose perspective is purely religious. It's hard to have someone who possesses a balance of the two." I'd be a fool to miss her hidden meaning. It was me, only me, that she wanted to undertake this project for her temple.

I didn't reply. I stared at the jade green tea and thought of something else.

Then her resonant voice rose again. "Is there something on your mind?"

"Hmmm—" I looked up and met her all-knowing eyes.

"Meng Ning, you don't look well. I can tell that something is bothering you, even the other day. If you need help, I'm here."

I said, lowering my gaze to avoid hers, "Yi Kong Shifu, I'm . . . very confused."

"It is natural to feel confused being alive in this illusory world."

After some silence, she cast me another meaningful, yet softer, look. "I suggest you stay here for a while—do some serious meditation to clear your mind."

I was surprised to hear this. "You mean—"

"You can come here and live with the nuns for a few days. The temple might help to settle your perplexity." She paused. "And of course if you don't like it, you can go home anytime. There's no commitment."

Seeing that I didn't respond, she smiled. "Think about it, Meng Ning. It'll only do you good. Moreover, during meditation, you'll be under my supervision."

To my surprise, considering that I'd never liked meditation, this time I instantly agreed. "Yi Kong Shifu, thank you for arranging this for me."

"Don't be polite."

28

The Private Retreat

M ichael had already called several times to ask about me, and
each time before we hung up, reminded me to start preparing
for our wedding. Yesterday I told him not to call for a while because I had to live in the nunnery for a few days to help Yi Kong
with her museum project and to meditate. He showed disappointment but understanding. "I'll miss your voice, Meng Ning. Please
call me if you have a minute."

I told Mother I was going to live for five days in Golden Lotus
Temple to help with a big event to get donations for the poor. Had
I told her the truth, that I was going to a retreat and would live like
a nun for a few days, she'd have thrown herself into a state of panic,
thrusting her pudgy finger at my nose and yelling, "Then you'll
shave your head and put on a loose robe and renounce the world.
After that, desert your mother and leave her to die in loneliness and
grandchildlessness!"

The next day I packed some simple clothes and daily necessi-
ties, then headed straight for Golden Lotus Temple.

Yi Kong put me in a small room by myself, close to the hall
where the nuns slept. She told me that the main purpose of this private retreat, besides meditation, was to live with the nuns and to
learn from them—their compassionate deeds, their rituals, chant-

ing, and, of course, the Four Great Impressive Ways of walking, living, sitting, lying.

Only the first day here, I'd already felt a tinge of regret. So many rules to follow and so many rituals to learn! I wondered how Yi Kong and the other nuns could look so peaceful and detached all the time.

My first assignment, to my great disappointment, was to help out in the *Xiangji Chu,* the Fragrance Accumulating Kitchen, to prepare vegetarian dishes—tofu, tarot, yam, bok choi, fungus, gluten, seaweed, anything tasteless that you could name. Chopping up carrots, celery, mushrooms, and taro into fine pieces was very slow work for me. Enviously, I watched experienced nuns arrange the food on the dish to look like a painting—smoked tofu piled up to represent mountains, chopped mushrooms, rocks, and noodles, rivers. Or a visual *koan,* riddle—rice balls with swirls inside, symbolizing endless transmigration.

Before the meal, I had to wash rice. One time a senior nun made me rinse and rerinse the rice for more times than I wanted to remember—until the washed-away sand equalled that on the banks of the Ganges River!

She looked at me with a deadpan expression. "Until not a single speck of sand is left. Washing rice is actually washing our heart and purifying our mind. We have to rinse and cook with one mind and one heart. Only after that can we have our mindful lunch."

She went on, looking even more serious. "Moreover, Zen cooking advocates three virtues: purity, freshness, harmony. That's why we're vegetarians. Because rich meat dishes confuse both our heart and mind, leaving no room for discipline and reflection. Not to mention the unnecessary killing of other sentient beings."

Her seriousness and her eagerness to lecture impressed me, but they also made me want to giggle. With an effort to keep my face solemn, I asked politely, "Shifu, do you mean rinsing rice is actually a form of meditation?"

"Yes, of course."

Now I couldn't help but tease. "Then, Shifu, is there any sleeping meditation, mindful sleep?"

To my surprise, her answer was, "Well, of course."

"You're serious? How?"

"Simple. You go to bed, focus on your breath, and empty your mind. Not only that, you'll fall asleep faster and more naturally and you'll be freed from nightmares."

But at night when I lay in my bed, my mind, instead of being empty, was visited by New York thoughts, like ghosts wandering toward me from eight thousand miles away.

Yi Kong asked me to meditate three hours at a time, both in the morning and afternoon. Every day she'd come into the room to burn incense, pay respects to the small Buddha statue on the altar, then sit with me. Sometimes, during the burning of one incense stick, we'd recite together the Heart Sutra or the Incantation of Great Compassion—to accumulate merit for suffering souls, dead or alive. Other times we'd chant—Praise to the Incense Burner, Praise to the Ten Directions, Fragrance for Discipline and Meditation, and, of course, the Heart Sutra—until I felt my mind being carried away by Yi Kong's powerful voice, toward another level of consciousness.

Sometimes during our *zazen,* sitting meditation, when Yi Kong noticed that I was becoming restless or falling asleep, she'd wake me up and lead me in walking meditation. During tea break, we would enthusiastically engage in conversations about arts and Dharma. This always made me feel achingly nostalgic, remembering the years when my world had known no man, no Michael, no Philip, no Lisa, no love, no confusions, but only Yi Kong and her beautiful art objects, and, of course, the always trouble-free, compassionate Goddess of Mercy.

This retreat brought back all the pleasant memories of earlier years. I still felt very fond of the nunnery. Of course, I admired Yi Kong the most, but my second favorite nun was the very young Enlightened to Emptiness. She was so simple and innocent that I secretly wished she were the little sister I'd never had.

But soon my fondness for the young nun was tested. One day, feeling restless during meditation, I decided to visit Yi Kong. A few steps before I reached my mentor's office, I took several deep breaths, smoothed my black robe, and tried to calm myself.

The door had been left ajar, and as I was about to knock, bits of conversation flowed into my ears.

A familiar young girl's voice chimed, "Wow, this is a master-piece!"

Then Yi Kong's authoritative voice. "It's skillful. But the face is too sweet. Guan Yin can look beautiful, but never sweet. Don't forget that Guan Yin listens to the tears of the world and then reaches out to help. So her expression should be compassionate, slightly sad rather than sweet."

I peeked in from the doorway and saw Yi Kong and, to my bitterness, Enlightened to Emptiness. A realization hit me—Yi Kong was teaching her to appreciate Buddhist art as she had me fifteen years ago! I could almost smell something bitter simmering in the air as another realization arose: Yi Kong seemed to be training Enlightened to Emptiness to be her Dharma heir!

Now Yi Kong was taking down an art book from the shelf and showing it to the young novice. The familiar voice snaked its way to my ears, asking the young nun the same question she had asked me years ago: "I'd like to teach you Zen painting; do you want to learn?"

"Oh yes, Shifu, I do!"

Though my decision whether or not to be a nun had occupied the very center of my mind, life in the nunnery was going on without me.

Feeling both sad and angry, I walked aimlessly for a while until I bumped into something lumpy and let out a loud *"Ai-ya!"*

"Hey, watch out, miss."

I looked up and saw a big-bellied man with an oily, vulgar face. I almost asked, *Mr. Vulgar, what do you think you are doing here in this nunnery?*

We eyed each other suspiciously for a few seconds before we whispered a simultaneous "Sorry." Then, to my utter shock and disbelief, I watched him drag his bulk into Yi Kong's office.

When I was back in my room, my mind was still possessed with that man's vulgar face and the question: what was he doing in Yi Kong's office? Certainly not appreciating art objects. Then a realization hit me so hard that I gulped—he's a big donor to the fast-developing nunnery! That's why Yi Kong had to entertain him!

On the final day of the retreat, while I was helping the nuns to sew meditation cushions, Enlightened to Emptiness came and told me that Yi Kong wanted to see me. I followed her to Yi Kong's office. My mentor was sitting in front of the Guan Yin picture, her face serene as usual. After Enlightened to Emptiness had closed the door and was gone, Yi Kong signaled me to take the seat opposite her.

After I sat down, she said, "How's your meditation going?"

"Fine, Shifu."

"I know you have never had a natural inclination toward meditation. But a lot of people don't. So don't worry about it. Just keep trying."

I nodded. She went on. "I have another plan for you." She paused to search my face. "That is, of course, if you like the idea."

"What is it?"

"The temple will sponsor you to go to China. Remember those pictures of the stone sculptures and cliff statues in Anyue grotto in Sichuan? I want you to document them for our nunnery." She shuffled some papers on the table. "And if we have enough money in the budget, we might even be able to publish your research later. We've already contacted the Circular Reflection Monastery there, and they're very happy to host you. Besides, Enlightened to Emptiness will also go with you as your assistant."

My heart sank a little upon hearing the novice's name. So Yi Kong was definitely going to train the young nun to succeed her.

"So do you want to go?"

"Of course, Yi Kong Shifu." It wouldn't pay much, if anything, but it would be my first actual job as an art historian.

29

Wedding Pictures

Two days before I was to leave for China, as a farewell treat I took Mother to a teahouse that had a soothing atmosphere and served the best kind of tea.

We sat down just as a young tea ceremony instructor had begun telling the story about the imperial Meng Ding tea.

"Once upon a time in the Qing Yi River," she narrated in her silken voice, "a fish spirit had been meditating strenuously for ten thousand years until she finally transformed into a beautiful young woman.

"One day, dressed as a farm girl, she went to gather tea seeds on the peak of the Meng Mountain and encountered a young man out collecting herbs. They fell in love the instant their eyes met.

"As a token of love, the fish spirit gave her tea seeds to the young man. The lovers vowed to meet again the following year at the mountain peak when the seeds would sprout. The fish spirit said to her lover, 'That will be the day of our marriage.'

"A year later, when spring came again, as they had pledged to each other, the fish spirit and the young man met again on the mountain and married. On their wedding night, the bride took off her white lace shawl and threw it into the air. Mist formed instantly to nourish the tea leaves he had planted. Ever after that, the tea grew luxuriantly, and the couple lived a happy life that was soon blessed with a son and a daughter.

"As good times rarely last long, so the fish spirit's marriage to a mortal was finally discovered by the Qing Yi River God, who ordered her to return to the river at once. Taking leave with tears and a broken heart, the young mother said to her children, 'You must help your father to take good care of the tea leaves on the mountain . . . and make sure the mist keeps moistening the leaves.'

"Sixty years passed like a horse-leap over a ravine. When the husband had turned eighty, and his children and grandchildren were all grown up, he found his never-ending longing for the fish spirit so unbearable that he jumped into a river and ended his life.

"So great were his accomplishments in tea growing that the emperor conferred on him posthumously the title Master of Popular Wisdom and Wonderful Compassion. The tea he planted on the Meng Mountain was honored as *gongcha*, Tea of the Imperial Offering."

After the instructor had finished the story and her tea ceremony demonstration, Mother looked relaxed and happy. She sipped her tea with an imperial air. "Ah, excellent tea. And what a touching love story!" Then she went on to praise the tale and the storyteller's pretty Chinese dress and silken voice.

Before I had the chance to say anything, she pulled my sleeve. "Meng Ning, I suddenly feel very hungry; let's find a place to eat."

"But, Ma—"

"Let's go. I'm starving."

We were walking along Waterloo Road. The weather was as hot as the Meng Ding tea. And as intoxicating.

Mother blurted out, "I really love that fish's story. So moving!"

Her eyes glistened and lost their focus. "The story has a sad ending, but at least the fish and the young man were able to get married and have two children; it was not that tragic after all."

In the shop window, my mother's reflection silently overlapped those of other pedestrians on the busy boulevard. Stooping old people, briskly striding young men, shuffling children, giggling teenagers in torn jeans, sweaty construction workers, middle-aged women straining with loaded shopping bags, shiny Mercedes sedans cutting off battered bicycles, packed buses, overloaded trucks lumbering, taxis swishing by, the overpass looming above . . .

The Ten Thousand Miles of Red Dust reproduced in the light and shadow of a silent movie.

How peaceful, this world of mirrored images, where people intersect but never interrupt, interact but never interfere. Now even my excitable mother looked happy and relaxed in the shiny, cool glass. The deep wrinkles around the eyes of her seasoned doll's face turned into fine lines, like subtle cracks on the glaze of an antique vase. Even her dyed black hair had a more natural shade. Mother seemed to have forgotten her hunger, her eyes absorbing the commodities displayed behind the glass.

"Hey, look, Meng Ning, Sally Yeh in a wedding gown!" Mother stopped in front of a bridal salon; her eyes fixed on a huge picture of the Hong Kong pop singer. "Very fancy, isn't it? French sixteenth-century classical court style." She was reading from a small ad next to the picture.

"Yes, but a distasteful imitation." Her easily distracted attention annoyed me.

Mother raised her voice to compete with the street noise. "Hey, look, she took the picture at the garden of Versailles, in France."

"Yes, Ma, it is the garden of Versailles, but not in France. Can't you tell the background is just a blown-up studio picture?"

Mother seemed determined not to be discouraged by any of my negative responses. "Hey, look how beautiful she is in her bridal makeup."

"No, too loud. Ma, don't you see that everything on her face is overdone? Too many colors on the eyelids, the nose shadow is too deep . . . and . . . you see those eyelashes? They're too long and too thick, too artificial! Besides, how come her grin is so big? In the past, women were not supposed to reveal their teeth when they smiled. A bride has to be bashful and demure, at least pretend and act that way, not baring her teeth immodestly like this—"

"It's theatrical," Mother said, finally cutting off my harangue. "Like in Beijing opera. You like Beijing opera, don't you?"

I did.

I remembered as a child how I was thrilled by the actors with their *lianpu*, multicolored face patterns. My tiny heart never failed to be captivated by patterns moving on the actors' faces as if a giant portrait were springing to life!

Mother had eagerly taught me how to recognize their symbols. White Face is bad, so be careful of him; Black Face is righteous, so pay respect to him; Green Face is cunning and touchy, so stay away from him; Red Face is brave and courageous, so applaud him; Gold Face is either an emperor or a nobleman, so emulate him.

But not until I grew up did I realize people can put more than one *lianpu* on their faces. That was more than my mother had taught me. And it takes one lifetime, or many lifetimes, to learn to strip away all the layers until you catch a glimpse of the truth. Or of nothingness, as you discover at the end of the tearful process of peeling an onion.

Now as I searched Sally Yeh's painted face, her eyes stared back at me from behind the glass, as if beckoning me to enter her dream-world. I wondered who was the real woman hiding behind this pretty mask, and whether she was really as happy about getting married as she looked.

My childhood efforts to identify *lianpu* still groped in a maze. For the human face, as constant as it seems, is in fact as capricious and camouflaged as the human heart.

I peeked at Mother. She was still studying the pop singer with great envy and absorption, oblivious to a giggling teenage couple and a band of four marching housewives pushing by her.

"Ah, how beautiful she is, wearing all her fancy jewelry," Mother said, hiding her bare hands behind her. "See, Meng Ning," she said, her voice soaked with feeling, "Sally Yeh is still single, so nowadays you don't have to get married to take wedding pictures. The newspaper says it's fashionable for young women to dress as a bride only to look pretty and to take pictures as souvenirs. I think you should also take pictures like this while you still look young."

I snapped, "But, Ma, I am not a pop singer, and this is just an advertisement."

Mother's face stiffened. "Of course you're not a pop singer.

You're better, much better!" Then she sighed, muttering to herself, "*Hai,* then why aren't there many men knocking at your door?"

I pretended not to have heard her. She went on, this time staring right into my eyes. "Meng Ning, don't act stuck-up and chase men away. And don't be overly choosy so you end up getting only the leftover rotten apples at the bottom of a moldy crate."

I remained silent. She gave me a chiding glance. "You're very pretty and talented, so I really don't believe there're no men prostrating at your feet. It must be your attitude. You know the proverb 'Gorgeous as the peaches and plums, cold as the ice and frost'?"

Seeing that I still didn't respond, Mother plunged on: "I have taught you many things, but never to snub men, especially the good ones like doctors, lawyers, or even engineers."

"Ma—" Suddenly Michael's face, looming large, squeezed out all thoughts in my mind.

"What?"

I blurted out before I could stop myself, "Actually, someone has just proposed to me."

Mother had a stunned expression, as if her teenage daughter had just told her that she was pregnant. "Really?"

"Yes."

She studied me with a puzzled expression, ignoring a withered old woman pushing through the space between her and the shop window.

"Is it true?" A smile was gradually blooming on her face. "Then why didn't you tell me earlier? Who is he?"

"He . . . he's an American."

"ABC?" She meant American-born Chinese.

"No, he's . . . white."

"You mean a white ghost?"

Although Mother looked happy having learned that someone had proposed to me, she didn't look pleased that he was an "old barbarian."

Because, in Mother's opinion, foreigners were synonymous with wantonness and debauchery. When she was in a bad mood, they would even be carriers of an unspeakable disease. When I'd prepared my trip to the States, she'd said, "Ah, very brave, go to America and deal with barbarians. I'll never have your guts, I don't want to catch AIDS!" Of course she didn't mean sex, but sitting on a chair someone with AIDS had sat on, that sort of thing.

"But, Ma, please don't use that ugly word. Michael is very nice to me and—"

"Mic Ko?" Mother pinched her eyes into slits. "When did this Mic Ko propose?"

"A month ago."

"How long have you known each other?"

"A few months."

Mother snatched a paper fan from her handbag, snapped it open, and fanned impatiently. "Too quick! That's typical American. Can't wait, everything rush, rush, rush! Instant tea, instant coffee, instant sex, instant marriage, instant divorce! Can't sit down for ten minutes to brew tea, spend another ten to appreciate the leaves, another five to smell its fragrance, and another five to sip. That's why Americans have no culture, because they have no time!"

After Mother had finished repeating the tea instructor's lecture and criticizing American culture, she paused to look into my eyes. "Ah, innocent girl. Love and marriage are never as simple as that. Don't believe the Chinese saying 'If you're in love, you'll eat your fill by drinking water.' I suffered enough from that with your father. And if it's with a barbarian, that's worse. Americans always think everything in their country is better than ours, except Suzie Wong."

She plunged on excitingly. "I had a friend who had a white ghost husband. Not only did he sweat like a coolie, he gobbled food like a refugee, roared with laughter like a huge broken bell struck by a lunatic, and embarrassed her women friends by washing his throat with wine and making gurgling sounds like he's doing you-know-what. One time during a banquet when he got drunk, he glanced at the women and said, 'How come when an old hag reaches fifty, she's still horny,' then, 'Don't worry if a girl's ugly, as long as she's handy.'"

Finally Mother concluded her harangue. "That's what people end up with when they marry a *gweilo*."

"Ma, but Michael is nothing like this. He's a doctor."

"A doctor?" Mother sneered. "Of what? Philosophy? Or poetry?"

"Ma, didn't you just worry that I would never get married? So aren't you happy now that someone has proposed?"

In the shop window, the golden twilight glistening in the reflection softened Mother's visage; sometimes I could see my face in her older one. Her robust figure turned more supple; even the deep purple suit she wore now spoke with a softer hue.

"Hai!" Mother sighed. "Meng Ning, of course I'm glad you're getting married. But . . . I'm also afraid."

"Of what?"

"That you'll be . . . unhappy"—she let out a long sigh—"like your mother."

A long pause. Traffic whizzed by. Restless people and speeding cars kept passing through her in the glass.

But Mother was fine. For nothing can hurt a soul in a mirage. As no one can steal the moon reflected on a river.

Mother had the same expression when she watched Beijing opera with me when I was a child. Now I certainly understood why she liked the painted-face actors so much, but got so upset when I aspired to be one.

However, I still couldn't fathom the way she loved me, even though I had shared the same roof and nearly the same face with her for thirty years.

Now in the shimmering reflection of the shop window, our eyes parted as swiftly as they had touched, like a pair of kissing fish. I gazed at my own face and found my thirty-year-old mother there, whispering to me all her girlish dreams, eyes fresh.

I wanted to love her back as much as she loved me, and much more.

I touched her elbow. "Ma, don't worry."

"Hai!" Mother sighed again. "I'm a very careful person, but see what happened to me with your father." She put a strand of my hair in place.

My mother could be very difficult in her own way, but despite being of the older generation, she had only occasionally nagged me about finding a husband.

Her remarks about the fish bones, about Sally Yeh, and today about the story of the fish spirit were the few times she had hinted marriage to me.

If I had not misread her face pattern, nor misinterpreted her dreams.

I said after a long silence, "Ma, although I said yes to Michael's proposal, I might still"—I swallowed hard—"break the engagement."

Mother's voice shot two octaves higher. "Turn down a doctor? *Are you crazy?* How many girls will be befriended by a doctor, let alone asked to be married?"

A middle-aged man cast us a curious glance.

My cheeks felt hot. I stammered, "I mean . . . Ma, I'll be careful . . . I mean, if Michael turns out to be bad, I can . . . always get a divorce."

Mother spat, "*Choi! Daigut laisi!* It's bad luck to talk about divorce before you're married!" *Daigut laisi* means "great prosperity and luck," to counteract anything bad that's been said.

"Ma, calm down. People are staring at us."

"Then watch your mouth and stop saying unlucky things."

"All right, all right."

We resumed walking along Waterloo Road and I began to tell Mother, amid the intense heat and noise, everything about Michael. Except, of course, my recent baffling experiences in New York, my confusion. After that, I took the engagement ring that Michael had bought me out of my purse.

Mother looked at the stone with envy. "Beautiful, excellent fire!" she exclaimed, then asked timidly, "Can I try?"

"Of course." Right in the middle of the busy boulevard, I slipped the ring onto her fourth finger, but it was too small, so I took it off and slipped it onto her little finger.

My eyes stung when I saw a big smile bloom on her face. "Ma, anything more that you want?"

"I only want my daughter to be happy," she said, giving me back the ring.

≈ 30 ≈

A Trip to China

My trip to document the art of grottoes in Anyue was scheduled to last for a month. Michael was not very happy upon hearing the news.

Across eight thousand miles, I could clearly sense disappointment in his voice. "Meng Ning, I know I can't stop you from going. But please take very good care of yourself and don't make me worry."

When he asked for my address and phone number in China, I said, "I'll be staying in a temple and there is no phone. Anyway, I'll try my best to find a phone to call you from time to time."

His voice suddenly turned distressed and alarmed. "You mean I can't reach you, not at all?"

"But don't worry, Michael, I'm traveling with nuns and Guan Yin. We'll be protected. Anyway, you have the temple's address, so you can write to me."

This time I really wanted to be left alone, not only to concentrate on my work, but also to clear my mind to make the most important decision in my life.

On October tenth, Enlightened to Emptiness and I took a flight from Hong Kong to Chengdu, the capital of Sichuan, and from there, a seemingly endless ride in a decrepit van to the Anyue grottoes.

Long before the van ride was over, any jealousy I'd felt toward Enlightened to Emptiness had dissipated. She was too innocent and too young for me to harbor such feelings toward her.

The driver, Mr. Qian, a volunteer from the Circular Reflection Monastery where we were going to stay, asked whether this was our first trip to China.

Enlightened to Emptiness uttered an excited "Yes!"

I said, "I've only been to Guanzhou. . . ."

"Then you'll be surprised to see the differences in the north," he enthused, "and I'm sure you'll like it."

But I was not so sure. What slipped past us among the sparse trees were low gray buildings decorated with two different kinds of banners: official admonitions such as *Let's build a civilized China,* and *Marry late, have one child,* or unofficial ones: clothes, towels, bed sheets, blankets, underwear, all fluttering lazily in the air. I saw a motorcycle pass with a large wicker basket containing dozens of chickens, squealing and flapping, their feathers scattering in the air while the vehicle drove toward their ill-fated destination. A boy was smoking in front of a store, under the watchful eye of his admiring father.

I soon dozed off.

At two o'clock in the afternoon, we finally arrived at the town and then, after another fifteen minutes' ride on a narrow winding path, the Circular Reflection Monastery. A fortyish nun with a round face came to answer the door. Mr. Qian introduced us and we exchanged bows. The nun, Compassionate Wonder, split a wide grin. "Our Shifu has been expecting you two the whole day. She's been very excited to have visitors from so far—me, too."

On our way to the dorm, Compassionate Wonder said, "You two are our first guests from Hong Kong. Our humble temple is brightened by your visit."

I almost chuckled. What was the big deal to have someone from Hong Kong? But I put on a smile and said, "I'm flattered."

Enlightened to Emptiness immediately threw in, "And I'm honored."

Compassionate Wonder let out a hearty laugh. "Ah, so Hong Kong people also have a glib tongue!"

Enlightened to Emptiness and I were led to different dorms: she was to live with the other nuns while I, a lay person, took a room in the dorm for Buddhist guests. I unpacked, took a shower, and then we were served snacks. Since my friend refused to break the monastic rule of no eating after noon, I was the only one to enjoy the steaming buns and fragrant tea in the Fragrance Accumulating Kitchen.

Around three, Compassionate Wonder took us to see the abbess, Beckoning Invisibility Shifu. I took an instant liking to this sixtyish, plump woman. Always smiling, she seemed to be soaked in the endless joy of the Dharma.

While Compassionate Wonder was busy serving tea and snacks, Beckoning Invisibility, her small eyes darting between my friend and me, said, "I was told many times how beautiful Hong Kong is, and today I finally have the chance to greet someone from there. How wonderful."

After returning her praise with our hands together in the prayer gesture and a demure "thank you but you overpraise," Enlightened to Emptiness and I presented to the abbess our gifts—a book on Buddhist architecture and a bronze incense burner carved with lotuses.

Only after several more rounds of politenesses, tea pouring, and drinking, did the abbess finally take us for a tour of the temple where she introduced us to the other Shifus and to the workers and volunteers. Around seven, Enlightened to Emptiness and I retired early to our dorms.

The next morning I woke up at six. Enlightened to Emptiness had probably awakened much earlier, for in my semi-wakeful state, I could hear chanting drifting from the Hall of Grand Heroic Treasures. After a quick wash, I joined the nuns in the kitchen for a breakfast of porridge, buns, and pickled vegetables—simple but delicious after my sound sleep. Then, with not much ado, we grabbed our belongings and set out for the grotto sculptures.

Four of us climbed into the same rickety van provided by the temple: Mr. Qian, the driver who'd brought us here yesterday; a lanky young man named Little Lam, who'd be our guide as well as help us with odds and ends during the trip; Enlightened to Emptiness; and me.

Yi Kong wanted me to survey at least three grottoes, and our first destination was the Sleeping Buddha Temple located in Bamiao Township, forty kilometers north of Anyue.

After about an hour, with a sharp turn of the van, Mr. Qian announced that we'd arrived. He said that he wouldn't join us for the tour, for he'd rather stay in the van with his favorite company—Longlife brand cigarettes.

I stepped out of the van and gasped. I'd never seen a Buddha so huge.

Carved out of an entire cliff, he was lying with his head facing east and his feet west. Little Lam came up to me and said, "Impressive, isn't it? The Buddha's length is twenty-three hundred meters."

I turned to pass this information to Enlightened to Emptiness, but saw that she was prostrating vigorously on the ground and mumbling—probably a *sutra* or Hail to the Buddha's Name. I also bowed and said a short prayer.

I walked here and there, shading my eyes while taking in different views of this gargantuan yet peacefully reclining statue, as well as the group of figures on its top. Two figures stood at the Buddha's feet—one was the warrior attendant and the other one a woman mourning his death.

Without delay, Enlightened to Emptiness and I got to work, taking pictures and writing down detailed descriptions of the statues' iconography: headdresses, facial expressions, *mudras,* postures, drapery, amulets, and other decorations. We transcribed inscriptions, worked out dates, and recorded damage. During our work, people hovered around us and interrupted our concentration with unending questions:

"Do you work for the cultural or the religious department?"

"You speak with an accent—where did you come from?"

"What's the brand of your camera. Nikon? Canon?"

"You married? Why not?"

"How many children do you have?"

"How much money do you make?"

One young man even looked over my shoulder and read aloud my notes. Knowing that I was from Hong Kong, a middle-aged woman asked me to teach her English.

Ignoring the distractions, Enlightened to Emptiness and I worked fast—we couldn't afford to waste time. At four in the afternoon, we'd already finished initial documentation of cave no. 44 with a double dragon sculpture, cave no. 54 with three Buddhas, and cave no. 59 with reliefs of *apsaras*—flying bodhisattvas.

A few hours later, the van driver, Mr. Qian, began walking restlessly outside the cave, so we knew it was time to go back.

The days passed with us getting up early, eating a large steaming bowl of noodles for breakfast, then riding out to the temple complex in the van with Mr. Qian. Little Lam soon stopped coming, having tired of watching us work in the caves. The days blurred together as we recorded the contents of cave after cave, then rode back home in the van. I ate alone most evenings, since Enlightened to Emptiness continued keeping her vow not to eat after noon. Then I would wash in water brought up in a large, stained, plastic bucket and go to bed.

I was happy to be using what I'd struggled so long to learn, yet I felt no desire to spend years in the remote dusty reaches of China. The place was so secluded, and the work so exhausting, that I truly achieved an empty mind. The confusion that had overwhelmed me in New York was letting me alone for now, but waiting, like the phoenix, to soar again.

On a hot day during the third week, we were working at our last destination of the day—cave no. 45 of the thousand-armed Guan Yin. This cave felt so cool that I gave out a sigh of comfort as I stepped in. I took out a handkerchief and wiped the sweat from my face, then I turned to smile at my young friend. "Shifu, wouldn't it be nice if we could now have a Coke with ice?"

"Hmmm . . ." She thought for a while. "But I'd rather have iced green bean soup—that's what really dissipates the heat."

"Not a bad idea, Shifu!"

Still laughing, our eyes caught the statue.

My friend gasped. I let out a small cry.

"Poor Guan Yin," I blurted out, "she has lost at least half of her arms!"

The young nun exclaimed, "And her whole face is gone!"

Seeing this heartbreaking sight, Enlightened to Emptiness immediately plopped down and did prostrations. I did them with her. After we'd finished, we stood up and scrutinized the mutilated Goddess.

Enlightened to Emptiness whispered to me as if fearing that the earless statue might hear our conversation. "Miss Du"—she was now counting the Goddess's outstretched arms—"there are only five left." Then she exclaimed, "*Ai-ya!*" and shook her head in dismay.

If all objects, like humans, have fate, then surely this thousand-armed Guan Yin's was not as lucky as the others who had the fortune to escape natural or man-inflicted damage. Then I thought of the Golden Body, dead for a hundred years, with the luck to be cared for and pampered like the living, or should I say, better than the living.

When I raised my camera to take another picture, I noticed the bare space on my left ring finger. Not wanting to take any risk that it might attract too much attention or even get stolen in China, I had left the engagement ring back home. Because of my hectic schedule in Anyue, I hadn't thought much about Michael. It's sad to realize the truth that human emotions are, like the stone statues, equally vulnerable to the lapse of time. Now ten thousand miles away, was I also out of Michael's mind?

My gaze fell on the two large holes in the Goddess's face. I stared at them as an emptiness started to gnaw at me. I didn't want my life to end up like the holes—dark, empty, forgotten.

I peeked at Enlightened to Emptiness, who was now snapping pictures with fierce concentration. Are all nuns' lives trouble-free like hers? I doubted it. She was just still too young to be enlightened to the machinations of this Ten Thousand Miles of Red Dust.

* * *

After three weeks of uninterrupted work on the sculptures, we felt so overwhelmed and exhausted that we decided to have some fun on the weekend—the last Saturday before we'd go back to Hong Kong.

"Let's start with the local market," I suggested to Enlightened to Emptiness.

She sighed.

"What's wrong, Shifu?"

"*Hai,* but . . ."

"But what?"

"You know, it's forbidden, actually not forbidden, but . . . inappropriate for a nun to go to the market."

"But Shifu, remember that all Bodhisattvas, after they have attained enlightenment, all come back to this dusty world, right in the marketplace, to help the others."

"Hmmm . . . OK , I'll go, but . . ."

"My lips are sealed."

In the midst of the crowded market we detected many stares and remarks directed toward us.

"Hey, a nun!" a teenage girl exclaimed, nudging her girlfriend.

"Mama, that woman has no hair!" a child pulled at her mother's tunic and yapped.

"What's that pretty girl doing with a nun?" a young man said to his friend, while throwing malicious glances at us.

A vendor smiled at my friend. "Miss, much cooler to have your head shaved, eh?"

Worst was when a plump man with missing teeth spat vehemently on the floor—a gesture to cast away bad luck. Some ignorant men believe that if they see a monk or a nun, especially in the morning when the day is starting, it will bring them bad luck. Shaved heads signify "nothing left," which might result in "nothing left" in their pockets and rice bowls.

I peeked at my nun friend. She looked a little upset.

"Shifu, are you all right?"

"Oh, yes. I've experienced worse," she said, resuming her spir-

ited stride. "One time a man even came up to knock on my head."
She smiled. "But most people are still very respectful to us."

Soon we squeezed into a stall crowded with children and their
parents and saw a display of candy figures: dragon and phoenix, as
well as the monk Xuan Zhuang, the crafty monkey and the lazy pig
depicted in the famous novel *Journey to the West.*

"Miss Du, look," my friend said excitedly, "he's making the candies."

The craftsman, a skinny, wrinkled fortyish man, ladled melted
sugar from a pot, poured it on a slab of marble, then, with a small
knife, started to pinch, pull, press, and cut the sugar. In just a few
minutes, human figures, animals, tigers, birds, fishes, even insects
were born under his dexterous fingers.

I bought the dragon for myself and the monkey for my friend.
"Shifu"—I handed her the candy—"Enlightened to Emptiness."

We chuckled. In the novel, the crafty monkey was named
Wu Kong—Enlightened to Emptiness.

Happily my friend licked the monkey's head, then said suddenly, "Oh, Miss Du, I don't think I'm supposed to eat this."

"Why not? It's vegetarian."

"It's in the shape of a monkey, after all!"

"Oh, come on, Shifu, it's not really an animal. No one from
Hong Kong will see us here. Relax."

"All right then," she said, noisily biting off the monkey's head.

Enlightened to Emptiness and I continued to lick and wander,
following the flow of the crowd. My friend looked completely en-
thralled by the diversity and animation of the market. Her large
eyes took in everything. Her pink lips let out excited oohs and aahs.
So young and energetic, she really should have had some fun in the
secular world before entering the nunnery. I wondered what made
her become a nun at such a young age and whether she ever felt regret. Had she ever tasted the flavor of being with a man she loved?

Memories arose in my mind of strolling with Michael in the
night market in Hong Kong. I remembered his hand reaching out
to mine, his asking me to take him to see a Chinese opera with a
happy ending, my teasing him about how I liked dogs, especially on
a plate. . . .

Then, we had been two strangers brought together by the fire. Now we were troubled lovers ten thousand miles apart.

"Miss Du—" Enlightened to Emptiness's high-pitched voice awakened me from my reveries. "Let's take a look here."

We were now in front of a book stall crowded with several young people and teenagers. My friend immediately plunged into flipping through pages of old books and movie magazines as well as cheaply printed books on astrology, physiognomy, palmistry, and cooking.

As I was about to suggest that we leave, I found the young novice's eyes shining bright and her lips moving soundlessly while she seemed to thoroughly enjoy herself.

I poked my head over her shoulder. "Shifu, what are you reading?"

Blushing, she tried to hide the book, but then handed it to me.

It was a martial arts romance comic book.

The blush still lingered on the young nun's face. "I've never read anything like this before."

"You like it?"

"Hmmm . . . sort of, but . . . I don't know."

"Don't worry, I won't tell Yi Kong Shifu."

Her face beamed. "Yes, I do."

The stall owner leaned forward. "Miss, I have other things very juicy. You want to take a look?"

Fearing that he might not have the discretion not to show something indecent to a nun, I tugged at my friend's sleeve, whispering, "Shifu, let's go."

❧ 31 ❧

Great Protector
of the Dharma

Back in my room in Circular Reflection Monastery, I found two letters on the desk. One was from the United States and the other from Hong Kong. So even before opening them, I'd already guessed the senders: Michael and my mother. Michael's had been sent a week earlier.

I felt a bit guilty that I first opened the one from the States.

Dear Meng Ning,

So far you haven't called me. I know you must be very busy, but please don't forget about me.

Recently my heavy workload really seems to be getting to me. In the last two weeks, I flew to attend meetings in three different states: Arizona, Florida, and Texas—all boring places. Of course, one of the reasons I felt despairing was because you were not with me. Otherwise I'd have enjoyed the trips, no matter how tedious the meetings.

How's your work in Anyue going? Please take very good care of yourself in such a remote place. Be sure to drink only bottled water. Don't even brush your teeth

with tap water. Also stay away from local doctors and
hospitals.

Since I haven't gotten a letter from you and you
don't have a phone, of course I wonder how you are. I
really miss you and worry about you. Maybe you have
written—mail from China takes a long time to reach
the U.S. Or maybe you tried to call and it never got
through. I know the connections from China to the
States are horrible.

Please call me collect and write to me.

I love you.

Michael

PS. When you're appreciating the beautiful
landscapes and sculptures in Anyue, don't forget to
think of me.

After I'd finished reading, I pressed the letter to my chest and
let out a sigh. The serenity I'd felt being tucked away in a remote
part of China crumbled at the thought of Michael, far away in New
York, lonely without me.

Next I ripped open the other envelope, slipped out the letter,
and saw my mother's large characters.

My beautiful daughter,

How's your trip? I hope everything's fine. But still,
be very careful in China and don't trust anyone there,
nor any *gweilo* in America, not even this Mic Ko. Although he's now your fiancé, he's still a *gweilo* after all!

Your grandmother once told me that in all foreign
devils' eyes, the most desirable woman is a combination
of a good cook in the kitchen, a polished hostess in the
living room, a great fuck in bed (excuse the vulgarity).
What exploitations! So now I'm glad that I've never
taught you how to cook, that we've been too poor to

own a house with a big, elegant living room for you to play hostess, that—as for the bed, all I can remind you is, *don't forget the cup of water!* You must think your mother is crazy, for what couple would really put that between them in bed, let alone now that you're engaged? But you better not slight an old woman's wisdom, like I did when your father and I were very young (he nineteen and I nine) on a wonderful evening in May!

I'm fine in Hong Kong. But Hong Kong is not fine. Although you've never shown any interest in either politics or economics, I'm sure you must have heard about the stock market crash. Companies closed, workers fired, people committing suicide. One manager plunged his big BMW into the sea just outside City Hall. Every day, banks are swarming with people desperately trying to exchange Hong Kong money for U.S. dollars. The black market skyrocketed as high as $12 Hong Kong for $1 U.S. Can you believe that?

Enclosed is an article in the newspaper I just happened to read and I think it might interest you. Are you having such a good time thinking about this *gweilo* American Mic Ko that you forget about your own Chinese mother?

Worriedly yours,
Mother

PS. One more thing. If you really love this Mic Ko, go ahead and marry him quick, because Hong Kong is really doing very badly. Women can starve by marrying a doctor of philosophy, but never a Western doctor of medicine!

2nd PS. I almost forgot to tell you that your Mic Ko called many times and I only understood half of his English. Sounded like he was complaining about you not calling or writing to him. Having had enough of his nagging, I told him everything—when you'll be back in Chengdu and the name of your hotel.

3rd PS. Do you not like this Mic Ko anymore? Or have you met someone better than him, like a Chinese Western doctor?

I muttered to myself, "Mother! Why did you give my schedule to Michael? I went to China to be left alone!"
Then my gaze fell on the newspaper clipping:

BIG SPONSOR DISAPPEARS, GOLDEN LOTUS TEMPLE
IN FINANCIAL TROUBLE

Au Yeung Wei, alias Sunny Au, Hong Kong bil-
lionaire and president of The Sun Real Estate Cor-
poration, has not been seen since he left his luxury
house in Clear Water Bay last Wednesday morning. A day before his disappearance, his company
filed for bankruptcy. It was rumored that he is now
in Europe, where he is said to have deposits of
more than three hundred million U.S. dollars.
Among the many organizations that will suffer
from Au's disappearance is Golden Lotus Temple,
of which, according to sources, he is the biggest
supporter. It is reputed that he has, since 1982, do-
nated over twenty-five million Hong Kong dollars
to the temple after he had learned about its Golden
Body. It is also reputed that he was so impressed
by the imperishability of the Golden Body that he
believed it to be his guardian goddess, not only for
this life, but also for his future ones. He wanted
the donations kept secret so he could be the sole
donor and have all the merit for himself.
With his disappearance and his company's fil-

ing for bankruptcy, the construction and expansion of the Golden Lotus Temple have also stopped. The chief nun, the Venerable Yi Kong, is still in Xian on a trip to recruit painters for the decoration of the Temple's Hall of Grand Heroic Treasures, and is not available for comment.

As I read the article, I felt like a stone was pressing on my chest. Was it possible that Yi Kong, who always gave me the impression that she disliked and distrusted men, got her main support for her temple from a vulgar businessman? And had this Sunny Au become the main sponsor, or *hufa*—great protector of the Dharma—only because he thought the Golden Body was his guardian goddess?

Suddenly a thought hit me hard. Could the vulgar man I'd seen dragging his big bottom into Yi Kong's office be Sunny Au?

Maybe the nuns' world was much more complicated than I'd thought, or would want to admit. I remembered during our quarrel, Michael had said about Yi Kong:

You really believe she got all her donations to build a school, an orphanage, a nursing home, and to reconstruct the whole nunnery only from women?

Then:

If she has no idea what it's like to be loved by a man, then how can she be so sure that that kind of love is illusory?

Feeling a headache coming, I reached out to turn off the bedside lamp, then plopped down on the bed. I flipped like a fish in a frying pan, but, exhausted as I was, sleep did not come for a long time.

The next day, since Enlightened to Emptiness would be going back to Hong Kong in the afternoon and I to Chengdu to sightsee, maybe do some research in the Sichuan museum, I invited her to have tea in my room. We took the tea bag provided by the temple and brewed ourselves tea with water from the temple thermos. Then we sipped the fragrant tea while chatting about this and that.

After a while, my friend suddenly asked, "Miss Du, your fiancé—he must be a very nice person, isn't he?"

Although I'd told her briefly about Michael, I was still taken aback by this question from a nun. "Yes, he's a very nice person, and very nice to me."

"What does he do?"

"He's a doctor."

"Wow, a doctor, how nice." She stared at me curiously. "What kind?"

"Neurologist."

"You mean he fixes people's brains?"

I chuckled and nodded. "I don't know much about medicine, so I guess so."

"Wow, he must be very smart to be in this specialty."

"I think so."

"Wow, Miss Du"—her large eyes shone intently—"you're so lucky."

A pause. Then I asked, "Shifu, you mind if I ask you something personal?"

She shrugged. "No, I have no secrets."

"How old were you when you became a nun?"

Her answer came as a surprise. "I was raised in Golden Lotus Temple."

"Were you? Then how come I've never seen you there?"

"Yes, you did."

"Really? I have no memory—when?"

"One time I came into the library when you and Yi Kong Shifu were looking at some paintings. Then Shifu introduced me to you."

"She did?"

"Yes. She said, 'Miss Du, meet our Little Cookie.'"

Now I vaguely remembered that plump little girl who'd loved cookies and who'd often peeked in the library to stare at Yi Kong and me. "Oh, I can't believe it—" I stared at the very slim young woman in front of me. "So you're Little Cookie!"

She nodded and smiled shyly.

I asked, "Oh . . . but you weren't an orphan, were you?"

"No. But my parents had seven kids, all boys except me. My father died young, my mother was always sick, and I was very naughty. So my grandmother, who decided everything in the family, made up her mind one day that I should be sent to live in a temple. She said this would help not only to discipline me, but also cast away bad luck, not to mention that it'd accumulate merit for the whole family."

"But, Shifu"—I scrutinized her—"I don't see any mischief in you, not at all."

"But that was what my grandmother thought."

"For example?"

"I once rubbed our cat's fur backward and pinched his tail."

I laughed.

My friend continued: "Another time I forgot to feed our pigeon so it died, its insides eaten away by mice, leaving a hollow shell. When my grandmother saw the dried-up bird, she hit me and screamed, 'Bad luck, a big black hole!'"

We laughed at this, then I asked, "Did your mother miss you?"

"Oh yes, she did, very much. When I was small, she visited me in the temple all the time, sometimes even stayed with me overnight without letting the nuns know. Then two years ago when I was fifteen, with my mother's consent, they shaved my head to become a nun."

After she'd finished her story, we remained silent. Then a question slipped out of my lips before I could stop myself. "Shifu, did you ever have a boyfriend?"

"Of course not!"

I studied her smooth skin, oval face, and large, curious eyes. "Do you ever . . . regret that?"

She seemed lost for an answer.

"I'm sorry, Shifu. Maybe I shouldn't have asked such a secular question."

"It's all right. You're a nice person, Miss Du. I don't mind." She paused. "Well, I suppose my answer is, I . . . I . . . have no idea."

That made sense.

"Hmmm, maybe I . . ." She bit her lip. "I really don't know." Then she added, her face flushed like a tomato, "Oh heavens, Yi Kong Shifu hoped I'd persuade you to take refuge, and now see how I failed!"

Did she? But knowing Yi Kong's unyielding personality, I shouldn't be surprised. Now I suddenly realized that letting me see the Golden Body and sending me here were to lure me back to the empty gate! She even wanted me to donate Michael's engagement ring to her temple!

Although she'd never imposed, Yi Kong's wish that I would be a nun in her temple was as clear as the twelve scars atop her bald head. As a nun she couldn't openly object to my falling in love and getting married, yet even here, over eight hundred miles from the Golden Lotus Temple, I could feel her pull, persistent as ever, toward the empty gate. She would think of it as compassion; she didn't want me to fall into the burning hell of human infatuation.

That's why "form is emptiness" was Yi Kong's favorite quote from the Heart Sutra. For, she taught, human passion, like all other forms on earth, will eventually turn into emptiness. When we see that all human suffering is caused by the impermanence of form, we are led to develop compassion. And for her, compassion was the most important thing in life—not shallow passion, like romantic love.

Maybe we can cultivate emptiness, but still live in the world of form. Maybe even have a boyfriend. Or maybe, after all, I didn't have to be a nun *to be a nun*.

Now I looked at Enlightened to Emptiness and remembered what it was like to be with Michael, to be kissed by him, to feel his warmth when I lay next to him in bed. Yes, no matter how our future would turn out to be, it's fortunate to have, at least once, a man in your life.

Then I ventured another question. "Shifu, do you like being a nun?"

"Yes, this is the only life I know." She smiled, then added, "But sometimes I also feel fed up with all the rules."

"Such as?"

She started to recite quickly. "We can't eat food in overly large mouthfuls. We shouldn't open our mouths when the morsel has not arrived. We can't eat food making the *susasu, thutyut,* and *phuphphuph* sound."

When I started to laugh again, she said, "Wait, Miss Du, I haven't finished. We, not being ill, will not make excrement, urine, phlegm, or snot on green grass."

Then we collapsed in laughter.

32

The Elevator

Around two-thirty in the afternoon, Enlightened to Emptiness and I said good-bye to each other and Little Lam drove her to the airport. After that, I bid farewell to all the nuns and took a taxi back to the city.

A few hours later, I arrived at the Chengdu Golden Cow hotel. Although the pillars and moldings were all painted gold to match its title, the hotel was an eyesore. Loud and cigarette-dangling-from-lips men were talking with violent hand gestures. Exhausted mothers were yelling to their kids to behave. Shabbily uniformed staff walked around slack-mouthed, grunting . . .

As I was hauling my luggage toward the counter, to my utter shock, I saw a familiar face appearing and disappearing among milling people.

Michael? I couldn't believe my eyes. Could it be Michael right here in Chengdu, in China, in front of my eyes? Or was it a hallucination?

Then Michael's tired face and gaunt body were quickly approaching me.

"Meng Ning!" he screamed. A few people threw him curious glances.

"Michael, is that you?!" It was now my turn to scream back.

Suddenly Michael was standing in front of me. A long silence. Then he said, trying very hard to suppress his voice and seemingly rising anger, "Meng Ning, why did you just shut me out like this? Do you have any idea how much I worried about you? My heart is torn when I think of the danger you might have encountered in China—all alone in the middle of nowhere!"

Now a small group of people started to gather around to watch this free drama between a Chinese woman and an American barbarian in a cheap hotel in this Heavenly Capital—Chengdu.

"Michael, please, people are watching. Let's talk later after we've gotten a room. Please . . ."

"Fuck these people! I don't care about them, I only care about you! Haven't you realized that? If I hadn't asked your mother, I'd have never found out where you are. How can you do this to me?"

"Michael, please, I'm so sorry, so terribly sorry . . . please lower your voice and . . . can we talk later?" I was scared and pleading. I'd never seen Michael so angry before.

He demanded, "Then answer me!"

My voice came out like a wounded animal's. "I . . . just wanted some time to think things over."

"Then have you finished yet?"

"Forgive me, Michael. I'm so sorry. Please . . ."

After some time, he finally emitted a soft, "All right," then pulled me to him to plant a kiss on my forehead.

The crowd applauded and cheered.

A middle-aged woman split a big smile, while quoting a popular Chinese proverb. "Yes, when a family is harmonious, ten thousand things will be prosperous!"

A cigarette dangling between yellowish teeth, a young man echoed with another popular saying—"Yes, fighting at the head of the bed and making up at its foot!"—to another loud round of applause.

Michael cast the onlookers angry glances, then turned back to me. "Are these people making fun of me?"

"No, Michael, they're happy that we stopped fighting! Please, let's go."

In silence, we lugged our bags to the counter, behind which sat a man in a navy blue uniform and a fortyish woman.

I said, "My name is Du Meng Ning, and I have reserved a room."

The man stared hard at me, then Michael. "Are you two going to stay in separate rooms?"

I turned to translate to Michael.

He looked pained. "Now, are you saying that after I flew all the way across the Pacific to see you, you want to stay in a separate room?"

"No, that's not what I mean. I'm just translating his question."

"All right, then tell him that not only are we staying in the same room, but also the same bed." Of course I left out "the same bed."

I said to the man, feeling ill at ease, "He's staying with me in the same room."

The guy's malicious small eyes ping-ponged between me and Michael. "You're married?"

Sensing that there might be trouble coming up, I again translated our conversation to Michael.

He frowned. "Tell him that we are husband and wife."

"But—"

"Just tell him, Meng Ning."

I turned to the man. "Yes, we're married."

His response came as a surprise. "Then show me your marriage certificate."

I translated that to Michael. "Marriage certificate?" He looked very upset. "Tell him we don't have it with us."

I told the guy. Face hardened, he put on an authoritative air and said, "Then you have to stay in separate rooms."

"But we're husband and wife." My voice sounded unconvincing even to my own ears.

Without losing a beat, he shot back, "Then prove it."

"I've told you that we don't have it here."

"Then where is it?"

"Back in the United States."

"Then why are you not traveling with your American passport but with your Hong Kong Entry Permit?"

"Because I haven't gotten my passport yet. My husband and I have just been married for a few months."

We kept arguing back and forth like this for a while before I translated everything to Michael.

To my utter shock, he lost his temper. Face flushed and eyes intent, he yelled at the man in English, thrusting his open hand toward him. "Listen, I'm not going to put up with this bullshit anymore—just give us the damn key!"

I didn't think the guy understood English, but the yelling worked. With a look of humiliation he handed Michael the key.

Then, when we were walking toward the elevator, I heard him complain to the woman next to him. "It's not my problem if the police come around here tonight and she fails to show their marriage certificate. And don't blame me if they stamp 'prostitute' on her reentry permit."

"Old Zhang"—the woman chuckled—"don't forget she's with an American, so, believe me, the police won't give them any trouble."

Walking toward the elevator, I imagined all eyes were upon us, as if on my forehead were engraved two large characters: *jinu*—prostitute; and on Michael's the characters *laofan*—old barbarian.

As the elevator door closed, cutting off the piercing gazes, a sense of safety immediately flooded the confined area. In this temporary refuge, we listened to the elevator's humming and felt its rising momentum to the fifteenth floor.

"Meng Ning." Michael reached toward me, his tone now soft. "Aren't you happy that I flew all the way to see you?"

"Of course I am." I looked at his sad face and felt a surge of love swelling inside.

"But you don't act that way."

"Because I still haven't gotten over the shock of suddenly seeing your face here."

"It's because you never called to let me know where you were. Please think more about me. Meng Ning, if you're really happy to see me, then show it—"

Before he could finish, a screeching sound slashed the air and swallowed his words. Then everything went black. I felt my heart leap into my throat as if I were plunging down a precipice. But I quickly realized it was the elevator plunging.

I grabbed onto the rail and fervently prayed, "Guan Yin, now please hear our sounds and come to help!"

Memories of my fall into the well flashed across my mind.

Would I die this time? Or would I miraculously survive, as I had seventeen years ago? While silently praying to the Goddess of Mercy, I heard myself blurt out, "Michael?" and I reached for him, still holding the rail with my other arm.

Then I was knocked off my feet by a strong jolt.

Fate plays games with mortals. I'd survived the well, and now this! This would be the end of everything, nun or not nun, married or single, empty gate or dusty world. I was going to die. I was dying, and Michael . . . Oh, Michael!

But the elevator had only jolted to a stop, and I didn't die. Silence roamed tortuously through the dark, expansive confine.

I tried to reach for Michael, but my hand touched only emptiness.

"You OK, Michael?"

"You OK, Meng Ning?" Our voices sounded simultaneously in the dark.

Then his voice, now pained, arose in the eerie obscurity. "I fell. My leg hurts terribly. . . . Meng Ning, I can't see you at all!"

This was the first time that I sensed fear in him.

I groped in the dark for a few seconds before feeling his body. He grabbed my hand. Though I tried to help him up, he seemed glued to the floor.

"I don't think I can get up. My leg hurts too much."

I knelt down beside him and put my arms around his shoulders.

"My leg . . ." He sounded very upset. "Damn, they may not even realize that we're trapped here."

"I'm sure those people at the counter will get us out," I said, surprised by the sudden calmness descending on me. Seconds later, my hands started to bang on the door.

Michael joined in the banging, but feebly. I told him to save his energy and kept banging until my hands hurt. But nothing happened; we were again engulfed in a dark, ominous silence.

"Michael, let's just wait. This is a hotel—sooner or later someone is going to use the elevator."

"All right," Michael said, sounding dejected, then, "Meng Ning, please hold me."

As I reached to embrace him, a tenderness rose in me, a different sort of tenderness than I'd felt with him before. I held Michael gently, aware of his neediness and feeling warmth grow in my heart and, to my surprise, between my legs. These were feelings I'd never considered—or even knew existed—when contemplating a life inside the empty gate.

In the darkness I smelled his scent of sweat and cologne; felt the texture of his cotton shirt, his warm breath.

I nestled his head tighter against my chest. His heart felt strong—but also vulnerable—beating here with me in the dark. A feeling of deep karmic connection with Michael rippled through me.

I thought of the phrase *xinxin xiangyin,* two hearts merge in one. I had known this Buddhist saying, but it had not meant much to me. And another that I had heard only recently, the fortune-teller's saying: With absolute sincerity, even metal and stone can be opened.

It was as if the moon, pure and luminous, slowly emerged from behind a cloud to light up the dark earth. I'd fallen in the well and fallen in love with Guan Yin; now, in a shabby elevator in a cheap hotel in China, I fell in love all over again—with a man. This fall, like the earlier one, had somehow pacified my mind. In Zen it might take a blow with the master's stick to trigger insight. For me it had taken two steep falls.

I'd never imagined that Zen would lead me to a life with one of the species called "man," which I'd so despised. I'd recognized my need for people, but I hadn't realized being needed myself. Just as Yi Kong was needed by her disciples inside the empty gate. Which, however empty, was still built upon the same ground of this dusty world.

"Don't let go of me, Meng Ning, please. Ever. You're all I have in life," Michael said, his voice much calmer now.

I touched his cheek. "I won't." Then I teased, "Though, as a Buddhist, I should Let-Go-and-Be-Carefree." Let-Go-and-Be-Carefree was Michael's Buddhist name.

He let out a nervous laugh.

I asked, "How's your leg?"

"It doesn't hurt as much now. With China's five thousand years of history, how long do you think it will take before someone will rescue us?"

Just then the light was snapped on and mingled voices were heard from above. "Hey, are you people all right in there?"

I yelled back in Mandarin, "Couldn't be better!"

I looked at my watch. We were only trapped in the elevator for seven minutes. But it already felt like a whole incarnation.

As soon as Michael closed the hotel room door behind us, he hugged me. He held me so tightly it seemed as if he were trying to squeeze out anything that might be between us. The world around us seemed to fall away slowly, leaving only him and me in the cocoon of this dilapidated hotel. We clung and kissed for what seemed an entire incarnation until he finally released me.

He said, "Meng Ning, are you happy to see me?"

I touched his hollow face as my heart swelled with pain. "Of course."

"Promise me you'll never run away from me again."

"Michael, I'm so sorry." Then I lied: "I did try to call you from a public phone, but it just never connected."

"All right."

Some silence, then I asked, "Michael, how's your leg?"

"It's a bit sore, but I think it's no big deal."

"Then let's go eat. I'm hungry."

"But I have my *dim sum* . . . right here," he said as he picked me up and carried me to the bed.

"Michael," I protested, "they might hear."

But he ignored what I said.

33

The
Peach Blossom Garden

The next morning, after breakfast, Michael suggested we visit the famous Le Mountain to see the big Buddha—to pray to him to bless our reunion in China.

The taxi ride toward Leshan was bumpy and dusty, as expected. Michael stared out the window, seemingly entranced.

"There's really not much to see, Michael."

"I don't care; I just want to see China."

His enthusiasm pleased me.

Some silence, then Michael suddenly pointed out of the window. "Here's something. Meng Ning, look—maybe it's a temple."

Partially hidden in thick groves, the building looked like a modest woman peeking out to the world through a crack in the screen of her private chamber.

It wasn't in our plan, but somehow I was intrigued by the half-hidden temple. I suggested to Michael that we take a quick look.

"I was just thinking the same."

So I asked the driver to make a detour. He made a U-turn onto a meandering dirt road and followed it for another ten minutes, frequently expressing doubt that we'd find anything. Finally, we spotted a flight of narrow stone steps and he pulled up and let us out.

"Miss, I'm afraid you two have to climb your way up. I'll wait here."

Slowly Michael and I made our tortuous ascent of the steep, heaven-bound, zigzagging stairs. The day was getting hot, but luckily, heavy canopies of foliage shaded us from the sun. It took us ten minutes before we finally emerged onto level ground, sweating and panting.

Michael smiled, wiping his forehead with a handkerchief. "We made it, Meng Ning."

Dressed in running shoes, jeans, and a pale green T-shirt, Michael looked relaxed and happy, blending perfectly with the tall bamboo and its dappled, dark green shadow.

We walked along the level path until we reached a moon-shaped gate made of old gray stones, the lower portion overgrown with plants. On top of the arched structure were large Chinese characters in seal script: Universe of Empty Nature. Once through the round gate, between patches of leaves we could spy fragments of a distant temple with upturned eaves. Inhaling the fragrance of unknown blossoms, I felt far from the dusty world, as if we had just found the fabled Peach Blossom Garden.

Peach Blossom Garden, a lost Chinese utopia, was the subject of a famous poem by the Six Dynasties poet Tao Yuanming, who, at forty-five, had become disgusted by his official life and decided to become a farmer. Thereafter, he enjoyed a simple life: he tended his garden, read, drank wine when he had a few coins to pay for it, and wrote poetry.

Tao Yuanming told of a fisherman from Wuling who used to boat along a nearby river. One day, forgetful of how far he had gone, he spied a grove of blossoming peach trees. He beached his boat and entered the garden. At once he found himself inside a secluded world forgotten by time. The small village was inhabited by farm families living simple, honest lives, unaware even of the passing of the dynasties over the centuries.

Tao's poem was immensely popular over the ensuing centuries, for it spoke of a paradise where people unselfconsciously appreciated the simple joys of spring: blooming flowers, singing birds, and the clouds passing over distant peaks. The Confucian moral rules were unnecessary because the people were naturally good. All lived for more than one hundred years because of their closeness to nature and freedom from stress. As the day grew late, the fisherman returned home, intending to revisit. Yet, though he knew the river well and searched earnestly, he could never again find the Peach Blossom Garden.

We approached the temple. Red paint was peeling off the wooden pillars supporting the bluish-green roof. Beside the entrance ancient pine trees towered like guardian gods.

"Michael, come take a look," I said.

We hurried up to the temple and peeked through the wooden-latticed windows. An antique bronze Buddha, unsurprised by my intrusion, stared back at me, smiling compassionately.

"Let's go in." He took my hand and we stepped inside the court-yard.

The first thing we saw was a plum tree with pink blossoms. As we looked up at the petals, Michael started to recite, "'In the past, we frequently met in the emperor's house. Many times, I heard you sing in the grand hall. Now south of the river, I meet you in this season of falling petals.'"

It felt strange to hear Du Fu's famous poem from Michael's mouth. I sighed, feeling lost in the familiar dream of a past life where we, as lovers, had lain down in a petal-strewn, sweet-scented garden, singing and reciting poetry.

The temple floor was well swept, leaving an impression of venerable age, but not decay. There were also inscribed stone tablets. I did my best to translate to Michael those I thought would interest him.

One told the story of a young man whose beloved, a village lass, had married someone else. Having recognized the delusive nature of worldly desire, he had taken refuge in this very temple.

After my translation, Michael shook his head. "That's not a good reason to be a monk—"

Just then a gentle voice breathed at our back. "Honorable visitors, may I be of service?"

We turned and saw a muscular young monk. He was clad in a gray top and pants, with a white sash tied around his middle, perhaps a touch of vanity to accentuate his lean waist. His manner seemed refined, his bald head glowed, and intelligence emanated from his almond eyes.

Placing our hands in the prayer gesture, Michael and I bowed respectfully. Then I said, "Shifu, we've just been looking around and appreciating the temple."

With equal respect, the monk bowed back with his hands together. "Thanks, you are welcome here," he said. "I apologize that I did not meet you at the gate. It has been a long time since we have had visitors. Stay as long as you like. Please join us for tea?"

"Thank you, Shifu, we'd love to," I said, then translated our conversation to Michael, whose face lit up instantly.

We followed the young monk through another moon gate. He pointed out a stone lion, an enormous bronze incense burner, and a tower with a green encrusted bell, so ancient it looked as if it had been last struck a thousand years ago.

Then, when we passed a small pond laced with weeds, the monk stopped and pointed to what I'd thought was a stone ornament covered with moss. "My honorable guests, I would like you to meet Perfect Merit, our enlightened tortoise. We believe he is the direct descendent of that tortoise who lived on the bed of the Eastern Sea and carried the Five Divine Mountains on his back."

Before I could express my amazement, he went on. "Perfect Merit has witnessed the vicissitudes of many lives and is older than the three of us together."

I translated this to Michael, and he exclaimed, "Is that so? How old—one hundred?"

I told the monk. He raised three fingers and smiled proudly. "No, three."

I asked, "Can we touch it?"

"Sure. He's achieved wisdom and compassion."

Michael and I stooped to pat the tortoise's shell, and the spiritual creature, instead of shrinking his head, cast us a slow soulful glance, as if saying, "Please leave me alone, you deluded mortals with your worldly entanglements!"

As I drank in the beauty of the place and inhaled its mingled fragrances, a sense of purity and freedom rose inside me.

The young monk led us from the sunlight into a cool, dim hall. Following him, we crossed another threshold into a sparse interior. The wooden furniture was plain and worn smooth. On one wall hung an ink painting of Bodhidharma, the founder of Zen, with an expression warning that he had no time for nonsense.

The young monk excused himself into an adjacent room.

The feeling here was quite special; there'd been nothing like it in the large cave temple that I'd documented with Enlightened to Emptiness. It was as if I'd somehow found myself in one of the remote mountain temples in a Song dynasty landscape.

Michael's thoughts were echoing mine. "When I first looked at Chinese art, I imagined myself in a temple like this. I never thought it would really happen." Smiling, he asked, "You think we'll be able to find our way back?"

"Who cares?" I smiled. Perhaps, like me, he hoped that somehow we could live together in this simple place far from the confusion of the real world. But of course, a monastery would be the last place I could live with Michael!

A pause, then I went up to take a close look at another hanging scroll. The ink pale, the style effortless, it portrayed a dozen elegantly crisscrossing plum blossoms; in between their branches a big moon peeked through. The poem to its left read:

When cold chills every crack, purity arises.
Now I realize I was the moon in a past life.

I kept savoring "I was the moon in a past life," until Michael asked, "What is it, Meng Ning? Can you translate it for me?"

After I did, he said, "If I were the moon in a past life, then you must be the Moon Goddess Chang E, who ascended to heaven and flew into my arms."

"Sometimes I wish I were Chang E."

Michael looked puzzled. "But what of her poor husband? Meng Ning, don't go away to the moon. China is far enough away. I need you here on earth. With me."

It felt strange to me, talking of earthly desire in this isolated temple. Strange to really be wanted by a man.

We went on joking for a while before my gaze was arrested by a piece of calligraphy. I went up to take a close look at the flowing characters executed in the running style.

> So I have looped around. From the preciousness of sensation to the harmfulness of being attached to it.

Intrigued, I wondered who had written this poem and what the motivation was.

I translated to Michael and told him my thought. He said, "I think it's just another Zen poem about nonattachment."

Just then the young monk returned. With tender respect, he helped another monk, old and wrinkled, who was inching forward with a cane. As slow as the turtle, Old Monk settled down onto a chair. His brown leathery face, brown robe, and brown cane blended in with the chair and the room. If a guest entered the room now, I bet he'd have taken Old Monk merely as another piece of antique furniture!

The young monk invited us to join them at the table.

Old Monk looked at us and split a toothless smile from a mouth like a dried-up well. His eyes, though yellowed and clouded, still penetrated, as if transmitting the law of Dharma directly from his mind.

Young Monk was now busy arranging the teapot, teacups, and dried fruit. When finished, he knelt at the altar table, muttered a short prayer, then offered his tea and fruit to the Buddha with utmost piety and respect.

I felt moved by this act of sincerity and devotion.

Then he poured another cup of tea and went to the old monk. To my surprise, he knelt down and offered him tea with the same piety and respect he'd paid to the Buddha.

After these offerings, the young monk, now looking relaxed, poured us steaming tea. Then he introduced the old monk to us as Master Detached Dust and himself as Eternal Brightness. Old Monk responded with an innocent smile.

Eternal Brightness said, "In comparison to our tortoise, my

Master Detached Dust is quite a young man at only one hundred and five."

I translated this to Michael. He exclaimed disbelief, but then bowed respectfully to Detached Dust. And, I believed, to the mystery of his longevity.

Suddenly the master spoke. "Do you two watch TV?"

This question from a one-hundred-and-five-year-old Zen monk recluse really took me by surprise—he should have long transcended the seven emotions and the five desires.

I translated to Michael. He said, "I feel sorry for him; he must be extremely lonely here."

Then I turned back to Detached Dust. "We have a TV, but we don't watch much."

The master surprised me again by saying, "I've heard about it, but I've never seen it."

"Master, you mean never in your whole life, not even *once?*"

"No."

Now this living fossil really intrigued me. "Aren't you curious to watch TV?"

Instead of directly answering my question, he smiled contentedly. "I have my garden, my *sutras,* the sky and the clouds."

I translated this to Michael and he said, "Ask him whether he's bored sometimes."

I turned and asked the master.

His reply was, "Night after night the moon shines on the pond."

Eternal Brightness eagerly chimed in. "Since his youth, Master's eyesight has been weak," as if an apology were needed for Master's not watching TV, and not connecting to the modern world.

"Then how can he read his *sutras?*" I asked.

"He'd already memorized most of them before he reached twenty." He paused, then added, "But Master possesses the Buddha eye."

I translated this to Michael and he nodded, looking deep in thought.

A brief silence. Then the young monk stood up, went to the cauldron, and held out a bamboo tray on top of which lay fat, snowy-white buns. The bun, hot and steaming in my hands, seemed alive and palpitating.

Michael, probably very hungry by now after our long climb under the sun, was devouring the bun and gulping down the tea with relish.

"Mmm." He raised his thumb to the monks.

Eternal Brightness smiled back politely, while Master Detached Dust cupped his mouth with his gnarled hand and giggled.

Then, seeing that I was not eating, Detached Dust cast me a meaningful glance. "Miss, eat! Eat while it's still hot." Then he added, "Don't wait till it gets cool."

Was it a metaphor for my being indecisive about marrying Michael?

I smiled at him, then split open the bun. Paste of red beans spilled to peek at the world outside and immediately I stuck out my tongue to take them into this Mortal's Field of Red Hot Passion.

When we finished our snack, Master Detached Dust said, "Honorable guests, I now have to work."

Work? At one hundred and five?

Seeing that I was staring doubtfully at his master, the young monk explained, "Master is going to tend to his garden." After that, he helped Detached Dust outside.

I told Michael about my conversation with the monks while we, amazed, watched Detached Dust at work. Though slow in his movements, he transmitted his special energy, his whole being spilling happiness. He moved deliberately but with a carefree air, watering, pulling out dead roots, cutting off yellowed leaves. He seemed not to feel the hot sun over his head or the baking earth under his straw-sandaled feet. He chanted in a faint voice as he went about his work.

Michael exclaimed, "Amazing! I hope I will live to his age and stay that active."

When Eternal Brightness came back to the room, I asked, "Shifu, don't you think that Master Detached Dust should . . . retire?"

"I've begged Master many times not to work, but his reply is always to recite the Zen rule: a day without work is a day without food. So"—the young monk shrugged and smiled wryly—"there's nothing I can do. He always tells me that by cultivating the garden, he's cultivating the Way. So how can he stop?" A pause, then,

"Master says that he's the guest of wind and dust. And his mind the ashes of dead fire."

We stood together watching Detached Dust.

Then Eternal Brightness spoke. "I must work also. Please stay in our temple as long as you like."

Suddenly I remembered the stone inscription in the main hall. "Shifu, that inscription about the young man who fell in love with a village girl, then took refuge after she'd married someone else . . ."

The monk had already guessed my question. "That young man is my master, Detached Dust."

I was shocked to hear this. "Oh," I blurted out, "what a sad story."

The young monk cast me a curious glance, then corrected me. "No. Master determined to cut off all attachment after he realized his folly of falling into the entanglement of human desire." He pointed to the calligraphy and recited, "'So I have looped around. From the preciousness of sensation to the harmfulness of being attached to it.'"

He turned to look out the window. "So look how happy Master is now." He smiled. "Moreover, that's why he lived to this ripe age."

I followed Eternal Brightness's affectionate gaze and saw Detached Dust now talking cheerily to an orchid.

"It's Master's habit to recite his mantra of Amita Buddha to the plants and rocks here. He believes they also have Buddha nature."

I turned back to the young monk. "So, Shifu, is this also the same reason you're . . . here?"

His face beamed. "Oh, yes. I am extremely fortunate, for Master was very strict in choosing his disciple."

Just then the old monk came in, studied each of us, and split a big, panting smile. "Tomorrow is another day; I'll take a nap today."

Eternal Brightness hurried to help him go back to his room.

After I'd translated everything to Michael, he said, "No matter how hard monks and nuns try to cut off from worldly desire, love still sneaks its way back in."

"What do you mean?"

Michael answered my question with another one. "The monk's love story is inscribed here in the temple, right?"

Not wishing to further disturb the two monks, we took our leave. The young monk walked us all the way to the level land and the steps.

Michael and I bowed deeply with our hands together. I said, "Thank you, Shifu. We really appreciate your and Master Detached Dust's hospitality."

Under the warm sun, his tanned, healthy face seemed to shine with wisdom and detachment. "You're welcome. Please come back and visit us again."

"We certainly will."

Michael asked me to tell him that he really enjoyed his bun and that he wished the Master good health and longevity.

I told the young monk and he said, "Thank you, but the master's health and longevity depend on karma, not men's wishes." A pause. Then he added, "By the way, it's master who cooked those buns, not me."

We silently picked our way down the long flight of steps. I felt depressed to leave this separate world of the small temple and plunge back into the dusty world.

Michael took my hand. "Meng Ning, let's hurry to the taxi. It's going to rain."

At the bottom of the steps, our taxi driver was fast asleep, curled up in the backseat. As we began to quicken our steps, the rain was already pelting mercilessly. We pounded on the door of the taxi, awakening the surprised driver, who quickly got out and let us, now dripping, into the back. Through the smudged window I watched the raindrops plunge, hiss, and bounce on the ground. I felt a rush of nostalgia. Their natural energy made me think of the two mountain monks. Their temple, though only up the nearby flight of steps, already seemed so distant. Would we have the chance to return to that simple beauty in this lifetime?

34

The Car Accident

After the pleasant diversion of the Peach Blossom Garden, we were now finally heading toward the famous colossal Buddha carved into the Le Mountain. As we drove, the rain abated.

The taxi driver caught my gaze in the rearview mirror. "Miss, you and your friend had a good time up there?"

"Oh, yes." I made my answer short, for I didn't want to share my intimate temple experience with this stranger.

But the driver couldn't keep quiet for long. As the car bounced up and down over potholes, he began to tell us stories about the big Buddha carved out of the Le Mountain. His eyes, flickering behind his thick glasses, kept peeking at us in the rearview mirror.

In a dramatic tone, he began. "Believe it or not, this Leshan statue is *really* a Buddha." Then he paused, for suspense, I believed.

I asked, "What do you mean?"

"Ah, you've never heard anything about it?"

"No," I answered abruptly. Still savoring my other-worldly experience, I wanted to be left alone.

Michael asked, "Meng Ning, what did he say?"

"Nothing."

"What do you mean, nothing? He surely is talking a lot."

The driver asked, "What did your *laowai* friend say?"

"He wants to know what you said."

He chuckled and paused to think. "Ah, so your *laowai* friend hasn't heard anything about it neither, eh?"

"I don't know, but one thing I'm sure about—" I could hear irritation in my own voice. "My old barbarian friend knows more about Buddhism than you do."

Instead of being offended, he smiled, his large, neurotic eyes locking my gaze in the mirror. "Ah, but I don't think so. I'm sure he doesn't know the fact that this Leshan statue is a real Buddha."

Feeling really annoyed now, my voice raised an octave. "Driver, just tell me what this 'Leshan statue is a real Buddha' is all about."

Michael took my hand. "Meng Ning, what's the matter? What did he say to annoy you?"

"Nothing."

Just then the driver spoke again. "When I say the statue is a real Buddha, I mean that it's alive with a spirit."

Now he had my attention. He paused to wet his thick lips, the color of coagulated blood. "During the Cultural Revolution, many times people tried to destroy the Leshan Buddha, but all failed."

"What did they do?"

"They climbed up the statue—that is, the mountain top—and tried to chop off his head."

"But that head's the size of a small house!" I'd seen many pictures of the famous Buddha.

"No, not that, miss." He chuckled. "It's because each time they tried, something happened—a comrade fell off the mountain and got killed; another seized by a panic so that he had to be carried down the mountain; yet another one had a massive heart attack and died on the spot. Finally the vandals agreed that chopping was impractical. A new idea was born; they climbed up the statue and tied sticks of dynamite around the Buddha's head—"

"Oh, no! Then what happened?"

Michael turned to me. "Please translate what he said!"

"Shhh! Let me hear the whole story first."

I prodded the driver: "Then what happened?"

"Be patient, miss. That's what I'm about to tell you." He took time to wet his lips, swallow hard, and after that, plunged on. "Then, when they tried to detonate the dynamite, it thundered. It had been a fine day, but suddenly there was a bolt of lightning!" He struck the steering wheel sharply. "And—"

Michael jolted. "Meng Ning, what happened?"

"Quiet, please, Michael, would you please let him finish?"

"I want to know what he's saying."

I ignored Michael's remark while searching the driver's eyes in the mirror. "And what?"

"And it struck everybody dead. Dead!" He spat out the window, then he lifted his hands from the steering wheel and stretched them wide apart, his excited voice echoing in the small confines of the car. "Their corpses looked like huge, roasted sausages!"

"Oh, my God!"

Michael's voice, now very upset, rose next to me. "Meng Ning, when you talk to him he takes his hands from the steering wheel—better stop asking him things. The road is still wet and slippery."

Just when I was about to warn the driver, deafening honks exploded. To my horror, I saw a car speeding toward us from the opposite lane. Our taxi swerved sharply and we all skidded to the side of the road.

Our driver stuck his head out and hollered, "You son of a bitch! Couldn't you wait to register with the King of Hell?!"

The other driver shot him a murderous look. "You dead man!"

He shot back, "Fuck your mother and stop driving like a lunatic!"

After that, he resumed driving, while casting a triumphant smile toward us in the rearview mirror.

"Jesus!" exclaimed Michael; then he patted hard on the driver's shoulder. "Would you please concentrate on the road and drive more carefully?"

The driver turned to ask me, "What did your *laowai* friend say?"

Before I could answer, Michael was fuming again. "Meng Ning, won't you tell him not to turn his head back, but instead look at the road ahead?!"

I told the driver and he said, "All right, all right. Miss, tell your *laowai* friend not to worry; I'm a very experienced driver." He added with a casual air, "I talk to my passengers all the time and nothing's ever happened."

A brief silence followed. I took the opportunity to translate to Michael everything the driver had told me about the Buddha.

Michael listened intently, and then, to my surprise, dismissed it with a laugh. "It's not at all Buddhist. Buddhas don't kill people."

Not wanting to incur Michael's wrath by distracting the driver, I kept my mouth shut.

But not the driver; he spoke again. "Miss, you know that the Leshan Buddha always responds to people's wishes?"

"What do you mean?"

"Many years ago before it was built, boats, when sailing past this mountain, had capsized. Then the villagers decided to carve a Buddha out of the whole mountain to subdue the devils. And after the statue was built, there have been no more accidents."

I translated this to Michael. He said, "It's nice that people believe that, but I think it's just coincidence."

"Michael, you're too scientifically minded. I like the idea."

"Actually, I sort of like it, too." He smiled.

A long meditative silence followed. Then the driver spoke again, this time turning back to stare directly at me. "Miss, if you ever have a chance to look this Leshan Buddha straight in his eyes, you'll find that they'll follow you wherever you go. Besides, if you stare at him long enough, you can see that he smiles—"

"Meng Ning. Is there some way you can convince him to keep his eyes on the road?"

After I'd translated to the driver, he chuckled. "Miss, *laowai* are famous for being nervous. Tell your friend to relax."

"Why don't you pay attention—then my friend will relax," I said, then translated to Michael.

"Good," he replied.

I started to translate our earlier conversation, but our driver turned back again, with a wide grin that showed a jumble of yellowed teeth. "Oh, miss, don't you worry about me. I started to drive thirty years ago, probably before you were born—"

Suddenly Michael screamed, "Watch out!" and pulled me toward him.

I saw a tall truck, like a mountain wall, crashing toward our taxi at full speed. In a split second, I heard frenzied honks, squealing of tires . . .

I didn't know how long I remained unconscious, but when I opened my eyes, the whole world seemed tilted. People—like phantoms—moved, talked, and hollered around our taxi in slow motion.

The driver, his glasses cracked and his forehead cut and bleeding, turned and muttered something comforting, but his words were lost in the buzzing and bustling of the people around us. My bones felt as if they were broken. Before I had a chance to gather up my thoughts, I saw rivulets of blood streaming from underneath me onto the floor.

I shrieked, "I'm bleeding!"

The driver spoke, his hand dabbing his forehead with a blood-stained handkerchief, "It's not you, miss. I think it's your friend."

It was then that I realized the blood was not mine, but Michael's. He sprawled next to me, unconscious.

I reached to touch him with my trembling hand. "Michael . . ."

But he didn't answer me and his eyes remained closed. A nerdy-looking man, his body half inside and half outside the car, was trying to stop Michael's bleeding with a filthy rag. Several others milled around giving useless suggestions.

"Oh, my God, Michael, Michael . . ." I touched him, but soon my mind was numbed by the quickly growing group of people now hovering around the car like vultures.

The driver got out of the car and moved toward me in the backseat. "Don't worry, miss, I think your *laowai* friend will be all right. I never hurt anyone with my driving."

"Shut up!" I yelled. "If you'd paid more attention—"

I lifted Michael's head, laid it on my lap, and gently rocked.

"Don't move him!" someone yelled as more people crowded around us to watch—as if we were animals on display.

Then I heard sirens wailing. Two policemen rolled up and got out of their car to look at us. Another police car arrived and more khaki-uniformed policemen jumped out and started to direct traffic. The crowd grew as thick and dark as the coagulating blood.

One fiftyish woman gestured wildly. "My heaven! Blood spilled out of the *laowai* like a slaughtered pig!"

A teenager slashed the air with a wide arc of his arm. "Wow! The truck driver flew up in the air just like a stuntman!"

I cried more.

Our taxi driver yelled to them, "Why don't you both shut up!"

I didn't hear the rest of the conversation. I kept holding Michael and involuntarily began to recite Guan Yin's name.

Right then the ambulance's piercing sirens overrode the crowd's noise. Several uniformed men jumped down from the vehicle and got to work. They put Michael and the truck driver on stretchers, threw blankets over them, then carried them into the ambulance. After that, they helped the taxi driver and me in. Then the ambulance sped away and brought us to the hospital.

To my great relief, Michael finally woke up. But because of all the commotion, we couldn't really hear each other talk. I felt a huge weight lifted from my chest when the doctor told me that his life was not in danger. He had a sprained ankle and a big cut on his scalp, which took twenty stitches to close, but fortunately, the X-rays showed no skull fracture. Because he had been unconscious, the ER doctor decided to keep him for observation.

I only had a few bruises and scrapes. After a wait of two hours, a young doctor in a stained, off-white coat quickly bandaged me and told me I could leave.

But I was not finished with the accident yet. Two policemen came and took me to the police station to give details of the accident and to verify both Michael's and my identity and the purpose of our trip. After that, I went back to the hospital. Michael, though awake and lying in bed, looked very weak and ill at ease. He asked where I'd been, and when I told him, he looked both angry and touched. "Meng Ning"—he reached to grasp my hand—"I'm sorry you have to go through all this."

A silence. Then when I was about to say something comforting, he'd already fallen back to sleep. While I stared at his bandaged head and his shrunken face, I kept telling myself that now I was no longer a young girl protected inside the Golden Lotus Temple.

That I was a woman responsible for Michael's recovery. That I had to be strong. Now, in China, where it was just him and me.

The hospital staff wouldn't allow me to stay overnight to keep Michael company, so I left the hospital at ten. A young nurse was kind enough to help me call for a taxi back to the hotel.

I cried my heart out in the dimness of the car. The driver, a fierce-looking man, scrutinized me in the rearview mirror and spat out, "You all right?"

I shot back, "Just let me cry in peace, will you?"

To my surprise, he shut up.

∽35∽

The Hospital

First thing next morning, I took a taxi to see Michael in the hospital. The large establishment was shabby, crowded, and stank of medicine. Beds were everywhere, not only in the wards but even along the corridors. Careful not to step on an outstretched arm or leg, I walked to the nurse's station and asked a skinny, bespectacled nurse the whereabouts of Michael.

"Bed number fifty-nine," she said after flipping through a few pages of the thick registration book; then she scrutinized me for long moments. "You're his girlfriend?"

I nodded.

"Then tell your boyfriend to be more cooperative with the doctors."

"What did he do?"

She didn't really answer my question. "Just tell him to show some respect for the second largest hospital in Chengdu."

Michael was asleep despite the noise around him. His neighbors, a fortyish man and an old woman, were engaged in a loud conversation. I went up to his bed, put down a plastic bag of fruit I'd bought at a stall in front of the hospital, then quietly pulled out a chair and sat down beside him.

While my eyes were caressing Michael's face, I was conscious of the curious glances cast in our direction.

Michael's head was bandaged and his face and chest, exposed above the white bed sheet, looked as gaunt as a chiseled bust. I watched the slight quivering of his lashes and the soft rise and fall of his chest. Seeing his masculine body now weakened almost like a child's, tears stung my eyes and rolled down my cheeks.

I'd been hearing all my life how the Buddha taught that life is uncertain. But it was different to see Michael, whom I'd blamed for always being in control of everything, now looking so fragile. Had it been just a little different, Michael would be as dead as Professor Fulton. Just as he lost his professor, I could lose him. As I was thinking, Master Detached Dust's husky voice suddenly rang loud and clear in my ear.

Eat while it's still hot.
Don't wait till it gets cool!

Had the old, wrinkled sage's words been intended as a Zen lesson for me?

Then a poem emerged in my mind:

Enjoy life to the full while you still can, never let the empty
wine glass face the solitary moon.

But how to enjoy it to the full? It seems so clear in poems, but not in my life. Then I remembered Michael's poem, *"All these thirty-eight years, all empty now, can the rest be full?"*

I wiped my tears, then took off my Guan Yin pendant to hold it in my hand and, just when I was about to recite the Heart Sutra to protect Michael, the middle-aged man, who'd been watching me as had the old woman, threw me a question. "Miss, this *laowai* your friend?"

I nodded.

He grinned insinuatingly. "Your boyfriend?"

I nodded again, feeling annoyed.

Now the old woman chimed in: "Miss, you're lucky to have a *laowai* boyfriend. Soon emigrate to America, huh?"

I really didn't know how to reply, so I returned a wry smile.

She went on. "Lucky you, miss, your boyfriend's handsome, too."

"Thanks," I muttered. *Please leave me alone!*

Now it was the man's turn. "But he's not well-behaved. He refused to take medicine last night."

"Oh, did he?"

"Yes. They were going to give him an injection, but he wouldn't let them."

I perked up my ears. "Then what happened?"

The old woman said, her cloudy eyes animated, "Your boyfriend had a big argument with the doctors and the hospital staff."

"What did they argue about?"

"I don't know." Old Woman cast a glance at her comrade. "We only understand the doctors; don't understand English."

The man's eyes brightened. "Finally the head doctor himself came, and tried to persuade your friend, but he screamed at the doctor." He looked at me to see my reaction, then went on. "Head Doctor Zhou was very mad. Just stalked out. Assistant doctor upset, too. Said, *'Hai, laowai* always means headache.'"

Now Old Woman looked at me and asked eagerly, "My daughter always wants to go to America—can your boyfriend give her English lessons?"

In order not to be rude, I said, "I don't know; you better ask him yourself."

"Good. Then you ask him for me when he wakes up."

Now the man cast his comrade a chiding glance. "Old Mother, I think we should stop bothering this young miss."

"All right, all right, I'll shut up." Pouting, she lay back on the bed, pulled up her blanket, and closed her eyes. Feigning sleep, I supposed.

The man unfolded his newspaper and began to read.

I took out the small book with the Heart Sutra that Yi Kong had given me and began to read it softly.

I'd been reciting and asking Guan Yin to grant Michael a quick recovery for I didn't know how long, when I heard a weak, "Meng Ning."

"Michael?" I put down my Guan Yin and the sutra on the bed.

Forehead wet with perspiration, Michael tried to sit up.

I grasped his arm. "Michael, let me help you."

He looked at me. "Meng Ning?"

"Yes, Michael." I touched his face and felt the bone. His cheeks were so sunken that it seemed to me his eyes were the only feature left on his face.

"How do you feel? How's your head?" My heart sank when I suddenly noticed his bandaged leg. "What about your leg?"

"I had a terrible headache last night, but it's not as bad now. My ankle is twisted." Then he pulled me close, wincing as he moved his arm.

"I was told you had a fight with the doctors."

"Not exactly a fight. I was just so frustrated that they wanted to give me an injection I didn't need. So maybe I raised my voice a little."

A silence, then I touched his cheek.

"When I woke up this morning, they served me some kind of meat porridge, so I refused to eat. Then when I asked for something vegetarian, no one understood me; they thought I was just being difficult. I felt completely helpless and scared. I'm a total stranger here and no one seems to care about me."

"But I'm here with you now, Michael, so you'll be all right."

He went on as if talking to himself. "I remembered how my parents died when I was young, leaving me all by myself. Meng Ning"— he put my hand to his lips—"the thought that I might lose you was so unbearable. . . ."

"But, Michael, I'm here and I'm all right!" I squeezed his large hand, which now seemed so vulnerable in mine. Then I felt something shift in my mind, something that perhaps I'd sensed but pushed out. I was no more the little girl protected and pampered in Golden Lotus Temple, but had to be a strong woman to help Michael recover in a place where he could not even speak to anyone but me. Overnight, our roles seemed reversed—now I was his guardian goddess, and he the child thrust under my protection.

One tear fell from the corner of Michael's eye and spilled onto the sutra.

"Damn," he groaned, picking up the book.

"It's all right, Michael." I took the book from him and examined it. The tear smeared right at the phrase "reflecting that all the five elements are but emptiness, transcending all sufferings." I showed it to him. "See, Guan Yin says we'll transcend all sufferings."

"I hope so," Michael said, looking lost in thought.

"I'm sure we will."

For the first time that day he smiled and the dingy hospital room seemed brighter.

At that moment, I felt overwhelmed with love for him. Suddenly I was almost glad about the car accident. I finally saw a place in his life—for Michael was not totally self-sufficient as I'd thought. Maybe nobody is. Even Yi Kong needed Sunny Au, the fat, vulgar protector of the Dharma. While I looked down at his now almost boyish face, the fortune-teller's words popped into my mind:

Inside you there's a spring of young yin *energy that you should put to good use by helping your friend. . . . He not only needs you, he needs the* woman *in you, not the little girl.*

Just then Old Mother poked her head toward us and asked, "Miss, can you now ask your boyfriend if he can teach my daughter English?"

Her comrade pulled her back and chided her. "Old Mother, stop your nonsense and let this miss talk with her boyfriend."

"My fiancé." This time I corrected him.

Although Michael didn't understand Chinese and had been in a rotten mood, he nevertheless smiled warmly at the two and said, "It's all right."

Old Mother threw another unexpected, irrelevant question. "Miss, you find everything you need?"

There was some silence before I said, softly, "Yes, and more."

❧ 36 ❧

The Missing Temple

Before we left for Hong Kong, Michael and I decided to visit Master Detached Dust and Eternal Brightness in their hidden temple once more.

We took a taxi and went by the place where we thought we'd first seen it. But it wasn't there. In one place, thinking we could see a corner of the old temple through a gap in the dense bamboo, we asked our driver to stop. Yet when we got out, to our disappointment, there was no sign of the path we had taken before. Unwilling to give up, we went back to the hospital to try to find our taxi driver. But he was not there. When we asked the porter at the hospital, he told us, "He left and we don't know where he is. Anyway, even if you could find him it's still no use, because I'm sure his license is already suspended because of the accident. Maybe they put him in jail."

PART FOUR

❦ 37 ❦

Bad Karma

After a few more days' rest in Hong Kong, Michael felt well enough to go back to the States. Before he left, we'd talked about our wedding plans. Now I wondered why I had ever thought of breaking the engagement and leaving him!

Suddenly there were all kinds of things to do. I knew I would have to ask Yi Kong to officiate at our Buddhist marriage ceremony, but in the meantime I occupied myself making arrangements: printing of invitation cards, trying on bridal dresses, ordering the banquet at a vegetarian restaurant. I was also desperate to see Dai Nam. Once back in Hong Kong, guilt welled up in me that my own karmic entanglements had kept me from doing much to comfort her after her attempted suicide.

One morning I took the MTR to Mong Kok, and from there changed to the train out to Golden Lotus Temple. I hurried past the stone garden and headed straight to Dai Nam's dormitory. To my surprise, I found her room empty. Alarmed, I half ran to the temple's new office compound to look for Enlightened to Emptiness. The young novice was arranging photographs of Guan Yin paintings on the desk. After we'd exchanged greetings and pleasantries, I plunged in and asked her about Dai Nam.

"The week after I came back from Chengdu, Wonderful Countenance Shifu left for China."

"Why, what happened?"

"Nothing special. Shifu refuses to talk." She frowned. "Shifu told us—in writing, I mean—that she wanted to go back to China to practice closed-door meditation."

"Did she say exactly where she was going?"

"No, you know Shifu . . . but don't worry, Miss Du. I'm sure she'll turn up again someday." Then she pointed to a photograph depicting a white-robed Guan Yin leaning on a rock by the river and asked, "You like this? This is Yi Kong Shifu's favorite Guan Yin painting. She's now in Suzhou. She said she'd see you later."

I was not really listening and barely glanced at the picture. My heart started to pound. I hoped Dai Nam was not trying to imitate the now mummified Revealing Mystery, who hadn't spoken, eaten, nor slept for her last fifteen years.

I thanked Enlightened to Emptiness, quickly left the office, and strolled to the stone garden. To relax, I inhaled the smell of the lush vegetation, appreciated the smoothly shaped stones, and listened to the poetic murmuring of the fountain. Then I realized I was not alone in the garden. The old woman, Chan Lan—Dai Nam's great-aunt—was sitting on my favorite carp-viewing bench. My heart raced. Maybe she knew where Dai Nam was. I hurried to sit down by her side. A trail of bubbles spread out along the water as a fat carp surfaced and flapped its tail as if to greet me.

"*Ah-po,* how are you today? Why aren't you practicing *qigong?*" Energy exercise.

Chan Lan smiled her toothless smile. "Just finished." She leaned close to stare at me. "Are you the pretty, unmarried girl?"

"I'm unmarried, but . . . I don't think I'm—" I patted her hand. "You have an excellent memory, *Ah-po.*"

She shook her head. "No good now, used to be excellent, can remember my grand-niece's birthday, the date she arrived in Hong Kong, the date I paid one thousand dollars to buy her passport . . ." She stopped.

I seized the chance to ask, "You mean Dai Nam? How is she? Where is she now?"

"No good. Doesn't talk and went to China."

"Because she wants to practice meditation on the mountain?"

"No." Chan Lan chuckled. "She went back to see her boyfriend."

This was not what I had expected to hear.

"*Ah-po,* I think you're mistaken, for she doesn't have a boyfriend. She's a nun!"

Chan Lan nodded emphatically, like a child trying to prove her innocence when accused of lying. "She does; he died long time."

I muttered to myself, "Dai Nam went to China to see her dead boyfriend?"

Chan Lan turned to stare at the fountain, her gaze becoming abstract. I forced myself to keep quiet and wait for her to speak again. Only the sound of water and an occasional croaking of a frog interrupted our silence.

"She was nineteen, the boy much younger, only fifteen. Poor couple! No good!" Her voice sounded as shrill and excited as a five-year-old's.

I asked softly, fearing that if I acted too eager I'd scare her out of talking, "I'm so sorry . . . how . . . did this happen?"

Chan Lan looked at me; her eyes flickered mischievously. "You don't know?"

"No, I don't. Please tell me. I'm her friend from Paris."

"Ah, Ba Li, yes, of course, my niece hates Ba Li. She said no good, too cold, no friend, no money, only arthritis—"

"But, *Ah-po,* you were telling me about Dai Nam's boyfriend."

Chan Lan's shrill laughter pierced through the humid air. "Ah, yes. See, my memory no good now. I used to remember my niece's birthday, my daughter's death day, my—"

"*Ah-po,* Dai Nam's boyfriend, how did he die?"

"Ah, sad, very sad." Chan Lan scratched her scanty white hair with her clawlike fingers. Then she hid her mouth with her hand and whispered into my ear, "Drowned."

My heart flipped, then suddenly something connected. "Was he drowned while swimming with Dai Nam to Hong Kong?"

"Yes, yes, miss, you're so smart." Chan Lan turned to look at me directly. "Swam seven times together and failed, succeeded at the eighth."

I was confused again. Was that boyfriend of Dai Nam's dead or alive?

"But, *Ah-po,* didn't you just tell me that he was drowned?"

Again she nodded emphatically. "Yes, but body arrived."

"You mean . . ." I felt a small explosion inside me as I spat out, "Dai Nam carried his body all the way to Hong Kong?"

"Yes, strong girl, eh?" Chan Lan touched my arm with her bony claws. "Carried body and swam for many miles." She leaned close to whisper into my ear, "Not only that, only half body arrived."

"How come?"

"Other half eaten by sharks. Bad sharks!"

My eyes stung. "Then how come the sharks didn't attack her?"

"Dai Nam lost him midway. Swam back for him but only half was left. Half still better than nothing, right, miss? So Dai Nam carried the shark's leftover dinner to Hong Kong. Hard trip, eh? But she had to because she'd made a promise."

"What promise?"

Chan Lan chuckled, then covered her mouth. "Miss, do I have bad breath?"

"No, *Ah-po,* you're fine. Please tell me what promise Dai Nam made to her boyfriend."

Something like a giggle wheezed from the space between her few teeth. "Ah, you don't know?"

Now I was starting to think of throwing this centenarian to the sharks. But then she spoke in time to relieve my frustration. "They took an oath that they'd swim together to Hong Kong. If one died, the living one would still carry the other to freedom." Suddenly Chan Lan looked sad. "Ah, shouldn't have sworn like this—bad luck—so it did happen!"

I patted her hand. "But it's all over now, *Ah-po.*"

"Hai!" Chan Lan sighed. "If the man hadn't died, my niece wouldn't have become a nun."

Of course. Then Dai Nam would have gotten married and had children, many many.

"Is that why she became a nun?"

"You bet. She said very painful. She told me if she is a nun, she won't attach." Chan Lan studied me for a few seconds. "Miss, you're smart; do you think they should make that promise?"

I didn't respond. I was immersed in my own thoughts. Now all the puzzles about Dai Nam seemed to be falling into place. The strenuous cultivation of nonattachment. The agitation behind her seemingly emotionless face. The attractiveness hidden under her plain, oversized clothes and thick glasses. The cold demeanor to seal in her mental turmoil. Burning off her fingers to show nonattachment. Forcing open her third eye to be able to see ghosts—perhaps her boyfriend's ghost. Her black-painted room. Her awkward squatting poses. Even her suicide attempt was not because she'd broken her vow by eating the wrong cake, but because she was still suffering.

Only at the moment she had pushed herself to the threshold of death was she relieved of her pain.

Buddhists say "to die in order to live." Suddenly I felt a swell of great compassion for my friend, together with admiration for her love and courage.

I turned back to Chan Lan. "*Ah-po,* since Dai Nam's boyfriend is dead, how can she go to see him?"

"Yes, yes, of course she can!" Chan Lan nodded her head like a pestle hitting on a mortar. "Boyfriend's grave overgrown with weeds. She went back to tend to it. Gone—three years' mourning. Also, my nephew—her father—died."

Now I understood. Chan Lan must have confused Dai Nam's departure for China now, with her departure a few years ago.

I put one of Chan Lan's stray hairs into place. "Dai Nam must have loved her boyfriend very dearly."

Chan Lan spoke again in her shrill, girlish voice. "Yes, yes. She told me the only man good and bad to her in China."

"What do you mean, good and *bad?*"

"Ah, you don't know?" Chan Lan's eyes twinkled. "He ruined her face when he was a kid; then he repaid his bad karma by being nice to her." She made a face. "But then he was drowned, so still too much bad karma unpaid!"

I felt a jolt inside. So Dai Nam's lover was the little boy who'd slashed her face for no reason and left her with the big scar?

Right then a nun approached us, smiling generously and beginning to tease her. "Ah, Chan Lan, you're gossiping again. Don't you know it's time for lunch? The other *ah-pos* are all waiting for you." The nun turned to me, still smiling. "Sorry, miss, it's time for lunch; maybe you can come back and talk to her later?"

As the nun helped Chan Lan to leave, I put my hands together and bowed slightly to both of them.

Chan Lan waved her bony hand, chuckling. "Miss, get married soon and have children, many many." When she was a few steps away, she turned back. "When you grow old, it's still better than talking to the four bare walls!"

The nun chided her affectionately. "*Ai-ya!* Chan Lan, stop lecturing others all the time!"

Watching the nun's and Chan Lan's receding backs, I felt tears roll down my cheeks. Michael's image emerged clearly in my mind. Again the clouds vanished and the full moon shone, silently reminding me that life is fragile and true love hard to find.

I swore that I would never let go of Let-Go-and-Be-Carefree.

❦ 38 ❧

Confessions

The next day after my meeting with Dai Nam's great-aunt, I asked Mother to sit down with me to plan for the wedding.

She looked uncomfortable.

"Ma, aren't you happy that I'm getting married?"

"Of course. But . . ." She sighed. "I worry because he's a *gweilo*."

"Ma, stop being racist! What's the difference, as long as Michael's a nice person? Besides, don't worry that you can't get along with him. He knows more about Chinese culture than most Chinese do."

Mother still looked upset.

Then I told her about Michael's erudition in Chinese philosophy and art, that he was a good doctor, and finally, how he had saved my life during the fire in the Fragrant Spirit Temple.

"Ah! This *gweilo* saved your life?"

"Ma, I've told you his name is Michael."

"All right, Mic Ko! So this Mic Ko saved your life and you've never told me that." She paused, seemingly in deep meditation; then suddenly her eyes widened. "But you know what? I think it's because you're a lucky girl. Remember the villagers in Yuen Long regarded you as the reincarnation of Guan Yin? That's why nothing can harm you. First you fell into the well, then this fire. Ah, so lucky, the Goddess of Mercy!" Mother looked at me admiringly while putting a strand of hair on my forehead in place. "So I think you're the one who saved his life."

"Ma, don't be ridiculous, how—"

"Why do daughters never listen to their mothers?" Mother sighed, shaking her head. "Because your aura protected him and made him do the right thing, that's how."

I wanted to argue, but stopped myself. If that was what she would like to think, why shouldn't I just let her enjoy her own notions?

"All right Ma, I saved his life." I chuckled. "Now why don't we start to plan for the wedding?"

Without answering me, Mother shot up from the sofa, dashed inside the bedroom, returned with a book in her hand, and plopped it down on the coffee table in front of me.

"What's that?"

"Tong Sheng, silly girl," Mother chided affectionately. "You think I'm not thinking about your wedding? I've got everything ready."

I flipped through the book—Tong Sheng, literally "Sure Win," is the most popular almanac for Chinese astrology. Mother always kept it in the house so she could look up and pick auspicious days, sometimes even moments, to do things right.

For Chinese, picking the right date is essential: for getting married, naming a new baby, starting a business, even starting a fire in the stove or getting a haircut.

"Thank you, Ma," I said, and, to show my respect for her, helped her to sit down on the sofa.

Then Mother and I, two generations with the same face yet different temperaments, sat beside each other in a respectful manner and turned the pages of destiny.

For the first time we became of one heart and one mind.

"Wait just another moment," Mother said. This time she hurried into the kitchen and returned with a tray.

She generously covered the coffee table with snacks, her favorites: roast melon seed, fried shrimp chips, pig-fat sweet cake, egg tart; and my favorites: Cadbury's Fruit & Nut milk chocolate, peanuts coated with fried fish skin, and preserved plums. To my surprise, she even brought out a dozen of my adored ginger flowers.

"To purify the air for relaxation," she said as she inhaled deeply from the velvety white petals.

"Ma—" I felt tenderness swelling inside. "Thanks for preparing all these."

Mother chuckled. "Ha, don't think that your mother is stupid. I'm not. You think I won't realize that after all, *gweilo* or not *gweilo,* you're getting married?"

Looking happy, Mother began to feast on the watermelon seeds. She would put the seed edgewise between her teeth, crack it open, slip in the whole seed, and spit out the husk in perfect condition, then noisily chew the kernel.

I'd tried, but could never learn how to split and eat the seeds expertly in one fluid movement as she did. I'd let the seed slip and bite my finger, or swallow the seed with the husk, or chew up both the husks and the kernel in an unpleasant-tasting mess.

Mother squinted at me triumphantly. "Ha, don't know how to do that, eh? Mind you, there're still a lot of things you don't know about your own mother. Anyway, let's have tea." She paused to pour us full cups. "Remember? It's the best Meng Ding tea I bought from that tea shop. I've also dropped in slices of ginseng to give you more *qi* to prepare for the wedding. Now, drink your tea. Let's read the Tong Sheng and pick the day for your marriage."

On the red cover of this Sure Win was printed the title *The Mansion of All Treasures,* and the logo "Encompassing Ten Thousand Items." Under the title was the bulging-forehead Longevity God surrounded by three colorfully clad children holding up the giant peach of long life. Hovering above the old man was the bat of good luck, and behind him, the deer of wealth.

The scalding Meng Ding tea, heightened by the delicately bitter ginseng taste, put me in a more balanced mood. But when I picked up the one-thousand-page almanac it felt like a brick in my hands, its pages crowded with obscure passages and complex diagrams. How to understand it?

I opened the string-bound book and found this:

Nov. 11. Do's: Make offering to ancestors, enter school, make friends, get engaged, get a haircut, sew clothes, see a doctor, move house, repair the ceiling, fix the door, clean the stove, buy a house, herd animals.
Don'ts: Brew wine, take off clothes, plough land.

Dec. 6. Do's: Make offerings, pray for fortune, go for a trip, get married, move house, start a business, plough land, fix the stove, take off clothes, bury.
Don'ts: Style hair, open a pool, go through a well.

I caressed the teacup in my palms, feeling its heat. "Ma, how are we going to read all these strange expressions? What does it mean by going through a well? What is it to open a pool? And how come a day is suitable for marriage but not for styling one's hair?"

"Ah, foreign-produced doctor." Mother replaced the lid on her teacup, then squinted at me with a chiding expression. "When it comes to ancient wisdom, you're but a child. Be patient, Meng Ning. Let's first turn to the page for the month you plan to get married, and then look for a suitable day. Of course you don't have to read through the whole book; in that case you can write a thesis and get another Ph.D. Besides, if this Tong Sheng can't help, then we'll look up another one. That's why I bought four versions. Smart, eh?"

Suddenly Mother chortled, jabbing her sturdy finger on one passage while emphatically spitting out a string of perfect husks. "Ha, ha, look at this! The day is suitable to get married, but not to roast food. How can newlyweds not prepare roast pig for their wedding?"

"But why not?" I asked, popping several peanuts into my mouth.

"Because roasted pig, especially baby pig, is proof of the bride's virginity!"

"Are you kidding?" I stopped chewing.

Straightening her lavender cotton pajamas, Mother picked up a pig-fat sweet cake and put on an authoritative air. "On the wedding night, only after the groom has verified his wife is a virgin, will his parents send roast pig to the guests the following day. Otherwise, everybody will know the bride was a wanton girl."

"That's stupid! The parents can still send out roasted pig, even if the bride is not a virgin. Who would know?" I said, washing down the peanut dregs with my tea and scorching my throat.

I grimaced and Mother scolded, "Watch out, Meng Ning! I've told you a hundred times not to drink scalding tea and you never listen." Then she nibbled at her pig-fat cake with great affection and went on. "Yes, the guests might not, but the gods do, because the newlyweds also have to offer the pig to them. . . ."

Mother eyed me suspiciously, dropped her cake, and blurted out, "Meng Ning, did you follow my advice to put the cup of water between you and your Mic Ko?"

"Ma! Please stop your nonsense and concentrate on planning for my wedding."

"All right, all right," she sighed, now picking up an egg tart. "*Hai!* But for me, neither the guests nor the gods knew, for I didn't even have a . . . ah, forget it."

I knew she meant the wedding she'd never had. I reached to pat her hand.

"But it doesn't matter anymore, for now my daughter is going to have a really big and fancy one."

"No, Ma, I don't want anything fancy, only something gracious, simple, and cozy."

Mother's eyes began to shoot out daggers. "No, Meng Ning, listen to me. You're going to have a big, fancy wedding. And you'd better get that French classical court–style wedding gown worn by Sally Yeh we saw the other day."

We kept arguing until finally I blurted out, "Ma, it's my wedding, not yours, so can't you just let me decide what to wear?"

Mother shut up right away. Suddenly I realized the reason she wanted something fancy was not for me, but for herself.

Feeling terribly guilty, I refreshed her tea. "Ma, I'm very sorry."

There was a long silence before she said, "I forgive you." She drained her tea to acknowledge my apology. "All right, now let's pick the day."

After Mother had consulted the four almanacs for quite some time, with a thick felt pen she circled the auspicious day on each of them as well as on the calendar propped up by the radio.

"But, Ma, it's too close. I don't think we have enough time to prepare."

Mother looked at me sharply. "This is the best day. Otherwise you have to wait a long time. Silly girl. Quick battle, quick victory. So never make a man wait till he changes his mind—you understand?" Then she squinted at me. "And don't ever discard ancient wisdom like you do old calendars."

I knew she said this because in the past, whenever she'd looked up the Tong Sheng, I'd sneer. "Ma, the only way to a sure win, according to ancient Daoist wisdom, is by losing. Less is more; we lose in order to win."

She'd shut me up by saying, "Tst, tst, lose to win? What kind of crazy logic is this? You lose your mind to win your mother's argument just to make her lose face?"

But now I felt happy to pick my wedding date as recommended by the Sure Win, for, like my mother, I couldn't afford to be careless, not at thirty, and not for such a big thing in my life.

I wanted to steer my marriage ship with Michael safely for ten thousand years.

"Excellent," Mother said. "This is the best day to get married, and you'll have a good, happy, and long-lasting marriage. With five almanacs arriving at the same lucky day, believe me, Meng Ning, there won't be any chance for mistakes." She cautiously sipped her imperial tea with a matching imposing air before she continued. "You see, Meng Ning, I really don't understand how some people are so foolish as to pick their wedding date at random without consulting our ancestors' wisdom."

Instead of responding to her unique logic, I sucked hard at a piece of ginseng, relishing its stimulating flavor.

"But too bad—" Mother suddenly caught herself in midsentence.

"Too bad what?"

"No, nothing."

"What is it, Ma?"

"Too bad—" she blurted out again, "that I didn't need to look up the Tong Sheng for my wedding, for . . . I didn't have one."

"Ma, I'm sorry."

A beat or two passed before she suddenly asked, changing the subject, "You remember No Name who became a nun?"

"Of course, Ma. What about her?"

"She did have a name."

"That's not surprising; what was it?"

"Li Yuan."

"Beautiful Cloud?"

"Yes." Mother's eyes darted around as she went on. "Besides, I've been lying to you . . . she was not the daughter of your great-great-grandfather."

"What do you mean?" My heart raced. "Then who is she? And . . . Ma, why are you suddenly telling me this?"

"Because—"

"Because what?"

Mother sighed. "Because since you're getting married, I'm obliged to make some confessions before you become someone else's wife and daughter."

Before I had a chance to tell her that she didn't have to worry that I'd be someone else's daughter because Michael was an orphan, she had already spat out, "No Name, or Beautiful Cloud, or whatever, was your father's fiancée."

"You mean the one for whom Baba was buying gold for their upcoming wedding in Grandma's gold store—where he ran into you after you two had lost contact for eight years?"

"Yes. It's sad that she ended up being a nun, but not my fault."

"You mean it's Baba's fault?"

"No, not his neither." Mother rolled her eyes. "It's Beautiful Cloud's."

"How?"

"Simple." She shrugged. "She was not attractive enough to charm your father, but I did, even when I was only nine."

I almost chuckled.

Mother ignored me. "But later when I lost my charms, then your father let himself be charmed by other more beautiful clouds."

I didn't respond, for that was not news to me. All those women at the gambling houses in Hong Kong and Macao, they weren't just playing cards with Father, were they?

Mother swallowed her egg tart. "So I also cheated on him."

I almost spilled my tea and fell off the sofa. "Ma, do you know what you're talking about?"

"Of course." She paused, then said, "You remember your little brother?"

"Of course."

"He's . . . only your half brother."

"What?!"

"His real father is a *gweilo*." Foreign devil. Barbarian.

"A *gweilo?* Ma, how could you! What are you talking about?" Now I felt myself not only plunge down a deep valley, but dash into pieces at the bottom, my brain spilled all over.

"Calm down, Meng Ning," Mother said. "Why not? Aren't you now marrying a *gweilo* yourself?"

I was speechless.

She made a face. "Don't panic, Meng Ning, it was nothing serious; just . . . one night . . . no, two . . . hmm . . . actually, maybe it was three-nights stand."

"Ma, are you sure you know what you're talking about?" My voice remained in the high register.

"Why does a daughter always sound so suspicious when her mother is telling her the truth?"

"Then tell me, who is this *gweilo*—an American?"

"Yes. He was an ambassador in the American Consulate—"

"An ambassador? Oh no, not possible!"

"If my daughter can charm a doctor, how come her mother's not good enough to attract an ambassador?"

"Ma . . ." My voice now sounded defeated. "All right, how did you meet?"

"That's what I'm trying to tell you. Can you just let me finish in peace?"

Mother sipped more tea, popped several shrimp chips into her mouth, and chewed noisily. "It was the year of the dog, when we lived in Wanchai. One late afternoon I went to the market to shop for food. Besides some meat and vegetables, I also bought two live chicks. I wanted to raise them to cook for the Chinese New Year, which was coming in three months. You know, it's much cheaper that way than if you buy them during the New Year. Your father, as usual, was not at home, probably in Macao gambling his ass off. I was walking along the pier and thinking about his gambling until I started to cry. Damn the year of the dog that made me work like a dog. I kept cursing and spitting into the angry waves below the pier. Since I was not paying attention, I bumped into a lamppost and fell. The vegetables and meat spilled all over the ground and all the chicks ran loose. I was busy getting up and then trying to catch them. Several Chinese gathered to watch, but no one helped. Then this *gweilo*—by the way, his name is Jim Si—"

"You mean James? James what?"

"How am I supposed to remember? It's been such a long time. Anyway, no Chinese can pronounce that last name, it's too crazy. And anyway, Jim Si put down his expensive-looking briefcase and helped me up; then in his expensive-looking suit he chased after the chicks and finally got them back for me, then . . . then—"

"Then what?"

"Then you know what." Mother's eyes suddenly went blank.

"You mean you did *that thing* with him, just like that? But where could it have happened?"

"In our apartment—where else could it have been?" Mother looked me in the eyes for moments without blinking. "It's just a few blocks from the market—"

"That . . . quickly? Ma, you hardly knew him!" I was yelling again.

Mother ignored my shock and went on, her expression turning tender. "Jim Si deeply moved my heart. He acted so gentlemanly, helping up a poor woman and chasing around for those filthy, fifty-cent chicks in his expensive suit in front of the Chinese onlookers. Since I couldn't afford to buy him a gift to show my gratitude, I thought I could at least offer him a cup of tea to show my appreciation. That was why I invited him to our house, not only for a cup of tea, but also to wash his hands and clean his clothes. After that, he came for one more cup of tea, and I went to his office for a cup of coffee and that was that."

"You mean you went to the American Consulate in Garden Road in Central?!"

Mother proudly nodded. "Very classy office, clean, painted all white with lots of sun and air and plants."

"And where did you . . ." I felt too embarrassed to finish my sentence.

So Mother finished it for me. "Meng Ning, silly girl, you're a painter, right? So you must know there're different angles to paint an object. So, by the same logic . . . there's also more than one way to—" She gulped down her tea and made a face. "To do you-know-what."

"Then what happened to him after that?"

"He said the consulate had to transfer him back to America. But of course he lied, for I saw him twice, by accident, several months after, with other women. When I tried to accost him, he pretended not to recognize me."

"I'm sorry . . . Where was I when all this happened?"

"At school, where do you think you'd be? You went to afternoon school, remember? It was cheaper."

"So he's . . . little brother's father?"

Mother shrugged.

"Ma! What do you mean? Yes or no?"

Mother nodded.

"Did you tell him that?"

"No chance. I tried to, but never made it. The guard by the consulate's entrance never let me in."

"Did Baba know about this?"

"I don't know—maybe yes, maybe no. Of course I didn't have the chance to tell him either."

"But couldn't he tell the baby was Eurasian?"

"Possibly, but not necessarily. Your little brother was only three days old when he died. How can one tell with a three-day-old?"

I suspected that Father had known, at least sort of. Otherwise how could he have taken little brother's death so lightly? I'd never considered that little brother's death, instead of a punishment for her love with Father, as I'd always guessed, was in fact the karma for her love with a *gweilo*.

Mother sighed. *"Hai!* Meng Ning, you understand now why your marrying a *gweilo* worries me?"

I didn't respond. A meditative silence, then she asked, tentatively, "Meng Ning, do you . . . despise your mother now?"

In fact, I didn't, not at all. Strangely enough, after I'd learned the secret, I even felt happy for Mother. Now at least her life didn't seem that miserable after all. She'd had some fun. Besides, I also admired her. This took courage, didn't it? Especially when it happened almost twenty years ago when Hong Kong people were very closed-minded and any contact with *gweilo*s was considered wicked.

I patted her hand. "Ma, I'm sorry . . ."

To my utter surprise, Mother said, looking almost cheerful, "But I'm not."

"Because you loved this James?"

"No, because . . . I had a good time."

Another silence, then I said, "Ma, I've always thought Baba was your first and only love."

Again, she surprised me. "He still is. Jim Si was only a small American adventure."

I put my arm around her. "You know what? When I said sorry, actually I didn't mean it. In fact, I feel happy for you. And . . ."

Just then I remembered something. I dashed into the bedroom, snatched out the jade bracelet from my handbag, then hurried back to Mother.

"Ma, I hope this will make you more happy." I felt choked with emotion as I handed her the bracelet.

"Meng Ning, where did you get it?" Mother scrutinized the jade, looking both surprised and pleased.

I told her it was a gift from Michael.

Mother caressed it with her plump, callused hands.

"What do you think? You like it?"

"It's a decent piece. But I think Grandma's one was better, greener and more translucent."

"Ma, try it on."

"But it's yours."

"No, it's too loose for me. So it's now for you."

But the bracelet refused to slip onto her wrist—it was too small. Simultaneously we sighed.

"I'm sorry," I said, now feeling completely drained.

Mother looked at me affectionately. "Meng Ning, you're such a lucky girl. This Mic Ko, you'd better be nice to him and treasure him as Grandma treasured her jade bracelet."

"You're not worried anymore?"

"Ah, Meng Ning, silly girl. Look at all this Mic Ko has done for you, even before you're married to him. Grandma was right, she could see that you'd fall in love with a nice man, marry, have many children and a good life." The corners of her lips curled into a mischievous smile. "Besides, you've been worrying about money and haven't found a job yet, and Hong Kong will soon go back to China, so it's good that this Mic Ko comes along now, not to mention he'll give you free medical care!"

"Ma, you think I'm marrying Michael because of this?"

"Maybe, maybe not. But it's still a bonus that he's an American and a doctor, don't you think?" Then she added, widening her eyes, "But, still, be careful. This Mic Ko is still a *gweilo* after all!"

We laughed.

"Meng Ning, about the bracelet. Why don't you donate it to that pretty nun who always appears on television?"

"You mean Yi Kong?"

"Whatever you call her."

"But I thought you didn't like her."

"Ah, silly girl. I disliked her because I feared you'd follow her to be a nun." Mother made a face. "In fact, I like her now; she's so pretty and gave you so much help. So I think we should pay her back by donating this to her temple. Besides, we can also accumulate more merit—"

"But, Ma . . . How do you know that she helped me?"

"Ah, you think your mother's a stupid old woman, eh? Of course I knew, I just didn't want to embarrass you. How could you have had the money to pay for your father's funeral, and pay back the debt to the Big Ear Hole? Of course I know. I always do." Mother winked. "Like your grandma, I have a third eye."

39

Ten Thousand Miles of Red Dust

Two days later, I rode the train to Golden Lotus Temple, passing the sights that had become familiar to me since my teens. But this time I was seeing Yi Kong to announce my wedding. How would she react—angry? worried? detached? Would she agree to conduct a Buddhist wedding for me? I also had determined to donate my jade bracelet to the nunnery, for this was to accumulate merit for Michael, Mother, and me.

I had called Golden Lotus Temple and asked for Enlightened to Emptiness. After I'd told her my wish to visit Yi Kong, she said, "You've got perfect timing, Miss Du." Her voice sent waves of vibration to me from the other end of the line. "For Yi Kong Shifu has just returned from Suzhou this morning."

Before I had a chance to ask what the purpose of the trip was, the novice's enthusiasm again swelled in my ear. "This time Shifu has brought back several architects to build an imitation Suzhou rock garden for our temple."

But wasn't the nunnery in financial difficulty after its benefactor had disappeared? I thought, but stopped myself from asking.

Yi Kong was already waiting for me when I entered her office. "Hello, Meng Ning," she said, looking up at me. Her face beamed, her hands choreographing several tiny antique Buddha figures on her desk. "Please sit down."

I sat down in front of her large wooden desk. Amidst her curios were set a teapot and two cups; rose petals floated on the steaming amber liquid. The aroma reached into my nostrils, then seemed to travel down my esophagus and deep into my chest. Beside the tea set was a ceramic plate with nuts piled into a small mountain.

Yi Kong said, "Let's have tea." As we sipped our tea and nibbled on the nuts, I started to give an initial report of my work at Anyue, then our conversation drifted around her work, her art collection, and her recent trip to China.

I'd been expecting her, as usual, to lecture me on the illusion of human passion and the delusion of human love. But, to my surprise, after we'd finished our second round of tea, she spoke not a single word related to these. Just when I was wondering if maybe this was the right moment to bring up my marriage, she flashed a lighthearted smile. And, instead of posing her usual question, *When are you coming to play with us?* she said, "You look good, Meng Ning. When are you getting married?"

This took me by surprise. Perhaps she'd acquired psychic powers from her nearly thirty years of meditation and was able to tell that I'd come to announce my marriage. Or, was *I'm getting married!* printed on my face like a poster?

"Hmmm . . ." I stuttered, "soon . . . Yi Kong Shifu." Then, following the Chinese saying that when you hit a snake, let it crawl up the stick, I asked, "And, Shifu . . . I'll be very grateful if . . . if . . ." I mustered up all my courage and blurted out, "You can take the time and trouble to perform a Buddhist wedding for us."

She looked at me for a few moments with her penetrating eyes, nodding. "Yes." Then, "What is the date of the wedding?"

"Early next year, February nineteenth."

"Then I can arrange for the wedding to be held at our new Hall of Grand Heroic Treasures." She lifted her cup to her lips. "Let's have more tea now, then I'll take you to see the murals in the new hall."

After we had finished our third round of tea and flattened the mountain of nuts, she stood up from her chair and cast me a side-long glance. "Well, be happy." Then, "Come, Meng Ning, let's go."

I hurriedly followed her out of the office. Together we strolled past the library, the nursing home, the orphanage, the elementary school, and the half-finished construction site. She walked steadily with her back straight and her head held high. On the way, half a dozen workers and passersby stopped to bow to her with their hands held together in the adoration gesture; she returned a nod and a smile. Though she'd put on some weight, her gait was still as graceful as a crane's. It pleased me to watch her heels mysteriously playing hide-and-seek from under her robe. I wondered what the arches of her feet looked like wrapped inside those soft slippers. The hollow of a bridge, or the curve of a fish?

"Here we are. This is the Hall of Grand Heroic Treasures." Yi Kong's voice cut off my idle thoughts. She was already stepping across the threshold into the hall; I quickened my pace to fall into step behind the undulating hem of her robe. Cold air blasted from within, raising gooseflesh on my arms. A mixture of raw wood, wet cement, paint, oil, and turpentine stung my nostrils.

The hall was huge—seven or eight thousand square feet. Round, thick red pillars like giants' legs soared from its four corners to the high ceiling above. The entire wall was covered with an enormous mural—a whirlwind of pink, gold, and periwinkle. Turning my head in a circle to take it all in, I discovered it was filled with goddesses; hundreds, possibly thousands of them: flying while strumming a mandolin, bowing a fiddle, plucking a harp, tapping a drum. I could almost hear the twang of a plucked string, the lingering echo of a vibrato, the wailing of a fiddle, the distant thunder of a drum. The goddesses' supple bodies and limbs curved in graceful arcs; their clothes with long-flowing ribbons rippled in between ornamental clouds. I could almost feel the sensuous caress of the silk strips against my bare arms.

"Very impressive," I said, dropping my gaze back to earth, to Yi Kong.

Except in some rare, lavish art books, I had never seen frescos so beautiful and complex. The entire wall from floor to ceiling was filled with Bodhisattvas, gods and goddesses, people of all sorts, birds and auspicious animals. This huge mass of human forms and animals moved gracefully in a seemingly endless procession. Elegantly dressed Guan Yins marched abreast with sumptuously attired emperors, empresses, and lords. Some Bodhisattvas rode on white elephants, others on lions, with birds hovering above and peacocks trailing behind, fanning their thousand-eyed feathers. Farther back in the procession strolled poets and scholars, followed by servant boys with stacks of books weighing down their backs. Farmers held spades; fishermen, buckets filled with squirming fish; woodcutters with axes resting on thick shoulders walked here and there. Sailors and pirates fresh from the sea hastily fell in line to join the long queue, soon approached by prostitutes with pouting lips and flirtatious smiles.

I let out a gasp. "Yi Kong Shifu, I've never seen a modern Buddhist painting so magnificent."

But as we came closer to the mural, I discovered that lurking in corners and shadows were the outcasts: beggars, lepers, cripples and, almost hidden from sight, the ugly and the diseased, the old and dying.

Suddenly I realized something. For my whole life I'd been obsessed with beauty, especially female beauty, beginning with my girlhood crush on Yi Kong. Chasing after these floating, transitory images had unsettled my mind, so that I'd neglected what was really meant for me in this life. But hadn't my obsession with beauty later extended itself to men? I didn't think I would have fallen in love with Michael—despite his rectitude and compassion—if he had been unattractive. I wouldn't have gone out with Philip Noble if he'd had greasy hair and a crude face. I wondered: Would I have forgiven my father despite what he did to our family, if he had been wrinkled and ugly? If Lisa was plain-looking, would I have so easily been taken in by her?

And yes, also Guan Yin. Whenever I visited a temple, I'd always prayed just to Guan Yin, so I could admire her elongated eyes, curving brows, and crescent-moon lips. It was not so much her compassion as her beauty that I'd worshipped.

At last I saw that I'd missed the real lesson from my fall into the well. Spirituality for me had always been connected to things beautiful. Enlightenment was a jeweled paradise, a multicolored wonderland where beautiful celestial maidens danced to ethereal music and drank sweet elixirs. I'd ignored that it also includes hell—smelly and filled with trash, filth, rotting flesh. Though I'd been told many times over that enlightenment leads not to heaven, but to where I was now, I'd never accepted it. Enlightenment happens in the Ten Thousand Miles of Red Dust—where sin and virtue, dreams and nightmares, truth and delusion, nun and not nun, *samsara* and *nirvana*, all exist together.

Yi Kong was right to teach that we shouldn't discriminate. Life just *is*. So it's pointless to reject the world, hoping to escape *samsara*—suffering. All we can do is keep to our ordinary mind.

So, what's all the fuss about?

I was feeling expansive when Yi Kong softly said, "Let's look some more," and resumed walking.

I reached to touch the Guan Yin pendant hanging around my neck.

Yi Kong cast me a meaningful glance. "Time never stops. It's been seventeen years since the day I threw the pendant to you into the well."

Then I thought of something else and blurted out, "Yi Kong Shifu, since you've always talked about the illusion of human passion, then you must have experienced—"

"No, nothing like that." She cut me off, her voice calm, her gaze as clear as a cloudless sky.

A light dawned in me, illuminating what had been in shadow before. There are different ways for people to see their "original face"—to perceive their different callings in life. Hers was to shave her head to become a nun—perhaps a worldly nun who gathered large donations for charitable projects. Dai Nam's karma was to taste bitter love, then become a recluse, far from this dusty world. And mine was to be awakened to the spirituality of this Ten Thousand Miles of Red Dust through the love and compassion of a man. All of us: Dai Nam, an ascetic nun meditating on a high mountain;

Yi Kong, ambitiously gathering large donations and carrying out huge projects; Enlightened to Emptiness, who, though happy in the empty gate, knew she would never have the chance to love; or me, simply a woman in the world, about to be married and starting a career—we were just a few of the myriad sentient beings struggling with our own problems and striving for enlightenment in this unsatisfactory world.

As we continued walking, my thinking shifted. I no longer felt small in my teacher's strong presence. Our karmas were about to diverge. Yes, Yi Kong had been my mentor and I would always respect her for that. But already the hold she'd had over me was weakening. Now I could feel sympathy for those parts of her life as a nun I'd only recently understood, like the need to attract donations from vulgar businessmen like Sunny Au. From there, my magnanimity continued to expand to the late Professor Fulton and his daughter Lisa, Philip Noble, even the taxi driver. . . .

Feeling free, I smiled.

Yi Kong cast me a curious glance.

As if my hands were directed by some higher force, I snapped open my handbag, took out the brocade bag with the jade bracelet, and handed it to her. "Yi Kong Shifu, remember you said the temple welcomes any nice stone?" I slid the bracelet out from the bag. "Here's my offering."

But Yi Kong didn't take it; she didn't even look at it. "Meng Ning, please go to the general office for any business related to a donation."

Embarrassed, I dropped the bracelet back into my pocketbook. Then, trying to fill the awkward silence, I asked, "Shifu, what's the title of this mural?"

"Ten Thousand Miles of Red Dust." She turned to face me and placed her hands together. *"A Mi Tuo Fo,"* she said, and was gone.

I had just given the jade bracelet to Enlightened to Emptiness and she was studying it like a little girl given a Barbie. "Thank you so much, Miss Du; it's very generous of you to donate this."

"You're welcome."

"Nan Mo A Mi Tuo Fo," Hail to the Merciful Buddha, the novice said as she walked me to the door.

I made a deep bow to her and she bowed back. After that, I stepped through the door into the courtyard, which led to the stone garden.

I was listening to the clicks of my high heels on the gravel path in the garden leading toward the temple's exit, when I saw my carp-viewing bench and suddenly remembered Chan Lan, Dai Nam's great-aunt. Where was she? As I was wondering, there appeared the familiar face of the nurse who had helped Chan Lan the last time I saw the centenarian.

I hurried up to her.

She smiled.

I smiled back. "Where is Chan Lan?"

"Oh, don't you know?"

"Something happened?"

"She died yesterday morning."

"What?"

"Miss, don't feel bad. She was one hundred and one; it was a happy death." The nurse scrutinized me behind her thick glasses. "Oh, by the way, we found in her drawer this letter for you from her great-niece the Wonderful Countenance Shifu. You're Miss Du Meng Ning, right?"

I nodded. "Thank you." I took it from her and saw my name in neat penmanship on the envelope. "Do you have any news about Shifu?"

"No. I only heard that she still doesn't talk." The nurse smiled at me and continued down the path.

After I'd torn open the envelope and fished out the letter, my gaze fell on a poem:

Hundred flowers in spring and a moon in autumn
Cool breeze in summer and snow in winter
If there's no worry in your mind
that's your good time on earth.

I held the letter to my chest and a sigh escaped from my mouth. Then I read the poem again and again, like reciting a mantra, until I'd memorized it.

Relief washed over me.

I knew Dam Nam was fine. And I knew that she'd know that I knew, too.

Epilogue

Three weeks later, Michael arrived in Hong Kong, this time to plan for our wedding. The meeting between Mother and Michael was, to my surprise and relief, cordial and comfortable. I could only say that once she had laid her eyes on Michael, it seemed her tongue had suddenly gone itchy and her prejudice against *gweilo* had been thrown beyond the highest heavens. It reminded me of the Chinese saying, "When mother-in-law sees son-in-law, her mouth water can't help but fall."

One late evening, I took Michael to see the newly constructed nunnery so he could meditate with the Buddha, Bodhisattvas, and all the sentient beings in front of the Ten Thousand Miles of Red Dust mural. Watching his half-closed eyes and his legs in full lotus position, I suddenly realized that Michael was the real Bodhisattva: alive, struggling for balance, patiently inhaling and exhaling, not a well-preserved dead nun clothed in gold and silk.

After we stepped beyond the threshold of the main gate, I turned back to gaze at the temple. Under the moonlight, everything looked as if in a distant dream. The crescent moon hanging on one of the ancient trees silently echoed the graceful arcs of upturned eaves. The windows, though ablaze with lights, seemed to seal in a thousand secret tales.

An unknown nun's shadow flitted past that of a huge bronze incense burner. I idly wondered what her reason was for willingly entering the empty gate and passing her life endlessly reciting *sutras* under a solitary lamp.

My wandering gaze fell on a *stupa* in the distance. This was the second time—the first was during the fire—that I noticed its sensuous shape like the curve of a woman's body. I stopped and turned to face Michael, feeling a tingling sensation rise in my body.

"Michael?"

"Yes?"

"I love you."

He pulled me toward him and kissed me deeply. "I love you, too, Meng Ning, very much," he whispered.

As we walked along together, I turned back to watch the nunnery's wooden gate and its mysterious skyline recede in the moonlight, feeling sad that part of my life was now irrevocably gone. Then I looked at Michael's beaming face under the moon's silvery sprinkle and felt my sadness overlaid by happiness that another kind of life was beginning. . . .

PETALS FROM THE SKY
MINGMEI YIP

ABOUT THIS GUIDE

The questions and discussion topics that follow
are intended to enhance your group's
reading of this book.

Discussion Questions

1. Why did Meng Ning consider becoming a nun?

2. What is the significance of these two early accidents: Meng Ning's falling into the well when she was thirteen, and the fire in the Golden Lotus Temple?

3. Although Meng Ning's true love was Michael, why was she also attracted to Philip Noble? Why do you think he tried to seduce his best friend's fiancée?

4. Michael is a scientifically educated medical doctor. How did he react to the visit to the fortune-teller?

5. How would you characterize the relationship between Meng Ning and her mother?

6. Meng Ning's father plagiarized poems and gambled away everything. Did he have any redeeming traits?

7. When Meng Ning found out her conservative Chinese mother had had an affair with an American ambassador and betrayed her father, how did Meng Ning react, and why?

8. What is the significance of the scarred nun Dai Nam's role in this novel?

9. How did Meng Ning's nun mentor, Depending on Emptiness, try to stop Meng Ning from marrying Michael? Why did she do this?

10. Buddhist temples sometimes preserve the bodies of famous monks and nuns. What is the motive for this custom and what is your reaction to it?

11. To what degree does Depending on Emptiness exemplify Buddhist virtues of nonattachment, compassion, and selflessness?

12. Why did Meng Ning finally decide to marry Michael instead of become a nun? What roles did the car accident and elevator fall play?

13. Enlightened to Emptiness, like many nuns, was given to the nunnery by her family before she had had much experience of the world. How do you feel about parents deciding for their children what sort of lives they will lead?

14. What do Meng Ning and Michael experience in the small temple near the end of the novel, and what is the significance of their being unable to find it again?

15. How is Buddhism depicted in the novel?